A CHIEF INSPECTOR
ST.GEORGE
MYSTERY

Peter Jamesson

Unplayable Lie

A Chief Inspector St. George Mystery

Sleeping Bear Press

Sleeping Bear Press
310 North Main Street
P.O. Box 20
Chelsea, MI 48118
www.sleepingbearpress.com

Printed and bound in Canada.

10 9 8 7 6 5 4 3 2 1

Library of Congress Cataloging-in-Publication Data on file
ISBN: 1-58536-088-0

To my son Kyle

Saturday

1

HEAVEN ON EARTH....

A deep blue midsummer sky...cottony white clouds hovering above Scotland's green Lothian plain...the sun following its prescribed arc toward the zenith in its endless westward journey...sheer heaven, all right....

At least to the sailplane pilot coming in silently from the north-west at 5,000 feet. Weather permitting, once a week he hitched a ride skyward from the small airfield abutting the A80 near Cumbernauld to revel in the miracle of unpowered flight. Gliding silently across the M8 and A71 stretching between Glasgow and Edinburgh, he never ceased to be awed by the view: the fields, hills, and woodlands; the country's two largest cities in the distance, fore and aft; the Firth of Forth away to his left; and towns like Bathgate, Armadale, Whitburn, and Linlithgow set about like chess pieces.

And of course, Livingston (population 38,000), the new kid on the block, so to speak, set in the M8 corridor some 14 miles west of Edinburgh, designated back in 1962 as the hub of the region's bur-geoning light manufacturing industry. A Scottish Silicon Valley with a science park having close ties to university research departments and easy access to train, auto, sea, and plane transportation. In fact, the town had become important enough to headquarter the "F" Division of the Lothian and Borders Police.

Following his usual flight plan, the pilot coaxed his spindly craft through a wide 360 as he banked off the thermals rising from the Pentland Hills. Coming around to his return heading, he spotted a small curl of gray smoke several miles west of Livingston near West Calder. Flying closer, he watched it transform into a thick yellow-brown cloud billowing aggressively from a lone flat-roofed commercial building set along a county road about a mile from town. Fire lapped at all sides of the structure. He noticed one car parked in front and another one racing south erratically before turning into a distant farmyard near Woolfords Cottages—no doubt to call in the alarm, he concluded. And a lone cyclist heading north. Mesmerized by the evil spectacle below, he circled again while flames leapt from the roof like antiaircraft tracers. Suddenly his craft bucked and yawed violently, and immediately he lost all visibility. He cursed—he had flown straight into the shifting column of hot ash rising from the conflagration. Though he was back in clear air in seconds, his Plexiglas windscreen was hopelessly fouled as the impotent dry wipers merely spread the sooty film back and forth.

Faced now with his own crisis, he quickly forgot about the burning building below him. His gut cramping tightly, he repeatedly checked his altimeter and compass in a desperate effort to set course for his home airfield many miles away. He tried to calm his voice as he radioed the tower for priority landing clearance. In answer to their query, he confessed that he had not checked the wiper fluid level before taking off. The tower's pause before sign-off told him they shared his concern: although instruments would get him back to the field, touchdown would be blind since he had no forward vision. His odds of fatally crashing were significant.

While the sailplane glided away far above them, two fire trucks from Livingston, their sirens wailing and lights flashing, peeled off secondary road B7008 out of West Calder onto the country road and rushed toward the conflagration. A mile behind them came a third truck, this one from Bathgate eight miles distant. Like Royal Marines storming a beachhead, the firemen sprang into action as the big rigs braked to a halt in the front parking lot.

"Whose car is that?" barked Chief Fire Officer McSwain to his dispersing company as he pointed to the lone automobile—a Mercedes—parked close to the front door. The fire's intense heat had already seared and blistered the front-end finish and had set the front tires ablaze. Recognizing the risk of the petrol tank exploding,

McSwain directed a team forward to hose down the car, release the hand brake, and roll the ponderous luxury vehicle back across the parking lot toward the grassy border.

"I think it's Mr. Pont's car!" shouted Capt. Bogan.

"Which one?" called out McSwain over the hissing whine of the blaze.

"The older one! He's probably inside!" yelled Bogan as he gestured emphatically toward the burning building.

McSwain cursed as he stomped impatiently along the spread-out battle array manned by men garbed in suits of 60 percent polybenzimide and 40 percent Kevlar and carrying oxygen tanks on their backs. Three men had already put on their SCBA masks in preparation for entering the building. Suddenly a loud WHOOOOMPFF! announced the collapse of the roof. The fire chief knew the entire structure was in its death throes and that any further efforts toward saving anything or anyone were equivalent to expectorating into the wind. The best they could hope for was preventing the release of any toxic agents.

Two hours later, with the fire completely suppressed, the firemen began packing their gear and retrieving their hoses. A shiny Range Rover roared up to the police barricades and was passed through. The vehicle charged up the driveway and into the parking lot where the driver jumped out and, after his initial shock, sought out McSwain.

"Mr. Michael Pont?" asked the brigade chief of the approaching civilian.

"No, no, no, I'm not," said the refined-looking gentleman as his eyes swept over the destruction with undisguised distress. "I'm Edward Cargill...I'm his cousin....The police called. Dear God Almighty..."

McSwain shook his head sadly.

"Complete loss, I'm afraid. Do you know where Michael Pont is?"

"Ah, yes, he's...spending the day up at St. Andrews. He's playing host...to some business guests of ours...He won't be back...until sometime this evening."

"Ours? You do business with him?'

"Yes, I'm the Chief Financial Officer for the company. Number Three man. He's Number Two."

"I see. Do you know where *Geoffrey* Pont is?"

"No, I have no idea—wait! Is that—?" said the new arrival as he spun around and pointed to the smoldering Mercedes.

"We found it parked right up at the front door."

"Dear God, it looks like Geoffrey's!"

"I'm afraid it is, according to the registration."

"But that means—if his car's here—then he's inside!"

"I'm sorry, Mr. Cargill, but I'm afraid it does look that way."

Edward Cargill began turning around and around as if looking desperately for someone.

"But...but your men, they're packing up, they're *leaving*; isn't someone going to check inside?"

"We are—tomorrow."

"TOMORROW! But he's in there!"

"Mr. Cargill, I'm sorry, but if he is, there's no question he's dead. There's nothing anyone can do for him."

"But you just can't leave him lying in there like...like...like some *roadkill!*"

Chief McSwain squared his shoulders and straightened to his full height.

"Mr. Cargill, we got here straightaway, considering the distance and all, and I can tell you this place was already an inferno. Anyone inside there was already well cremated by then. Now the roof has come down and the walls are almost sure to follow. I'm not going to add to the mortality list by sending my men in there until a structural expert has examined what's left. I'm sorry, sir, but I'm firm on that."

Visibly distressed, Cargill paced around in tight circles, rubbing his head as though it ached.

"And this expert will be here when?"

"Tomorrow."

"But that's Sunday!"

"I know, but I've already sent word. He'll be here."

"Why not tonight? Why wait?"

"Because you can't tell a bloody thing in the dark. This isn't exactly Pinewood Studios, now is it?" and with that McSwain marched away to immerse himself in the final preparations for departure. Edward Cargill stood still, emotionally numb, staring first at the ruins and then the violated Mercedes. Minutes later all was ready, and Cargill reluctantly returned to his Rover and followed the fire trucks back to the county road, leaving the barricades and the funeral pyre under the watchful eye of West Calder constables.

Tuesday

2

VALISE FIRMLY IN hand, Chief Inspector Byram St. George stepped nimbly from the railway carriage onto the crowded platform in Edinburgh's Waverly Station. His train, the *Flying Scotsman*, had covered the 378 miles from London's Kings Cross Station in under five hours—more than enough time for a leisurely meal and a catnap. Sated, refreshed, and in reasonable spirits, the man from Scotland Yard slowly worked his way through the throng of people hustling on and off the train and headed toward the main lobby where "someone" would meet him. He had not the foggiest notion who that lucky person might be, only that the Yard had assured him he would not be abandoned. Then his superiors had hustled him out the door and on his way.

He heard a few whispers of "Look! It's him! I thought he died!" but kept marching on. Though he saw no resemblance himself, passersby not infrequently mistook him for the late actor Sebastian Cabot. Must be the mustache and beard, he thought, but I'll be damned if I'll remove them!

He knew his vexation about this trip had been all too evident when his immediate superior—the Assistant Commissioner/ Criminal Investigation Department—had bestowed upon him this confounding assignment. He also knew he must expunge all such feelings of annoyance, persecution, and self-pity if he were to perform to his own high standards. Still, as he approached the cathedral-like rotunda, he fumed that this was a bloody poor way to start a case: showing up like some anonymous waif with only a satchel in hand and a few bob in his pocket.

Pausing at the rotunda's perimeter, he scanned the crowd but saw no familiar faces. He was about to go sign out a rental car—department budget be damned!—when he heard a familiar call.

"Chief Inspector!"

He turned to see Det. Sgt. Laurence Poole striding hurriedly toward him.

"My God, Laurence! It's a pleasure to see you!" exclaimed St. George as he shook his adjutant's hand warmly. It occurred to him that only once before had he seen his youthful aide in casual clothes. "What in thunder are *you* doing here? I distinctly recall ordering you onto holiday."

"Yes, sir, that you did, and I went. Been up here visiting relatives on my mother's side, but the Yard called last evening. Since I was in the area, I got my marching orders but with a promise of compensatory time off next month. So here I am."

"Ach! They always say that. Well, my friend, you have my solemn word that I shall see to it they live up to that commitment. Even if I have to stash you in my own digs."

"Yes, sir. Thank you."

"You have a car?"

"Yes, sir. A rental authorized by the Yard. Subcompact, I'm afraid."

"Surprised they didn't reserve a pair of scooters instead. Even cheaper."

"I guess," Poole said, "I was just relieved it wasn't a bloody rickshaw."

"Hah!" was the Chief Inspector's hearty reply as he followed his assistant of the past three years out to short-term public parking. Within minutes they were clear of Edinburgh and headed west on the A71.

"We've got lodgings at the Squire's Inn in Bellsquarry just past Livingston," Poole said. "Nice place, cozy, adjacent rooms, but thick walls so I doubt I'll hear your snoring..."

The sergeant focused his eyes on the road ahead, his face expressionless, while St. George shot him a withering gaze. From long experience, Poole knew when his mentor would accept a gibe and when not. He also knew how much his boss enjoyed puffing up and acting offended. The two men went through such repartee at least once a week.

"Did our patron saints tell you why we're on this goose chase?" asked the Chief Inspector.

"No, sir, just that you were popping up for a look-see and that we're meeting the lead detective on the case—a chap named Dougall—this evening in his office in West Calder. Seven o'clock. He's to send a car around."

"Good. Maybe we can finagle our way into using his vehicles for the duration rather than this rolling coffin."

"I hoped you'd say that. So if I may ask, what's going on?"

"Something very queer. You know, three times before I've found myself closeted with both the Commissioner and the Home Secretary, and each time the matter was put forth straightaway and to the point. No shilly-shallying. I knew exactly where I stood and what was expected for my efforts. But not this time."

"Oh?"

"They told me essentially *nothing*. Such ambiguity! Such pirouetting! You should have heard them! We are concerned, yet we're not quite sure there is really anything to be concerned about. It's purely a local matter, and yet, worst case scenario, there *might* be profound ramifications for the national economy and, oh yes, national security. We have every confidence in the abilities of the local authorities, and yet we'd appreciate it ever so much if you could just drop whatever you're working on right now and pop up there for a day or two. Nothing major, just a once-over to check things out, although should you feel it appropriate, do not hesitate to initiate a full-scale inquiry, albeit with a low profile. Your ride is waiting downstairs to take you home to fetch some things and then on to the station. What rot!"

"I'd say it sounds like someone's scared out of their knickers."

"Agreed. Even worse, they parried all my direct questions as though brandishing an épée. They made absolutely no effort to alleviate my obvious disquiet about the entire assignment. I would have thought that, as a senior man with a good record, I would have warranted better treatment. But no, just hie yourself up there and we'll stay here and man the breastworks. Bloody hell! Felt like a damned cadet, I did. So to answer your question, Laurence, something damned queer is going on, and, yes, the graybeards in London are worried about it."

"So why all the ruckus?"

"A bloody fire, of all things—and the man who died in it. Destroyed a computer plant. I guess it was nearly the complete package. Manufacturing occupied about three-quarters of the floor space. The rest was divided between the business office and the computer labs in Research and Development. Total workforce of 30 people, almost all of them high-tech white-collar. Completely self-contained operation."

"What about the local force?"

St. George shook his head in disgust.

"That's just it—I haven't the slightest doubt the Lothian and Borders Police could handle the matter perfectly well. But here we come, riding into the Valley of whatever, for Queen and country..."

"So who requested the Yard?"

"Strangely enough, they were vague about that, too. You know how our betters like to preen and strut about when our assistance is requested. Well, there was none of that. I hesitate to say but, as a result, I sensed there is quite a bit of divisiveness on this end up here. Consequently, let's just say I think we would be well advised to keep our mouths shut and just listen and remain very neutral until we see how things lay. In fact, I would appreciate it very much if you would simply play dumb. They may be on their guard around me but hope-fully not around you."

"Darn! And I was so much looking forward to strutting around and showing off!"

St. George snorted and looked over at his colleague while stifling a smile. "We all have to endure disappointments in life. This won't be your last."

"Yes, sir....Well, here we are."

Poole pulled up beneath the carriage porch of a modern hostelry designed to mimic a Dickensian caravansary. St. George went ahead to sign in while Poole continued on to the car park. Minutes later, they rode the elevator to the third floor where each man adjourned to his own room to freshen up before meeting in the lobby for dinner.

There was little conversation during their meal as both men sub-scribed to the notion that silence was the best testimonial to good food. To their collective mind, people who talked incessantly through dinner either had no appetite, wholly disliked the entree, or were selfish oafs desperate for attention. Poole concentrated on a hearty stew while his mentor nibbled on a sandwich. Over dessert, they commented on the furnishings, particularly the darkly-stained, imitation, rough-hewn beams spanning the ceiling 10 feet over their heads. Then St. George, to be courteous, inquired how his aide had spent his aborted holiday. With precious little to recount, Poole soon switched the subject back to their mission.

"I wonder what sort of reception we'll get."

"Officially, a very proper one, I'm sure. You know, the more I think about it, the more I wonder if the impetus for our invitation came from London, not here."

"How so?"

"Well, as you alluded to before, we have no jurisdiction outside the London metropolitan area unless someone formally requests our assistance. Yet, as I think back on it, the emphasis quite clearly was on *London's* concern for what may or may not have happened. Bass-ackwards, if you ask me. Very possible that something deucedly serious may be involved."

3

STANDING BENEATH THE front portico while waiting for Inspector Dougall's car, the two detectives savored the mild evening air as they continued their conversation.

"It's all about arson, you know," St. George said. "What someone once called a crime 'easy to commit, quite hard to detect, and maddeningly difficult to prosecute.' Indeed, some experts take the view that the advantage actually lies with the arsonist both before *and* after the event."

"Why so bleak a view?" Poole queried. "I thought we had made great strides through forensics."

"In many ways we have. The pessimism derives, apparently, from the fact that most fires are not diligently investigated. That's the claim here, in fact. An insurance investigator named Walcott works for the company that carries the policy on the burned plant. He was once a working fireman and reputedly knows what he's about. A family illness forced him to abandon his low-paying fireman's job for something more remunerative. Anyway, the fire here happened Saturday morning. He was called in Sunday. He didn't like what he saw, spoke his piece, alienated the local authorities, and filed his report. The next thing you know, the Secretary of State up here is giving the Home Office an earful and today I'm stuck with the bloody case. Given that background, I'm sure you understand why I was so pleased to see that you would be here to share my misery."

"Oh, *thank* you, master! May I hope that also includes a flogging?"

As St. George smiled broadly, a black police sedan swept in from out of the darkness, its driver calling out their names through an open window. As he reached for the rear door, St. George said quietly to Poole, "Again, let's play dumb."

"Aye, aye, sir."

Their driver, a senior constable nearing retirement, introduced himself and thereafter remained silent, concentrating instead on exhibiting his best behaviour for these important gents from that *other* capital. The last thing he needed were any complaints that might jeopardize his pension.

As a distant church clock struck the hour, the men from Scotland Yard stepped inside the West Calder police station at 9 Polbeth Terrace. The uniformed desk sergeant promptly thumbed them over to another constable for delivery to their host. They found Inspector Brian Dougall standing somberly outside the station's small conference room. His sad face matched his suit, which looked badly in need of pressing. After the first introductions, their host ushered them inside where they encountered Chief Fire Officer McSwain decked out in his full dress uniform. Standing beside him was another dressed-out senior officer, Chief Superintendent Reginald Stallings, Commander, "F" Division, Lothian and Borders Police. After a second round of short, crisp handshakes, everyone took a seat. During the brief but heavy pause that followed, St. George thought the small humorless room reeked of hostility. Then, as though playing white, Stallings made the opening move.

"Officially, Chief Inspector and Sergeant, we welcome you. We're always pleased to assist the Yard in any investigation. Whatever men and resources you require are at your disposal."

St. George hesitated but a split second—did the man say "at your disposal"?—before responding in his most amiable tone, "Thank you, gentlemen, but we were of the impression that, ah, we are to be at *your* disposal."

"Not ours, surely. Our investigation of the Viscount fire was complete and thorough. As far as we are concerned, the matter is closed."

"But your request to the Yard…"

"No such request came from my office," the district's top cop said as he stiffened noticeably.

"Nor mine," said McSwain, jaw set, eyes darting toward an uncomfortable Inspector Dougall sitting at the end of the table. Stallings also bestowed his own disapproving gaze upon the apparently disfavored policeman.

"Afraid we have Inspector Dougall to thank for that," continued the top cop. "Not the first error in judgment, I'm afraid."

For his part, Dougall merely clenched his teeth, stared at the table, and offered no rebuttal. It was abundantly clear to both London men that the local detective had already suffered his superior's expressed displeasure.

"But I understand," St. George said, "that the insurance company for Viscount has serious doubts about the cause."

"Not the company," Stallings said, "just one very crass, very ambitious investigator. Fellow named Walcott. He could not care less for the truth; just wants to save his company a bundle of money. Probably get a hefty bonus if he does, I'll wager."

"Wouldn't surprise me if he came in this week and offered to change his report for a price," added McSwain.

"He's asked for a bribe?"

"Not yet, but give him time."

St. George made a show of frowning.

"The fact is, Chief Inspector," Stallings said, "our joint examination of the fire produced absolutely no suggestion whatsoever of arson. Absolutely none. Short circuit knocked out the alarm system and sprinkler controls. Simple as that. And as tragic. But an accident nonetheless. And Mr. Pont is no longer with us and nothing can change that. However, rebuilding the plant will at least preserve his memory. So as far as I'm concerned, my department has signed off on it."

"So have I," said McSwain. "Here's a copy of my report."

Poole wasn't sure whether the fireman tossed or threw the stapled report across the table toward the senior Yard man. St. George ignored the document.

"You're saying Inspector Dougall did not have good cause to make the request?"

"He did not. I'm sure he's anxious to explain his version to you. However, I'm equally sure you will concur he allowed himself to be conned by this man Walcott. Thanks to which we've had more calls from London than we can count. All of it needless, quite needless. Well, I think that about covers it. Be assured, Chief Inspector, I would not commit my reputation to something without a firm foundation."

"*Nor would I*," added McSwain.

"We would never think otherwise, gentlemen. However, seeing as we *are* here, we might as well look about and be done with it. I understand we're set for tomorrow morning?"

"9:00 A.M.," said McSwain. "I'll be there."

"I have meetings," Stallings said. "Besides, I see nothing more I can add. It's open and shut. Anyway, Inspector Dougall has the responsibility to see this through, so I'll leave you in his care."

With that, the two service chiefs rose to their feet, shook hands with St. George but not Poole or Dougall, bade everyone a polite "Good night," and left the room.

* * *

The remaining three men continued standing, not speaking, until they heard the commanders leave the building. St. George turned to an embarrassed Dougall.

"Shall we sit down? I think, under the circumstances, it would be appropriate to hear your side of the story."

"Oh, yes, right, thank you," replied the detective as he almost fell into his chair. "No question I've been on the hot seat. Probably get the sack...but that's my problem. The sad irony is that it's all come about from trying to better myself. Better late than never, I thought."

"How's that?"

Dougall rubbed his face with his two hands as though trying to wash away his troubles.

"Well, I've not been the usual success story. I started in Edinburgh and worked my way up to Detective Sergeant. I had a few miscues—dumb mistakes—along the way, and so I was branded as 'likely not to advance further' and was loaned out to Narcotics. One day I was serving as bailiff for a stash that was being introduced as evidence in a big case. I was in the waiting room with the stuff, it was a slow day, the lawyers were having at it and dragging things along, and Nature called. You know how it is. So I took a 30-second break, down and back in a flash, but when I returned, the stash had been nicked. We caught the bloke downstairs going out a back door. However, the defense claimed that the stash was tainted because the chain of custody had been broken. Said it was inadmissible and the court agreed. Case got thrown out and me with it."

St. George had been watching the man closely and now pursed his lips.

"Yet if you were sacked, how could you be here as an inspector?"

"Because I resigned. Got hauled before the Chief Constable and read the riot act. Told my resignation would be welcomed. So I did. I mean, getting the sack on paper would brand me for life. Resigning at least left the door open a smidge. So I worked private security for two years while I took courses part-time and then applied when a position here came open. They had their doubts but I think they were impressed that I had taken the course work, and so I was brought on and then last year I made Inspector. Got to be honest with you, I don't think I would have gotten in anywhere else. But this is one of the smallest districts and traffic is our big thing."

"So what created this problem for you?"

"Well, I continued reading and studying, trying to improve myself like I said, to make sure no one ever regretted bringing me on board. But I guess, in this case, it's possible I've read too much into everything."

"That can happen, I suppose, but tell me...do you really believe that?"

Dougall looked somberly at the two London men and his features hardened.

"No. No, I've been over it a dozen times, and I'm convinced Walcott is right. No matter that all the others say otherwise. That fire was set."

"What about your supervisor here?"

"Superintendent Boyd? He's away on holiday. However, I've heard he's voted *in absentia*."

St. George nodded sympathetically. He knew full well how departmental politics operated.

"I'm sure you wish to get home, but despite the hour, might we prevail upon you to brief us on this place? The layout and so on?"

"Certainly. I thought you might want something on it," the detective said as he reached behind and removed a folded sheet of paper from a back table. Once opened, it displayed a diagram of the grounds and the factory's floor plan. Dougall pointed out the guard booth on the two-lane main drive, the parking lot in front, and the receiving dock in back. Nearby was the bottled gas repository where a fresh supply was trucked in every other week. A clutch of offices and the R&D section nestled along the west wall while the manufacturing area occupied everything else.

"The bottled gas exploded?"

"No. That section sustained the least damage—all the lines, valves, and couplings were intact. The tank itself would not have ruptured unless there was a break, but they hosed it down anyway and kept it relatively cool as a precaution. The building itself was of standard construction, all to code, proper insulation, and all that. No indications of any shortcuts. The usual power and water; normal sewer lines to septic tanks; repository tanks in the rear for toxic waste—pumped out and carted off weekly. Place was about 10 years old."

"Who sounded the alarm?"

"A who and a what. The plant's computerized alarm system shot off a signal by microwave to the fire station. They don't rely on phones lines being intact. Then a woman passerby saw smoke pouring from the place and called from a farm down the road."

"What about the security guards?"

Dougall went on to explain that the plant's security people worked only during regular weekday business hours and spent their time primarily directing visitors and deliveries. He had learned that Geoffrey Pont was adamant about not having the place look like a Kremlin fortress. The dead man's view was how could they expect customers to put full faith and confidence in electronics if they themselves did not?

"You're saying security was completely automated?"

"Essentially. They erected a symbolic wire fence around the perimeter which I understand carries no current. Security came from hundreds of motion and pressure sensors, thermal detectors, infrared and laser beams, sonic sensors, you name it, all over the place. And all of it built right into the building as it was constructed. No drilling holes and tunnels after the fact. So no one could later come in and follow a cable and sabotage anything. That's why they felt it was fail-safe. They believed the place was as tight as your Number 10."

"But what about breakdowns? Maintenance problems?"

"Statistically highly improbable, they claim. Used top of the line materials for everything. Estimated lifetime of 20 years minimum. By then, they expected to have begun expansion and remodeling."

St. George's eyebrows rose in apparent disbelief. "Cameras?"

"None. Considered unnecessary gadgetry."

"What about power loss?"

"Automatically triggers an alarm," Dougall said. "Backup lithium batteries for the computers are routinely tested and then changed every six months. Petrol generator at the rear of the property for the rest. Actually happened once several years ago when there was a regional blackout. Power was gone for three or four hours. The backup systems here came on-line within a split second. Worked flawlessly."

"Anyone ever penetrate this security system?"

"No, sir."

"What about false alarms? Maybe squirrels, foxes, rabbits?"

"None."

"Remarkable!" said the Chief Inspector as he leaned back in his seat.

"Perhaps not. My understanding of their theory is that, in the midst of so much open ground, such animals would have little reason to approach the building itself. Thus, eating outside was strictly prohibited so no scraps or crumbs would be left behind to attract scavengers."

"Did the security guards signal arrivals to those inside the building?"

"Not directly. Just handset radios. Limited range by design. Cell phones were thought too vulnerable to eavesdropping."

"What about alarms? Any direct connection at all?"

"No, sir, just the radios."

St. George shook his head in disbelief.

"The woman who reported the blaze...did she describe the fire in any detail? Color of the smoke, perhaps?"

"No, sir, I doubt it."

"*Doubt* it? I don't understand."

"Well, remember, she called the fire station, not us."

"So...?"

"Since we didn't field the call, we had no record of it."

"Yes, but you did call the fire department, surely, and inquire?"

"Yes, I did."

"Fine. So then," said the Chief Inspector softly, "may I suggest you ring her up and ask her."

Poole thought Dougall paled a bit.

"Ca-can't do that, sir. I'm afraid no one there took her name or number. Or address."

The Chief Inspector clasped his forehead.

"What a lost opportunity! And you haven't pursued this?"

"Well...there was nothing to pursue."

Shutting his eyes, St. George gripped the edge of the table, and took a slow deep breath. *Oh, biofeedback, please work*, prayed Poole.

"Use the radio, man! The newspapers! The grocery shoppers! A simple notice would do—Will the person who did such-and-such please phone your office at this number. My God! Can it be any simpler?"

The hapless detective could do nothing but look down at his shabby shoes as St. George's voice now became quiet and menacing. "How many farmsteads in the area?"

"Several, uh, maybe a dozen."

"Well then...unless they've all been hoisted aboard alien spacecraft, I should wager one of those residents will tell you that a strange woman came to them last Saturday and asked to use the bloody phone. And they can probably provide a description unless she wore a ski mask and fatigues and carried a MAC-10 at the hip."

Poole winced at the cutting sarcasm.

"Yes, sir. Quite right, sir. I'll get a man on it right away."

St. George nodded and said, "Sgt. Poole and I will wait..."

It took a few seconds for Dougall to get the hint. But then he was up, out of his chair, and headed for the squad room. St. George rolled his eyes heavenward but foreswore further comment, keeping his thoughts to himself as he looked first at Poole and down at McSwain's report.

* * *

When Dougall returned, the Chief Inspector asked, "Which came in first—the electronic signal or the phone call?"

"The signal. At 10:05 A.M. The call came in at 10:10."

"The firemen got underway when?"

"10:09 from Bathgate; 10:10 from Livingston."

"So they were on the road when the call came through."

"Yes."

"Which might account for the lack of interest in the caller...after the fact. They arrived on-scene...?"

"In 12 minutes—at 10:22."

"Meaning the fire burned unattended for that time."

"Yes, sir."

"Admirable response time, I'd say. According to Chief McSwain's report, the blaze was fully mature by the time they arrived."

"Yes, sir. Had already set the Mercedes on fire—it was parked right up at the front door."

"Sounds like the blaze moved quite rapidly. I mean, the security system detects the first few wisps of smoke, radios in the signal—the phone call follows shortly thereafter—but then, after a mere 12 minutes, the place is an inferno. Is that not suspicious?"

"I expressed concern about that but was overruled. Everyone else insisted there was nothing unusual about the fire's progression with nothing to impede it."

"Meaning?"

"Meaning the sprinkler system didn't work."

"Reason?"

"Short circuit."

"But Walcott disagreed."

"No. He agrees the fire caused the short circuit. He says arson caused the fire."

Dougall went on to explain that McSwain had checked whether the alarm system itself had malfunctioned. Because the company that installed the hardware had gone belly-up three years earlier, another vendor did the inspection. Despite all the wreckage, they found no signs of sabotage or mechanical or electrical failure.

The Chief Inspector folded his arms across his ample abdomen.

"Mmmmmm. The security system—did it monitor comings and goings?"

"Yes. Worked several ways. Logged in who opened up and who closed the place. Monitored people passing through each entrance. Employees entered and left through the front while deliveries were taken in the rear."

"Fire exits?"

"McSwain said they were unlatched but not open. He feels the air conditioning and the laminar flow operations supplied extra air and so inadvertently helped spread the blaze."

"You mentioned pressure sensors ... where?"

"Under the concrete pads at the guardhouse and beneath the sod all along the roadway and perimeter of the parking lot and grounds so pedestrians couldn't sneak around the barricade. Then again inside the front entry."

"Employees ... special IDs?"

"Yes. A generic affair with a magnetic strip which allows them access to the grounds and then through a separate gate inside the building into the work area."

"Generic?"

"No individual numbers or codes. Just an 'open-sesame' device. So the total number leaving at the end of the day must equal the total number entering."

"Isn't that rather primitive?"

"Suited their purpose," Dougall said. "We checked all the logs thoroughly. No discrepancies until Saturday, of course."

"Oh? How early Saturday?"

"9 o'clock."

"Did the cards give the employees access to the building?"

"No. Only the Top Five, as they're called, had such cardkeys. That's the two Ponts; the chief engineer James Barrows; the head technician, a chap named Manning; and the dead man's secretary. The two guards rotate duty and share a special card which is kept in a strongbox in their booth. The six-digit code to the box is changed every month."

"The special cardkeys ... individually coded?"

"Right. No duplicates exist and so the log records exactly who passes through and when."

"Did they ever hand off their cards to each other?"

"No, sir. It's totally forbidden and taken as a matter of honor. They rotate weekly as to who opens and closes."

"What if someone becomes ill? Or has to leave? Oh, well yes, of course, their departure would be counted. But what if their car breaks down and they cannot leave the grounds before closing time. Then what?"

"Any of the Top Five can override the system at the main console next to R&D."

"Hmmmpf! Any attempt to steal the keycards?"

"Never."

"All right, anything more about the front door?"

"Two doors actually. Outer and inner with a four-foot vestibule between. Sensor in the outer door coordinates with a pressure sensor beneath the floor beyond the inner door to record comings and goings. A deadbolt lock in the outer door is operated only by the special cardkeys which also turn the security system on and off. The employee cards will not work."

"How does the sensor work?"

"Well, I'm no mechanic, but what I understand is that whenever the outer door separates from the doorframe, a signal registers. Then the pressure pad just inside the inner door trips a second signal with the first step inside. The sequence lets you know at once whether the person was entering or leaving and when."

"1-2 versus 2-1."

"Yes."

As for several people entering or leaving together, Dougall said the VES executives were not concerned with groups of people but with after-hours break-ins and individuals trying to stay behind after closing. Moreover, supposedly VES received very few visitors and, with the small workforce, everyone knew everyone else by sight and sound. The final cog was the loyalty of the employees who had been with the company since its inception.

"Did they, by chance, consult a professional security firm or the police?"

"No. Not that it would have changed their minds."

"You indicated the logs showed no problems on Friday."

"Correct. None at all and none for the entire week. Walcott's company insisted on print-outs for then and for random days over the past few weeks. In each case, the guard arrived first and opened the driveway and then the front door. Within 15 minutes, the first employees filed in and registered with the time clock. Then at 5:00 P.M., everyone left with the guards locking up and leaving the premises by 5:30. Just as it was intended."

St. George nodded. "What about janitorial? Maintenance?"

"No one works overnight or weekends. Their products are so specialized that they do not require extra shifts. But I understand that will all change when the new project starts. Anyway, the cleaning crew and maintenance people arrive at 11:00 A.M. and are out by 5:00 as well. Only the Top Five are authorized to be in the building after closing."

"Anyone work late Friday evening?"

"No. Geoffrey Pont was the last to leave—it was his week to lock up. The guard followed him off the grounds."

"Any indication that the guard's passkey had been used Saturday?"

"None. Only their fingerprints are on it and the log shows no record of its being used after Friday afternoon."

"But clearly this Pont fellow got inside Saturday morning."

"Yes, using his own card. No one else's. Oh, and I forgot: neither the temperature and humidity logs inside the building showed any disturbances. That's critical for all their computers and such."

"Right. OK, when was Mr. Pont's entry recorded?"

"I'll show you," said Dougall who now unfolded a long sheet of computer paper which displayed monotonous columns of codes and times until well after sunrise Saturday morning. Poole got up and stood by his boss's shoulder to view the record.

ACCESS	ACCESS	TIME	TEMP	HUM	TEMP	HUM	TEMP	HUM
		0650	18.0	36	21.1	34	20.4	36
		0700	18.0	36	21.1	34	20.4	36
		0710	18.1	36	21.1	34	20.4	36
		0720	18.1	36	21.1	34	20.4	36
		0730	18.1	35	21.1	34	20.4	36
		0740	18.1	35	21.1	34	20.4	36
		0750	18.1	35	21.1	34	20.4	36
		0800	18.1	35	21.1	34	20.4	36
		0810	18.1	35	21.1	34	20.4	36
		0820	18.1	35	21.1	34	20.4	36
		0830	18.1	35	21.1	34	20.4	36
		0840	18.1	35	21.1	34	20.4	36
		0850	18.1	35	21.1	34	20.4	36
	GP(O)	0851						
		0900	18.2	35	21.1	34	20.4	36
		0901						
		0901						
		0901 (E)						
		0901 (E)						
		0902						
		0902						
		0902						
		0905 (E)						
		0905 (E)						
		0905 (E)						
		0910	18.2	35	21.1	34	20.5	36
GP(E)		0917						
		0920	18.2	35	21.1	34	20.6	35
	GP(+)	0920						
	GP(O)	0920						
	GP(+)	0920						
	GP(O)	0920						
		0930	18.2	36	21.1	34	20.6	35
		0940	18.2	36	21.1	34	20.6	35
		0950	18.2	36	21.1	34	20.6	35
		1000	18.2	36	21.1	34	20.7	34

"We've had the software company look it over. They say it represents a malfunction in the hardware, not the program."

"Of course," St. George said, "otherwise they might have to pay out."

"No, we pressed them on that. They said what's there is typical of either a power surge or a power loss. But we can rule out the latter because the alarm would have rung and everything would have switched over to the batteries and the generator."

"Power surge like a lightning strike?" asked Poole.

"Yes, as well as a number of other possibilities. However, there was no lightning that day. Or the night before."

"What about tampering?" St. George said.

"None."

"Even in a company packed full of computer geniuses?"

"Right,' answered Dougall. "No altered codes or unauthorized entries into the system."

"But they have incoming phone lines, do they not? Or rather, did?"

"Yes, sir, but only to the office suite and then to the individual officials. R&D was completely isolated. There was no way anyone could use the phone lines to tap into the computer system."

"Internet?" asked Poole.

"Just one page for advertising. One e-mail account to the office terminals. They were not buying or selling on the Web; they didn't have to."

"Fax machine?" St. George inquired.

"Yes, sir. Designated phone line as usual."

"So someone in the office or the plant area could not go to a terminal and call up the R&D section or the security system files."

"Correct."

St. George stared at the aberrant record for a long minute, his face the picture of one who has just bitten into something rancid. "Perhaps you'd be so good as to explain these columns for us. And these letters?"

"Right. The time is local military time. The right three pairs labeled 'temperature' and 'humidity' give the readings for the work area, R&D, and the business offices, respectively. Climate controlled all the way as you can see. Temp's in Centigrade, comes out to around 65 degrees Fahrenheit on the low side and 70 degrees on the high."

"Humidity is in percent?"

"Yes. The 'access' columns are for access to the grounds and the front entrance, respectively. As for letters they use the Top Five's initials. 'GP' stands for Geoffrey Pont, 'MP' would be Michael Pont, 'JB' would be James Barrows, and so on. 'E' means 'entry' and 'X' means 'exit'."

"The pluses and zeroes?"

"Turning the alarm system on and off with the cardkey."

"At the front entrance."

"Yes."

The Chief Inspector frowned.

"This first access at the door at 8:51 A.M.—what does this mean?"

"Gibberish, I'm afraid. He really arrived at 9:17."

"How do we know?"

"It's consistent with the time when we believe he left home," Dougall said. "Besides, there was no way he could gain access to the grounds without passing the guardhouse. That's why that earlier entry is spurious. It's really the only explanation that makes sense."

"So say the software people as well?" St. George challenged.

"Yes. The point is that, except for the 9:17 entry, we cannot rely at all on this record from about 8:30 onward."

"What about these times of 9:01 and 9:02 without anything beside them?"

"More gibberish, I'm afraid. What we're left with is Geoffrey Pont arriving at 9:17, going inside, and never coming out."

By now the Chief Inspector was scowling. "And the fire started some 40 minutes or so later."

"Yes, sir. If I may say so, sir, one reason why they discounted arson by another person was that there would have to be records of a *second* entry to the grounds, and a matching exit. But there's none either way."

St. George pursed his lips and nodded. "Now I can see why you and Walcott are pariahs around here. You're saying Geoffrey Pont torched his own plant."

"Yes, sir. And, of course, the Number One motive in that event is collecting insurance."

"He or VES in financial straits?"

"None that anyone will admit to. Deserves further investigation, though, in my opinion."

"Another question about the security system: how do we know the malfunction did not begin hours earlier, perhaps at midnight?"

Dougall was visibly pleased at having the ready answer.

"Because the temperature and humidity readings remained constant throughout. You see a slight drop in the work area, as they call it, in the early hours before dawn and also in the offices that are on the west side and so the last to be lit by the sun. The R&D suite has the tightest control of all. But had there been a problem, the record would have stopped right then."

"Have the cardkeys for the Top Five been accounted for?"

"Yes, sir," replied Dougall with growing confidence. "What was left of the dead man's was in his coat pocket. Chief Engineer Barrows was out and about all day but had his card with him. Same for Head Technician Manning who was home. The secretary, an officious harridan named Edith Sperling, was supervising a neighborhood garage sale. Fifth person was the younger brother Michael Pont. He was playing golf."

The Chief Inspector's eyebrows shot up.

"Really. Where, may I ask?"

"St. Andrews."

"Really!"

"Actually he was hosting three Japanese businessmen who had come in Friday for the signing of some big contract. He had spent that day, however, in London, got back in the evening, and then drove up early Saturday morning. Had his card with him. Standard protocol."

"Pardon me, "said Poole, "but there was nowhere closer to play?"

"You must forgive my associate," groused St. George, "but he has yet to experience the passion for the game. A congenital defect of some sort, I suspect...You see, Laurence, they did not have to play there, they had the *opportunity* to play there. St. Andrews is the Wimbledon of golf. Playing at St. Andrews is a once-in-a-lifetime experience. Now it happens that the Japanese are fanatical about the game, and you may have read how much Nipponese capital has gone to purchasing some famous American tracts such as Pebble Beach. So for the Ponts, what better way to curry favor with their new associates than to provide them with a round of golf on the most hallowed turf in the game? Stroke of genius, I'd say." St. George turned to Dougall and asked, "The Old Course, by chance?"

"Yes, I believe so."

"Michael Pont has a membership somewhere up there?"

"No, sir, it was his brother, the dead man. The Royal and Ancient."

"The R&A, no less," said St. George, eyebrows raised. "Very good, indeed."

"Yes, Geoffrey kept his membership though in recent years he had less and less time for playing as the company became more and more successful. Frequently fell to Michael to play social host."

"But if the plant closed down on weekends, why couldn't Geoffrey have gone up there?"

"I don't know; he just planned on not going. Had it all set for Michael to do the honors. At least that's what everyone says."

"About going out to the plant, did Geoffrey leave any messages with anyone? Notes? Voice-mail? E-mail? Whatever?"

"No, sir, not even with his wife."

"Anyone aware of something troubling him?"

"Not that anyone can recall."

"Lawsuit, perhaps? What's that term...infringement?"

"No, sir, nothing like that," Dougall said. "The Sperling woman checks all his mail. Nothing untoward or unusual came through this past week or the week before. She thought he seemed a bit pensive but chalked it up to the impending visit by the Japanese."

"Was there a private line into his office?"

"No, sir. He considered that an extravagance."

"So you're telling us that no one knows why this highly successful businessman went out there all alone Saturday morning."

Glancing at Poole, Inspector Dougall firmly shook his head. "No sir, no one."

"Hmmmpf! Didn't anyone find that very strange?"

4

RECEIVING NO REPLY except a weak shrug, St. George slapped his thigh, got to his feet and paused to smooth the wrinkles from his coat before picking up McSwain's report.

"Well, Inspector, we thank you for the briefing. You've been thorough and what you say certainly sounds plausible. As for tomorrow, rest assured that we come with no preconceptions. Beyond that, I guess things will just have to fall where they will."

"Fair enough. Constable Cobb will take you back. He'll also fetch you in the morning."

Poole was acutely aware of his superior's unusually crisp "Thank you" and exaggerated politeness and courtesy as Dougall accompanied them outside to their car. The local detective seemed puzzled that their driver was nowhere to be seen.

"Oh, one more thing," said St. George. "May we have a copy of the *postmortem?*"

"No," Dougall said. " I mean I'm sorry, there is none."

"Not the original. A Xerox copy."

"We don't have one."

"Well, then..." St. George said with a quick furrowed glance at Poole, "would you please have one of your people run one off for us?"

"What I meant was we don't have an original to use."

"No original? But you have jurisdiction. The man died just down the road from here."

"Yes, but we have no report. There was no post."

"Wh-at?" St. George said softly, his single word hanging ominously in the air. "You're telling us that no autopsy was performed?"

"None. I wasn't aware of it at the time—I was busy out at the scene with Walcott—but apparently they took him straightaway to Edinburgh—h-he lived there."

"No *autopsy?* But how...?"

"From what I've heard—no direct word, mind you—but they felt he was too far gone to need one. As for identification, they had his wedding ring, watch, lighter, belt buckle..."

"Belt buckle?"

"Yes, he had one commissioned with a big 'V' for Viscount. And then there were the dental records."

"But the body, surely it's still on hold?"

"Oh, no, cremated Sunday night. Memorial service is tomorrow."

"What the bloody hell—!" escaped from the Chief Inspector's lips just as Constable Cobb came up to inform Dougall that he was wanted inside for a call from the Chief Superintendent. The detective quickly bid them "Good night" and hastened into the station before St. George could say another word. Cobb then respectfully opened the rear door for a seething Chief Inspector while Poole went around and let himself in the other side.

5

After the completely silent ride back to the Squire's Inn, St. George stormed into the lobby while Poole tarried to confirm the morrow's pickup with their driver. Catching up, he found his boss talking with the bellman who was gesturing with one hand while simultaneously holding the other discretely at his side, cupped palm face-up.

"Sergeant!"

"Sir?"

"This gentleman says we have visitors awaiting us in the pub. Did you make any such arrangements for us this evening?"

"No, sir, none," replied Poole, puzzled and a bit concerned.

"They said they would await your return," urged the fidgeting bellman. "They've been waiting almost an hour."

"Oh? I see...and who might 'they' be?"

"Businessmen, sir. Friends of yours, perhaps?" the bellman answered, his open palm inching higher as though he sensed his tip might be slipping away.

"Huh! Well then, I suppose there is nothing for it but to go greet our fan club!"

St. George passed off a few large coins to the bellman, deliberately dropping one in the process. The bellman tried to act nonchalant as he quickly bent over to pick it up while the two Scotland Yard men crossed the lobby and entered the pub. They at once espied a man rising from among a group of six well-dressed civilians seated around a large corner table. The man came forward, smiling all the way, his eyes never leaving the new arrivals, but forgoing any handshake.

"Chief Inspector! This way, please."

They followed the factotum to the table where the others now rose to greet them with restrained yet polite smiles. One man with luxuriant gray hair and wearing an impeccably tailored summer-weight wool suit was obviously the leader.

"Chief Inspector, good evening and welcome to West Lothian. My name is Silas Muir."

After Muir and St. George exchanged handshakes, head nods completed the introductions. An extra chair was brought over for Poole who nevertheless found himself sitting second row.

"May we get you something?" Muir asked as he seated himself regally.

"Thank you, no, perhaps another time...I'm afraid, gentlemen, you have us at a disadvantage. We were not expecting anyone. What brings you here to see us at this hour?"

"Well, sir," said Muir, suddenly very somber, serious, and sincere, "it has to do with that terrible business out at the Viscount plant. I'm the Chief Executive Officer of the Lothian National Bank in Edinburgh. We've handled the Pont family accounts for years. You just met Mr. Forster. He's Executive Vice President of our bank. We also carry the note for the company's original financing and oversee their books as well. These other gentlemen..."—Muir motioned with a broad wave of hand—"...are the leaders of other businesses with major interests throughout the region and who directly or indirectly do business with Viscount and expect to do more in the future."

"I see," said St. George as he looked each man in the eye. No one blinked.

"We appreciate the effort you've made to come here," Muir continued. "We felt the least we could do was to welcome you in person and to answer any questions you might have."

"Certainly the more information one has, the better," St. George said affably.

"Exactly! And nowhere is that philosophy more vital than appreciating the full economic impact Viscount Electric Systems has had and must continue to have on our region."

As if on some silent cue, the other businessmen nodded emphatically.

"As you know, Viscount is a small but full-service computer component operation from modifying chips to specialty software to circuit boards to everything in-between. The only thing they don't do is manufacture the case or assemble the computer itself. They're extremely well run and growing. Indeed, I may say that, in the foreseeable future, their importance will be measured *nationally* as well."

More heads nodded en chorale.

"So, as crass as it may sound, it is absolutely critical that we get this tragedy behind us and move forward and get Viscount up and running as quickly as possible. For *everyone's* benefit."

Muir had leaned forward in his chair, as though to add emphasis to his last remark, reminding Poole of a pushy insurance salesman who had once invaded his parents' home. Poole also noticed how, in counterpoint, his boss struggled to look professorially studious and contemplative.

"So time is of the essence."

"Pre-cise-ly," said Muir who was visibly pleased that this London copper had grasped his message. "You've been told of the YAMATSU project?"

"No. Perhaps you could fill us in."

"Well, that's what has put the urgency to the whole situation," began the banker. "For several years, VES and a Japanese company called YAMATSU have been competitors and have pretty much split about two-thirds of the Western world market between them. Some time back, they each independently tackled the same design problem but from different directions. Well, if you'll excuse a bit of Scottish pride, *our* boys worked out the missing link before the Japanese approach—even though they say it was quite by accident. Anyway, before you could say 'sushi,' the two companies were talking cooperation and finally merging for a joint operation. The whole process would be difficult and costly for either one going it alone, but together, with economies of scale, lack of duplication, the whole timetable can be accelerated. Puts the new product out on the market more than a year ahead of anyone else. An outstanding accomplishment."

Silas Muir again paused to permit his associates to nod en chorale.

"This past week, the top three men from YAMATSU came here to sign the final papers setting the joint venture in motion. That happened Friday. No one disputes the fire is a setback, but if we can give YAMATSU some assurance that VES will be rebuilt and operating within six months, everything stays on course."

"Is such an ambitious recovery feasible?"

"Oh, yes, quite," Muir answered while nodding emphatically. "Modular construction makes all kinds of things possible."

"And if there is some delay?"

Muir's countenance suddenly was pure anguish. "Absolute ruination for VES *and* the region. The standard escape clause—which we *never* thought would *ever* be needed—allows the parties to go their separate ways. YAMATSU has informed us that more than a two-month delay will invoke that clause. As well as the subparagraph which would force VES to pick up all the legal expenses."

"But why the hurry on their part?"

"They claim that the joint operation would miss the targeted market opening, after which the project would be moot. Although officially we vigorously contest that position, in truth, they are completely in the right. So should the worst occur, we would have absolutely no redress anywhere."

St. George nodded ponderously, like a jurist hearing complicated arguments from the bench. "I see. Correct me if I'm wrong, but then the insurance proceeds are needed to pay for the rebuilding and refitting."

"Unfortunately, yes. Comes to a few million pounds, sterling. As promising as the project is, no bank will extend any significant amount without tangible collateral."

"What about your bank?"

"We're already committed to the full allowable extent."

"What about intellectual property? The software?"

"Worthless without the hardware."

"And that's why the insurance company's position presents a problem."

"Indeed," Muir said. "This bastard Walcott's got us over a barrel and he knows it. He's a shyster and nothing more. Bastard will get a hefty commission if he can get his company out from under their rightful responsibility to honor their coverage. Oh, yes, his people stand righteously behind him—I know, I've called them—but I have no doubt he's just positioning himself so he can strike a deal for himself."

"Deal?"

"A bribe, of course."

"He has suggested such?"

"Not yet, but he will. He lobbied that poor Inspector Dougall and inveigled him into calling you people. Just his way of creating pressure not only here but in the nervous old Nellies in London. Damned extortion is what it is!"

The nodding heads now uttered muffled, "Hear, hear!"

"I see," said the Chief Inspector, as though growing comfortable with the situation.

"So we simply cannot have Geoffrey Pont blamed for the fire. If he is, there's no payout. And without a payout, there can be no more VES."

St. George nodded slowly as though thoroughly absorbing the banker's dripping sincerity.

"On behalf of all concerned," Muir hurried on, "may I implore you to not be hasty in your examination? I have no doubt that Walcott and his people will exert as much pressure as they can, say whatever they must, to influence your decision. So stay whatever extra days you need, the bank will cover the cost. Here's my card...I can be reached through that number at any time."

St. George took the card without looking at it and slipped it in his coat pocket. He noticed how the banker's eyes followed the card to its destination.

"Very well, Mr. Muir, we shall certainly take everything you've told us under advisement. And may we, in turn, thank you gentlemen for taking the time to come here. We do appreciate your cooperation."

Knowing the Chief Inspector's abhorrence of insipid, vapid, corporate byplay so prevalent in modern life, Poole fought to conceal his puzzlement at his mentor's almost obsequious, overblown courtesy toward the six businessmen. *What self-control!* he marveled as he watched the social minuet draw to a close.

"It's been our pleasure," the banker said, sitting back, his mission accomplished.

"But now if you will excuse us," said St. George, shoving his chair back, "we've a long day ahead of us tomorrow."

"Of course," said an obviously pleased Silas Muir as he rose to his feet. As though choreographed, the others followed suit. The banker and St. George again shook hands. "And again, call me anytime should you need anything."

The executives smiled politely as they passed by but said nothing. Once the entourage had filed out of the pub, Poole started for the door himself when St. George tugged on his sleeve and motioned for him to follow to a small booth. Once seated, neither man said anything until their server had left with their order for two beers.

"Well, Laurence, were you impressed?" asked St. George, his face rigid.

"I'm not sure."

"Oh, come now! Confronted by these wealthy, self-made alphamales emitting that unmistakable aura which says, 'A mere policeman? Is that the *best* you could do with your life?' Like being hauled before a council of church elders. Surely you picked up their dictum, 'Be good, children, and do as we say.' What rot!"

"Well, I did notice how no one expressed concern for the deceased or his widow."

"Indeed. Maybe they're saving it all for the memorial service tomorrow. And that pompous ass Muir! What was fairly reeking from everything he said was that they wanted nothing to stand in their way of increasing their personal wealth. But then again, why should we be surprised that money drives this whole affair?"

Like the pause button on a VCR, the two coppers waited until the server delivered their beverages before resuming their conversation.

"I'm counting mine as medicinal," said St. George, nodding toward his drink. "Count yours as you wish."

"Medicinal?"

"A sedative if I'm to get any sleep tonight. And it also gives me an excuse to stall before going to my room where I might be tempted to make some intemperate phone calls to London. Better to let some time pass."

"Really now. That bad?"

"Well, what have we? London's charge is to shove the toothpaste back in the tube. Our instructions from Herr Muir is to leave it out. Either one damned near impossible. And making matters even worse is that we cannot do anything meaningful until we have first eliminated all conceivable accidental causes for the fire. Amazingly simple undertaking in some people's minds."

"But *all* set fires leave clues lying about, don't they?"

"That they do," replied St. George after a swallow. "But on Day One, not Day Five. I can tell you this: had we encountered such dereliction in London, I would have popped off right then and there. However, to my everlasting credit, my remarkable inner self sensed the ramifications here precluded any self-indulgence, and so miraculously I held my tongue."

"Yes, your restraint was duly noted," said Poole with a slight bow. "What still boggles the mind is how Stallings and his Edinburgh superiors could have settled for such gross misconduct...or ineptitude."

St. George nodded. "I'd say someone exerted enormous political pressure to subvert such venerable established procedures. I mean, it's one thing to decide against a post, but quite another to hurry up and destroy the body. Raises suspicion, does it not?"

"I was also taken by the passion of Superintendent Stallings and Chief McSwain—almost as though they've taken the whole thing personally."

"Well, they have," said St. George who paused for another sip. "Stallings did say he was staking his reputation on the result."

"Yes, but even with such hyperbole, isn't that an unusual stance?"

"Indeed it is, which tells me this is rapidly becoming an unusual case. Might even be a two-beer case. Wait here, I'm going to raise some cash."

Puzzled, Poole stayed put and sipped his beer as his boss left for the lobby. He glanced casually about the cozy establishment that this night was sparsely patronized. The only activity was the departure of a young couple and the arrival of a burly, though nondescript-looking man sporting spectacles who took a seat in another corner. For a moment, Poole thought the man was watching him. Probably a reporter, he concluded as St. George returned and handed him a wad of money.

"Scottish notes?"

"Yes. From the Royal Bank in Edinburgh. One of three banks permitted to issue their own currency."

"So why, may I ask, do we have these?"

"We are in a very subordinate position. True, we are within the boundaries of the United Kingdom, but Scotland is an entity all unto itself. Has its own government and a judicial system not like our own. So here we are, two Englanders poking our noses into a local matter which some people in authority obviously hold very dear to their hearts. We've already seen that our presence is not wanted or welcomed. At the moment, our only ally is a disgraced born-again inspector of questionable ability who's posted to an out-of-the-way station house."

"You make it sound rather bleak."

"Well, perhaps I'm being a bit melodramatic, but we will need all the help we can get if we're to do this thing fairly. And the quickest way to sabotage such an effort is for the people here to become sorely passive-aggressive. So, in my view, there is no surer means of igniting such negative reactions than to go around dropping Her Majesty's British currency all over the place. Rather a blatant reminder of who conquered whom...you know, shades of Robert Bruce. Remember, there is still strong sentiment up here for genuine full independence."

"So using local currency shows a measure of respect."

"Exactly. Can't hurt, can it? Ah, well, if you're finished, shall we adjourn?"

"Aye, lead on McDuff."

They rode the elevator in silence, bid each other "Good night," and went to their respective rooms. A minute later, someone knocked cautiously on Poole's door. He opened it to find the burly man from the pub, minus his glasses, standing there in equal surprise.

"Oh, sorry. I thought this was the Chief Inspector's room."

"And you are—?"

"Walcott. Ansel Walcott."

6

POOLE LED THE way next door, knocked, and once inside, completed the introductions. Both detectives were impressed with the insurance investigator's firm grip and forthright, positive manner. St. George offered the man the lone armchair in the room while Poole took the stool at the dressing table.

"I thought we'd be seeing you tomorrow," said the Chief Inspector as he sat on the bed.

"That is the plan, and I'll be there...it's just that I thought it important to confer with you beforehand. I might not be allowed on the premises tomorrow."

"Why not?"

"Well, Superintendent Stallings may feel I no longer have a reason to be there."

"No problem," said the Chief Inspector. "He's already informed us he has more important work elsewhere. McSwain, however, will be present."

"Right. I see you've met Silas Muir."

"Yes...but we did not see you..."

"I had planned on waiting for you in the lobby, but then Muir and his colleagues showed up, and I beat a retreat to my car until they left."

"It sounds like you and the good banker share the same antipathy."

Walcott showed a wan smile. "He's a very influential man in

Edinburgh. Been the Pont family banker for years. Their relatives, the Cargills, as well. Very set in his ways. Very formidable opponent."

"Why an opponent?"

"He's been exerting pressure on my company to reject my report."

"How do you know that?"

"I have word from associates at the home office that he's been burning up the wires to my superiors. Even had some solicitors calling on behalf of their 'concerned clients'—those other men you met tonight. But what has me worried the most is that now my own calls are not being returned."

"Are you suggesting your superiors could be intimidated or bought off?"

"If you had asked me a week ago, I'd have said certainly not. Now I'm not sure. I've never been out on a limb like this before."

"I see. Tell me, could you be bought?"

"Never! The very idea!"

"Well, it was suggested to us earlier this evening that all this puff and nonsense about arson was simply your way of positioning yourself for a bribe to change your report."

Walcott shook his head vigorously and wiggled in his chair. "That's McSwain, all right. Yelled it right to my face, he did. Well, I can tell you, they couldn't give me enough money to put up with all this grief. I've had my tires slashed, I've received threatening phone calls, so now I work out of a room in Edinburgh and drive a different rental car every day."

"Surely you exaggerate!"

"Hardly."

"Any idea who's behind all that?"

"Unfortunately, no. Let's just say I'm persona non grata in these parts. I've even taken to wearing fake glasses."

"Can't say that I blame you. You've met this Muir fellow?"

"Yep. Him and his Four Horsemen of the Apocalypse."

"His *what?*" Poole exclaimed.

"The four sycophants who accompanied him tonight. Names are Cole, Bambury, McMann, and Behan. Powerful men in their own right in West Lothian and Mid-Lothian yet they seem especially beholden to Muir for some reason. My guess would be ultrafavorable loans or mortgages somewhere along the way. Ostensibly they stand to do a great deal of future business with the Ponts. Forster, of course, is Muir's gopher."

"Remarkable. So how did you meet these men?"

"I was called to an audience Sunday evening at Stallings' office in Livingston. Muir was there as were the others. He tried to reason with me, as he put it, about the economic significance of the Pont operation and how it would be fully understood should I wish to reexamine my findings. The cheek of the man! It was quite intimidating, all the same."

"What did the others say?"

"Grunted here and there. Muir was clearly the one setting the agenda."

"So how did you end it?"

"I thanked them for the additional information, but told them that what they conveyed did not change the physical findings out at the site and that my report would stand. And with that, I bid them farewell and withdrew. That night my tires were slashed and the calls started."

"Remarkable! Well, Sgt. Poole and I received our arson education at the academy quite some time ago, and I'm afraid we've had little contact with that crime since. So, despite the late hour, we'd certainly welcome a refresher course on the basics...if you have the time..."

Walcott smiled. "My pleasure...no telling what may happen tomorrow. Well, as you recall, the basic axiom is that a fire starts when some type of burnable material comes into contact with a source of ignition. That contact is designated the point of origin which, in turn, is located at the apex of the 'fire cone'. Think of that as the bottom tip of one of those cone-shaped paper cups at water coolers. The cone demonstrates how the blaze spreads upward and outward from that original point of origin. Therefore, one should see the most severe damage at the pointed apex because that's where the fire burned the longest."

"Right," said St. George as he and Poole nodded in unison.

"So we need to be alert for signs of anything which enhances or expands or accelerates this process. The most classic sign is multiple points of origin, called hot spots. Nature simply does not start equally intense blazes within a defined space. Period. Then there is the presence of a foreign container, exposed electrical wiring, unexpectedly open or shut doors and windows, concentric burn marks –"

"I'm sorry," Poole interrupted, "those are...?"

"Concentric marks result from a puddle of flammable liquid burning off from the periphery inward. Again, never happens in nature." Walcott paused while Poole said "Ah." and then continued. "The last thing we look for are 'trailers,' which are irregular areas of scorching along the floor that pass *around* objects such as floor lamps or heavy furniture. They represent the deliberate spilling of a liquid to guide the flames from place to place. The kind of thing you see in the cinema."

St. George inquired, "You are aware that Chief McSwain covered these points in his report?"

"I am, and he's correct as far as he goes."

"But you feel there's more...."

"I *know* there is, but it will be easier to show you tomorrow than try to describe those findings tonight."

"May we presume that you photographed what you saw?"

"Absolutely. Couldn't risk some energetic chap getting in there and clearing everything away. Oh, there is one more thing—silly really, but I should mention it only to illustrate the lengths to which Muir and company will go to write this whole thing off as accidental."

"And that is?"

"It's absolutely unbelievable," said the insurance man. "On Sunday, they argued the point as a probable cause for the fire. Mind you, McSwain's report says 'unspecified origin' and the death certificate states 'accidental', but that's not what they lobbied for."

"And that was...?"

"Spontaneous human combustion."

* * *

The two men from Scotland Yard could only gape in disbelief.

"It certainly was nothing of the kind," continued Walcott. "But they argued and argued with the medical examiner and then tried to get me to state the same. I absolutely refused to do so and that's when I knew I had to get my report in pronto."

"Amazing!"

"Question—" said Poole with a cautious eye toward his boss, "but why could it not be spontaneous combustion?"

"Two reasons. First, in genuine human spontaneous combustion, the surrounding environment is left wholly untouched, not burned to the ground as what happened to the Viscount plant. Second, the body is calcined; by their own description, this one was not."

"Calcined?" said St. George.

Walcott chuckled. "When the body is ignited by some *external* source, as in formal cremation, it is called *preternatural* combustion. Cremation involves prolonged temperatures around 950 degrees Centigrade. For comparison, remember water boils at 100 degrees. The key point is that external burning does not consume the entire body. The flames char the surface but do not penetrate through and through. So generally, bones remain intact and so must be pulverized into fine ash in a crenulator, which is nothing more than a revolving drum holding several iron balls."

"Ouch!" said the Chief Inspector. Walcott smiled again.

"However, in *spontaneous* combustion, the body *itself* is the source of ignition. The fire completely converts nearly the whole body to ash. Usually, all that is found are the ends of the extremities much as one finds the ends of logs in a grate. This unique process is called *calcination.*"

Poole raised his hand. "So you're saying the body was not consumed and turned into ash but was only charred."

"Correct. 'Burned to a crisp' was how they put it."

St. George: "Did you see the body yourself?"

"No. They extricated it first thing Sunday morning. I could not get here before noon. Besides, I had no right to view it. Just here to assess the building."

"We understand the remains were cremated that same evening."

Walcott nodded. "That's what I heard. Sounds positively ultraefficient!"

St. George paused a moment as though giving Walcott an opportunity to expand his answer. However, the insurance man remained silent. "So what happened after you filed your report?"

"My office said 'Sit tight,'" Walcott replied. "After that, I've just hung around trying to keep a line on things. Then earlier today I got word that two blokes from Scotland Yard were coming up and I was to meet them out at the site tomorrow at 9:00 A.M."

"So how did you find us?"

"My office had the details. And then I checked, discreetly, of course. Remember, I'm an investigator."

"Well, sir, we thank you for tracking us down," St. George said. "And for your discourse. I'm sure it will prove most useful."

"I hope so. Got kind of a tall order facing you," Walcott offered as he rose to his feet, his hosts doing the same.

"Oh? How so?"

"Well, in the Lothian and Borders jurisdiction, we get some 500 cases of fireraising each year. Only solve about one of every six. Percentage is a little better out here in the country. On the other hand, of the handful of murders, 100 percent get solved. But don't let me discourage you."

"Hah! Perish the thought! Just what the sergeant and I relish—an uphill battle against impossible odds. Right, Laurence?"

"We wouldn't have it any other way."

* * *

Amid good-natured chuckles and handshakes, the locally unpopular insurance man departed. After a few seconds, at the Chief Inspector's behest, Poole stepped into the hallway to be sure their visitor had left the floor.

"Spontaneous combustion?" whispered Poole as he returned to find St. George pacing the room, his hands clasping and unclasping behind his back. "Makes one think that somebody's downright desperate."

"Well, some things are certainly clear. One, these factions are playing for high stakes. In the end, there will be a winner and the rest losers, no ties. Two, in that regard, banker Muir described merely the tip of the iceberg. Three, London knows a damned sight more about this matter than what they told me or even intimated. Note well, Laurence, that when the Home Secretary bothers to busy himself in such a matter, be assured that he is not alone, that others are waiting in the shadows to follow events. Four, we are clearly on the spot, all of which must then raise the obvious question –"

"What?"

"No, *why*. I'm not an arson investigator. I'm a *homicide* man. *You're* a homicide man. *We* are homicide men. So why have we been sent here to work an arson investigation?"

"Well, to rule out murder, I suppose."

St. George stopped and thought a moment.

"But note that no one has even mentioned murder. Stallings and Muir are petrified that the dead man will be blamed for the fire. On the flip side, Walcott and his company are anxious for him to be so designated. And somebody, somewhere, put the idea into the heads at Whitehall that all was not as it appears. I suspect it centers around the missing autopsy and the apparent hurry to cremate the remains."

"Perhaps a conspiracy?"

"No," answered the Chief Inspector, "I seriously doubt it. What I've seen thus far suggests amateurish incompetence rather than a sophisticated, coordinated plot. But that give us all the more reason to remain alert tomorrow."

"In that event, we should probably retire."

"Yes, yes, you're right, you go ahead. I'm going to call London and give a few people a sleepless night."

"Oh, one final thing ..." said Poole.

"Yes?"

"I wonder ... do you suppose our driver got instructions to report whatever we say?"

"You're thinking of Cobb being late and that call for Dougall? Oh, yes, yes, of course, I'm sure they both did. Mum's the word, mmm? Good night."

Wednesday

7

WEDNESDAY MORNING, POOLE awoke at dawn, puzzled that he had not slept the remaining hour until his alarm would sound. He lay back to doze but found himself getting restless and, after some time, realized that the early daylight was fading. Getting to his feet, he peered between his window curtains and winced upon seeing the heavy dark clouds gathering overhead. Thankful for his foresight, he hurriedly dressed and dashed out to the rental car to retrieve the galoshes, raincoats, rainhats, golf rainsuits, and umbrellas expropriated from his grandparents. With the boodle safely in his room, he then bathed, shaved, and redressed before joining his boss in the dining room.

"Say nothing!" St. George said as he held up a cautionary finger. "You are not late. I am early for a change. Sleep well?"

"Yes, thank you. Actually, I've been up for a while," whereupon Poole reported his covert activities, pausing momentarily to place his order for a fried Scotch egg and coffee.

"Rain, you say? Lord, I never gave it a thought."

"Well, I checked with the weather service before I left home; 50 percent chance."

"Thank goodness one of us was on the ball. I guess I was too busy feeling sorry for myself."

"I borrowed my uncle's golf rainsuit. He's about your size.

Thought maybe…"

"That's very considerate, Laurence, thank you, and no, I'm not embarrassed about my size as you can tell from my breakfast."

"Anything from London?" said Poole.

"Yes, some. Had the pleasure of rousting the AC no less. Emphasized that I was reporting directly to him in keeping with my private brief from him and the Home Secretary—he did not appreciate that reminder—and that I needed the weight of his office to expedite my request for information."

"Which I'm sure he appreciated."

St. George grinned. "Anyway, about an hour ago came the information I wanted. Silas Muir is the power broker he makes himself out to be. In these parts, he's the man to see if you want to finance a project. Apparently brought several very lucrative projects to fruition over the past few years. Brought his bank quite a return on investment. All of which has given him power and influence of the highest order."

"In other words, he can do no wrong."

"At least inside the bank. He's accustomed to giving orders and to being obeyed. So let's say you have a project to develop, well, you're well advised to seek out Silas Muir and invite his bank to participate. Conversely, his 'thumbs-down' can kill any deal."

"You inquire about any others?"

"Oh, yes. The man Forster is highly regarded as an office operative, a technocrat, if you will, but not leadership material. So Muir has no challengers within the bank. The other four gentlemen are all respected business leaders who have at various times joined Muir in his ventures and have profited handsomely as a result."

"An economic high council of sorts."

"Pre-cise-ly, as Herr Muir would say. Also confirmed that Stallings and McSwain are who they are—no elaborate spending, no unusual habits, so no indication why they are so blind to any possible outcome except accidental fire and death. Oh, and our friend Inspector Dougall checked out as well—Good morning, Inspector!"

Poole just had time to look over his shoulder to see the local detective approach their table and take an available seat.

"Looks like it's going to be a bit damp and nippy," Dougall said, his nervous smile reflecting his anxiety about the imminent confrontation out at VES.

"We're prepared, thanks to the good Sergeant here," said St. George as he swallowed the last of his juice. "Can we get you anything?"

"Thank you, no, I ate earlier. Didn't have much of an appetite."

"All right. Any overnight developments?"

"No, sir, not yet."

"Very well," said the Chief Inspector as he laid down his napkin, "let's settle up and get out there and be done with it."

"Uh, sir?" said Poole.

"Yes, Laurence?"

"I believe my breakfast is coming right now. Might I have a few seconds with it?"

"Wha—?" replied the Chief Inspector before he broke into a sheepish grin, apologized for his inattention, and invited Dougall to retake his seat. "I'm so accustomed to being the last to finish..." To dramatize his intention not to rush, the Chief Inspector leaned back in his chair and ordered crullers and coffee for himself and Dougall who politely switched his beverage to low-fat milk.

As for Poole, he expressed his appreciation with a smile and a nod and then diligently devoured his meal, all the while pretending not to notice his mentor's five clumsy attempts to check his wristwatch surreptitiously under cover of a forced conversation on local traffic problems. In the end, all three took their last swallows at the same time and rose as one before heading for the exit.

* * *

The two Scotland Yard detectives stood under their dripping umbrellas and stared at the charred, warlike ruin before them. Suddenly, Ansel Walcott materialized out of the gloom and joined them. No greetings were exchanged. At last, mindful of the discomfort of the assembled people awaiting his assessment of the scene, St. George murmured a few words to Dougall who in turn nodded to McSwain and Deputy Chief Bogan. With the civil servants aggressively projecting their professional facades, the group moved en masse a few steps closer to the burned wreckage. Then, in the steady drizzle, McSwain began his resume with the comment that, upon the brigade's arrival, there was nothing for his men to do but allow the blaze to burn itself out.

"There were no odors of any kind," he continued, "and we found no trailers, no petroleum puddles, no empty containers, and nothing showed under UV."

"UV?" asked Poole. "You mean ultraviolet?"

"Right," answered McSwain with a bit of importance. "It picks up fluorescence from flammable liquids. If anything was there, we would have seen it right off."

"Thank you."

"All the windows were properly closed and fastened. We found a side door and a rear door unlatched but not open. We learned that was part of the emergency exit protocol. Happened automatically. The point is we found nothing blocked or barred, nothing held open, no exposed wiring, no remodeling underway, so no soldering irons, blowtorches, or the like. Hotplate and microwave in the employee lounge were in working order. Air conditioning units were intact as was the laminar flow unit. We believe that they fed air to the blaze and helped spread it."

"Could the building be sealed off into compartments?" St. George asked, immensely thankful to Poole for the golf rainsuit and galoshes. Completely dry beneath, he felt like an astronaut on a spacewalk.

"No. Wouldn't've helped, though."

"What triggered the alarm, would you say?"

"Heat and smoke. The signal itself was nonspecific. They just wanted us out here at the first sign of trouble, no matter what."

"Of course."

"As for the electrical systems," McSwain said, "all receptacles were intact, properly installed. Thought they might have melted, but they didn't. Fuse boxes were intact. No sign of a power surge or overload."

"Pardon me," said the Chief Inspector, "but did I not hear that one of the software companies said the irregularities in the security system printout were due to a power surge?"

"Within that system, I can't say. What I'm referring to is something involving the main buses. All the primary and secondary circuits were secure. No tampering anywhere. No clocks lying about; no batteries; no radios save the one in the employee lounge and which belonged there. No residues such as wax, paraffin, soap, no matchboxes or match stubs, no broken bottles. The mess in the assembly area was completely natural. The point is everything *belongs*, if you get my meaning. No sign of foreign particulates that could be tested for nitrates. Nothing to suggest a Molotov cocktail or any accelerant. Most chemical containers in the plant were intact, all things considered, as was the line from the bottled gas tank in the rear. The level of burn was fairly uniform throughout; lowest point about three feet above the floor, except for the body. No sign of multiple origins."

"The body ... on the floor?"

"Yes. It's quite clear he caught fire while standing and then collapsed—as you'd expect."

"Any possibility that he died first and was already on the floor when he caught fire?"

McSwain blinked three times. "Uh...that's not really within the realm of reasonable possibilities, let alone probabilities. We believe the fire started in the ceiling, spread laterally through the building, and then broke through, catching Mr. Pont as it did in the office area."

Poole marveled how his boss was again putting forth professorial impartiality. He wondered how long it would last.

"And no tampering with the alarm system?" St. George inquired.

"None at all. No malfunction, either. You're leading to the short duration of the blaze. We believe the air conditioning system and the broken windows inadvertently created a substantial backdraft. The place became a virtual fireball."

"Broken windows?"

"Rather cheap glass used. Won't stand up to much."

"Were any company files removed from the premises last week?"

"We checked that right off," the fire chief answered. "Nothing there as it turned out. The younger Pont heads up Research and Development and customarily takes work home with him. Gets more privacy there, he says. He showed us the material he had taken on Thursday—routine stuff as far as we could tell. No relation to their Japanese project."

Poole noted that the questions and answers were coming faster. Perhaps just because everyone wanted to get out of the weather and away from there.

St. George: "Did he have a tendency to stockpile his work? You know, 'to-do' piles that gather a day at a time?"

McSwain: "No, sir. Seemed to be very organized. Just takes home what he needs and brings it back the next day."

St. George: "Right. So once the structural engineer gave the go-ahead, your men went in and found the body."

McS: "Correct. Right smack dab in the middle of the offices. Lying between the desks. All curled up he was. Horrible thing."

St.G: "How do you mean 'curled up'?"

McS: "Drawn up—like when they're cremated. You know, fetal position."

St.G: "That badly burnt?"

McS: "To a crisp. If I may speak frankly, worse than a pig on a spit."

St.G: "Around on all sides, then."

McS: "Pretty much."

St.G: "Clothes burned away?"

McS: "For the most part."

St.G: "Tissue as well?"

McS: "Correct."

St.G: "Was there *any* clothing, anywhere, that was spared?"

McS: "Just that in contact with the floor."

St.G: "Which was carpeted."

McS: "Correct."

St.G: "Was the carpet beneath the body burnt as well?"

McS: "Just singed, as you might expect. Means nothing, of course, because obviously the fire there was extinguished as soon as contact was made. Lack of oxygen."

St.G: "And at the edges as well?"

McS: "Couldn't really say, what with all the mess around. Nothing really stood out."

The Chief Inspector nodded ponderously and scrunched up his face. Perhaps a bit overplayed, thought Poole, but effective for the circumstances. When would his boss spring the trap?

"Interesting. Would you say the office area was burnt as badly as the rest of the plant?"

"It was," said McSwain, his jaw set forward, satisfied with having kept this London copper at bay.

"How about the lungs—soot in them?"

In his peripheral vision, St. George noticed that Dougall suddenly became very interested in his wet galoshes.

"Lungs?" said McSwain. "I suppose so. Why wouldn't they?"

"You've not seen the Medical Examiner's report?"

"No, but I was there when they checked him over. Did it right there inside their van."

"I was referring to the autopsy."

"Autopsy? What autopsy? Didn't need no bloody autopsy to tell you what done him in. The M-E said it was all plain as day...and it was."

"No autopsy? In a death under suspicious circumstances?"

McSwain drew himself up to his full height and mustered as much swagger as he could.

"Wasn't my decision."

"But you could have insisted!"

"Not for me to say if the M-E says otherwise. Like I said, if you'd seen him...seen it...you'd know why."

"This is impossible!" cried St. George as he looked first toward Poole and then Dougall. Turning back, he continued. "And they cremated him the same day?"

"They did. Wasn't much to it. He was almost cooked through anyway. Thing was, he was so bent over, there was simply no way to get him into a casket unless you cut off the limbs. Hell, I'd'a done the same thing if it were my kin."

"So who gave the go-ahead for the cremation?"

"It was his cousin, Mr. Edward Cargill. He had come out here when we were fighting the fire."

"Hmmmpf! You realize the problem by not having the lungs examined..."

McSwain looked daggers at his English antagonist and then stared steadfastly at the sopping wet ruin.

"Not as there is one."

"If soot were found in the lungs, then he inhaled smoke and thus was alive when the fire started. But if there was no soot, *ergo* no breathing, then he was already dead. And if he was already dead, then we're left with how and why...and who?"

The fire chief remained silent but his tight lips and moving jaw betrayed his anger at the devastating implications of the Chief Inspector's remarks.

"So in the absence of an autopsy," St. George continued, "we're left with four possible scenarios."

McSwain turned his head, but it was Bogan and Dougall who, in unison, said "Four?" as Poole brought out his notepad and began scribbling on it.

"Yes. Number One—Mr. Pont is in the office suite, probably trapped there by the smoke and fire. So he's standing there when the fire breaks through the ceiling and ignites his clothing and quickly spreads around his upper torso. He falls to the floor and dies while his clothes continue to burn. But it is the upper body clothing that should burn, not his legs or shoes, and that's what puzzles me. How did they become as burnt as the rest of him? But then we have

Number Two—Mr. Pont is trying to torch his own place—"

"No!" exclaimed McSwain. "That's outrageous!"

"Bear with me, Chief, bear with me...he's trying to set the fire, he spills some fuel on himself, he accidentally catches fire. But that should be limited to one arm and the most burning should be on the upper trunk. Again, leaving the legs relatively free of damage...which conflicts with the evidence you described. Wouldn't you agree?"

Jaw again firmly set, McSwain replied, "There's a logic to it."

"All right. Which brings us to Number Three—Mr. Pont is already dead when the fire starts. Someone pours fuel all over his body which I would guess is propped up against something, probably a desk or chair. His body thus becomes its own crematorium which fits with the evidence as described, namely the nearly complete destruction of the body and the clothes."

"Problem with that," said McSwain smugly.

"Yes?"

"There's no record of any second person entering or leaving the plant or the premises."

"Indeed...which leaves us with Number Four: self-immolation."

"Self-what?" Bogan asked before McSwain could stop him. Standing to the side, Walcott watched, open-mouthed in amazement and delight.

"Suicide. Buddhist monk-style. Vietnam in the 1960s. Doused himself with fuel and then lit the match. Fits everything."

"No! Now wait a minute!" shouted McSwain. "That's impossible!"

"Oh? Why? The evidence you present does not fit your theory of events. But Number Four does. And apparently no one knows why Geoffrey Pont came out here so no one can refute the idea that he was suicidal."

"No, I tell you! Never! It can't be!"

"But you have no proof, Chief, do you? You see the problem? And that's not all. There's something else...you mentioned that the electrical receptacles did not melt despite the intense heat."

"That's right," replied McSwain cautiously.

"And the greatest scorching came down to three feet from the floor."

"Yes."

"What are those receptacles made from?"

"Alloys. Aluminum, tin, nothing fancy."

"At what temperatures do those metals or alloys melt?"

"Pure tin around 230 degrees Centigrade, aluminum and its alloys at 400 degrees and higher." The skeptical look on McSwain's face told Poole the fireman sensed another trap was coming but had no idea from where.

StG: "You described the body as mostly cremated, and yet formal cremation requires more than 900 degrees Centigrade. So if there were 900 degrees at floor level to consume the body, then how come nothing else at or near floor level melted?"

McS: "Well, it's quite simple. You see ...well, I mean...well, ahem, uh, well..."

StG: "Again you see the problem." The Chief Inspector started to turn away and then stopped. "I'm sorry, do you have anything else?"

McS: "You have my report."

"Thank you. Right...Mr. Walcott, I believe you have something you wish to show us?"

McSwain favored both men with a contemptuous glance before the insurance investigator led the group around the corner to the west side of the building where he stopped by the broken windows of the main office suite.

8

"CHIEF INSPECTOR," WALCOTT began, "I would like to draw your attention to three things. The first are these glass fragments down here in the grass."

Only St. George, Poole, and the insurance investigator bent over for a closer look at the numerous bits and shards lying some five feet from the wall. "Now granted, firemen were stepping all around here, so many larger pieces have been broken, but that did not affect what I wanted to show you."

"Tempered glass?" said St. George.

"No, sir, just simple decolorized window glass. Inexpensive, as Chief McSwain indicated. But look at these larger pieces—notice the smooth, curved edges. They're called 'mirror edges.' There's no originating locus, no point of impact for these like you find with a missile. To create these fracture lines, you need heat...or an explosion...or both. Next, consider this: panes which simply fall out will drop straight down and come to rest along the base of the wall—not five feet away. So what gave these pieces such momentum?"

"And your opinion is?"

"That there was an explosion coincident with the start of the fire."

"Nonsense!" said McSwain who had been standing by silent as a statue. "You get hot air trapped inside, builds up pressure, sure it can blow things a bit when it lets loose. I've seen it lots of times. But that's no explosion."

St. George looked back at Walcott who was shaking his head.

"Uh-uh. This was an outright detonation, not just a cloud of expanding hot air. Check this out...you'll see where I've made a few small scrapes on this blackened part of the windowsill."

"You've tampered with evidence!" snorted McSwain.

"Not at all. And besides, since you wouldn't do it..."

"Gentlemen! Please!" said St. George before nodding to Walcott. "Now go on."

"If you check the depth of the burn here and on the inside, you'll find they're the same."

"Meaning they were exposed to flame for the same length of time."

"Exactly. Now that can only happen if the panes came out at the start of the fire. Before any heat buildup. Hence, a detonation or explosion."

"All right, duly noted," said St. George. "And the third thing?"

"If you press up against the wall, you can view the window frame tangentially. You'll see that the frame is misshapened."

"Simple heat distortion!" McSwain snapped. "Commonplace!"

"However," Walcott said, "heat distortion normally produces an undulating, rippled effect. Here, you'll notice that the entire frame is curved *convexly*, forcibly bent *outward*—again secondary to an explosion."

"And you draw what conclusion from all this?" coaxed St. George.

"No simple fire could have produced such an explosion. And this was not a fireworks factory or a fertilizer plant dealing with cagey combustibles. There can be no doubt that an accelerant was used. And we know which one."

The drone of the falling rain only partly obscured McSwain's muttered obscenity as St. George asked Walcott if he had anything else to present.

"Yes...inside."

Walcott tactfully asked Dougall for permission to enter the burned wreck because, as a civilian, he had no independent authority to cross the blue-and-white ribbon barrier stretched across the entrance. Without looking at McSwain, the detective uttered his gruff assent, and they set off, closing their umbrellas at the entrance. Amid frequent nervous glances up at the fractured and fragmented ceiling, the group crossed the blackened threshold behind Bogan, who led them along debris-laden hallways and around and over fallen

beams and partitions. St. George found the experience claustropho-
bic and momentarily fantasized about submariners awaiting depth
charge assaults on their leaky craft. Slowly, carefully, step by step,
they penetrated deeper and deeper into the labyrinth of devastation.
All the while McSwain said nothing as though letting the destruction speak for itself.

When they reached the office area, St. George spotted a dark cav-
ity with two large partly-covered white porcelain objects resting on
the floor.

"What in the world...?"

"The loo for the office staff," said the fire chief. "One stall for
each. Ceiling came down with the roof. Over here's where we found
him."

The Chief Inspector paused to silently imagine what the scene
must have looked like. Then he stepped over to where McSwain was
pointing and then moved on to where Walcott demonstrated his cut
in the charred window frame.

"I see. And you said you know the accelerant used?"

"Yes. They use quite a lot of acetone here to clean some of their
equipment. There were three 15-liter carboys back in the work area—"

"Bollocks!" snorted McSwain. "They just burned like everything
else."

"Delivered only last week, it turns out," said Walcott. "Chief
McSwain is right: two of them exploded and burned, but the third
only melted because it was already empty. Empty after less than a
week? I think not. Splash about 15 liters of acetone...a flick of the
lighter found in the victim's pocket, and you have arson."

"But chemicals leave traces. There were none."

"You wouldn't have any with acetone. Instantly vanishes into water
and carbon dioxide. Only way you'd ever know any was here was if it
had been made with radioactive carbon. But that's high-tech research
stuff. Commercial grades are clean."

McSwain cursed, started to stomp out of the area, but then stopped,
hesitated, and turned back, apparently determined not to be run off.

St. George said nothing further as he now meandered about, picking his way over and around dripping wet debris, glancing every now
and then at the ceiling with its exposed beams, rafters, insulation,
wiring, and ducts. Despite water damage and litter, the floor appeared
generally unharmed by the catastrophe. While his companions hud-
dled to one side to escape the rivulets of rain trickling through innu-

merable gaps in the roof, St. George asked McSwain about the sprinkler system.

"Structurally intact but inoperative at the time. The blaze knocked out the electrical system controlling the sprinklers so when the alarm sounded, nothing happened."

St. George nodded. "Had the sprinklers ever been tested?"

"Not since installation. Never any reason...and besides, how could they have all that water pouring down on all that expensive equipment?"

"Right."

St. George continued on until he found himself next to the destroyed lavatory. Aloud, he judged that the presence of the urinal identified the men's facility.

"That's odd...the roll of paper is nearly gone," he said, pointing with his closed umbrella to the sodden, soot-covered spool in its holder.

"Why odd?" asked Poole who felt more courageous than anyone else present.

"Well, one of the perks of being top dog is always having a full roll of paper. Check if you're ever in the Commissioner's office. Like you see there in the ladies' stall. Could be merely lazy maintenance—except one would expect that sort of problem in a much larger operation."

As the group exchanged puzzled glances, St. George used his umbrella to raise the lid of the men's toilet.

"Hmmmpf! The bowl is empty."

"What?" said McSwain.

"There's no water in the bowl. Soot and ash on the lid but not inside. Tells us the lid was down at the time of the fire. So why is there no water in the bowl? Laurence, give me a hand, will you?"

The two men shoved aside some soaked plasterboard and lifted off the tank cover. The flotation ball was lying inert at the bottom. The tank was empty. They checked the next stall—both the tank and the bowl were full of clear water. At the Chief Inspector's behest, Poole reached down and checked the empty toilet's inlet valve—it was open. St. George ordered it closed. A close examination revealed no crack or leak in the empty toilet. With minimal prompting, McSwain dispatched firemen to check the other four toilets in the building. Minutes later, they were back.

"All plumb full, sir."

"Inspector Dougall, may I suggest you have your people photograph each toilet to document the water level in each bowl and tank and time each photograph. Also, close the other inlet valves. Especially let no one touch these two toilets under any circumstances. Chief McSwain, in all seriousness, have you ever known your men to use such facilities after a fire rather than waiting to return to their station?"

"Are you suggesting one of my men relieved himself here?"

"I'm *asking* you if one did. It's extremely important."

"Of course not!"

"Will you please canvass your men just to make sure? I'm not trying to insult anyone. It's vital that we know."

"All right," snarled McSwain, the very idea galling him. "Deputy Bogan, poll your men."

"Yes, sir. Be easy enough to do."

"Secondly, Chief, did you have anyone shut off the water during or after the fire?"

"Not at first. But once we saw it was a loss, Deputy Bogan sent a man round."

"And he did shut it off?"

"Yes. Standard outside valve for such emergencies."

"He told you personally?"

"No, he would report to Deputy Bogan."

St. George looked at the subordinate who seemed genuinely puzzled.

"Yes," said Bogan, "I believe I recall Stephens coming back and telling me he had done so."

"Chief Inspector," said McSwain, "what the bloody hell do toilets have to do with anything?"

"Simply this—someone shut off the water before flushing this one. Flushing it twice, to be exact. I wager some of the missing toilet paper went down with the water."

"But I just told you that we shut the water off after we got here."

"And I submit the water was shut off *before* you got here. In fact, *before* the fire."

"If I may..." interjected Walcott, "...alluding to what Chief McSwain said earlier about not wanting water dripping down on all their precious equipment, they also would not want a flood. Places like this often have an inside emergency valve. Has anyone checked that?"

From the pained expression on McSwain's face, it was evident no one from his brigade had even considered the possibility. In a flurry of commands, he mobilized his men and set them to working their way through the rubble toward the inside corner of the east wall where the main water line entered the building. The debris field was considered too hazardous for the others to follow and so they waited at the entrance in nervous anticipation. After some minutes, Deputy Bogan called out for McSwain who disappeared into the maze. More minutes passed and then Bogan returned.

"It appears that there is a second valve; simple lever device set just inside the wall in a small utility room. Controls the flow to every-thing—counters, spigots, lavatories, sprinklers. And it is completely in the closed position. But none of our men have touched it."

"It's clear then," said St. George as a crestfallen McSwain reap-peared. "Someone shut off all water to the plant prior to the fire. That person then used the toilet paper and flushed the john twice. Why, we don't know. Was that person Geoffrey Pont? Possibly. Thus far, the only thing standing in the way of Mr. Pont being proclaimed the arsonist is the lighter in his pocket."

"How so?" Deputy Chief Bogan challenged out of curiosity rather than anger.

"Someone on fire is not going to take the time to close his lighter and put it back in his pocket."

"Unless he had already lit a wick of some kind," suggested Walcott.

"Very true," replied the Chief Inspector who then motioned to McSwain. "Chief, may I see you over there for a moment?"

9

POOLE AND WALCOTT waited discreetly out of earshot until McSwain marched away and began barking orders to his men. With rainwater cascading off his rainsuit like a miniature waterfall, St. George approached them.

"So, Mr. Walcott, all said and done, how do you read all this?"

The insurance man visibly puffed up with pride.

"Well, I've got to say first that I should've picked up on that toilet bit and the inside valve."

"Perhaps, but then, better late than never, what?"

"Right. Well, how do I read it? I was struck by this all happening on a weekend. When no one was supposed to be on the premises. I understand that only the dead man and four other people had unrestricted access and that the security computer recorded only the dead man's entry on Saturday. And then, with the man himself being the point of origin and no one having any idea why he was out here...you put it all together and I say the bloke came out here to do mischief and got hoisted on his own petard. An inside job gone wrong. Of course, your version about suicide is much more sensational. Either way, makes no difference. See, I don't need to solve the whole thing to do right by my employer. So my company is going to write this one down as arson by the deceased."

"But no actual paraphernalia were found and the lighter was—"

"Really doesn't mean much. I mean, who knows what was done here before I arrived Sunday? A fireman with specific instructions could clean up the scene in a matter of minutes and no one would be the wiser. And then what if the dead man was a genius of sorts—who's to say he didn't come up with something really clever that would be consumed by the fire? Or destroyed by the water putting out the blaze?"

"You're suggesting someone *planted* the lighter in the man's pocket?"

"Hey, I know a case where that kind of thing was done. But like I said, for my company's purpose, I'm done here. Thanks for all your help. You've been great. And good luck."

With farewell handshakes exchanged, Walcott strode off into the gray drizzle while St. George and Poole turned to face Inspector Dougall who was bustling toward them.

"Loo all secured as you wanted, sir. Photographer will be out here within the hour."

"Excellent! Next we need to set up a murder room. May we use your conference room at the station?"

"A *murder* room? Oh, yes, oh certainly, of course. We've never done one here before. I mean, for real."

"Really. Well, now's the time, I'd say."

"Right. We'll set it right up."

"Next we'll need appointments with the family and the top staff. Where's Michael Pont working now that this place is down?"

"They're operating out of a storefront in Livingston. He's spending his time there when he's not with the widow and his cousin in Edinburgh. Remember the memorial service is today."

"Mmmm, yes. All right, next I need a phone, preferably your office right now, to call London, and then Sgt. Poole and I need lunch. Can you recommend some place?"

Twenty minutes later, the Chief Inspector was phoning his report to the AC/CID who seemed surprised, alarmed, and finally worried by the information.

"And I need Marcus and his van up here *now*," St. George enunciated into the mouthpiece. "Absolutely. He can requisition what else he needs from the forensic lab up here but I must have him here in person. I cannot insist any more forcefully...because if murder was done, and I believe it was, then the killer has perhaps an insurmountable head start. Compounding that is the fact that too many people up here are too close to the situation and seem to have ulterior motives for subverting the process. So I need him *desperately* if we are to salvage this thing at all. No, sir, I am *not* exaggerating. Thank you, sir, that is most appreciated. And there is one other thing. I shall require a briefing by both 5 and 6, tomorrow if possible. It's quite easy to see the international ramifications to all this. Right. Thank you. Well, I believe there's a great deal of money behind it. Very good. Thank you again."

Poole grinned. "Dr. Woolsley will just *love* pulling up stakes like that."

"No doubt, Laurence, but besides you, he's the only one up here I can absolutely trust. Remember what I said before about our working in a foreign land. After our success this morning, we're going to be even more unwelcome. I daresay we're likely to replace Ansel Walcott as the object of their collective disaffection. So we best be careful what we say and how we act at all times. In fact, I believe I must ask you a favour..."

"Certainly."

"Act dumb and stupid and just sit back and observe and listen."

"I thought that was my job description."

"Hah! Of course you did. No, my hope is that anyone working against us will be so busy watching me, they won't be on their guard around you."

"All right. But then, can I ask a question?"

"Of course."

"That talk about suicide. Self-immolation. I can see it in theory, but you weren't really serious, were you?"

"Yes and no. It fits nicely with arson by the deceased so it didn't cost anything to throw it in. But my purpose was to throw a scare into people who had already tried to sweep this matter under the rug as spontaneous combustion. You saw McSwain's reaction. Perhaps these same people may be more pliant and willing to talk truthfully if they believe there are now two chances, not one, to hang the arson on the dead man. We'll see."

"Oh, and one other thing," Poole said, "if permissible. What did you say to McSwain out there?"

St. George smiled. "I merely suggested that there was still time to submit an amended final report in lieu of his original draft. He grasped the idea at once."

"Ah, the old instinct for self-preservation!"

"Indeed. Well now, let's find Cobb and do lunch!"

Insisting that their driver join them scored points and provided them with a light diversion during the meal. Back at the station, they found everyone edgy: Chief Superintendent Stallings had arrived and was waiting for them in Superintendent Boyd's empty office. Learning that the top cop wished to speak privately with him, St. George asked Dougall and Poole to check on the murder room's progress. No sooner was the door closed than a dour Stallings began, his brogue more evident than before.

"I've received word you believe arson was committed."

"I do...and it was. There can be no doubt."

"You're certain one of the firemen could not have used the facility?"

"Certain? No. Highly improbable? Yes. There is also the matter of the missing toilet paper."

"You can't be serious!"

"Oh, but I am. And the closed emergency valve. I'm fully aware what's at stake, and I would not make such a statement lightly."

"With all due respect, Chief Inspector, you haven't begun to know what's at stake."

"Really? Then please inform me."

"I'm talking about the effects on the economy around here."

"What I've seen looks quite prosperous. You're saying things are in a downturn?"

"They will be...word of this gets out. Yes, that damned valve, I must admit that is worrisome. No way anyone could have shut it off after the fire started. So I guess your side carries the day."

"My side? I thought as fellow policemen we were on the same side."

"Yes, yes, yes, of course, it's just that—never mind. Right. You're going to do things as you see fit. No doubt of that. So, since Superintendent Boyd is not due back from holiday until next week, I've assigned Superintendent Wallace from our Livingston office to be your liaison."

"Thank you, that's most considerate. But if I may make a request...?"

"Of course."

"Inspector Dougall has been quite forthright about his past problems and shortcomings and yet apparently has endeavoured to improve himself. May I ask that he continue on with us here? He knows the case, and I'm thinking that perhaps working the thing through, doing all the scutwork, might provide him with some additional training along the way which, in the end, may make him a better officer. At the same time, I think Superintendent Wallace would be just the man to coordinate things for us in Livingston and Edinburgh. Especially for appointments with the family. This afternoon, if possible."

Stallings took but a moment to decide.

"Sounds reasonable. If you're sure you won't mind putting up with Dougall..."

"Quite sure. I think he really wants to do better."

"Very well. Let's inform him."

With that Stallings marched out of the office and retrieved his junior detective from the embryonic murder room.

"Yes, sir?" Dougall said, standing at attention with an anxious eye toward St. George.

"The Chief Inspector and I have decided that you will continue working this case to its conclusion. He expects excellent work from you and anything less he's to report to me. Are we clear on that?"

"Yes, sir! Right, sir!"

"Superintendent Wallace will serve as your control officer, keep him posted, call him for anything. He'll coordinate matters with the family."

"Yes, sir. Right, sir."

"Very well. Carry on."

Stallings turned on his heel, gave St. George a curt nod, and strode out of the building.

10

THE STOREFRONT ON Almondvale Road, according to Superintendent Wallace, had once been the district office for one of the Edinburgh newspapers. However, economies of scale and improvements in local transportation had made the near-suburban depot unnecessary. So for the past several months, the space had lain dormant. Now a half-dozen standing partitions separated rented furniture and other office accoutrements into a cluster of workstations. *Like a damned rabbit warren*, thought the Chief Inspector upon first sight.

Greeting Dougall and his two London associates was a handsome man, late 30s, trim athletic in build, clean-shaven but for a neatly mustachioed upper lip, and bearing the saddest face St. George thought he had ever seen. Dougall introduced him as Michael Pont, brother of the deceased. After weak handshakes, Pont led them past a receptionist into the sitting area behind the second partition where they found another man introduced as Edward Cargill. The sandy-haired cousin, who reminded St. George of a dandy, rose to meet them. The two men accepted the Chief Inspector's official condolences with quiet nods.

"We also want to thank you gentlemen for agreeing to meet with us so soon after the funeral. Were matters not of the highest import, we would not have imposed ourselves upon your grief until later."

"Yes, well, I was against it at first," said Edward. "I mean as if the entire day isn't miserable enough, all this damned rain made a sham of the graveside service, it did, but Michael correctly pointed out that keeping busy with the company and your investigation was our best means of coping at the moment and so here we are."

"You'll have to excuse my appearance," Michael said. "We've had little sleep the past few days trying to keep things afloat. Mainly being here to answer the phone. Can't take a chance on voice mail. People get the word and they want immediate answers."

"You can do everything from here?" said St. George as he accepted an unfolded metal chair from Poole and sat down. The sergeant and Dougall then followed suit.

"Just messages for now. Lucky for us, Edward here had a line on this office and a small warehouse in Edinburgh where we can store inventory for the time being. It's literally day-by- day."

"Correct me if I'm wrong, but doesn't your work involve a lot of software as well? Did you lose that in the fire?"

"What was there, yes," Michael said. "Fortunately, anyone with a brain keeps all critical files backed up. For our basic programming and platforms, Geoffrey kept a full set of discs at home and another in the Lothian National Bank in Edinburgh. So we're safe there. What we really need is the hardware to get going again."

"But that's where you present us a problem, Chief Inspector," Edward said.

"Really?"

"Yes, we've had word of your investigation this morning. Result was most disappointing."

"Well, gentlemen, to put it bluntly, there is nothing for it—arson was committed. And except for one detail, the case looks hard against your brother being the culprit."

"But *suicide?*"

"It's as easy to say that as to say 'accident.' Most importantly, without the body to examine, it's going to be difficult to prove murder and thereby refute the insurance company's verdict."

"*Murder?*" gasped Michael. Both cousins looked shocked.

"It's the only alternative."

"But how? He was the only one to enter the building."

"That is a problem to be sure. A major problem. However, the blaze clearly had chemical assistance, and so if your brother set the blaze, then what happened to his paraphernalia? Surely there was no opportunity for someone to go inside and remove such evidence."

"So how do you propose to overcome this obstacle?" said Cargill, frowning like a skeptical cleric questioning Copernicus.

"Well, since no one examined the lungs, we cannot know if they were free of soot. Had they been clean, then murder would have been the only answer."

"So why aren't you out beating the bushes for the arsonist?"

"Edward! Please!" Michael said, slouching back in his seat. "Chief Inspector, we know that you people are just doing your jobs, but for four days we've been whipsawed by this whole tragedy, thinking first one thing and now this. How can we help?"

"For now, by providing us with as much background on your company as possible. For example, how did you gentlemen start VES?"

Michael swept his hand through his hair.

"Well...in fits and starts. Geoffrey got the basic concept while I was still at university—St. Anne's—and when I received my degree in computer science, we concocted an idea for our first program and set about getting financing. Our own family funds were modest at best, and what the banks would provide left us a couple of hundred thousand pounds short. Then galloping to the rescue came this man here, Sir Edward of Cargill, who supplied the balance and we were off and running. We haven't looked back since."

Cargill shook his head. "I merely recognized a good thing when I saw it. Bloodline notwithstanding. It was a sound investment. The added benefit was having total family ownership and control. No outsiders whatsoever meddling and adding their tuppence! I think that has made us even stronger."

"Hear, hear," Michael said.

"Your new deal with the Japanese—does that dilute that control?"

"Not at all," said Edward. "VES is simply a copartner of a new company which will run that new operation. VES remains inviolate."

"Are there any shareholders besides yourselves?"

"Yes," Edward replied, "my brother and two sisters. Necessary to satisfy some government regulations. They hold no more than a few percent and vote by proxy whenever they bother to find a stamp. Otherwise Michael, Geoffrey, and I vote 95 percent of the shares."

St. George pursed his lips. "Then they're not equally allocated?"

"Essentially," Michael said. "Amounts to the same thing. Geoffrey and I each vote 30,000 and Edward votes 35,000."

"So your voting goes either three-zip or two-to-one."

"Most often the former," said Edward.

"Seems like you've developed a most amicable and workable troika."

"I think so," said Michael.

"Oh, definitely," Edward added. "Though as you might expect, some outsiders are so jealous that they would try to make you think otherwise."

"Might there be some reason beyond jealousy?"

"Such as?" Michael asked.

"Oh, perhaps a former business associate bent on revenge. Someone who swore to get even. Or maybe just a competitor out to gain an advantage."

Michael Pont shook his head. "None that I can think of...Edward?"

"No one I could mention without inviting a lawsuit. They'd call it libel or slander or whatever. Besides, the ones I'd think of would *never* go to the extreme of arson...or murder. Haven't the stomach."

"Even if it meant scuttling your deal with the Japanese?"

"Good thought, Chief Inspector," Edward said, "except that no one around here, or anywhere for that matter, had any inkling about the deal. The entire negotiation was very confidential."

"To bring up an unpleasant point," St. George said to Michael, "with your brother dead, who votes his shares?"

"I'm not sure—why are you looking at me that way?"

"Oh, sorry, no offense intended," replied the Chief Inspector. "I was just taken aback by your claim not to know the provisions of your brother's estate." For Poole, it was a rare instance when his mentor had so transparently telegraphed his skepticism and surprise.

"Well, I really have no idea what his will provides. Besides, who would have thought that it would become a consideration before the millennium? All I know is that he intended to leave his estate to a trust."

"I think it was a pass-through trust, Chief Inspector," Edward said. "I don't know whether Myra—Geoffrey's wife—now votes the shares or not. We meet with the solicitor tomorrow afternoon."

"I just know I don't automatically come into them," Michael added as a postscript.

"I see. How long has this Japanese deal been brewing?"

The two cousins looked at each other.

"Seven months?" Edward asked.

"More like a year," Michael said. He stood up suddenly and began pacing listlessly about the enclosure. "At first there was a very faint, very delicate inquiry, if you will, through several intermediaries. Ostensibly about the Germans and market share here in Europe or some such drivel like that. I completely missed the significance of it, but Geoffrey picked it right up. I don't know whom he contacted or how he did it—he kept it all very much to himself—but a few months later we began receiving formal inquiries, letters, relayed conversations, and so on. Mostly about VES in general. Nothing was mentioned about the project we were working on."

St. George asked, "Which happens to be what, may we ask?"

"Are you gentlemen versed in computers?" Michael said.

St. George: "I'm afraid my expertise ends with the 'start' button and the 'escape' and 'enter' keys. Sgt. Poole is quite proficient—at least that's what he tells me."

Dougall merely shrugged his shoulders.

"Well," Michael said, "it involves increasing the number of conductive elements on the circuit board. Rather tricky. Anyway, we figured it out before our primary Japanese competitor did. Company called YAMATSU Ltd."

"Had there been any reciprocal visits before Friday?"

"Yes, two. Midlevel ones, nothing to attract attention. Our Chief Engineer James Barrows went over. So did Ted Manning, our Chief Technician. He really didn't know what the whole thing was all about. His job was to go over our technical readouts with them so they'd know our two plants and sets of equipment were compatible. Then they sent their corresponding numbers over here."

"So you top three stayed out of the picture until the last minute."

"Right," said Edward. "It's not unlike formal diplomacy. If one of us principles had gone along, protocol and etiquette would have meant our being met by our opposite number, rank for rank. The newspapers would have had wind of the whole thing in no time and we'd be done for. As it was, we did not actually meet everyone in person until the papers were ready for signing."

St. George continued, "So then it was the top three men from YAMATSU who came here."

"Yes," Michael said. "Ironically, they had already scheduled trade talks in London and had let it be known their plans included a brief trip to St. Andrews. So they figured that would provide the perfect cover for a quick diversion to West Calder for the signing before anyone was the wiser. Then they would continue on north."

"So they were already coming..."

"Yes. Brought their entire retinue to London but then came up to Edinburgh with just a skeleton team. Fooled everyone. Of course, Geoffrey's arrangements made it all possible."

"What about security people?"

"Left most of them in Edinburgh as decoys. After all, everyone, especially the media, expected that the executives would not stray far away from their bodyguards."

"Rather gutsy, I'd say. Who would have imagined all that intrigue?"

"Oh, all the cloak-and-dagger was quite necessary," said Edward. "As you may know, the French and the Israelis are the most active practitioners of industrial espionage in the world. Make the Eastern Bloc look like pikers. In fact, they've even given the lofty Americans fits."

"You don't say," said the Chief Inspector. "I presume everyone took precautions."

"Of course, but it still happens."

"By the way, Mr. Pont, I understand you missed the signing on Friday. You must have been disappointed."

"Yes, but Edward covered for me admirably. I had to spend the day in London meeting with one of the banks handling the financing on the secondary market. Just a bit of trouble-shooting is all. Were it about anything else, I could have handled it over the phone, but you know how bankers love to be stroked and made to feel important. Especially when they *are* important and they know it. I wanted to be sure nothing was really amiss at the last second and I wanted to score major points with them by putting in an appearance. So yeah, it was a major inconvenience, but it paid off."

"Any local banks involved?"

"Well, the Lothian National Bank in Edinburgh has handled our affairs from the beginning. Also been our family bank as well. As a matter of fact, they're directing the overall financing for the project."

"Strange that your bank didn't intercede for you and save you the trip. I was raised in a family where we insisted on getting every penny's worth of service," said St. George who, in fact, had been an orphan farmed out to numerous foster homes.

"Well, as a matter of fact, on an earlier occasion, I broached that very idea with the bank's president, fellow named Silas Muir, and it was he who stressed the importance of personal attention. And I must say, he was right."

St. George smiled and then turned to Edward Cargill.

"So then you were present Friday."

"Yes."

"How did your cousin Geoffrey seem that day? I mean, aside from the normal tension one must feel on such a mementous occasion."

"He seemed quite normal to me."

"Was he preoccupied? Forgetful? Distracted in any way?"

"Not that I could tell. Why do you ask?"

St. George ignored the question and went on. "Did he express any thought about returning to the plant that night or over the weekend?"

"None at all."

"Did he leave any word for you?"

"No."

"You, Mr. Pont?"

"Nothing beyond what I already told Inspector Dougall here. That we had switched to the Old Course. And that the signing had gone well."

"You didn't call your brother to reply?"

"In fact, I did, but there was no answer. However, I knew he and Myra had plans to go out and so I didn't pursue it."

St. George nodded as though he understood perfectly the nuances of such social graces. "How did the YAMATSU people make their way up here?"

"By private plane."

"Would we be correct, Mr. Pont, to assume that your London journey was equally discrete and inconspicuous?"

"Absolutely, and not just from the standpoint of the press. We would have lost face with the YAMATSU people if they thought we might have money problems. So I traveled alone by rail."

"Then how, Mr. Cargill, did you explain Michael's absence on Friday?"

"We lied."

11

"OH?" REPLIED THE Chief Inspector whom Poole could tell was trying mightily to appear casual at the disclosure.

Edward went on: "We told our Japanese friends what they wanted to hear—that Michael had flown on urgent notice to Madrid to meet with some potential investors. For possible third-world expansion. They like that sort of thing: people aggressively pursuing money. Anyway, blah, blah, blah, his return flight was postponed and he would not get back until Friday evening but he would drive up in time to play golf with them the next morning."

St. George turned to the surviving brother. "And you did follow the next morning?"

"Yes."

"Do you carry a membership at St. Andrews?"

"No, but Geoffrey has been a member of the R&A for years. Also set up a temporary membership for me so we might use the clubhouse."

"Why did he not go himself?"

"He hasn't played for several years. Totally absorbed with the business. And like the rest of us, he was rather vain about not wanting to make a spectacle out of himself. So he tabbed me."

"Michael's too modest," said Edward. "He's sort of our roving ambassador. It was only natural that he play with our new partners.

And why not? The man's almost a pro!"

"Oh, come now…" said Michael as he brushed off the compliment.

"No, really. Plays damned near level par most of the time. So what would be better for our Jap friends than to play with someone far better than they are? Automatically improves your own game, right? It was perfect for the YAMATSU people."

"And how about yourself?" said St. George to Edward.

"Me? I do pick up the clubs twice a year or so for some charity events where I'm the dubber bringing up the rear. Tennis is my game though I'm really no good at that, either. But it gives me exercise. Michael, on the other hand, has got it made—bachelor, freewheeling, unattached, and able to just chuck the clubs into the left seat and be off. I do feel jealous at times."

St. George turned back to Michael and asked, "You played the Old Course?"

"Yes."

"I'm envious. Always wanted to."

"A policeman play golf? I never heard that combination before."

St. George smiled politely at the jibe. "First time on the Old Course?"

"What? Oh, no, played it once several years ago. Usually play the others; the New Course three times, the Jubilee twice, and the Eden three times. The Strathtyrum, no, because it's geared for the struggling player, shall we say. All occasions were business outings again, though generally we entertain our people down around here. Ironically, the Old Course was not our original assigment."

"Come again?"

"Well, about six weeks ago, when it was apparent the deal would work, the YAMATSU people told us about their upcoming visit to London and their plan to hie up to St. Andrews for golf on Saturday before returning home Sunday. But then they reported not being able to secure lodging or tee times on such short notice, and that's when Geoffrey swung into action. Got them a luxury two-night hotel package which normally includes guaranteed prime-hour tee times. Except no advance Saturday reservations are accepted for the Old Course or any of the others. So Geoffrey had no choice but to accept a time on another course, quite popular, two miles distant, the Dukes Course, which the YAMATSU chaps welcomed with good grace. As an extra added bonus, he threw me in as the substitute fourth as well as stand-in host. All quite fortuitous as it turned out."

"Pray tell," said the Chief Inspector, his interest undeniable.

"Well, Geoffrey still wanted one of the traditional courses if at all possible. Now it happens you can phone the day before for a Saturday reservation on the New Course. So last Friday morning, at his behest, another R&A member indeed secured a Saturday morning time. And released the other reservation, naturally. But that's where the good fortune came in because the New Course has a handicap limit and the Japanese fellow whom they would have brought as their fourth carries a handicap four strokes above the allowable maximum. So he would have been denied playing privileges right there at the first tee. Can you imagine the uproar that would have caused?"

St. George smiled and said he could.

"Anyway," said Michael, "when the Japanese arrived here, he's got this surprise for them that they are going to be truly on the Links. Made them even happier to be working with these Scots."

"So how did you get on the Old Course after all?"

"Ridiculously simple as it turned out. Geoffrey had his R&A chum sign us up for the Friday afternoon ballot and we won."

"I was there when the call came through," Edward said. "You should have seen the looks of awe and respect on those YAMATSU boys' faces when Geoffrey up and tells them he has yet another surprise and that they're now playing the Old Course. Masterstroke, I'd say."

"Indeed," said St. George who turned back to Michael. "And so how'd you play?"

"Pardon?"

"Your score Saturday? Oh, by the way, Inspector—" St. George said as he swung around to Dougall, "surely you know of your famous namesake up there."

Dougall shook himself alert. "I don't quite follow..."

"Chap named Maitland Dougall. Made quite a name for himself. Seems he and some other lads were about to tee off in the Autumn Medal in 1860, when a ship foundered offshore. They all dropped their clubs, jumped into boats, and took off the crew without losing a man. That all done, he teed off and went on to win."

"Really?" said the dazed detective while the two cousins piped in with "Amazing" and "You don't say."

St. George then returned to his subject. "I'm sorry to digress, Mr. Pont...right, we understand you had to drive up Saturday morning."

"That's correct."

"Did you receive any calls or e-mails or other communiqués from your brother before you set off?"

"On Saturday? No, sir. None whatsoever. He did leave me a message Friday night about the switch to the Old Course. But for Saturday, I wish to hell now that there had been one. Might have been able to stop him."

"From what?"

"From at least going out there, no matter whatever reason was on his mind."

"Yes, quite. Your drive up—how was it?"

"Not bad. Good weather so I exceeded the speed limit most of the way. It's simple, really—just pop across the Forth Road Bridge to A921 and then swing onto the A915 and, before you can say Auchterlonie, you're there."

"And you found your YAMATSU people?"

"Yes. They were booked at The Rusacks."

"Ah, yes, I know the place. On Pilmour Links."

"Right. Once we teed off, they dismissed their liaison man. He was responsible for having everything ready. In our absence, I suppose he just wandered around town. Anyway, he was waiting alongside the 18th green when we finished."

"Do you speak Japanese?"

"Me? Heavens no!"

"Or you, Mr. Cargill?"

"Never."

Again to Michael, "Did the YAMATSU people speak English?"

"A bit. Enough social words overall to enable everyone to smile at each other. The Number Two man, chap named Sameki, spoke passable English. What I suspect is that those boys understand a lot more than what they let on. Of course, maybe it was just the golf."

St. George smiled. "And then you had their interpreter at hand."

"Yes, quite. He also took on the role of photographer to document their play, starting with the traditional business pose on the first tee with the clubhouse as backdrop. The hotel also sent a man over to videotape their tee shots and then later their play onto the 18th green. Otherwise, it was still photos on each hole. Especially of the Number One man putting out. Made no sense to me but they were very serious about it."

"They included you in the pictures?"

"They wanted me in the first tee photo but I declined. I told them I was honored, but the record was of *them* playing, not me, and that no one in Japan would know who I was. After some translating, they understood and appreciated my taking a subordinate position. They liked being the center of attention anyway."

"So when did you tee off?"

"10:10. Their pecking order was very important for them. The top man was Tamura and Number Three was Suchawa, and after every hole, they did all this bowing back and forth. And no matter Tamura's score, he always teed off first. They might claim they're becoming more Westernized, but in my opinion, they were pure samurai from beginning to end."

"So what was your score?"

"What? My score? As it happens, I didn't keep a card; I was too busy playing diplomat. After all, I feared any miscue on my part could scuttle the entire project. Well, maybe not the whole thing, but you know what I mean. It was my job to see that they finished their trip in grand style."

"Oh yes, of course, but surely you must have kept track in your mind somehow. I mean, after all, playing the Old Course..."

"Well, yes," replied Michael Pont sheepishly, obviously embarrassed to discuss his athletic prowess. "I shot a 76."

"No! Capital! Excellent!" exulted the man from Scotland Yard. "It proves once again how an appropriate distraction relieves tension and allows one to play better. You have my admiration and my envy, sir."

"Oh...well, thank you."

"I told you he was good," chimed in Edward.

"And tell me," St. George pressed, "that first time? Could not have been nearly as successful."

"Ah, no, no, it wasn't...shot an 86."

St. George nodded vigorously like a schoolmaster whose pupil had just recited Tennyson's *Ulysses* with perfect timing and inflection. "From trying too hard and not being familiar with the terrain. I've heard that any ball landing off the fairway will bounce toward a bunker."

"True enough," said Michael.

"That doesn't seem fair," complained Edward. "At least, in tennis, play is self-contained."

"Which is the benefit of keeping one's ball in the short grass," St. George said, ignoring the cousin. "Tell me ... you know, I've always found the High Hole fascinating. Saturday, how did you play it?"

"You mean the 11th?"

"Yes. The carry over Strath bunker."

"Shot par," said Michael with a quick smile of pleasure at the memory.

"Fantastic! On in regulation?"

"As a matter of fact, yes. Five-iron. Why do you ask?"

"I played quite a bit when I was younger, so I can fully appreciate what you accomplished. I must say, I truly envy you."

A now frowning Edward Cargill coughed dramatically. "Chief Inspector, our family has just sustained a great tragedy and is facing possible financial ruin and you sit here and talk about golf? I must object in the strongest terms."

"Not to fear, Mr. Cargill. Besides my genuine interest, it's been my experience that sometimes a drastic digression frees up memory which otherwise can be frozen by an overwhelming catastrophe such as you have experienced. So in fact, Michael, I would next ask what the YAMATSU people did after completing their round?"

"They returned to London that evening. Flew home Sunday."

"And yourself?"

Michael Pont glanced in sequence at Poole, Dougall, and his cousin before answering.

"In anticipation of a favorable outcome, I had previously scheduled an appointment in Edinburgh with someone of the female persuasion. Consequently, I did not return home until shortly after 1:00 A.M. I checked for calls and that's when I heard Edward's message about the fire. God, what a shock!"

"After I got home from Myra's," interjected Edward, "I rang him several times. I was unaware of his social plans—though he certainly has no obligation to clear them with me. A bachelor deserves his privacy. At any rate, he called me back when he got home."

"Why did you not call him up at St. Andrews? Leave word there?"

"It was a business decision. Geoffrey was already gone and burdening Michael with the news could not change that. Rather, we judged it critical that for the outing to go as smoothly as possible, the Japanese should be kept unawares. So we decided not to inform Michael until he returned."

"And who, may I ask, are the 'we' you speak of?"

"Myself, Geoffrey's wife Myra, and Silas Muir."

"I see. Thank you." St. George quickly turned to Michael. "So what did you do once you heard Edward's message?"

"What could I do? It had all been over for hours. I called Edward right away, of course. I suggested going to see Myra again, even as late as it was, but he sensibly pointed out that she had been sedated and needed the rest. It was clear nothing could be accomplished until daytime."

"Were either of you present when the body was found?"

"Yes," answered the cousins in unison.

"Did either of you view the body?"

"I couldn't," said Michael as he quickly looked away.

"I did not at first," said Edward. "Later, at the morgue, somehow it seemed less real, less personal, and so I did it as a matter of formality. No way you could recognize him, however. There was so much damage."

"Features obliterated, I would imagine."

"Oh, yes, and much of the rest as well. Besides some of his personal possessions, dental records left no doubt it was he."

"About the severity of the burn damage, did you happen to notice whether everything was charred or were there areas relatively untouched?"

Edward's eyes flared in anger. "Yes, I suppose from a policeman's standpoint that is a reasonable question...though had you asked me at the time, I probably would have swung at you, badge or no badge. But all right, as I remember, the clothes on the right side, the flank area, were fairly intact. I mean, you could still see the weave, the color of the pants..."

"I see. Tell me, have either of you received word from the YAMATSU people about the tragedy?'

"Yes, we have," Edward said. "I sent word Monday through their economic attaché in London. Would have been terribly bad form for them to learn about it on CNN."

"And their reply?"

"At first, the customary formal condolences. Very proper and correct. No frills. Then yesterday, Tuesday, came their first query about our future plans. No doubt their embassy people had been very busy collecting what information there was. Of course, thanks to the efforts of your man Walcott, we were up in the air about what we could tell them."

"How did they contact you? By letter? Fax?"

"Phone call from London. Again low-key and discreet. Their attaché had already talked with Silas Muir. They were concerned about delays."

"Now wait a moment, I'm confused," said St. George as he shifted in his seat. "If a separate company is producing the new product, why does VES have to be up and running?"

"Because," Michael said with a sigh, "we're to produce some integral components for the new product. Later on, as the market expands, we'll need a new R&D over there as well."

"So you cannot afford to have VES lying fallow."

"Precisely," said Edward.

"But surely they realized the ashes were barely cold."

"Yes, but the yen and the pound sterling respect no one."

"I assume, then, that you're up against a deadline of some sort?"

"Yes," said Michael.

"Very much so," added Edward.

"Do you face some sort of penalty if you're not up and running?"

"Yes," Edward replied. "Each side must accomplish certain things within the next six months or the deal is off. Point of fact, until Saturday, it seemed everything of importance either had already been done or would be completed shortly and so it was only a paper formality. Now, it's the real thing. Anyway, the kicker is that should either party fall more than 60 days behind the agreed-upon schedule as specified in whatever subparagraph, the other party may cancel out without penalty, the party in default to bear all costs. Like I said, fairly standard terms. But my God, who would have thought the clock would start running Monday?"

"There's something even more critical," Michael said softly as he leaned against the back of a chair. "We are in a highly competitive field, Chief Inspector, not only in terms of product but in personnel. As you may know, our employees have been with us from the very beginning. They are very loyal, very trustworthy, and very good. The danger is that, should we give them any reason to think that we may not recover or that we will recover late but in a weakened condition, they have every right to seek positions elsewhere. And now that the word about the fire is out, our competitors will be lined up along the perimeter fence trying to sign our people away. If that happens, we have a very bleak future. So it is essential that we can publicly announce our resurrection in the shortest possible time. And I think you can see why talk of arson does not help us in that regard."

St. George nodded somberly. "Indeed. Well, I can assure you that we want to clear this matter up as expeditiously as possible. There is one thing we would like your thoughts on, distasteful though it might be for you both...the fact that arson occurred means that the act was premeditated. And its occurrence within 24 hours of the signing of your new agreement cannot be taken as simply coincidence until we have examined all possible avenues. Furthermore, it is possible that the thing has been in the works for months. So I ask you to consider this scenario: A competitor wants to gain an advantage over you; they lock you into place by negotiating a joint venture; along the way, they learn what you know and what you are capable of producing; and then, once having that information, you become expendable and—voilà!—a catastrophic fire."

The two businessmen were dumbstruck.

"That's awful!" gasped Edward. "I never thought for a moment—"

"I can't accept that," said Michael, vigorously shaking his head. "I know there's logic to it, but remember, I played golf with those people! Behaviour on the course mirrors behaviour in the boardroom. Cheat at one, cheat at the other."

"Your point is well taken, Michael, but we must still consider the possibility. And, unless your man Tamura was a very good player, he did cheat if he teed off first on every hole."

Michael said nothing but began pacing again while Edward slumped in his seat, his refined face again filled with worry.

"In this regard," said St. George, "I must implore both of you to say nothing to your opposite numbers at YAMATSU. Or to anyone else. In the meanwhile, I shall ask Whitehall to look into it. Now, aside from manning this office, how will you be dividing up responsibilities?"

Michael Pont slowly returned to his seat and sat down.

"Not all that much differently from before," he said quietly. "We three all worked well together. You used the word 'troika' earlier — quite apt, actually. We held our Executive Committee meetings at least three times a week. Usually Monday, Wednesday, Friday. Had others as required. We covered everything about the business, reviewed all areas, so that each of us would be in a position to provide cross-coverage should something arise."

"Which, until now, it never did," said an increasingly morose Edward.

"Granted," Michael said, "we had our own areas of primary responsibility...domains, if you will. Mine is R&D; Edward's is finance, insurance, and investments; and Geoffrey's was the day-to-day operations. Mind you, we made it a point to stay current with the other areas. So, to answer your question, we're prepared to step in and pick up the slack. Our staff will provide us all the support we'll need."

"Very commendable," said St. George. "And I should think enviable."

Both men shrugged.

"Have the YAMATSU people given you a firm deadline?"

"Not yet," Michael said. "But it's coming."

"I expect that next week we'll hear," added Edward, "unless we can disclose something affirmative before then."

"Theoretically," Michael said, "we have six months to meet the schedule. However, it will take all of that to rebuild and retool. So we really need to be back in operation in three months. Four months at the latest. It would not be difficult for us to fall 60 days behind."

St. George cleared his throat and asked, "All right, then let me broach this wholly unpleasant proposition. And believe me, we must cover it. Geoffrey either was in financial trouble privately or he discovered a flaw in the joint operation that would go badly against Viscount Electric Systems. So he torched the place either to gain cash flow or to cancel the project."

"Preposterous!" cried Michael as he jumped to his feet. "Outrageous!"

"Absurd!" spat Edward as he sat bolt upright.

"Now just listen, please, because you will have to answer these claims at some point, possibly even to the YAMATSU people—and answer them convincingly. It would seem to me a safe assumption that Geoffrey knew the layout better than anyone, correct?"

"Absolutely."

"Of course."

"And he had unrestricted access, agreed?"

"As did we all," said Edward.

"And now the crux of the matter—he secretly went out there, with no one aware of his plans, he had his lighter with him, and the fire began at or very near his body."

"That pig Walcott!" snorted Edward. "Well, I can squash some of that right now."

"Please do so."

"Insurance is not at issue. We have carried the same amount of coverage adjusted for inflation with that company for the past 10 years. And the coverage is for replacement costs only. We have taken out a new, second policy to cover the new building for the new project, but that is totally separate and apart from VES in every way. So, in short, none of us would gain a sou by burning down our golden egg."

"Well put," said St. George, nodding approvingly. "Thank you. And believe me, that's the kind of answer you're going to need to head off speculation. Now then, what about someone using the fire to cash out the business? Rather than sell it?"

"You mean take the proceeds and not rebuild?" Michael asked.

"Exactly."

"Rubbish again," said Edward. "The policy provides only replacement costs. There is no option for anything else. If we don't rebuild, we don't collect, period. And if it seems odd that we opted for that kind of policy, let me just say that the price was right."

"So none of you would receive anything personally."

"No."

"Wait minute," Michael said, stunned, as though he had seen a ghost. "I just thought of something. What if Geoffrey went out there for whatever purpose and stumbled onto something? What if he caught somebody trying to set the fire?"

"Died a hero's death, in other words," said Inspector Dougall who had sat listening in rapt attention.

"Sure, why not?" said Michael.

"The same problem, I'm afraid, as laying the guilt at Geoffrey's feet in the first place," answered St. George. "What happened to the paraphernalia?"

"The other bloke took it with him," said Edward.

"Except the security system did not record anyone's exit. Absolutely no one."

"What we heard," Michael said, "was that the system was not reliable for the hour preceding the fire. So one can't really say one way or the other."

"All right, then consider this proposition...you've heard the World War Two II expression, 'loose lips sink ships'?"

The cousins nodded.

"Could your brother have inadvertently confided in someone harbouring his own private, opposing agenda? Say sometime in the last six months? Or how about either of you? Perhaps you might have spoken to someone who—"

Edward Cargill slapped his hand to his forehead, his mouth agape. "Oh, my God, no!"

12

VISCOUNT'S PRIM COMPTROLLER looked as though someone had just slapped him with a dozen paternity suits.

"Oh, surely, that cannot be it!" cried Edward. "Certainly not...I mean...but how can we know for sure?" He looked at his cousin with unabashed anguish.

"Burklund?" Michael asked quietly as he gazed with equal concern at his cousin.

"Yes. Oh, my, my yes," Edward answered as he rubbed his forehead.

"Could one of you please elaborate?" St. George coaxed.

Edward Cargill scrunched around in his chair as he fought to regain some composure.

"Well...some time ago—guess you could say months, actually—I was approached by a major player in the computer industry named Harald Burklund. Swedish national, heads a consortium based in Stockholm though he's lived in London for years. Sort of like that Egyptian chap who owns your Harrod's. He carries a good reputation for being aggressive but careful. He's someone not to be taken lightly. During our conversation, he expressed an interest in buying shares in VES and later even voiced the idea of buying it outright."

"Was he serious?"

"Only halfway. Those kinds of things are done all the time. You know, feelers here and there, probes to see what kind of reaction they might generate."

"And what was your reaction to his overtures?"

"At the time, nothing. I mean, that was the last thing on our minds—bringing in some outsider. However, as a responsible Executive Committee member, I mentioned it to my cousins later that week. Good business requires that you not ignore a fully-capitalized buyer or investor. After all, our value and thus our sale price would skyrocket once the project was underway."

"Were you not concerned that this fellow Burklund contacted you just as your company was undertaking the new project?"

"Oh, no, not in the least. First of all, no one outside our inner circle had any knowledge of what we had in mind. So he could only be on a fishing expedition. Again, that kind of thing happens all the time in the circles in which I travel. You're at a foundation dinner, a conference, a seminar, a meeting somewhere, and someone comes up to you and you exchange ideas and comments. That's all. It sometimes reminds me of the lawyer's courtroom trick of asking an outlandish question just to see if the witness might volunteer something useful. It's all probing; nothing more."

"I see...," said the Chief Inspector. "Please don't take this personally, I'm not asking it to be accusatory...but how certain are you that this Burklund fellow sought you out and not the other way around? That perhaps you sought him out?"

Edward emitted a grim chuckle.

"I won't say I've never played the game, Chief Inspector, but not that time. No, he approached *me*. You see, from the very beginning, the three of us were keenly aware of the risk of letting something slip out. So we took great pains to avoid it. And may I say this—had I been guilty of such an indiscretion, I could not have brought it to the table without exposing myself."

"He's absolutely right," Michael said. "He told us about Burklund's remarks and we concurred with his assessment that the Swede actually knew nothing about the YAMATSU project."

"Had you heard of this Burklund before that?"

"Oh, yes, but indirectly...through the industry trades."

"So did any of you contact this Burklund sometime thereafter?"

"No. And I'm sure Geoffrey did not," Michael said.

Edward added, "I had strictly casual contact off and on, as before."

"Did he probe any further?"

"Not once. Which should not be surprising. A responsible, skilled CEO will not be so obvious. He would show his hand and the sale price would shoot up. The best CEOs always act as though information caught them by surprise and that they just happened to be in the right place at the right time. Everyone knows better, but we all pretend it was just good luck. After all, outward appearances are still what count."

"So is this Burklund now aware of developments?"

"Yes," said Edward. "I phoned him as a matter of respect. Despite our friendly contacts, we're hardly peers. Sounds a bit like the American Mafia, I guess. It was only a matter of time before he read about it off the wire services."

"Would he have any reason, incentive if you will, for VES to fail?"

"No," said Edward, shaking his head. "His people have nothing similar in development so there's no competition. In fact, we're a supplier to one of his subsidiaries. He gets a fair price from us so losing us would cost him substantially. And burning us down—if that's where you're going—would simply drop our value to him and he'd have to look for another supplier. As for any buyout, he'd have to spend a fortune to rebuild and retool, only to lose out in the end because the YAMATSU people would have left."

St. George's eyebrows drew closer. "I see, but how can you be so sure he has nothing similar in the works?"

"The grapevine."

"The same grapevine that knew nothing of your YAMATSU venture?"

Edward's patrician face went blank.

"Point," said Michael morosely. "Maybe we did give something away."

To Edward: "What was his response to your call?"

"Condolences," replied the cousin, still shaken. "Little else he could really say."

"Do you think his interest in VES will continue?"

"No, because it really wasn't there in the first place," Michael said. "However, what he did say originally gives us an entree in the future, should we need one. But first, we want to—we *need* to—show the world some *positive* action, something tangible, such as clearing up the mess."

"Well, I've called for a forensics team to come up from London. They should start work tomorrow. Probably require one or two full

days on-site, after which I see no reason why the scene cannot be ·
released to you without restriction."

The two cousins expressed their unenthusiastic understanding.

"There is one other matter," continued the Chief Inspector in his
best professional manner. "A delicate one, I still need to explore,
however, I'm afraid...specifically, the haste to cremate the body."

Michael Pont looked ill while Edward fidgeted and cleared his
throat.

"No haste," said the cousin, his lips drawn thin and tight. "It was
nothing more than common decency. After all, the poor wretch was
burnt to a crisp! Sorry, Michael."

"No, no, no, go on, he has to know. Just doing his job."

"You saw the body in the morgue," the Chief Inspector said to the
cousin.

"Yes. The Medical Examiner and Chief McSwain said a formal
viewing was totally out of the question. His limbs were all drawn up.
Damn unholy thing, I tell you. The only decent thing was to spare
Myra and Michael any more pain, so I made the request and signed
the consent."

"*You* signed? But you're not—"

"Myra gave me emergency power of attorney for that sole purpose."

St. George now got to his feet, stepped to the edge of the nearest
partition, looked out toward the front window, and then turned
back.

"Mr. Cargill, you faced an awesome responsibility what with
Michael being away and, as you explained, out of touch. You had to
notify your employees that there would be no work on Monday. You
became acting CEO."

"Yes. I had Barrows' number and those for Manning and Mrs.
Sperling. We divided up the roster."

"Did you contact anyone else?"

"The insurance company, of course. And utilities."

"Your bank, perhaps? Considering the serious financial ramifications?"

"Well, yes, I called Mr. Muir. Only seemed natural...as you said,
the financial consequences. Need to cover the payroll."

"What time did you reach him?"

Edward glanced at Michael. "Oh, quite early on, I think. Around
noon."

"Did he have any suggestions?"

Again Edward glanced at Michael. "Well...I can't recall exactly. So much had happened."

"Was the power of attorney his idea?"

Edward looked blank for a long moment.

"Chief Inspector," Michael said, "what difference does it make?"

"Only that I should caution Mr. Cargill to be careful before taking credit for too many things. The press for an early cremation has wrought the very crisis you wished to avoid. There was absolutely no reason the remains could not have remained in cold storage. But destroying what was left of the body has deprived us of extremely important evidence. Specifically, lungs free of soot would prove he had not inhaled smoke, and thus he could not have set the fire. So at the very least, anyone recommending the cremation exhibited extremely poor judgment. And the local officials who allowed that travesty to occur have much to answer for as well. Mind you, as concerned as you are with public perception, the rush to destroy the remains might be looked upon in some quarters as highly suspicious. You see the problem?"

Subdued and chagrined, the two cousins nodded slowly.

"Silas Muir thought it best," Edward said softly, like a scolded schoolboy. "That's all I can say."

"Well, gentlemen," said St. George as he signaled to Poole and Dougall to stand, "I think that will be enough for the moment. Thank you for your time and cooperation. You've been most helpful. Again please accept our condolences. Inspector Dougall will need formal statements from you both—you can schedule them with him. We will keep you advised of any new developments. Oh, Michael, by the way, we'll need the name and address and phone number of your Edinburgh contact of the feminine persuasion."

"Of course. I would only hope that her identity need not be broadcast all over the UK."

"Only if for some reason she has to testify in court to support your alibi."

"That won't be a problem. I can write it down for you now if you'd like."

"Yes, please. Thank you."

"Come to think of it," Edward said while Michael was writing on a message pad, "since you're checking alibis, I can show you our receipts for Saturday. Took the family for a day on the town."

"Thank you. Perhaps Inspector Dougall can send a constable round for them."

"Right. I'll get them together as soon as I get home."

Dougall accepted the notepad page from Michael and led the way to the door.

"Oh, one more thing," said St. George as he stepped on the threshold, "was anyone sick at the office last week? Something intestinal? Flu? Diarrhea, perhaps?"

"Good gracious, no, not that I recall," Michael said. "We've always been a healthy lot."

"Anyone have a peptic ulcer? From stress and what not? Maybe Geoffrey?"

"Oh, heavens no! He was too ornery to have an ulcer."

"Ornery?"

"He could be very stubborn at times."

"Obstinate, I'd say," added Edward. "As for ulcers, I think he gave them rather than received them."

"Why do you ask?" Michael asked.

"Oh, the thought just crossed my mind. Well, gentlemen, thank you again. Until later…"

13

THE DEAD MAN'S home sat in the midst of a fashionable Edinburgh neighborhood where wealth was evident but not flaunted. St. George found such restraint appealing. As he and his party were shown into the ground-floor drawing room, the lady of the house joined them. Myra Pont exhibited remarkable composure though the tension etched in her face betrayed the fragility of that self-control. During the introductions, her visitors conveyed their condolences.

"Thank you, gentlemen," replied the widow of five days as she motioned for them to take their seats while she perched on the edge of a brocade chair as though posing for a formal portrait. "Your news has been quite unsettling. I'm not sure how I should feel about it."

"In what way?" said the Chief Inspector.

"Well, just when I've begun to come to grips with Geoffrey being gone, you raise this specter of him burning his own factory and perhaps deliberately destroying himself in the process. Given the choice, I'd much prefer him murdered. Either way, it's all quite terrible."

"Yes, ma'am, and we're sorry to have to broach such distasteful matters at this time in your grief, but because some parties stand ready to blame your husband for everything, we thought it best to press our case if there is any chance to prove otherwise."

The widow began wringing her hands and plucked a crumpled handkerchief from a pocket in her dress.

"So Geoffrey's death was *not* an accident?"

"We cannot say positively at this time, but there is reason to suspect not. What's allowed the uncertainty to fester is the absence of an autopsy which would have told us whether there was any soot in his lungs from smoke inhalation."

"You mean if he were dead before the fire, then he could not have inhaled anything."

"Yes. But since we cannot undo what has been done," St. George said, "perhaps the two things protecting him from an adverse verdict are the absence of any fire-setting paraphernalia on the premises and that his lighter was found in his coat pocket. Rather hard to do that if you've set the blaze, only to catch fire yourself. At any rate, to be thorough, we must explore all conceivable explanations—some good, some bad, some favorable, others not so. I hope you will not be offended. Above all, what we need first is to learn as much as we can about the man himself."

Myra Pont straightened up, sighed, and said, "Ask what you will."

"Thank you. Have you any idea why he went out there Saturday?"

"None whatsoever."

"He made no mention, gave no hint, perhaps Friday evening, that he might?"

"None. He was quiet—he had been all week—but he would be, of course, considering the meeting on Friday."

"The one with the Japanese."

"Yes."

"Did he discuss that meeting, or even the project itself, with you?"

"Only in general terms."

"From his manner...his words...his posture, could you perceive how he felt things were going on the project?"

"Well...yes and no. This past week, no, because he had something else on his mind. It might have had something to do with the financial reports he worked on each evening. I mean, when they signed the initial agreement some months earlier, he was positively ebullient. He was a bit transparent that way."

"So this week was different?"

"Yes, but I don't know how much to read into that."

"Please do not mistake my intent in asking, but how do you know they were financial statements your husband was reading?"

"Because I could see columns of numbers behind pound signs and decimals and sums and so on. I've briefly seen the company's statements before."

"I see...Was he accustomed to going to the plant on weekends?"

"Not since they were first up and running."

"So would it be a fair statement to say you were surprised to learn that he had gone out there?"

"Oh, yes, definitely."

"We understand that you went out shopping that morning. Had he left any message for you? Maybe a Post-it note? Something scribbled on a pad?"

"No, nothing."

"Could he have left a message on your answering machine?"

"No. I checked that right off when the word came."

"Could someone on your staff have erased it?"

"We have no staff except Marta who comes in weekdays and a butler for social events. Only Geoffrey and I worked the machine."

"So the first you knew of his going to the plant was when they informed you of the tragedy."

"Yes."

"In retrospect, was there anything that morning which might even remotely have indicated his interest in going out there? Or maybe somewhere else?"

"No. You may already know, gentlemen, that Geoffrey and I have gone our separate ways for years. We've always had high regard for each other, but after three miscarriages and a stillbirth, we grew apart. I actually became afraid to have children, and for Geoffrey, the company had become his child. It was quite evident we were not cut out for the typical family experience. We also realized that adoption was as ill-advised as divorce. So we elected to leave things status quo. And in return for my placing no constraints on his world of electronics, he did the same for my interests which center around the humanities."

"Interesting...and I must applaud your candor."

Myra Pont merely nodded her acknowledgment of the compliment.

"So would it be a fair assessment to say that your marriage was now an economic convenience?"

"Yes and no. We loved each other in ways not usually thought of. And we each got a trophy spouse for social occasions and I got a generous lifestyle. It obviously wouldn't work for everyone."

"Of course, the next question must be...were there any outside relationships for either of you?"

"You mean lovers? Oh, yes, occasionally but very discreetly. That was our first consideration."

"And was Geoffrey discreet?"

"I'd say yes because I really have no idea who he saw or when or for how long. Even if he saw anyone."

"So the two of you did socialize together..."

"Oh, yes, all the time. Only our closest friends understood our arrangement. In fact, we were to have dinner with the Prescotts Saturday evening. To celebrate the agreement. They're probably our dearest friends. Absolutely precious people."

"What about dinner Friday evening?"

"We originally planned on dining out, just the two of us, but Geoffrey pled fatigue and so we stayed home and called out for Chinese. There's a place in the market not far from here with the most delightful Mandarin cuisine. Ironically, Geoffrey mentioned that at some point we would have to acquire a taste for Japanese fare, for when we had to go there."

"Sensible thought. We're, of course, looking for anyone who might have had some reason—real or imagined—for wishing either your husband or the company harm. Former employees are a prime source of worry, naturally, but we also must consider—"

"Former lovers; yes, I understand. I'm afraid I cannot help you there. My last relationship was some two years ago. It ended amicably."

"Did the other party feel the same as you about its termination?"

"Oh, yes. I was in Milan for a course in art history. A nice man from Leeds was there as well. A one-month interlude, nothing more."

"I'm not trying to pry, Mrs. Pont, but sometimes the second party secretly does not share the same sentiments as the first. So that leaves the door open to stalking..."

"That's completely out of the question. I've received no phone calls or letters since then."

"All right. Then there's the flip side: the man wishes to court you but finds your husband standing in the way."

"Again, Chief Inspector, I've had no further contact with that man in any way. And certainly no one has called me since the fire. I really don't see myself as a Helen of Troy."

St. George could not suppress a quick grin. "Very well. But please let us know if someone does. It may be nothing or it might be significant."

"I will."

"As far as you know, your husband fully intended on going to the Prescotts Saturday evening?"

"Yes. In fact, he called them Thursday afternoon to confirm our coming. They understood how he was being a bit superstitious about not wanting to count on the final result before it was accomplished."

"Hmm, quite. You mentioned earlier that he seemed to have something else on his mind last week. Did he say what it was?"

"No."

"How could you tell he was preoccupied—was he given to mood swings? Depression,even?"

"No, just distracted. Not really listening to me. I had to repeat some of the things I said."

"Must have been somewhat aggravating."

"Not as much as you think. It was standard behaviour for him when he had something important on his mind. I learned long ago that once that something had passed, I would have his full attention once more."

"Were there degrees of this...distraction? Was he harder to bring around at some times than at others?"

"Oh...I suppose so, but right now nothing stands out. If you're asking about last week, I don't know."

St. George nodded sympathetically.

"Since he contacted the Prescotts on Thursday, he must have felt quite comfortable with the upcoming meeting the next day."

"Oh, yes, quite."

"Yet he remained distracted Friday evening."

"Well, yes...I guess so. No more than the other evenings, however."

"And he was not home Saturday morning when you left to shop."

"That's right. He's almost always sleeps until 9 or 10. But he was up and gone by the time I arose at 9."

"If something had come up Friday afternoon, if the meeting had not gone well, what would he have done?"

"If he were going to be delayed, he would have called me. He was very courteous that way."

"And if matters had soured at the meeting? If nothing was signed?"

"He probably would not have come home until very late. Either that or come home and sulked. Which, if you're wondering, would have been very consistent with past behaviour."

"Did your husband have any business or investment dealings with the Prescotts?"

"No. He believed that such activities were the surest way to ruin a friendship."

"Had he experienced that misfortune in the past?"

"Personally, no, but he had seen it happen to others."

"Did he always leave work at the same time?"

"No, he might sign out anytime during the afternoon. Usually close to 5, though."

"He always came straight home?"

"Generally, though not infrequently he would drive downtown to meet with Silas Muir and others concerned with the Japanese project."

"Besides his distraction of last week, can you think of any change in his routine over the past month?"

"No. I've thought about that a lot, but no, nothing."

"Was he in the habit of returning to the plant after hours during the week?"

"Only rarely and then it was to retrieve something he had left behind. Work of some kind. Reports, analyses, I guess. That's more Michael's habit—taking work home."

"So would it be correct to say that the financial reports Geoffrey was working on here last week were sort of out of the ordinary for him?"

"Yes, you could say so. Although at the time I just assumed they were part of the project."

"Ah, yes, of course. Where did he review these materials?"

"In his study. It's just off the living room. You're welcome to see it, if you'd like."

"Yes, please, we would. But first, has anyone been in there since the...since his death? To tidy up, perhaps?"

"No," said the widow, her lips suddenly thin and tight. "I have no intention of making it a shrine, but right now I could not bear to go in there. And I've let no one else inside, either."

"Perfectly understandable. By the way, how did you learn that the deal had been signed?"

"He called me straightaway. He sounded genuinely relieved."

"Did he mention that the Japanese were on their way to St. Andrews?"

"Yes. I think he was as much concerned about having that come off well as he was about the deal itself."

"He carried a membership there, correct?"

"Of the R&A, yes."

"Why did he not go up himself?"

"I asked him that months ago when he made the reservations. It was a matter of silly male pride. He had never been a good golfer, and he hadn't played for several years because he was so caught up with the company. Never found the time. He was sure he would play poorly and he felt it was important to have someone play well in front of their new partners. So as usual, he had Michael substitute for him. In fact, a few years ago, they actually got one small contract because Michael so impressed and entertained the guests that they just had to sign on."

"It happens," said St. George as he smiled. "But I'm still puzzled—why did he not go up and just be the gallery?"

Myra Pont flashed a wan smile.

"That's exactly what I asked him. He said the Japanese would insist he play and not doing so would show a lack of respect."

"So he wasn't disappointed about not going?"

"I think deep down he was, but he also felt relieved that Michael was going to be there."

"We understand Michael missed the signing. Down to London or somewhere?"

"Yes. I believe he got back some time that night and then drove up to St. Andrews the next morning."

"Was Geoffrey upset about him not being present? You know, full complement on hand and all that?"

"Not at all. Something with the banks down there. Again, Geoffrey was quite relieved that Michael agreed to handle it."

"When Michael returned, did he phone your husband?"

"Yes, he did, in fact. I took the call. He said the trip had gone well. However, Geoffrey had said he did not want to be disturbed and so I gave Michael the word and he rang off."

"Your husband came home straight from the plant?"

"Yes, about 6 P.M. We ate about 7."

"6 P.M.? A bit late was he?"

"Not considering what had transpired, no. Ceremony ran overtime and he wanted to finish the work for the week."

"You said he was tired."

"Yes, but also excited. He pretty much held the floor when he first came home. Couldn't shut him up if I had wanted to."

"And after that?"

For the first time, Myra Pont looked away if only but for a moment.

"I hadn't thought about it but now, with all your questions, I'd have to say he was actually very quiet the rest of the evening. At times, perhaps even daydreaming. I put it all down to fatigue."

"How did the evening end?"

"I read some and watched the news and then retired. Somewhere around 10 o'clock. Geoffrey spent the time in his study. As I was heading upstairs, he came out of the kitchen—he had gotten himself a soda—I congratulated him again on his success and he said 'Thank you,' and then, you know, it's strange, I just remembered...yes, he said something very puzzling. He said 'So much for Act One' and raised his glass to me in a toast. Then he went back into his study."

With that, Myra Pont broke down into tears. Before anyone could proffer a chivalrous handkerchief, however, she regained her composure and waved them away.

"Was that the last time you saw him?" St. George prodded gently as he retook his seat.

"No," came the weak reply. "I awoke early and found his bed unslept in. We keep twin beds if that's important. I came downstairs and found him asleep in the study."

"How was he dressed?"

"In the same clothes he had worn that evening."

"Did you wake him?"

"No, I didn't have the heart. I thought he had quite earned his rest."

"With the two of you going your separate ways, were you in the habit of leaving messages for each other?"

"Occasionally. Usually we simply discussed our plans over breakfast and dinner."

"Who fixed breakfast?"

"I did if we were both up. Otherwise each to his own."

"And Saturday?"

"I don't remember seeing any dishes."

"Changing the subject, how well did your husband get along with Michael and cousin Edward?"

"All right. I don't think there ever was any problem. After all, Geoffrey was the driving force behind the company. However, I could tell whenever he lost a vote because he would come home and pout."

"Are you referring to the executive committee?"

"Yes."

"I understand that together Geoffrey and Michael held 60 percent of the shares, Edward 35 percent, with the remainder divided among Edward's siblings."

"That's right. Something about qualifying for some tax exemption or other consideration, I'm not sure."

"It seems the three of them worked things out quite well."

"I suppose so."

St. George cocked his head like a terrier that has detected rustling in the grass.

"Pardon me, are you saying they did not?"

"Oh no, no, it worked out very well. Viscount has been a great success."

"Forgive me, but I must be sure I have this clear in my mind...it sounded like you did not fully agree with the idea that the three of them were equally responsible for that success. Am I wrong?"

Myra Pont regarded the Chief Inspector for a long moment before looking down at her hands.

"My point is...that one cannot *truthfully* say that the *three* of them ran the company."

"Not even as the ruling Executive Committee...?"

"Oh, officially, yes, for form and all that, but Geoffrey was the company's heart and soul."

"So they were not a troika."

"Hardly. In the beginning, Michael was critically important to the operation. He was the brains behind their first product, but after that, the well ran dry. Although he carries the title of 'Director of Research and Development,' he's been living on his reputation ever since. If you want my opinion, I think the real performer has been Michael's Number Two man. A man named James Barrows."

St. George paused to give Poole time to jot down a few notes. During the hiatus, Myra Pont looked languidly about the room as though seeing it for the first time.

"For someone who has kept herself far removed from the company, you have considerable insight into its operations."

"Well, while I did not intrude in my husband's business life, I did listen when he wanted to ventilate."

"I see. Did he ever say that he thought Michael had lost his touch?"

"He would never come right out and say that. Family loyalty was very important to him. But I'm sure he felt disappointed that Michael was less and less available to assume more and more of the mantle. And now and again there were things Michael said—I can't recall any examples for you, you'll have to forgive me—but they made me think he was covering up for his lack of performance."

"You mean like excuses?"

"Or reasons. Explanations. Always explanations."

"Interesting. And how about Mr. Cargill?"

Again Myra looked down at her hands.

"Edward is strictly window dressing. I believe the Americans have an expression—fifth wheel. Although he's a relative, to me he's always epitomized the adage that old money is never as sharp and cunning as new money."

"Old money?"

"For several generations. The Cargills have spent decades waiting for a place on the Honors List. Geoffrey's—and Michael's—mother was a Cargill. However, their father, James Pont, was a merchant who was strictly middle class. The Cargills believed that their sister married below her station but were decent enough to be discreet about their displeasure. Anyway, when the boys were trying to fund Viscount and were a couple of hundred thousand pounds short, the Cargills stepped in for a 40 percent share and Edward's brokerage to receive all of the company's insurance business. Because the other Cargills could care less, they allot Edward effective control of that 40 percent share. So, in sum, he's done very well for very little work."

"Interesting. So the voting ... Michael and Edward merely followed Geoffrey's lead?"

"Until about two years ago," answered Myra who now stared intently at the drapes hanging on the far side of the room. "Yes, Michael dutifully supported his brother while Edward came along for the ride. But as Michael's effectiveness—or should I say productivity—waned, he began espousing divergent viewpoints, and then Edward found himself kingmaker. Sometimes he'd vote with my husband, sometimes not. So whenever Geoffrey came home sulking, I knew Edward and Michael had ganged up on him."

"Aside from sulking, was there any other way your husband reacted to these defeats?"

"Not really, except that once he finished talking about it, he didn't want to be disturbed. Then by morning, it was all forgotten."

"Did you ever hear of any serious arguing?"

"No. If any occurred, Geoffrey never mentioned it."

"Did Edward or Michael ever contact you to pressure your husband on anything?"

"Never. However, I think they both knew I wouldn't stand for it."

"Does the Executive Committee continue to run things during this interim?"

"You mean Michael and Edward alone?"

"Yes."

"Yes, they're in charge. Edward told me an emergency provision allows them to manage until Geoffrey's estate is closed."

"Have you any idea of the company succession?"

"No. I would think there must be something in the charter."

"Has anyone approached you about voting your husband's shares yourself?"

"Oh, God, I hope not!" cried Myra, her eyes flashing fear, not anger.

"May I ask you why?"

"Chief Inspector, what I know best is how to be a lady, not a company executive. And the first rule for a lady is not to make a fool of herself privately or publicly."

"I hope this does not sound impertinent," St. George said, "but I would respectfully disagree with you about your capabilities. I think your performance, given time, would be more than satisfactory. However, we don't wish to detain you any longer than necessary, so allow me to carry on with this question: If you do inherit his shares, what do you plan to do with them?"

"Oh, Chief Inspector, I wouldn't have the *faintest* idea!"

"So would it be fair to say you would consult someone?"

"Oh, yes."

"Such as?"

"Oh, I don't know, it hasn't actually come up, but I suppose Silas Muir would be the obvious first choice."

"Had your husband entertained any thought of changing the company charter?"

"Not that I know of. Of course, I'm sure he wouldn't have done anything, let alone say anything, unless something awfully drastic had happened."

"A very deliberate man, then."

"Oh, quite," said Myra. "Purposeful might be a better word."

"Not impetuous."

"Never."

"Did your husband share your views about Michael's diminishing contribution to the cause?"

"I don't know that he was aware of my opinion. I made a point of keeping my thoughts to myself unless he specifically asked. Again, remember our agreement about not meddling. Had I expressed myself, I would have crossed the line. As I said, I saw my role as listener, not speaker."

"While listening, then, did you ever hear him voice any qualms about Michael continuing on as head of R&D?"

"Not as such. He muttered now and then about a lot of things, especially after being outvoted, but then just as quickly, everything seemed to be patched up and they moved on. There were times when I know he felt frustrated and pined for the old days when he held free rein."

"Did he ever express any feelings about Edward?"

Myra rubbed her hands for a long moment as though working on a stain. "Edward was just so much window dressing as far as Geoffrey was concerned," she replied. "Served a useful purpose, a vital purpose, certainly, when they first got started, but thereafter has never been anything exceptional. Good secretary could do what he does, in my opinion. I think Geoffrey agreed but was more comfortable trying not to view it that way."

"I see. Well, Mrs. Pont, we thank you for so graciously giving of your time. You've been most helpful," said St. George, rising to his feet, his companions following his lead. "We shall certainly keep you informed of any developments."

"You're more than welcome," said the widow as she remained seated. "But Chief Inspector...now that I've answered your questions, would you answer one or two of mine?"

"Certainly, as best as I can."

"What did you mean about my husband's lighter being in his coat pocket?"

"Just that it was found there. Those wishing to tag him with the crime are quick to point out that a lighter provided him with a ready source of ignition to light the fire. My contention is that, had he been caught by the fire as claimed, he would not have had the presence of mind to replace it in his pocket while himself was on fire. He would have dropped it. So to me it seemed more logical that its presence was simply coincidental. There is a counterargument, however, that he used the lighter to ignite a delayed fuse of some kind. Somehow we have to resolve the conflict."

"I see..." said the widow, frowning and biting her lip.

"Was there something in particular about the lighter?"

"Well, no, I was just curious...because he gave up smoking eight months ago."

14

AFTER SHOWING THE policemen to the study, the widow withdrew to another part of the house. Stressing that they would touch nothing, St. George led the way inside, instructing Dougall to keep a running inventory of the things they saw. The centerpiece to the snug, masculine room was a highly polished executive desk near the broad bay window. On top was a closed but unclasped briefcase. A small side table held a computer and its keyboard and mouse.

"Let's save the briefcase for last," said the Chief Inspector as he began to slowly orbit the room.

Photographs were everywhere, even occupying considerable space on the bookshelves. One man appeared in all the pictures: average height, a bit chunky, clean-shaven, hair always well-cut, conservative sideburns, dapper, well-dressed no matter the setting, sharp crease in his slacks, collars smooth, well-set ties, a man who appeared very organized at all times. St. George commented that, compared to the photos of business groups, most noticeable was the man's broader smile in the golfing pictures. Adding to Geoffrey Pont's personal sense of order was the orderly appearance of the room as a whole—desk clear, pictures all squarely aligned, books all even with the shelf edge, nothing lying about, no litter, nothing open and unfinished, nothing casual anywhere. An empty humidor sat on the small table behind the desk.

"What we have is an achiever," St. George said, coming to rest. "A man who was very neat, very tidy without being a fop, someone with a pronounced sense of order, of what is right and wrong, someone who always took great pains to be prepared, who did his homework, who enjoyed his golf..."

"Seems a bit compulsive," ventured Dougall.

"Perhaps, but then are not computer people very detail-conscious? I submit we can read several important facets of this man's character from this room. The first, and dearest to my own heart, is that he genuinely loved to play golf. Therefore, for him to abandon the game in favor of VES was extraordinary. His work became his passion, and as Mrs. Pont just stated, the company became his child. Second, he was a gregarious chap who was not uncomfortable in close proximity to others. In none of these pictures is he leaning *away* from anyone. Also, as his widow pointed out, he was transparent about his feelings. Third, he was someone not given to sloppiness in clothing or conduct. Rather than 'compulsion,' perhaps we might consider 'control' instead. So with that in mind, what do we have? Laurence?"

"He never undertook anything lightly. As she mentioned, he was very deliberate. So whatever he was reviewing here last week was something serious."

"I'd agree. Inspector?"

"Had an ego. He's in every picture and yet I've seen only one of his wife. Typical, I suppose, for a successful CEO."

"Consistent anyway. You might add pride and vanity because of his fear of not playing well before the YAMATSU people. I would also wager the clothes he's wearing in those pictures are top-of-the-line. Laurence?"

"Starting late Friday evening, he broke with custom. Despite the complete success with YAMATSU, he continued working in here presumably on the same financial reports that he had studied all week. It's possible they had nothing to do with YAMATSU. And then he never bothered to go to bed, he just stayed in here in his street clothes and fell asleep. That would suggest that only something extraordinarily important would keep him at his post."

"Exactly!"

"I wonder if he changed clothes Saturday morning?" said Dougall.

"Good question," St. George said. "Go ask Mrs. Pont right now."

While they waited, St. George poked around the table and desk drawers with his rubber-tipped collapsible pointer that he had received as a birthday present from Marcus Woolsley. It allowed him to probe and snoop without contaminating anything or leaving prints. All the while he regretted not saying 'please' to Dougall.

"Nothing locked. See any sign of a safe, Laurence?"

"Nope. Pictures aren't big enough. Under the carpet most likely."

"We'll have Dougall request the local lab to come out and survey."

Just then Dougall returned to report that Saturday there were no soiled clothes upstairs in the clothes hamper or in the laundry room. She was not sure if any suit was missing.

"*Damn*, if we only had that bloody autopsy! All right, so, in the absence of evidence to the contrary, the man left here unkempt and slovenly. Possibly unshaven. *Quite* out of character."

"So whatever was on his mind," Dougall said, "was either the Japanese deal or something equally as important. Or maybe more so."

"I think you've nailed it, Inspector," said St. George, in his peripheral vision catching the local man's startle at the compliment. "So how do we find out what it was? Would you mind checking his phone records? Here and from the office? Past week or so? Not foolproof but there's a chance he called someone about the problem."

"Right. Will do." Dougall then added, "There's one other thing—what about his comment about 'Act One'? A dying clue of sorts?"

"It's tempting to think that," replied the Chief Inspector. "Was 'Act Two' those financial reports? And were they the reason he went out to the plant? Or was that Act Three? Best we leave such speculation alone for the time being but let's not forget it, either."

"Yes, sir."

"Now then...the sergeant and I have determined that none of the drawers in this room are locked. So shall we see what they contain?"

Putting on standard latex exam gloves, the detectives explored each drawer but found nothing out of the ordinary. Finally, all that remained was the briefcase itself. Closing his pointer to its shortest length, the Chief Inspector nudged it under one clasp and lifted the lid until it settled into its upright position. Inside there were no financial statements, either bound or loose-leaf, and no computer discs. Rather, the dominant item was a current national newsweekly that was devoid of any articles on Viscount Electric Systems or YAMATSU or anything dealing with computers, chip technology, superconductivity, or other esoteric topics. Nothing was highlighted, underlined, circled, boxed, or checked. Nothing had been cut out. There were no jottings in the margins. Two disposable pens and a pocket-sized appointment book completed the inventory. Perusing the small book revealed nothing to indicate the dead man intended on going to the plant on that fateful morning. Collectively disappointed, they lowered the lid.

"Mrs. Pont said she saw financial statements," said Poole. "Where are they?"

"She said she had seen *Viscount's* statements before," countered St. George as he stroked his chin. "It's equally possible the ones last week were from somewhere else. But as you pointed out, either way, where are they? Moreover, did she see formal printed financial statements or did she see something on the computer screen there? Inspector, would you please bother her again and find out? Thank you."

"If they were computerized, then they must have been VES files, right?" offered Poole.

"Logically, yes. Especially since the company computers are not connected to anything off the premises. So he could not have linked up and downloaded from here—Ah! Inspector!"

"She saw both printed statements and what appeared to be documents on the computer screen. She also informed me that she's not a computer person and has no intention of ever using one."

"Hmmmpf! Well, let's see what we can find." St. George nodded to Poole who reached over and first moved a tiny switch on a lunchbox-sized device set alongside the CPU tower. A small green light appeared and then he switched on the monitor and the CPU itself.

"A combination power surge protector and standby storage battery," the sergeant said as he pointed to the device. "Run your power through there and it builds up a charge that gives you ten seconds to shut things down if the main power fails. That way you don't crash your files."

"Really," answered the Chief Inspector who had not the slightest idea what his aide was describing. However, as with supervisors everywhere, he made it a point never to let on that he was in the dark. He watched as the machine hummed and the TV screen blinked into life and first showed a few black-and-white screens filled with C-prompts and other jargon and then the main platform came on. A few desktop icons were clearly visible. None was labeled VES or Viscount.

"There's the word processor and some personal finance management stuff and the wastebasket and his internet connection."

"My computer?" queried St. George, pointing to an icon bearing those words.

"Yes, sir, it displays all the hardware plus the bells and whistles on your machine. Well, let's go inside..." whereupon the good sergeant directed the mouse cursor to the lower left corner of the screen. He clicked and right away a short menu popped up. Even quicker came a window asking for a password.

"Blast!" St. George said. "Makes sense, however, with him being a computer whiz and all. Next task for you, Inspector—find the password."

"I'll wager it's not the same one Michael and Edward use at work."

"Logical, though considering their overconfidence about security, I would not be surprised. You'll have to bother the widow once again when we leave—for his personal effects this time."

"Already have those at the station."

"Oh, yes, of course, you would, wouldn't you? In the meantime, we need to call for a forensics team. I'd suggest running it through Superintendent Wallace since we're in another jurisdiction. Oh, and we need the computer taken to our station—sorry, Inspector, I mean your station."

Dougall chuckled. "No problem. I'll go make the call now."

* * *

During the ride back to West Calder, St. George snuggled into the rear seat, lowered his head, and dozed contentedly. Poole nudged him awake as they pulled up to the station.

"James Barrows should be here momentarily," Dougall said as they debarked. "I had my people call him when we left the store. In the meantime, I'll check on the murder room."

"Thank you," said St. George as he stretched beside the car before following Poole inside. They were in Dougall's small office browsing through the local paper when the inspector popped in to say all was ready.

The Chief Engineer for VES entered the murder room to find St. George seated at the head of the conference table and Poole nearby on the far side. The witness chair was at the opposite end by the door with Dougall taking his place across from the sergeant. Youthful, unobtrusive, and alert, James Barrows displayed a closely-cropped haircut bordered by a receding hairline. He was, in fact, the exact opposite to the stringy-haired stereotype St. George had expected. In truth, as the seasons came and went, so did the man's beard and sideburns, customarily untrimmed and unkempt. However, in deference to the present circumstances, he had elected to arrive clean-shaven.

"Thank you for joining us," said the Chief Inspector at the conclusion of the introductions. "In view of the hour, we shall conclude our business as quickly as possible."

"No problem. Glad to help. Got nowhere to go anyway. What do you want to know?"

"You've been at Viscount how long?"

"Right from the beginning."

"And how long have you held the office of Chief Engineer?"

"Same time. Straight out of graduate school at St. Andrews as a matter of fact. Started out as mostly a figurehead title because Michael was the resident genius. But since then, you might say I've grown into the role."

"How did VES happen to land you?"

"Quite simple, really," Barrows said. "Michael had contacts at the university, and even before I was giving any serious thought to job searching, I got this letter and then a phone call. After that, everything just seemed to happen. I can tell you one thing: Being able to get in on the ground floor of a successful enterprise is a sweet deal."

"In what way?"

"Well, over time you get to become an important cog in the machine. And that translates into influence. You begin to see that much of what is produced bears your imprint."

"Yes, but I should imagine that, beyond professional satisfaction, there should be financial rewards as well."

"Oh sure," Barrows said, "and I've done all right. You know the conventional wisdom that says us hackers don't know how to have fun. Well, I guess that could apply to me because I've spent very little of what I've made."

"Have you ever been offered any company stock?"

"No, that's all held within the family. And that's fine with me because I've seen too many of my peers run themselves into the ground chasing pounds or dollars or what have you. I don't want all the responsibility that goes with it. You see, my work requires that my mind be unfettered. But having to keep one eye on the balance sheet would stifle me. No thanks."

"Yet surely someone with your qualifications could command quite a salary elsewhere, could he not? Plus stock options, patents, and so on?"

"Possibly. Let me give you an example. One of my friends from the university went to IBM, drew more income from the start than I'm making now, and nearly went bonkers after one year. Had to quit. And that will haunt him the rest of his working life because it's part of his permanent record. No sir, money couldn't buy the satisfaction I get from knowing I'm important to these people. As a result, I sleep very well at night."

"Pardon my asking," said the Chief Inspector, "but you don't sound like a resident Scotsman. American, by chance?"

Barrows flashed a quick smile. "Canadian. Vancouver originally. My mother came from Seattle. My father was Canadian; a stock analyst; 12 years her senior." Barrows named a famous international brokerage firm. "Spent several years in Toronto and then transferred to their London office. We travelled around a lot and when the time came to go back to America, I decided I wanted to stay here for college. It's worked out fine."

"Only child?"

"Three younger sisters. I was glad to get away from all the bickering."

"Family doing well now?"

Barrows stiffened. "I suppose. My father and I exchange e-mails every once in a while, mother sends a letter now and then when she's sober, and last I heard the girls were out chasing husbands. Beyond that, I consider them a past life. Period."

"I see. Well then, getting back to the matters at hand...your comment about growing into the role of Chief Engineer...would you say you've replaced Michael Pont as the top man in R&D?"

"Not the way you describe it. I've not campaigned at all. I was green as grass when I started, and so naturally, working around Michael, I gained valuable experience. Gradually, as Michael was called away more and more, I was given more responsibility."

"I see. From your insider's perspective, how well would you say the three top men worked together?"

"Well enough. I think the success of the company speaks to that. However, I'm not the fly on the wall you may think I am. I make it a point not to eavesdrop."

"Right. We've heard two very different assessments of their working relationship: A) that they worked cohesively as equal partners, and B) that Geoffrey did the real work while the other two merely came along for the ride. Your vote?"

"Get to put my tuppence in, do I? Well, I'd say neither was correct. The whole operation is...was...too involved for one man to control everything. Geoffrey had a flair for day-to-day operations, all that detail crap and such; Michael did his thing in R&D; and Edward watched over the finances. Each was important in his own domain. They met about three times a week to go over things, review income and outgo, the usual."

"Regarding Michael being called away more and more...could we say that *you* have been the acting director of R&D?"

James Barrows looked from officer to officer before answering.

"Chief Inspector, I had nothing to do with Geoffrey Pont's death. No doubt you already know I have no alibi for that morning. But you must believe that I had no cause to do anything of the kind. I did not covet Michael's position or his title. Reason Number One: you're right, I already run the department. It is my department. So why knock off poor Geoffrey to get what I already had minus the hassles?"

"The salary?"

"Not enough to compensate for all the business crap you've got to put up with. Completely contrary to my wants and desires."

Dougall spoke up, "Why would Geoffrey's death gain you the official position in R&D?"

Barrows looked at the local detective as though the copper had sprouted horns.

"Well, obviously Michael would move up to first chair. I'd move up to his. Simple."

St. George coughed softly and resumed his questioning. "From your present position, you've been familiar with the YAMATSU project?"

"Of course."

"Are Michael and Edward as well versed on the subject?"

"Michael is, of course, even though he's been away a great deal. Edward has never had a head for science or mathematics and was satisfied just knowing how to spell YAMATSU."

"Is Michael as fluent in the essential details as you?"

"Hah! Of course not! Whose brainstorm do you think sparked the whole thing? In truth, though, everybody contributed something."

"But it sounds like Michael contributed very little."

"Naw, that's not right. I concentrated on the nuts and bolts and he did a lot of other things."

"Such as?"

"Talking to bankers, investors, and so on. I mean," Barrows said, "you've gotta have somebody out there who knows computers. But I'm not a talker or a party guy. Michael is. I was in on the private technical meetings."

"Have you ever attended any of their three-way meetings?"

"The Executive Committee? A few. When we started to take the YAMATSU thing seriously."

"Touchy subject, perhaps, but have you ever felt excluded? Even snubbed? Rich man, poor man, that sort of thing?"

"Not my style. Besides, I've been too busy working."

"Was the YAMATSU project common knowledge among the other employees?"

"Not really. We kept it under tight wraps. Of course, RAD is a hush-hush place anyway and so everyone knows we're not going to tell them anything."

"You just said RAD—is that another version of—"

"Yeah, R&D. Saves time."

"A chap named Manning was also involved, I understand?"

"Just regarding machinery and tooling. Our secret is not so much *what* we use as *how* we use it. The individual components give no clue as to the final product."

"Permutation rather than combination."

"You got it."

"Can you think of anyone in your world of computers who might bear a grudge against VES?"

"No one. From what we had produced and what industry forecasters predicted for us, we were thought to be two years behind the big boys. Consequently, we presented no threat to anybody. However, with the YAMATSU project, we will leapfrog all the others, only no one outside the company realizes that."

"Might not someone have suspected you were on to something?"

"I suppose it's possible, but I wouldn't know who."

"Could the Japanese have leaked word?"

"I seriously doubt it. Had they done so, first the trades would have carried the story, then the Internet, and then we would have been swamped with people wanting to buy in. That would have cost them a bundle and they know it. Would have required honorable hari-kiri."

The Chief Inspector's eyebrows rose for a moment and then fell. "Consider this scenario: the Japanese learn a wealth of information through your negotiations and decide VES is expendable and decide burning you down is cheaper than buying you out."

"You might have something there if the Japs hadn't gone through with the land deal. However, if the project fails now, there's nobody to buy the land except the farmers. No, it's in their best interests to see this thing through. Fact is, we both stumbled upon the Golden Goose."

"So you feel certain that no one from VES or YAMATSU leaked word to hostile third parties?"

"I do. There was just me, Geoffrey—God rest his soul—Michael, Manning, and of course Edward."

"And Silas Muir?"

"Who?"

"Banker from Edinburgh?"

"Name doesn't ring a bell. If he brought money, then he went through Edward."

"I see. Tell me, have you ever had occasion to go out to the plant on weekends?"

"No, not for—aw, hell, there you go again, trying to get me to say something like 'Oh, yeah, I go out there every Saturday.' Well, I don't. I haven't for several years. Not since we first got running."

"Not even in the weeks leading up to last Friday?"

"Especially then. What was so great was how we anticipated *everything*. We had all the bases covered, all the answers figured out beforehand. So there was no last-minute hustle. No midnight oil."

"Ever take work home with you?"

"Never."

"How about the other three gentlemen?"

"Edward? Perish the thought. Michael? Occasionally. Same for Geoffrey."

"And where is home by the way?"

"Bathgate. South side of town. Actually I'm about a mile from Michael's place. He's up in the hills there in a nice development. Sort of a chalet-type place."

"You've been there."

"A couple of times. Company Christmas parties, that sort of thing."

"Do you two ever socialize at other times?"

"Not really. We teach separate classes at West Lothian College in

Livingston. Off now for the summer, of course. And we bike together sometimes. He does it for punishment; I do it for enjoyment."

The Chief Inspector's brows curled. "What do you mean, 'punishment'?"

"Just that he gets into these fitness binges every now and then and so he bikes around for conditioning. Breaks up the monotony of walking and exercising, he says. He's kind of an all-around athlete."

"But you're a devotee."

"You bet. Got the skintight pants with the padded crotch, the helmet with the rearview mirror, the shirts, the water bottles, the works. I was quite serious about competition when I was younger—before I got equally serious about my work. Came close once to qualifying for the Tour de France."

"Really now. That's most impressive."

"Yeah, thanks, but it doesn't fit on a resume."

"You said earlier that you had no alibi for Saturday morning. Why?"

"Because I don't. I was out biking back and forth to Glasgow. Ate lunch there."

"But why use the word 'alibi' when no one has accused you of anything?"

"Because that's what cops are after when they bring you in for questioning, isn't it? I mean, my boss dies in the fire and no one is going to care where I was or what I was doing? Especially now that you guys apparently think he might have been murdered?"

"Your point is well taken, Mr. Barrows. Very well, when did you learn of the tragedy?"

"Edward called me. Well, he left a message on my answering machine. Then Michael called late."

"I see," St. George said as he unfolded the computer printout. "Would you please look at this for me? Have you seen it before?"

James Barrows took the security system document and perused it quickly, his eyes darting over the columns of numbers.

"I've seen this data. They ran a copy off once they reached RAD."

"A thought just struck me," St. George said. "How could anything have been operational after the fire and all the water?"

"Simple. You may have noticed how the building is slightly raised above ground level. About a foot. Well, the computer that runs the security system sits in a waterproof well beneath the floor of RAD. All we had to do was hook up a new power source and a printer and we were in business."

"Ah! So does this printout suggest anything?"

"Not directly. It's gibberish after 8:00 A.M. We all talked it over—
you know, us, the cops, the hardware people, the software people."

"Taking just *your* opinion now, does gibberish seem the most plausible verdict?"

"Yep, more than any other. You may not believe this, but I'm a
dunce when it comes to electronics. I can find the wall outlet and
the 'ON' switch, but that's it. Just give me a powered-up system and
I can fly."

"So you were not involved with the system's design or installation?"

"Nope. That was all Geoffrey and Michael. They fiddled with it
and made some modifications to simplify things and it's worked."

"Would it be possible to tamper with the system?"

"Nope."

"Why not?"

"They allowed for limited points of access for maintenance and
repair. So there is, or was, minimal to no chance of unauthorized
access."

"What if something happened to the wiring midway between
such points?"

James Barrows exhaled as though he were forcing himself to be
patient with a slow pupil. "Extremely unlikely in the first place.
However, the conduits are large enough and the corners rounded so
that you can pull wires and cables back and forth. No problem."

"What about hackers?"

"Somebody from the outside? Nope. Our main computers have no
outside lines, no modems, nothing. There's a small one on Edith's
desk and on Geoffrey's that handles e-mail. Incoming power passes
through two transformers that jacks the power up and then back
down. No signal could survive. So there's no way for anyone to tap
into any part of our system. If we need to send anything, we fax it."

"But faxes are not secure," said the Chief Inspector.

"Right. Anything critical we send by bonded courier, we mail, or
we hand-carry. No chance of an intercept."

"I see," said St. George as he took back the printout. "Sounds
secure, all right. So if some outsider sought confidential information,
a trade secret as it were, he'd have to get it personally from someone
on the inside."

"Absolutely. A traitor. But we have none. There was plenty of opportunity for someone to blow the whistle on the YAMATSU deal but everyone kept mum."

"Leading up to Friday, were you aware of any change in Geoffrey's behaviour?"

"If there was, I missed it."

"Did he seem preoccupied at any time? Distracted? Perhaps pass you in the hall and not speak to you?"

"No. As a general rule, I didn't see him that often, but when I did, he was always focused but never impolite."

"What do you mean 'focused'?"

"Well, no matter what he had on his mind, he'd always acknowledge you if he saw you."

"Had his work habits, his hours, changed in any way in the last few weeks?"

"Not that I could tell, but then I wasn't at his side. Edith could tell you more."

"Did he ever express any private concerns to you about the company or others working there?"

"No."

"Did he ever express any concerns about your own work there?"

"No."

"Can you think of any reason why he would want to burn the plant?"

"Absolutely none. He had every reason to keep it going."

"Any reason why he would want to kill himself?"

"None."

St. George nodded and stood up, followed by his compatriots.

"Well, Mr. Barrows, we thank you very much for your time and cooperation. If you happen to recall anything else, please contact Inspector Dougall. In the meantime, please remain in the area or notify the Inspector should you need to travel."

James Barrow remained sitting, legs crossed, a crooked smile on his face.

"I'm it, aren't I? Don't deny it. I can read people like a book. I can see it in their eyes. I can see it in yours. All three of you. Especially the Inspector here. You've pegged me as your Number One Suspect."

St. George looked nonplussed.

"Oh, come on!" continued Barrows. "I worked there, I had unlimited access to the building and the computers, I knew all about the

YAMATSU deal, I had the perfect setup for selling company secrets, and I've got no alibi for that day. No witness to place me somewhere else. And they don't bring in a chief inspector from Scotland Yard unless they think somebody popped Geoffrey and set the blaze to cover it up. So yeah, here I am. Who else could it be, right?"

"You're very perceptive, Mr. Barrows, but also very premature. There are as many if not more items pointing to the deceased having died by his own hand. I'm not sure what prompted this display of self-flagellation, but it's duly noted. As before, please keep the Inspector apprised of your whereabouts."

"You mean every day?"

"Only if you're traveling. If you wouldn't mind, that is. Surely you can see that as one of the principals in the company, you're a valuable witness."

"Oh, I see...yeah. OK, sure, no problem."

Poole noticed that Barrows had begun fidgeting with his hands. "Are you sure?" he asked.

"Huh?" Barrows said, reacting to words from an unexpected quarter. "Well, yeah, of course I'm sure. I mean, well, you really mean every single day?"

"Yes," said St. George. "Is there a problem?"

The three detectives just stood and waited as the computer engineer's anxiety mounted.

"Well, I might need to go to London for a day. You know, by train. Or plane. Maybe stay overnight."

"What day?" Dougall asked as he turned to a fresh page in his notebook.

"Well, uh, tomorrow actually." He coughed. "And maybe Manchester and Glasgow. Well, I guess that might take another day or two."

"Where can we reach you?"

"Uh...well, I'm not sure...because I'm not there yet, am I? I mean, I'm not sure what hotel I'll stay in. I can call you from there...if that's all right."

"Interesting." St. George said, sitting down. "You're visiting three major business centers...industrial centers at that. Interviews, perhaps?"

James Barrows blanched and his forehead suddenly glistened with sweat.

"Yes," he rasped whereupon the other detectives retook their seats.

"Clever maneuver, sir, I'll grant you that," said the Chief Inspector as he sat back and crossed his legs. "Take the offensive, maybe even be a bit offensive along the way, a touch of arrogance, and then challenging us to name you as a prime suspect before we've got all our evidence. All in the hope we might be embarrassed into letting you go your way without interference. Sort of reminds me of the old adage that the safest place for a criminal to hide is inside a police station. That aside, the obvious question must now be why a dedicated, selfless, valuable, loyal employee is embarking on an itinerary filled with job interviews?"

Barrows swallowed hard as though the saliva would not go down. He also found it hard to look any of the coppers in the eye.

"It's not that I want to leave. I just thought it prudent to cover my bases."

"Why?"

"Because the scuttlebutt is that VES is finished no matter what happens."

"Scuttlebutt from where?"

"From my network. Colleagues on the Internet. All of us have PCs and modems at home. They've been asking point-blank questions and I couldn't put them off any longer. How could I pretend that all will be well when no one has the slightest idea when they'll even start cleaning up the mess out there?"

"Have you leaked any information?"

"No!" Barrows said with a vigorous shake of his head that sent a sweaty mist flying into space. "That would finish me for sure. No, I've broken no confidences."

St. George pursed his lips as he tented his fingers over his chest.

"Your predicament is understandable, Mr. Barrows. To the extent that I can, I commiserate with you. However, such meaningful interviews are not set up overnight. After all, you're not some entry-level person walking in off the street. You're aiming for a position of high responsibility and equally high reward. Interviews for such jobs are anything but spontaneous. It requires making just the right contacts over *days*, even *weeks*. It means having prepared and mailed out resumes *in advance*. So, in short, you must have done all that well *before* the fire."

Viscount's resident computer genius wiggled in his seat and then buried his face in his hands. The room remained still except for the impotent whimpering sobs coming from the witness. After a minute, thoroughly distraught, Barrows looked up at his inquisitors.

"You're right. I started working on them three weeks ago."

"Why?"

Barrows sniffed and then reached behind him for a tissue and blew his nose.

"Because I thought it was the smart thing to do. Don't get me wrong...everything at the plant was going well, there were no problems—there *are* no problems—not with YAMATSU or anything else, no hitches, no breakdowns, no glitches, nothing. It was just a feeling I had."

"A premonition?"

"Yeah, right. Well...maybe not that dramatic, but a worry, a concern, nonetheless."

"About what?"

"That we were going to be snookered by the Japanese."

"You had seen something that caused you concern?"

"No, nothing I could put my finger on."

"Did you say anything to anyone?"

"No."

"Why not?"

"Because they were all so taken with the whole thing. And they were right to do so from the face of it. But, well, you know how everyone the world over knows what sharp businessmen the Japs are. So here we are, we've got three local businessmen—Geoffrey, Michael, and Edward—all good Scotsmen and true, who have never once done business outside Great Britain. Now I ask you, would you match their collective business savvy against that of the YAMATSU crowd? Would you think their acumen was adequate to give VES a fair shot at parity in this deal?"

"You said nothing to your own family?"

"I have no family. They're all dead, and I'm not seeing anyone."

"So fearing the deal would backfire, you hedged your bets."

"Absolutely. Wouldn't you?"

St. George sat upright.

"Under the circumstances, Mr. Barrows, we'll have to require you to reschedule those interviews. You can tell them the truth—you're a material witness and must remain here. Inspector Dougall will still need to know where to reach you."

Barrows wiped his brow and stared at the floor.

"But I'll be ruined."

"Why? If you've not betrayed any confidences, not delivered up any trade secrets, not conspired with the enemy, I fail to see why you should come to any harm."

"The people I'm supposed to talk to won't like being canceled. They'll never talk to me again. And then when Michael and Edward find out I sent out those resumes...damn!"

"Well, Mr. Barrows, I see nothing for it but your remaining here and available. And yes, in light of what you've told us, upon reflection, I must say that you are a suspect. Accordingly, I'd advise you to retain counsel should we need to get back to you. Until later...Oh, there is one more thing...your riding togs, you have at home?"

"What? You mean from Saturday?"

"Yes. You've ridden since?"

"No, no, of course not. Not with what happened. Uh, no, I took them to the cleaners Monday. Got some grease on the pants. Otherwise, I would have simply washed them at home. As usual. Why do you ask?"

"I understand cyclist attire is notable for its racing colours. May I inquire what yours are?"

"Well, the shirt is yellow and the pants are black. Helmet's white. Why?"

"In case we come across a witness who saw you pedaling to and from Glasgow. Or perhaps ... the plant. Good day."

15

COBB DROPPED OFF the two weary Scotland Yard men at the Squire's Inn. They no sooner entered the lobby when the same bellman as before approached them. As earlier, the money hand was palm-up but this time held in front as though this would make the handoff more secure.

"Your friends are back. Only three this time."

"Really? Have they been waiting long?"

"Only 20 minutes or so. They don't look very happy."

"It's truly amazing, Laurence, this age of modern communications. How quickly it disseminates unwelcome information," St. George said, pointedly ignoring the open palm.

"Huh?" said the puzzled bellman as the Chief Inspector proffered a Scottish note and walked on with Poole at his side.

They found Silas Muir, his associate Forster, and the man called Bambury hunched around a small table. Before Forster could react, the detectives were upon them. Though standing to greet them, an angry Muir made no effort to shake hands and simply motioned them to their seats.

"Chief Inspector, I'll come right to the point. I received word of your verdict late this morning. I could not be more shocked. I thought we had come to an understanding. Surely a reasonable man of your experience would have the good common sense not to go caterwauling about this absurd idea of arson when there is not one shred of evidence to back it up! None whatsoever! I really must protest!"

"Really?" replied St. George smoothly. "On whose behalf?"

"What? What do you mean..."

"On whose behalf are you protesting?"

"Well...uh...on behalf of *everyone*. The least we could have expected was that you would keep such a nonsensical idea to yourself."

"As nonsensical as a man simply bursting into flame?"

"It's happened!" Muir shot back. "The upshot is that poor sot burned to a crisp and that's all that matters."

"Oh, really. May I ask, have you conducted your own forensic examination of the scene and the body?"

"Of course not! Don't be ridiculous!"

"Yet you're so certain what the outcome should be."

"Two very senior and very capable investigators have signed off on the case, sir! That should be enough!"

Without warning, St. George smacked the table. "WHAT ROT! The fact is your infernal meddling has created the Frankenstein monster which you claim you want to avoid. You could not possibly have done more to feed the idea that Geoffrey Pont set fire to his own building. Oh, yes, Mr. Muir, you've served your clients in exemplary fashion! Would that we all would be so lucky! And your desperation in seeing any investigation thwarted must raise serious questions, sir, as to your real motives. Well, we will tolerate no more of it! I will also tell you that you are teetering on the brink of being formally charged. Need I remind you that such citation would necessarily bring your bank to the media's attention?"

Muir was speechless.

"Finally, I'm afraid you've been seriously misinformed." St. George said. "I'm not applying for a job with you, I don't have a loan from you, and I don't work for you. And so, unlike Mr. Forster here, I do not report to you. Is that clear?"

Even in the pub's dim light, Poole could see their three visitors flush. A thoroughly chastened Silas Muir struggled manfully to regain some modicum of superiority before answering.

"You've made your point."

"Good. Now...Sgt. Poole and I are launching an investigation into the death of one of this area's prominent businessmen. And that investigation includes obtaining whatever information we deem necessary to gain a thorough understanding of the circumstances surrounding this tragedy. Like you, I prize efficiency. Therefore, seeing as how you and your associates have taken the time and the trouble to come out here, I think we can do no less than go over that information right here, right now."

"Now?" gasped the banker and his colleagues in unison.

"Yes. We need more details about why Viscount is apparently so much more important than its counterparts in Livingston, for example. About why prominent people, people in top positions of authority, have abrogated their responsibility to the law and have seemed unduly anxious to ignore what may have happened here all for the sake of real or imagined future economic gain. Quite a shameless scenario. Indeed, there really is quite a lot to delve into."

"I-I-I don't know what you mean," said Muir as a few strands of elegant gray hair slipped out of place.

"Failing to perform an autopsy. The rush to cremate the man's remains. That was your idea, I believe. To the man on the street, all that would suggest the most sinister implications. What the Americans so grandly call a 'cover-up.' Only full disclosure and *prompt* full disclosure can avoid that. You know a great deal about the company and what so far has been left unstated regarding why this YAMATSU deal is so critical to everyone. The time has come for you to divulge that information."

"I'm sorry, but such material is highly confidential and has no bearing on the fire or Geoffrey's death."

"Correction, sir. It is *my* purview to determine what pertains and what does not. Of course, we could always talk with the YAMATSU people directly..."

"No!"

Embarrassed, Muir then added that the less the Japanese knew right now, the better.

"Then I see only two practical options: Either you and your associates answer our questions now...or under subpoena from the Lord Advocate in open court with full press coverage. Which would you prefer?"

Banker Muir leaned back, squeezing the chair's arms as though trying to hold himself in place lest he assault this arrogant copper. Slowly the man's fury subsided into mere anger.

"If you insist, we'll do it your way. But you must assure me that what I say remains confidential."

"I'm sorry, I cannot. This investigation will become a matter of public record if the Crown brings someone to trial. On the other hand, we have better things to do than scour the countryside for petty scandals. In point of fact, the fire has actually taken the matter out of your hands."

Muir leaned forward, plunked his elbows on the table, and rested his face in his hands, defeated. In a moment, he sighed, sat erect, and spoke as if contemplating his own funeral.

"All right. What do you want to know?"

"Sgt. Poole, will you please take Mr. Bambury and Mr. Forster to another table and do the honors?"

"Yes, sir," said the junior man, inwardly enjoying the annoyance and embarrassment of the previously cocky businessmen.

"I'm afraid I can't stay," Bambury said, chin up, nostrils flared.

"Then leave your card with the sergeant and we'll stop by your office tomorrow."

"I'm afraid that won't work. I have meetings all day."

"Well, then, perhaps a subpoena will help open up your schedule."

For a long moment, the copper and the CEO stared each other down...and the CEO blinked.

"I suppose, if it doesn't take forever..."

As Poole led his interviewees to another corner table, St. George produced a small notepad which he flipped open to a blank page. Muir grimaced at the realization that this copper was intent on recording his revelations for posterity.

"So that there is no misunderstanding," began the Chief Inspector, "the question before us is, if Geoffrey Pont did not set the fire, then who did? Which really asks, who murdered Geoffrey Pont? With that in mind, before we discuss the company itself further, I'd like your professional opinion on the abilities of Michael and Edward as the surviving officers and directors to run the company."

"You can't suspect them!"

"Mr. Muir, we not only include them on our list, but you as well. Surely you can fathom that we cannot rule out anyone if we're given incomplete information."

Muir tugged at his cuffs and straightened himself in his seat without taking his eyes off his antagonist. The bastard had him cornered and they both knew it.

"Very well...They're totally different individuals. Apples and oranges."

"I gathered that. But they comprise two-thirds of the operational committee."

"You're asking an impossible question."

"I am? How so?"

The banker glanced furtively around the room and leaned forward conspiratorially. "If my answer were to be overheard, it would have the gravest, most dire consequences."

"Forgive me, but it strikes me that *everything* you're involved with is of the greatest moment. I'm afraid you've played that card once too often. Let's try it again."

"I'm serious!"

"So am I."

Silas Muir grimaced as he ran his fingers through his hair and squirmed in his seat.

"But you know how porous police departments are. Press leaks all over the place."

"Really? You have that problem up here? If it will make you feel any easier, I'll speak personally with the Chief Constable tomorrow."

"Bah!" snapped Muir with a sharp wave of his hand. "Damn it all, you're really going to hold me to it, aren't you?"

"All the way," St. George said. "Permit me to point out something as a neutral outside observer. For all intents and purposes, VES is dead in the water. However, I very much doubt that industrial spies are lurking about like touts, eavesdropping on every syllable to establish their betting line. I also haven't seen any news crews loitering nearby. So I think the circumstances right here are the best you could ever have. And the sooner you answer our questions, the sooner you'll be on your way home. However, as the sergeant and I are staying here, we have all night."

St. George wasn't sure whether it was a growl or a chair sliding against the wood floor that he heard just before Muir spoke in a strained whisper.

"Chief Inspector, despite your jibes, I cannot emphasize too much how severe the ramifications are of this disaster! It is absolutely essential that we leave the business world with the indelible impression that VES management will carry on as before."

"You're saying that competitors are watching like vultures from the treetops for any sign of weakness."

"Exactly! In fact, in strictly business terms, if this tragedy had to happen, then it could not have come at a more fortuitous time."

16

IT WAS THE Chief Inspector's turn to be stunned.

"WHAT? Geoffrey Pont's death a bonus?"

"No, no, no, of course not! I'm saying that, thank God, the deal was consummated beforehand. The project's course is now set—on autopilot, if you will. As you've no doubt realized, Geoffrey was the driving force behind it. He conceived it, nurtured it, arranged virtually everything, brought it all to fruition. The whole thing bears his imprint. So if VES rebuilds *promptly*, then we don't miss a step, and it makes no difference who is at the helm."

"But if there were a delay in rebuilding and therefore returning to full operation, the capabilities and qualifications of the top men become paramount."

"Precisely," said Muir with evident sadness.

"So then it must follow that you feel uncomfortable with either Michael or Edward or both in charge."

"I will say nothing further. That at least leaves me with some deniability. In any case, you have the picture."

"I see...and yet you sit at the very heart of the enterprise, do you not? The leader of the bank which is overseeing all the financing?"

"We have taken on a great responsibility."

"Does that not grant you unequaled influence with the principals?"

"Major influence, but nothing close to absolute."

"All right. Next problem: You've helped steer the helm to the point that top Japanese businessmen come all the way here to sign the necessary documents. So I am puzzled why you panicked when they recovered Geoffrey's body?"

"I did not panic!"

"Come now, Edward Cargill does not have the mettle, all by himself, to pressure the police and the medical examiner to declare the cause of death as something as absurd as spontaneous combustion."

Muir's face became even more grim.

"And then I cannot imagine." St. George said, "Edward pressing to have the remains vaporized before the family has been allowed the customary grieving period of a few days? And contrary to your previous disclaimer, Edward stated specifically that the idea for the cremation came from you."

The banker remained mute as the indictment continued.

"And then add to this little encounter tonight your tantalizing offer to us to spend a few leisurely days here at your expense."

"That was not a bribe!"

"Must surely be a sweeter deal than you offered Walcott."

"That was not a bribe, either!"

"So say you. I think a jury would feel otherwise. The upshot of all this is that you've acted as though you have something to hide."

"NO! Nothing is improper! Check the YAMATSU documents if you wish—they're perfectly in order! They're impeccable!"

"I have no doubt. But again the intensity of your reaction is striking. You're obviously under great pressure from some quarter. So I have to think, what could cause a banker such anxiety and worry? Clearly, only money—either his own or someone else's."

St. George caught the frightened look in Muir's eyes. He sat and waited.

"All right, you're quite right. There is a great deal more at stake than just getting Viscount back up and running in the shortest possible time."

"Please elaborate."

"Perhaps I can best illustrate the matter this way. You've been to shopping malls?"

"Of course."

"And you've noticed how there is always at least one major retailer? Often one at each end, sometimes a third in the center?"

"Yes."

"Those are called anchor tenants. They are the big attractions that draw in the customers in volume. Alongside the anchors, you have the smaller specialty stores that the customers might not otherwise seek out. Too much work. Do you follow me?"

"Yes."

Muir paused to take a deep breath. "The same principle applies to light industry, specifically to industrial parks. Not the huge, smoke-stack affairs of yesteryear, but companies dealing with miniaturized components such as for computers. An entire assembly line can fit into a building a block long. So you start with one major outfit, per-haps a Motorola, and then you add others alongside until you have a cluster of companies all separate and yet all interrelated and some-times interdependent."

"You're describing Livingston."

"*Precisely*. Been extremely successful. And as the old saying goes, nothing breeds success like more success. There are companies from all over the world begging to get in. Now, you've probably wondered why the Ponts stuck their plant clear out in that field, miles away from Livingston."

"Cheap land, I suppose."

"Correct. As businesses prosper, land prices soar. Takes a king's ransom to get an acre in Livingston these days, I can tell you. However, Viscount was put out there for more than just the price of the land. As I'm sure you've noticed, there's open ground all around it. And West Calder and its rail station are merely a stone's throw away. So is the A71. A hop, skip, and a jump north or south gets you to the M8 and A70."

St. George smiled.

"Ah! You see it!" cried the banker. "Exactly! Some time back, a few farsighted individuals realized that Livingston could not stretch out west forever. There is such a thing as becoming too big, too sprawl-ing, too cumbersome. So they made the decision to develop a *second* science-and-light-industrial park around West Calder."

"And Viscount was the anchor."

"Yes!"

"Would I be correct in presuming that you were one of those far-sighted people?"

"You would."

St. George nodded and scribbled some notes. "So then may I next presume that what's involved concerns all those acres surrounding

Viscount?"

"You may. A limited partnership has carefully, quietly, and economically purchased several hundred of them. There are options on another 200. The Ponts themselves own 75 acres immediately adjacent to the west. That is the acreage for the YAMATSU addition."

St. George took a paper napkin, laid it before the banker, and asked him to sketch out the extent of the new science park. Muir obliged, and when he was finished, St. George whistled softly.

"So it would be bad for future development for the anchor company to no longer be in business."

"*Precisely*. In the world of high finance, impressions and perceptions are extremely important. Should you sustain a setback, you must counterattack at once as though the adverse event had no effect on you whatsoever. You must act aggressively as though you have so much money that nothing can faze you. Otherwise, you will be perceived as weak either in spirit or the pocketbook, and your entreaties for further business will be rejected."

"You make it all sound so *machismo*."

"Because it is," Muir said. "Stop and think—you never see top executives wearing tight-fitting slacks or trousers. They always sport very loose, sometimes almost baggy apparel. Why? To leave the subliminal impression that their masculine equipment, shall we say, is so bulky and therefore powerful that they need the extra room. Simply a matter of strutting bulls in the pasture."

"So you're saying the partnership would lose its investment if Viscount folded."

"Or was not up and running in time to save the YAMATSU project. Same end result. What small peripheral company will want to build next to a burned-out ruin?"

"Who is in this partnership?"

Muir hesitated, took another deep breath, and sighed.

"The bank has a 35 percent share."

"And?"

"I have a 5 percent position and serve as managing partner. Forster over there and another vice president named Ridley are in for 2.5 percent apiece. Other bank officers make up another 10 percent."

"So your bank has a 55 percent stake in the outcome."

"Correct."

"All right, who else?"

"Mr. Bambury and others hold 30 percent collectively."

"That makes 85 percent."

"The remainder come from various private individuals."

St. George nodded as he jotted down the numbers.

"Let's assume everything works out...what do you project as your return on investment?"

"Four-to-one. Perhaps five."

"Within...?"

"Five years maximum. Even more in the next 10 years."

"Impressive. We shall need a list of everyone in the partnership."

"But you already know the major players. The others should remain top-secret."

St. George raised his eyebrows.

"Damn! All right, I'll run it off."

"I'll have Inspector Dougall pick it up. Fax and e-mail can be intercepted."

"You're going to speak to each one?"

"Either I or Sgt. Poole will, yes."

"Have you any objections to my notifying them first? Might save panic calls to me that way."

"No, unless we discover that all their answers are worded the same."

"I'm smarter than that, Chief Inspector."

"I would hope so. We shall also need the financial records for VES as well as for Geoffrey, Michael, and Edward."

"Now that's impossible!"

"Oh, not again. Is *everything* always 'impossible' with you? The records are surely on disc."

"Yes..."

"Well, we need them. I should like them by midmorning. In fact, you can include them with the partnership roster."

Silas Muir appeared stricken and he took two deep breaths before answering.

"Oh, all right, they'll be in the Comptroller's Office. Make it 9:30."

"Thank you. One final thing...we understand that Edward secured all of the company's insurance business in return for his family's funding a major portion of the company's original financing."

"That's correct."

"Some people have implied that he does little else besides manage those accounts. Is his business really that limited?"

"It is."

"And...?"

"This is all highly confidential, all of it ancient history, but it's disclosure would—"

"Yes, yes, I know, more extreme consequences for the nation and the world—this case seems to contain nothing else. All right, so what's the big secret?"

Silas Muir looked as though the Chief Inspector's jibe had actually punched him.

"It's about Edward. He was young, he was just starting out, his enthusiasm for getting a leg up on his peers got the better of his good judgment, and so he engaged in some trading that was, well, sort of not kosher."

"Insider trading."

"Synonyms do come in handy at times, don't they? However, note that I never said those two words. His participation was minuscule but sufficient to bar him forever as a full trader from any of the exchanges. The compromise was that, in exchange for not being prosecuted, he would not seek a full seat but he could manage his family's accounts. Subsequently, handling all the VES work brought his income up to tolerable levels."

"So he has more at stake in the future of VES than one might think. Interesting. Who takes over as CEO?"

"The Executive Committee operates with complete authority for two months and then they have to decide."

"Time enough for matters to either clear or become hopelessly entangled," St. George said.

"Which is the next problem once we get past this emergency. I'm sure Michael will want the post. Geoffrey's shares go to his wife. At his request, I reviewed his will before he signed it. She has never shown any interest in the company except as a source of income so there's little chance of her trying to come in and take over. However, that does not preclude her from casting a vote, especially an uninformed one."

"What if she does not vote her shares? What if she abstains?"

"Then it's Edward's 35 percent against Michael's 30...unless somehow Michael could sign up all of Edward's siblings to make 35 percent for him as well—which is damned near impossible."

"So Edward would be in control."

"Yes. A rather frightening prospect. Myra selling out to either Edward or Michael would assuredly rip the company asunder. Worse even is the chance that Myra could sell her shares to some outsider.

Certainly there would be no shortage of takers. However, if we are back up and operating, then my bank's influence could keep matters on an even keel."

"If you would entertain something hypothetical: what would happen if Myra died?"

"What? That's absurd—no, no, it's not, I see your point. Well then, her shares would be divided between the surviving directors. Next of kin have right of first refusal."

"Then Edward would have an additional 15 percent to give him fully half to Michael's 45 percent."

"Essentially. Whether the division was proportional or equal, the siblings would get anywhere from a few percent to 10 percent. Still, you would not expect them to vote against Edward, so the outcome would be the same."

At this point, Poole came over to report that he was finished questioning Bambury and Forster. Reminding Muir that someone would pick up the VES and partnership records in the morning, the Chief Inspector rose to his feet, thanked the banker for his cooperation, and accompanied Poole out to the lobby elevator. As they left the pub, neither detective heard the sotto voce comments "bastards" and "fat slob."

* * *

Agreeing to reconvene in the dining room in a half-hour, the detectives retired to their respective rooms to shower and change clothes. During that interval, Poole alternately heard either nothing at all or his mentor's angry bellowing baritone coming through the wall. The latter, he knew, were more calls to London. He could not make out the words but had a good idea of the expressions being used. As he stepped into his trousers, a sharp double-knock on his wall signaled that his presence next door was required at once. St. George used the same signal on the walls, windows, and doorsills back at the office, and it always meant the matter was urgent.

"Yes, sir," said Poole as he entered his boss's room without knocking.

"I've just been on the horn to London ..." the Chief Inspector's gaze dropped two feet. "Pardon, but are you planning to go downstairs like that?"

"Huh?" Poole said, who then looked down to see that his trousers were unzipped and gaping. "Oh, yes, certainly, sorry, sir."

St. George smiled at his flustered aide. "Walk around that way and they'll never show us any respect."

"Yes, sir."

"Good. Now that *you're* ready, let's eat!"

On the way down to the restaurant, St. George summarized his calls to London as "a fine kettle of smelly fish." Viscount Electric Systems had some small but lucrative government contracts, and so the company's health was central to that of many others. All as Silas Muir had emphasized. Worse yet, however, was that "none of the ninnies" in Whitehall being paid handsomely to monitor such goings-on had foreseen anything the scope and importance of the YAMATSU joint project. The West Lothian people had done a clean end-run and had caught London by surprise.

"As for Silas Muir," continued the Chief Inspector, "there can be no doubt that his sole interest—and those with him—is in washing the decks clean and getting on with business. Evidence be damned."

"Well, whenever I got around to money, Bambury and Forster clammed up and referred me to Muir. I think they're genuinely scared of him."

"Hah! What a loverly bunch of coconuts. Whether Muir's the ringmaster, the ringleader, or the ring around the tub, we'll just have to wait and see."

Poole chortled loudly then promptly apologized for his outburst. "Well, if there was foul play," he added, "do we count these men as suspects?"

"Good question. Projects like these are more volatile than the stock market. The merest hint of suspicion would have dire financial consequences for any or all of them. Anything, absolutely *anything* untoward would create the very delay they dread. That being the case, what motive could drive them to even hire the job done? Muir emphasized how Geoffrey was the prime mover of the entire operation, so assassinating that prime mover and destroying the plant is completely counterproductive to what these men are after. Which is ever-increasing wealth."

"Unless someone has a private agenda."

"Exactly. At any rate, Whitehall is very concerned about this affair and we now have carte blanche. Including my visit tomorrow with '5 and '6. I'm booked on a 9 A.M. flight. Cobb will take me to the airport. Ought to be back by late afternoon. However, if you and Dougall will meet me, we'll question Michael's lady friend on the way home.

In the meanwhile, I'd like you two to survey the companies in Livingston about how the business community regards VES. Should give you a full day. Oh, and Marcus will be here in the morning."

"Just when you're bailing out..."

"Well, Laurence, it's a thankless task, but some one has to do it."

"Which? Go to London or mollify Dr. Woolsley?"

"Both."

Thursday

17

THURSDAY DAWNED BRIGHT and cheerful, and after breakfast, the two detectives reviewed the day's agenda with Dougall before St. George and Cobb headed for the airport. Particular importance was attached to arranging an interview with Edith Sperling for later that day. They were reviewing Superintendent Wallace's letter of introduction that Dougall and Poole would present to the CEOs of the major Livingston companies when they heard a commotion out in the lobby. The Chief Inspector's eyes came alive as he heard a familiar voice: "I was told to report to CHIEF Inspector St. George. Would that august personage be on the premises?"

St. George stepped into the corridor to see a tall, thin, middle-aged man standing before the desk sergeant in his "aggravation posture": wide stance, arms akimbo, palms up, jaw jutting forward. Detecting movement in his peripheral vision, the newcomer spun around to glare balefully at the Chief Inspector, his undisguised displeasure fairly radiating into the room.

"BYRAM ST. GEORGE! You bloody son-of-a-bitch! You unmitigated scoundrel!"

"Marcus, old friend! I'm delighted!"

"Bloody well you should be! The ARROGANCE you have, pulling God knows how many strings to hie me up here! Like I'm some... some...some..."

"Marcus, *believe* me, all I did was ask that they send up the *best* damned forensic man in all of Britain. Nothing more."

"Well, I'm *not* the best damned forensic—"

"You're not? Oh, then *do* forgive me!" St. George said, clasping his hands over his heart in mock contrition. "A thousand pardons! There's been a *terrible* mistake! Of course, you wouldn't be up to the challenge. How silly of me...certainly you may return to your simple London practice at once. Here, I'll write a note for your office and we'll plod ahead."

Marcus Woolsley cursed.

Poole stood back and watched the Yard's Medical Examiner fume in piqued silence as St. George fumbled around on a nearby desk for a notepad. He never ceased to marvel how these good friends played some version of this scene time and time again in case after case. The tableau lasted but a moment until Woolsley broke into a face-shattering grin and the two men shook hands warmly.

"Byram, why the bloody hell do you persist in doing these things to me? I'm not the ringmaster of some traveling road show."

"For the simplest of reasons, Marcus: I need your help. Come this way," the Chief Inspector said as he led the new arrival back to the murder room. Along the way, Woolsley feigned surprise at seeing Poole and exclaimed "Oh, no, not you, too!" Poole's response was to wring his hands and grin fiendishly.

"All right, it's about the fire, yes, I've read all about it. What I don't understand is what you think I can bring to the case."

Whereupon, behind closed doors, St. George told him.

* * *

Inside a plain letter-sized envelope, Muir had sealed the land partnership list and the discs containing the Lothian National Bank's VES files. The envelope quickly found a home in one of the Chief Inspector's coat pockets. The Yard's financial experts would analyze the material while the spy agency officials briefed him and the AC/CID on both VES and the Swedish entrepreneur Harald Burklund. With fingers crossed, St. George prayed he would return with a surfeit of answers.

As his London driver delivered him to the "New" Scotland Yard complex at 10 Broadway just off Victoria Street, he felt a twinge of nostalgia for the old digs on the Thames Embankment. In the early days of his career, before all operations were transferred to the new facility, he had been briefly assigned to its predecessor. In fact, in 1890, the Thames building opened to replace the original Metropolitan Police headquarters established in 1829 at 4 Whitehall Terrace through the efforts of Home Secretary Robert Peel. It was not mere coincidence that officers were originally dubbed 'peelers' and 'bobbies.' And the very name 'Scotland Yard' came from the building's location in Great Scotland Yard, which had been the site of a medieval palace reserved for Scottish royalty during their state visits to London.

Though it felt good to be back on his home turf, he shrugged off the sentiment and made his way to a small conference down the hall from the AC/CID's office. There he found his superior waiting with two very plain but intense businessmen. He guessed one to be in his forties and the other in his fifties. The younger man pierced him with an unflinching gaze from solid brown eyes while the older man seemed a bit diffident, making eye contact for only a polite moment before looking elsewhere. The younger man moved stiffly as though uncomfortable with the setting and the situation; the older man seemed more at ease, yet cautious and informal, as though attending a corporate cocktail party. The younger man fit the Chief Inspector's stereotype of the paranoid counterespionage operative, fanatical in his devotion to his department and his idealistic perception of his country, while the older man had the seasoned aplomb which came from surviving many internecine wars and covert missions. The result was a semidisinterested posture, all the while preoccupied with misdirection and disinformation. Thus, St. George decided the younger man was MI-5, the older man MI-6.

He was right.

MI-5 was introduced as Mr. Hunt and MI-6 was introduced as Mr. Springer. As though the Chief Inspector were contagious, neither man shook hands with him but merely uttered professional greetings.

The AC/CID's opening remarks contained St. George's least favorite word: appropriate. A prissy word, he had long contended, but one now indelibly attached to the realms of administration and law, a term that granted absolution to anyone who otherwise might be forced to take a stand or confront an issue. *Don't defeat Napoleon, Lord Wellington. Do only what you deem 'appropriate.'* All of which went far to explain why St. George had stubbornly refused to accept any administrative post, if only for a trial period. He had long ago

learned that a manager's day was filled with such cutesy words and
phrases and blatantly insincere cordiality. And then there was the
endless sitting and conferencing. His favorite expression came from a
famous American CEO who opined that the hallmark of a poor
manager was someone who was always in meetings. (No offense,
Assistant Commissioner.) To the contrary, he, St. George, was a man
of action, his physical frailties notwithstanding. If shackled to a
desk, he knew he would quickly wither and wilt and die.

At the AC's behest, St. George summarized what little hard information he had before passing the shoe with the bland comment that
"Actually, gentlemen, determining what role extrinsic forces may
have played will greatly assist us in resolving this matter." Right away,
the tight, pursed lips of the two spies told him that was not what
they had expected to hear. They had come to acquire information,
not provide it. Why should this surprise you, he mused; these people
held their secrets like lockets containing strands of hair from loved
ones, long dead. The AC/CID quickly tumbled to the same conclusion
as the spies tried to take over the meeting by asking obtuse questions implying that Scotland Yard's intervention was presenting a
threat to national security. The AC tried ineffectually to fend off this
gambit and St. George felt compelled to crystallize the situation.

"Gentlemen!...I came here under the impression that we all were
working under the auspices of the same sovereign. However, if I am
mistaken, please say so. And if neither of you wishes to assist us in
this matter, then come right out and say it so we can continue our
investigation." Left unsaid, as everyone knew, was the threat of an
unfavorable report quickly making its way upstairs through the relevant bureaucracies, perhaps reaching even as high as Number 10
Downing Street. Because neither spy wanted to be seen as being
'soft,' Messrs. Hunt and Mr. Springer performed a brief pas de deux
of whispered conversation before agreeing to cooperate.

Over the course of the next 10 minutes, St. George learned that
VES had never engaged in any questionable practices of any kind.
The Pont company's overseas activity had been slight and their government contracts had as yet no international ramifications. That
would all change drastically when the YAMATSU venture got
underway. As for YAMATSU, while not the largest conglomerate in
Japan, they were also not the smallest and in Asia had sufficient
power to conceal whatever they pleased. MI-6's conclusion: It was
highly unlikely that anything akin to that power could be brought to

bear on British soil.

Mr. Hunt of MI-5 pointed out that, as of that day, no known saboteurs nor any known terrorists had entered the country for the past 12 months. He noted that the terrorist gains nothing from an isolated incident, that he craves witnesses, carnage, and widespread publicity. All of that was clearly lacking from the VES 'event,' as he called it. MI-5's conclusion: Any saboteur would have to be a homegrown product and a sleeper.

"What about other services?" the Assistant Commissioner inquired. "Mossad? CIA?"

"Only if they hired someone already here to do it. Which brings us to Gerald Burke. Man's a known industrial spy and saboteur. Only he's been too careful and clever to leave enough evidence lying around to convict him. Our information is mostly word-of-mouth. But he's a firebug, prefers that to explosives though he's used both. Thing is, he dropped from sight four days before your event. We'll keep looking for him and let you know."

As for Harald Burklund, both intelligence services had dossiers on the man: completely legitimate, very diversified, no moves into new markets for more than nine months, none into computer components, had never worked for British Intelligence, believed not to be working for Swedish Intelligence or anyone else.

"Perhaps a bit too good to be true?" St. George offered.

Hunt had an immediate response. "We've kept tabs on him as we do all major importers-exporters. The docks, airports, transshipment points, everything. Always been aboveboard. Scrupulously well-documented manifests. Never tried to send out anything even remotely sensitive or prohibited. While that may sound unduly favorable, we prefer the view that he's so bloody successful and profitable he doesn't have to cheat."

* * *

By 1 P.M., Sgt. Laurence Poole had put in a full day's work. He, Dougall, and Superintendent Wallace had covered the major offices in Livingston and its environs. The superintendent's letter of introduction had proved particularly effective, and Poole was sure St. George would send the man a personal note thanking him for providing it. The verdict seemed nearly unanimous: Viscount Electric Systems was an up-and-coming enterprise that, with proper guidance and strategic alliances, might someday become *the* power to be reckoned with regionally and nationally. At present, however, the company was viewed as little more than a quirky interloper among the established gentry. None of the three officers had detected the slightest hint that anyone knew of the YAMATSU project prior to the Friday signing.

As for Edith Sperling, the woman was under her doctor's care but would see them and St. George late that afternoon.

After a leisurely lunch, Poole drove out to the VES site to see if Woolsley might require any assistance or moral support. After passing through the police cordon, no one paid him the slightest attention. He meandered about the grounds, certain he could literally feel the despair still emanating from the jungle of blackened debris. Even the bright sunlight could not dissipate the aura of deep sadness enveloping the place. The St. Bart's van was parked near the front door, open but unoccupied, meaning the good doctor was somewhere on the grounds. He no sooner began peering inside the vehicle than one of Woolsley's lab men emerged from the ruin carrying two handfuls of sealed sample bags. Before he could finish saying "Good afternoon" to the man, out came the Medical Examiner himself trailing three more assistants in his wake. Somehow, despite all the junk underfoot, the man controlled his lanky frame so well that one might have thought he was simply walking down a sidewalk. Removing his fireman's helmet, he fixed Poole with his customary baleful stare.

"I knew it! Your boss just cannot stand the thought of me working unattended for more than a few minutes. It's a wonder he doesn't send someone to tuck me in at night."

"Not at all. I had some spare time and thought I'd drop by and see if I could help."

"Oh, sure. Your paterfamilias has the greatest nerve of anyone I've ever known. He knows that analyzing all this stuff will take weeks but still he sends you out here to see if you can hurry us up a bit. Rubbish! The Lord God Almighty would have a migraine trying to meet such expectations."

"Well," Poole said, "you do seem to manage..."

Early on, Poole had recognized how much the Yard's vaunted Medical Examiner relished the role of put-upon martyr. So it was not unexpected that the two men suddenly broke out laughing.

"I tell you, Sergeant, that man has taunted my ego so much I can refuse him nothing. No matter what the problem, he knows I must rise to his challenge, and I think that's what aggravates me the most. He *knows* I'll do whatever he asks. And I can't get genuinely mad at him because he's always so damnably polite about it. What I fear is that you're going to follow in his footsteps."

Poole smiled and was about to reply that he hoped so and then thought better of it. "Surely you also know how terribly much he values your help."

Woolsley paused.

"Yes, I guess he does, though he'd never tell me to my face. Well, as long as you're taking confession, hear this but damn your soul to Hell if you breathe a word of it to anyone: I *thrive* on it."

"No!" said Poole, feigning shock and surprise.

"Oh, yes. Like this impossible situation here. There's no doubt Byram and that man Walcott are correct, but I cannot help feeling there's evidence that's been overlooked. Anyway, we're almost done with the office, picked up a few odds and ends, and getting into the work area. Probably finish up tomorrow. Thanks for the thought, but there's really nothing for you to do—except intercept calls from your boss."

"Right. Well then, see you back at the hotel this evening."

Woolsley gave a quick wave before climbing into the van to begin work on the latest batch of forensic samples.

Poole returned to his car, passed through the checkpoint, and returned to the West Calder station where he found a constable unplugging the phones in the murder room. His puzzled query brought a prompt but courteous answer.

"Well, your boss got recalled to London to get his arse chewed, so you're not going to be needing these any more."

"What? The Chief Inspector went to London to confer with MI-5 and MI-6."

"Who?"

"The spy agencies."

"That's not what Chief Stallings said. Told us to wrap things up."

"This is ridiculous! Hold on, I'll call London and get word for you directly."

"Can't do it from here. Maybe from your hotel if you like. And, meaning no offense, but I don't think it'll do you much good. My orders come from Chief Stallings himself. Now, if you'll excuse me..."

Muttering "bloody hell" under his breath, Poole jumped in their rental car and rushed back to the Squire's Inn.

Meanwhile, Dr. Marcus Woolsley was wiping his brow as a shiny official car swooped into the VES parking lot and came to rest near his van. He hated surprise visits because working in close quarters always made him sweat. And then, as he would tell his friend St. George, "When I sweat, I stink, and when I stink, the girls won't dance with me." He also felt embarrassed to appear disheveled before any other official, including the uniformed one marching up to him.

"Dr. Woolsley!"

"Yes?"

"Fire Chief McSwain here. Good afternoon."

"Same to you. What can I do for you?"

"Nothing really. Rather I'm here to inform you that your services are no longer needed here. The Chief Inspector has been recalled to London—made a complete mountain out of a molehill, he did—and this case is now closed. So thank you for making the effort, but your work is finished and I'm sealing off the building."

Woolsley stood and stared, his countenance a mixture of amazement and concern.

"Recalled you say? Not that I've heard. The investigation is just getting started."

"No, no," said McSwain, shaking his head. "I'm afraid not. You were brought here under the false assumption that a crime had been committed. However, we now have proof otherwise."

"Well, what about the dry toilet? What about the closed emergency valve?"

"All explained away. The Chief Inspector insisted we poll our men and we did. One of my men did close that valve after the fire was out and he did use the commode and the toilet paper there. Been reprimanded for it, but there it is. Nothing here at all. Now, if you'll excuse me, we must get about securing this site."

"Just a moment, please..." Woolsley said as McSwain started to walk away, "you're positive one of your firemen used the commode and the paper."

"Yes. Have no reason to doubt him."

"Just one thing you should know then."

"What's that?"

"We have then a much greater problem."

"Oh? How so? I see no problem."

"Well, sir, we've retrieved much of that used toilet paper from the sewer line. And it's all bloody. So that means your fireman had bloody diarrhea."

"Wha-at?"

"And if he doesn't have fulminant inflammatory bowel disease — like ulcerative colitis — then it means he's got either dysentery, typhoid fever or ... *cholera.*"

Woolsley fought hard to maintain his most austere professorial manner as he watched the fire chief's stunned reaction. "And you know what that means..."

"Well, uh, no, I'm not sure..."

"It means we have a public health emergency on our hands. Those are three of the most highly contagious infectious diseases known to man! They're killers. We'll have to quarantine the entire region and track down everyone your man has come into contact with. Come on, we've got to get your man to a hospital!"

"WHAT?"

"Come on! God man, at this late date, the bug may already have reached Edinburgh and Glasgow! Time is critical. Come on! I'll help you."

"No, wait!" McSwain said as he watched Woolsley start to close up his van.

"What is it?"

"Quarantine?"

"Absolutely. West Calder, Livingston, Bathgate, the whole area...unless your man's movements have been restricted to one community. Has he been on other calls since Saturday?"

The fire chief paled.

"Hold on, wait a minute, he seemed OK when I talked with him earlier today."

"Means nothing. They wax and wane every day. But come on, we'll get him to a hospital, get him tested, and treated."

"No, hold on there, this is all too much...Tested?"

"Serum and fecal tests for the bacteria, endoscopic exam, antibiotics. Of course, we'll have to notify London as well. Public Health Act."

"No, wait! Wait a minute! Let me go back and quiz him some more. Timmons is prone to exaggeration at times. Likes to think he's helping out, you know."

"Chief McSwain, we can do all that while he's being examined."

"But...what about the bloody paper?"

"Well, if your man's clean, then it means you've got a murder on your hands...and you'd want to solve a murder, wouldn't you?"

"Well, uh, yes, of course, if you think that's what's really going on here. I mean, if you're sure..."

"Well, there's no time, man! If your man used the loo, he's sick as hell and threatening everyone else. We've got to act!"

"Well, well, now, wait a minute, Doctor, Lester does exaggerate at times, like I said, and he may have done so this time, so I think I best go and talk with him again."

"Are you sure?"

"Yes, yes, I mean, the idea of dysentery around here, create a bloody damned panic, it would, so I'd better go have another talk with him again...can't be raising any false alarms..."

"Well, you're right about that."

"Carry on as you were."

"Very well, Chief. Until later..."

Marcus Woolsley broke out into a wry smile as McSwain's car disappeared from view.

* * *

An urgent message from Dougall awaited the Chief Inspector upon his return to the AC's office. At 8:30 A.M., Saturday, from his home, Geoffrey Pont had called the office of the exclusive London law firm of Bagwell and Brohm. Minutes later, he had left home for the plant, never to return.

Dougall had phoned long distance to learn that they were open only Monday through Friday and that today both principals were on the premises. He had left word that the Chief Inspector might pay a visit. Asking the AC's assistant to call Dougall and acknowledge the message and then alert the lawyers that his arrival was imminent, St. George hustled downstairs and climbed into a police sedan for the 30-minute ride to the solicitors' suite of offices, which he found no less ostentatious than those of other prosperous lawyers. The wait was only momentary before he ushered into the private office of Leslie Brohm where the greeting was formal, correct, and guarded.

"You're here about Geoffrey Pont, I hope?" the lawyer said, worry etched in his face.

"Quite. You've heard about the tragedy, then."

"Yes, but only what I can get out of the papers and off the telly. Nothing from up there. But how does Scotland Yard fit into the picture? I thought you blokes were restricted to London."

"That is correct, but we were invited to participate. And the reason we needed to see you so urgently is because it appears Geoffrey called your second line here early Saturday morning. Not the main reception number, but directly here to your office."

"Yes, that's quite right."

"Would you please tell me your relationship to Mr. Pont? In other words, why would he call you in the first place?"

"I'm his personal *and* corporate solicitor. I drafted the original articles of incorporation of VES and directed him to some international colleagues for the new project. I've also advised his brother Michael and his cousin Edward Cargill now and again."

"I see. May I inquire what he said?"

Leslie Brohm showed a wan smile. "Under normal circumstances, such a question would be inappropriate ...

(That damned word again!)

"... for reason of confidentiality, notwithstanding the other party being dead. But in this case, I have no such reservations because he really said nothing."

"Come again?"

"Well, we get in at 9 and take our first appointments at 10. My first task, even before the mail, is to check my messages. And come Monday morning, there his was."

"Asking to see you."

"Yes...well, more of a statement really. Not a demand, just a statement of fact. He needed to see me first thing on Monday, very urgent, utmost importance, but to remain very hush-hush between us and no one else. Which is why he used my back line extension. He wanted me to set aside one hour."

"But he declined to state the nature of the problem, of his concern."

"That's correct. He said he would be here waiting for us, meaning when we open at 9 o'clock. Well, no show by 9:30 and we became puzzled and so I called the plant but was intercepted and told the number was out of service. Tried his home as well as Michael's and Edward's but no one was taking calls."

"Had he tried contacting you earlier in the week? Voice mail, e-mail, the post?"

"No, I haven't heard from Geoffrey for months."

"Was he in the habit of ringing you here in your office?"

"Rather than going through the front? No, this surprised me, I must say."

"He did not call you at home? Your cell phone, perhaps?"

"No. I never give out those numbers. Unlike our criminal law colleagues, we actually can do nothing on weekends and holidays because we need access to government officials and documents and libraries and so on."

"Meaning your field is...?"

"Corporation law, specializing in communications and subspecializing in computer ventures. This thing called the Internet is simply going to explode within the next 10 years, mark my words. We expect to be major players by then."

"Very impressive. So you're saying that even if he had reached you Saturday morning, there was nothing you could have done until Monday."

"Correct—unless there was a crime of some kind, of course."

"How familiar were you with his YAMATSU project?"

"Barely. Geoffrey just said they were entering a joint venture with this Japanese concern and needed someone well versed in international commerce and so on to draft the deal. The details were unimportant to me since I was not to be a part of it. So I never inquired and he never volunteered. As it is, all that the lawyers deal with is basic contract law plus taxation liability, grievance resolution, dissolution, and intellectual property rights. The actual nuts and bolts have no meaning."

"Would software come under intellectual property?"

"Oh, absolutely, especially if you were the one who wrote it."

"Do you still have his message?"

"No, I erased it right away like I do all my messages."

"Would you mind if I took your machine with me so our lab people could see what they could extract?"

"Yes, I would mind. Sorry, I see your point and on the one hand I concur but the rest of the tape contained confidential messages from other clients. I'm afraid I'd even have to contest a writ."

"Well," sighed the man from Scotland Yard, "I tried. OK, failing that, I'll turn you into the analyzer. How did Geoffrey sound? Worried? Frightened? Scared? Angry?"

"And all the other synonyms. No, really, he seemed rather neutral. 'Professional' would be the best description. Terse. Abrupt. Yet insistent."

"Any sense of panic? Fear?"

"No, none."

"And you say he did not specify what he was worried about or what he had in mind in coming to see you."

"Correct."

"Any chance he could have dealt with it over the phone?"

"Well, we'll never know, will we? But I should imagine he thought not since he seemed determined to come here and see me in person. One thing about Geoffrey Pont: once he made up his mind, he followed through. No matter what."

18

THE LONDON MEETINGS had gone well, the flights down and back had gone well, the hot dog at Heathrow had been tasty, the snack he had smuggled on board and the airline's beverage had temporarily satisfied his appetite—yet none of them attenuated his rage at Silas Muir's duplicity.

It was bad enough when, following the spy meeting, he had opened Muir's envelope to show the AC the investor list only to find the banker had omitted the shares remaining in the hands of anonymous investors. That had merely whetted his anger. What put him over the top came two hours later when he returned to the Yard from Leslie Brohm's office to find the AC embroiled with various officials within the Home Office regarding shutting down the West Calder investigation. St. George at once found himself under detailed interrogation about the validity of the his claim of arson and he quickly learned how banker Muir had lobbied numerous officials in Edinburgh and London to remove him from the case. However, in the end, his vigorous defense combined with cellular phone corroboration from Woolsley solidified his portfolio and produced the mandate he had wanted in the beginning.

Now a dangerously quiet Chief Inspector led Poole and Dougall into the Lothian National Bank and the hushed inner sanctum occupied by its top executives. First he introduced himself and his two companions to the middle-aged receptionist. He then showed her the list and informed her that the list was incomplete, and that, therefore, he must have an audience with Silas Muir at once. With a quick but restrained flexing of facial muscles meant to pass for a smile, the woman, a veteran of countless corporate wars, immediately played dumb and replied, "Oh, I'm sorry, sir, Mr. Muir is working on his report for the Board. He cannot be disturbed. Perhaps if you'd like to leave him a note?"

His eyes blazing, St. George retorted, "No, madam, I would not like to do that. I tell you what, why don't you go in there right now and inform him that unless he sees us forthwith, I shall call in the press right this minute and see if they can obtain full disclosure. They might even take your picture."

Her eyes showing alarm, the woman hesitated and opened her mouth as if to say "No."

"And you can forget about pressing that button under your desk. We *are* the police."

The woman excused herself, hustled over to the closed oak door, rapped twice, and entered. In seconds she was back, motioning the three detectives inside. They found the banker hulking behind his desk like a cornered badger. The scowl on his face said they were not welcome.

"I'm not one given to accommodating threats, Chief Inspector."

"Really? Well, I think you'd have to agree that was clearly the only way we were going to get past Cereberus out there and obtain the complete list."

"You have the essentials there. You need no more."

Poole flinched as his boss took a very slow, very controlled, very smooth deep breath before responding.

"Mr. Muir, I am quite fed up with your obstruction of justice. You may be an emperor within the walls of this building, but beyond them you are a meddler. And a meddler under ever increasing suspicion. In point of fact, your attempts to remove me from this investigation are not appreciated by me or my superiors in London. So be advised that I have referred the matter of your misconduct to the Chief Constable."

"No!"

"And unless you want to discuss the matter with him while under arrest, you will produce that complete list NOW!"

Muir literally trembled with anger as he gripped the edges of his desk. After a tense moment, he stabbed a button on his phone console. The receptionist's querulous voice answered at once.

"Get Barbara in here NOW."

A tense moment passed as the two men stood glaring at each other. Then another woman entered the room, received a terse order for the master list, and promptly disappeared. Despite the carpeting, the detectives could hear the brushing footsteps running down the adjacent corridor. Within seconds, she was back, handing a thin manila folder to her boss. A sharp glance from Muir sent her scurrying from the room. The banker slipped out a sheet of paper and handed it toward St. George who refused to take it.

"A copy, please. We'll not take the original."

His eyes flashing semaphored obscenities, Muir rang his receptionist who breezed into the room and took the page. During her absence, St. George looked nonchalantly about the room while Muir never took his eyes off his antagonist. Upon her return, the woman handed the fresh copy to St. George, laid the original on the desk, and again left the room. As the Chief Inspector carefully read the page, his eyebrows shot up.

"The mists clear...Chief McSwain one percent; Chief Supt. Stallings one percent. No wonder they reacted so passionately. Rehearsing for their roles as security guards at the new complex, are they?"

"It's poor taste to disparage such men. They've invested a major part of their savings. Gives them every right to be concerned."

"But to the point of obstructing an investigation?" St. George asked. "And at your behest no less? You've suborned two fine professionals, Mr. Muir. I hope you find satisfaction in that. And here's Harald Burklund, 10 percent. How interesting. Yes, you've had quite a lot to conceal, all right."

"Are you satisfied? If that's all, I have work to do."

"This will be adequate for the time being. But in closing, let me say just one thing..."

Poole and Dougall could have heard the words even out in the waiting room.

"STAY...OUT...OF...MY...WAY. Do I make myself clear?"

As the detectives reached the open door, St. George paused and turned around. He was frowning. The banker had not moved.

"Wait a minute...something's not right, something doesn't match...something's out of proportion..."

As St. George took a few steps toward the desk, Muir pulled back like he was expecting a physical attack.

"All right—your bank, yourself, and a few of your fellow officials are investors...but that alone should not generate the desperation, the animosity, and the hostility you've consistently demonstrated."

Muir's narrowed eyes never left the senior copper. However, Poole thought they had lost much of their hardness.

"There's *got* to be something more," St. George added.

"There's nothing more. You've got it all." Both men knew 'damn you' was tacitly implied.

"Something that's putting extraordinary pressure on you..." St. George continued as he looked at the page again. "You know, if I were on a bank's Board of Directors, I would be comfortable with, say, a 10 percent stake in a venture like your partnership here. Maybe even 15 percent. But a whopping 35 percent? Ah, that's it! The fear in your eyes tells me that is the problem. Your board doesn't know about the extra 20 percent, does it? You've put them on the hook for a whole bundle more. Probably leveraged it, no doubt; I understand that's what all the clever boys do nowadays. So, yes, if VES goes under, you'd have a lot of explaining to do. Maybe even have a bit of trouble balancing the books?"

The strain and anguish on Muir's face was almost unbearable to see.

"Then for your salvation, sir," St. George said, "perhaps you'd best pray we find ourselves a murderer." With that the Chief Inspector turned on his heel and marched from the room with Poole and Dougall following in lockstep behind him. Just as they passed the receptionist, they heard her say into her intercom, "Mr. Muir, the Chief Constable is calling. He says it can't wait."

19

ST. GEORGE REMAINED uncommunicative during the journey back to the Squire's Inn. All he would acknowledge was Dougall's report that he had discovered Geoffrey Pont's password and that he and Poole had visited Michael Pont's girlfriend on their way to the airport. Bottom line: the woman backed up the surviving brother's story to the minute.

Thankful to be the driver, Poole could not tell whether his boss was sulking, brooding, meditating, or simply fuming over banker Muir's outrageous behaviour. Only when they pulled up to the Inn did the Chief Inspector roust himself and insist that Dougall join them for an early dinner. Twenty minutes later, seated at their table, St. George waited until their server had taken their orders before he spoke in a remarkably relaxed voice.

"I've called London. I'm returning there again tomorrow thanks to that damned Muir. I'm interviewing Burklund and hopefully we'll have some word on the financial reports. In the meanwhile, Inspector, you say you uncovered the password..."

"Yes, sir, found it in his wallet. A piece of three-by-five card with the name Macbeth in small case."

"Interesting. And thereafter you found what?"

"Just that it gets us through. I wanted to wait until you returned... in the event something inadvertently got deleted."

"Hah! Sensible move! Self-preservation never hurts. Very well, you say we meet Edith Sperling at 7 P.M.?"

"Yes, sir. Only about 20 minutes from here."

"Then perhaps we can examine the computer after that."

"Yes, sir."

"And have you had any results tracing the woman caller?"

"Yes. Placed the ads like you suggested. Got a bunch of crank calls right off but then she phoned. She said she was driving down the road and saw smoke and flames. She rushed on to a farmhouse and called in the alarm."

"Driving south?"

"Right."

"Had she ever been to VES?"

"No. She's not from the area. In fact, she was supposed to be someplace else—if you get my meaning."

"I don't. Please elaborate."

"Her husband did not know she was up here visiting her lover."

"Ahhh, Lady Chatterly rides again. Does she know any of the Ponts or Cargills? Or Barrows?"

"None. Or so she claims."

"How about other employees at VES?"

"Again none. Also has no family or friends up here. Granted, we didn't have her on a polygraph, but she didn't sound disingenuous."

"Well, at least we can bring her in later if needed..."

"Uh...no, we can't. Now wait, Chief Inspector, before you explode. I repeatedly told her how important it was, but she steadfastly refused to give us her name or address or where she was calling from. Traced her anyway to a call box in Glasgow. She said she couldn't take the chance of her name being made public."

St. George clenched his teeth and sighed.

"So we will not have her testimony."

"No, sir, unless someone turns her in. Even then she'd deny everything."

"Blast!"

"Pardon," said Poole, "but she called from Glasgow and Barrows claims he rode to Glasgow on Saturday. Maybe they're an item."

"A stretch but, yes, a possibility. All right, Inspector, did she mention seeing anyone on the road?"

"No cars, no pedestrians; there was a cyclist somewhere north of the place."

"Could she describe him?"

"Thought he was wearing a yellow shirt."

"Really now...interesting. What about the fire itself? Color of the smoke?"

"Wasn't black, she knew that for sure. Wouldn't commit to anything more than probably grayish."

"What about farmsteads? Any luck?"

"Yes. Family near Woolford Cottages got a surprise visit from a well-dressed lady Saturday morning. All excited, wanted to use the phone to report a fire. Problem is, they paid more attention to the fire than to the woman and couldn't give us much of a description. Even tried composite sketch. Nothing. Couldn't agree on hair color except that it wasn't red."

"Her car?"

"Only that it was black, moderate size. Couldn't agree whether four-door or two-door. Nothing about the plate. Pretty much a wash."

"Well, you tried. Might go back tomorrow on the chance they may remember something."

"Will do."

"Anything from the other employees?"

"Nothing useful thus far. The other three secretaries were very careful not to appear as gossips but that's about all they could contribute. Specifically, no one reported Geoffrey doing anything more than merely speaking to them in passing. Rather abrupt compared to normal but they each attributed that to the pressure of the upcoming deal."

"How much did they actually know about the project?"

"Remarkably little. Just that VES was about to land a big contract with a foreign company."

"What about Manning the technician?"

"Bookish fellow. What's called a 'geek' in most quarters. Strong mechanical sense to go along with his computer knowledge. His office is in the center of the manufacturing area. Aside from playing engineer in designing new products, he's their primary troubleshooter. If he can't solve the problem, he knows who to call in."

"And had he called in anyone recently?"

"No, sir. No problems of any kind. Haven't been for several months."

"Speaking of calling..." said the Chief Inspector who then commended Dougall on his initiative concerning Geoffrey Pont's

London phone call and then related his interview with solicitor
Leslie Brohm. When he finished, he asked the local detective for his
conclusions about Geoffrey Pont's as-yet-unexplained behaviour.

"Well, I'd say he did four things highly out of the ordinary for him.
First, he took work home with him several days running, especially
during what was probably the most important week of the entire
year. The YAMATSU people coming over and so on. I'd say that
indicates whatever he was reviewing was bloody important to him.
Whether it concerned VES or a person or his own portfolio, we can't
say. Second, he worked all Friday night and never went to bed. Again
whatever he was reading took precedence over normal habits. Third,
he made this call to his company solicitor Saturday morning,
demanding to be seen first thing Monday, again something that
seems odd just after his YAMATSU triumph. And fourth, he went
out to the plant on Saturday morning. All in all, I suppose you could
say it's possible one thing had nothing to do with the other, but I'll
wager they're all tied in."

"Laurence?"

"I agree. And while Mrs. Pont could not identify the financial
records as belonging to VES, what else could they be? If he were
reviewing his own portfolio, why go out to the plant? And this lawyer
is not his close friend, not someone he calls all the time for informal
advice, but the guy who set up the VES corporation, so why call him
unless the problem has to do with VES?"

"Yes, that thought occurred to me as well. Inspector?"

"It just struck me. Geoffrey's worried about something at the plant.
He's gone over financial statements night after night. He calls his
lawyer. My question is this: why did he not call his brother? Or his
cousin Edward? Why did he not confide in them? Instead, he calls
neither one. He calls a neutral third party hundreds of miles away."

"Odd, yes," St. George said. "He could have left word on their
answering machines, but they claim he did not. For the moment, we
must assume they are telling the truth. Otherwise the alternative is
that he called one or both and they are denying it because they are
guilty."

"So where do we go from here?" said Poole.

"Well gentlemen, until we have further data, I suggest we focus on
the dead man. To begin, either Geoffrey Pont was the intended victim all along or he was an accidental and incidental casualty.
Therefore, I submit we face no less than 12 solutions to this crime,

starting with..."

Poole flipped open his notebook and readied his pen as St. George counted on his fingers.

"...Number One...Geoffrey Pont tried to burn his own plant and died by accident. Ansel Walcott's theory. Despite our ideas to the contrary, we have not yet proven this false."

"Have to be a Thor Bridge type of problem, I'd say," commented Poole.

"Quite. From a practical standpoint—

"Excuse me," said Dougall, "but what's a Thor Bridge?"

"Inspector, for shame!" said St. George good-naturedly. "You haven't forgotten The Great Detective, have you? The patron saint of policemen everywhere?"

Dougall was nonplussed. "I'm sorry, I don't..."

"Sherlock Holmes, man! *The Problem of Thor Bridge.* Laurence, will you do the honors?"

"Yes, sir. Well, you have this wife who's insanely jealous and wants revenge against another woman who is completely innocent. So she invites the woman to meet her on a small bridge near the estate. But she gets there first, ties a weight to a cord, and hangs the weight over the railing. She then ties the other end to a gun which she uses to blow her brains out. The weight pulls the gun from her hand and over the railing and into the water. The innocent woman is thus accused of murder."

"In the present instance, if Geoffrey were responsible for the fire, what happened to the necessary paraphernalia for starting the fire? Or in terms of the story, what happened to his weight and cord and gun? Unfortunately, the only way we're going to put this option to rest is to come up with a murderer."

"Yes, sir, I get the point. Thank you. And I quite agree."

"Right. Then we have Number Two...Geoffrey Pont, for reasons almost certainly financial, hired someone to torch his plant. Perhaps he went there to let the man in, perhaps he fiddled with the security system to cover their actions, but either by accident or from a falling-out with his accomplice, he died. The accomplice then improvised and removed his goods from the premises. How he covered his tracks remains to be divined....

"Number Three...the YAMATSU people hired the job done. Perhaps to seize the market all for themselves. Something made Geoffrey Pont suspicious and he went out there and was ambushed, overcome, subdued, murdered, whatever, and died. This is where my visit with MI-5 and MI-6 comes in. They see no threat from outside the country. Inside is another matter. Turns out there's a known industrial spy and saboteur named Gerald Burke who's dropped from sight. They're to keep us posted..."

"Anarchist?" said Dougall.

"No, he's apparently apolitical. Just does it for the love of fire and money. Other questions? No? OK, on to Number Four: Harald Burklund had it done. As one of Silas Muir's hidden investors, with VES out of the way, he could put his own plant in its place. As I said, I'm going to question him.

"Number Five...simple extortion by person or persons unknown. As the CEO, Geoffrey would have been the one contacted for the payoff. With the YAMATSU deal pending, he had no choice but keep the threat and any payoff secret. Therefore, as the driving force behind the company, he would conceal the problem from everyone. Even Michael and Edward. Perhaps he suspected one of his current employees and went out to the plant to check files. He stumbled onto the crime and was murdered."

Poole raised his pen. "What about the financial records he was reviewing?"

"They might have—no, scratch that—they *probably* contained evidence of wrongdoing. Odd that no one else knows anything about them."

"Or has shown any interest, " said Poole.

"Unless they're concealing that information," added Dougall.

St. George nodded and continued. "Number Six...extortion having *everything* to do with YAMATSU. Not a threat to the plant, but a threat to expose malfeasance in management that would squash the deal. That would cover two other items: why he did not notify the police, and why he placed that cryptic call to his London lawyer. I mean, you must always hold suspect any calls to lawyers, mustn't you?"

A few smiles spread around the table.

"Number Seven...Myra Pont hired someone to kill her husband. She was either jealous of his affairs or resented the time and money he had sunk into VES. Or her lover from two years ago is still in the picture. In which case, let's surmise there never were any financial statements—she made them up as a diversion. Another possibility— the mystery woman calling in the fire alarm—"

"Is Geoffrey's mistress or his accomplice," Poole said.

"Yes. The only negative is she would have assured her anonymity by not making the call at all. Perhaps it was regret or remorse for something she had done. Like having the affair. Or killing him."

"Could her husband have killed Geoffrey?" Dougall asked.

"Possible, I suppose," replied the Chief Inspector. "Confronting Geoffrey at the plant, killing him, and then setting the fire to cover the crime. If the woman lives in the Lothian area, her husband may even be a VES employee. And then while still at risk, Inspector, the woman calls you out of continued regard for her dead lover? A bit too pithy for my taste..."

Dougall took his rejection well, thought Poole. Or maybe he's just used to being told 'No.'

"Number Eight...Michael, Edward, and Barrows all conspired to kill Geoffrey and burn the plant to scuttle the new deal. Perhaps they discovered YAMATSU would replace them once the project was underway. So while Geoffrey would surely continue on in some capacity, the same could not be said for these three. Here we should note that neither Michael nor Edward are looked upon favorably in the business community. So what was their future? Dismal, I'd say. Anyone feel otherwise?"

Shaking heads were the only answer.

"Number Nine...Michael and Edward decide to eliminate Geoffrey, scuttle the YAMATSU project, and frame Barrows for the murder. After all, they both have airtight alibis, while he has none. Again, there would be a hired accomplice such as this saboteur Burke...."

"Number Ten...James Barrows did the deed all by himself. Motive possibly some irregularity in the department accounts. Or perhaps Geoffrey caught him trying to sell secrets to a competitor. And remember that Barrows had already sent out resumes to cover his future. He certainly would have no problem manipulating the security system to cover his movements. That the cyclist supposedly seen by the mystery woman wore a yellow jersey cannot be discounted. In my opinion, his disclaimer about not coveting a share of the company's wealth and stock rings hollow. I think he's deeply resentful, in fact."

"I would be," offered Poole.

"Number Eleven...Michael Pont hired it done. He himself could not be directly involved because of (a) his solid alibi and (b) we have no motive. He is the beneficiary of no insurance policy. Geoffrey's death potentially leaves him at risk should VES fail. So he has all the reason in the world to see matters move ahead. And finally....

"Number Twelve...Edward Cargill hired it done. Motive? Perhaps Geoffrey caught him mismanaging the company's insurance premiums. Or trying to sell out. Or maybe Edward has delusions of grandeur and thought he could stage a coup and somehow acquire full majority ownership. Through his contacts within the industry, did Edward seek out the saboteur Burke or someone similar? Have I left anyone out?"

Poole grinned. "Just the upstairs maid."

20

"MRS. SPERLING HAS had a terrible time through all this and I should caution you that I reserve the right to terminate your visit at any time."

So said Dr. G. Austen, longtime family physician to the woman and her late husband who lived but seven doors away and had answered her call for assistance upon learning of Geoffrey Pont's demise. The London men saw Dougall bristle and realized the last thing they needed was having two stubborn Scotsmen squaring off over prerogatives.

"I assure you, Doctor," replied Dougall, "that we would not intrude upon the lady's grief were it not of the utmost importance."

"If you don't mind my saying so," Austen replied, "I don't see how that could be. The man's gone and buried and now we have to move on."

"I'm afraid there's a bit more to it, Doctor," said St. George. "The man was murdered." The physician's jaw dropped as did Dougall's at the bald declaration. "I hope you would agree that the more we can learn about Mr. Pont and his movements for the past week or so, the better our chances of catching his killer."

With mumbled agreement, Dr. Austen bade them enter and then led the way to the dining room where they found their hostess waiting for them.

Geoffrey Pont's secretary still wore her mourning clothes and made no effort to smile as she greeted the three detectives. By way of preamble, she stated that Pont's death had been very hard on her and that she was very grateful for Dr. Austen's support. She disclosed that he had even escorted her to the funeral and the graveside services. St. George was impressed by the way she had not only seized control of the meeting but had taken pains to secure the good doctor's allegiance for the duration. This lady, he thought, has been around bigger corporate boardrooms than the one at VES.

"Pardon me," said Dougall, "but you said 'graveside'? It was my understanding the body was cremated."

"He was, but surely you've heard of placing an urn in a vault alcove."

"Oh, yes, of course. May I ask how many people were there?"

"We filled the church for the first," Edith said, "but the second was private for only the closest. And now I would like to know why you gentlemen are here. Superintendent Wallace was rather vague, I thought, but I got the impression you people had some doubt about the circumstances of Mr. Pont's death. It was an accident, wasn't it?"

Oh, baby, you're good, thought St. George as he silently composed a quick prayer of thanks that poor Dougall was leading the interview.

"That's what we're working on, ma'am," said Dougall. "There's evidence that suggests there may have been foul play."

The woman stiffened, her lips pursing tightly until they were bloodless, as she stared away from them toward a far window. Already past 60, she seemed to age another 10 years right before their eyes. Then just as quickly, she regained her composure and relaxed, took a slow deep breath, and looked again at her visitors.

"Mr. Pont was very important to me. He was very fair, very gracious, always polite and courteous, even under the most trying circumstances, never made a show of his wealth or position, never acted like so many employers do these days. Besides my personal grief at his loss, his death leaves me with a very bleak future."

"If you'll forgive me for asking," Dougall said, "how might that be? The company will go on. Michael Pont and Edward Cargill said so yesterday."

"Inspector, despite our modern times, you must realize that there are not many openings in business offices for older women. Professional qualifications and experience do not compensate for youth and beauty. I suppose one reason I admired Mr. Pont is that I was gratified he took a chance on me. My husband of 30 years had died and Dr. Austen had prescribed work as the best way for me to occupy my time. We were childless, you see. I had been secretary to some of the busiest executives in Edinburgh but had retired to help care for my husband in his final years. Fortunately, Mr. Pont needed someone with my experience and so I have been with the company since its inception. Even before the building foundation was laid. For the past few years, it appeared that I had found a very secure place. But now that's all changed.

"You ask how so, and I'll tell you. Mr. Pont was the driving force behind this company. Make no mistake about it. Yes, they had their Executive Committee and Mr. Muir and Mr. Forster joined them on the Board of Directors..."—St. George's eyebrows shot up—"...but the man whose judgment and guidance got us to where we are ...where we were...was Mr. Pont. I'm saying nothing against Mr. Michael or Mr. Edward, but it's just not the same. Were Mr. Pont alive, I would have no doubt we would be rebuilt and be up and running. But without him, I just don't see that happening. And that means I'm out of a very good job."

Dougall was about to press his question when St. George interrupted.

"Mrs. Sperling, our purpose in these inquiries is to learn as much about Geoffrey Pont as possible. To get to know the man as much as we can. We believe that is our best chance to catch the people responsible for this catastrophe. Unfortunately, this means sometimes digging into painful matters such as your own perceived misfortune. For example, Inspector Dougall was correct when he stated that Michael and Edward are working very hard to rebuild and rebuild quickly. However, I am struck by your pessimism. Are you saying Michael and Edward want you out of the company?"

"No, it's not that. I'm just another one of the secretaries to run errands for them. I doubt they will notice my absence."

"Then I must express my puzzlement why you will not be returning? Has there been talk of staff reductions?"

"No, to the contrary, some Viscount people will be moving over to the new project. People will have to be brought it in to replace them."

"Are you slated to move over?"

"No. As far as I knew, I was to remain with Mr. Pont."

"So...why your certainty that you're unemployed? I don't understand."

The veteran secretary looked down and began rubbing her hands.

"It's so embarrassing..."

"Madam, we're not here to embarrass anyone, we're here to learn, and I believe you have much to teach us about your boss. I ask you to please do so."

Edith Sperling regarded the three detectives with tearful eyes which she dabbed at daintily with a lace handkerchief she had produced from somewhere.

"Because they didn't call. They haven't called. Oh, yes, they were very polite at the services, but that was all. No word, no mention, nothing."

"About what?"

"About working. About setting up the temporary office in Livingston. But they chose not to call me, the one who was the natural choice; I would have been had Mr. Pont been alive. But no, they called in Mary Gates instead."

"She's the receptionist we saw there yesterday," Dougall explained.

"And you see that as a dismissal?"

"Of course. Wouldn't you?"

St. George shook his head. "No, ma'am, I would not. From a strictly business standpoint, I should imagine the executive secretary was the obvious first choice. But I believe they are very aware of your grief and did not want to impose those added responsibilities on your shoulders right now. I rather think they were being very considerate. They know they're going to need you in the near future."

The way Edith Sperling repeatedly blinked her eyes told Poole she had never considered any option beyond a personal affront. She looked at Dr. Austen who nodded and said, "Makes sense to me." That brief moment changed the entire encounter, and for the next 20 minutes, the lady was a fount of information about the daily workings of the VES central office suite. The first portion, of course, was a restatement, in stages, of why the late Geoffrey Pont had been a saint. Then the detectives heard in considerable detail why Mrs. Sperling was indeed first among equals relative to the other employees and especially the other secretaries. Gradually St. George brought the subject around to the previous week and the events leading up to the climactic Friday meeting with YAMATSU. Among the questions about final preparations for the official signing, he interspersed a few seeking to learn if Geoffrey Pont had asked her to retrieve any files for him. The answer was 'no.' Did he take any files home with him that week? No, he had not done so for years. Had he expressed any frustration or disappointment or concern that week? Nothing you would not expect under the circumstances. Seeing the question forming in her eyes, he switched tack.

"It's our understanding that Michael's trip to London was a last-minute sort of thing."

"That's right."

"I imagine that both he and Geoffrey were disappointed that he could not be present for signing."

"Geoffrey took it in stride as did Michael."

"A bank matter, I believe, secondary market financing or some such...?"

"Yes, that's right. Michael announced late Thursday that he had received word that the London bank had some question or other. He said it might be do-able over the phone, but he thought that, with matters so close to fruition, he had best tend to it in person, and Mr. Pont agreed."

"And Michael returned sometime Friday evening and continued on up to St. Andrews Saturday morning."

"That was my understanding."

"So it was left to Geoffrey to carry the day, so to speak."

"Yes, but he was quite up to it, believe you me. Forgive my saying so, but Michael would have been window dressing. He's gone so much of the time. Has been for the past couple of years. On company business, of course, developing new contacts and keeping old ones, but it involves playing a lot of golf and going to receptions and parties. Hardly a burdensome life..."

"Indeed. To wrap up Friday, then, did Geoffrey leave you with any orders or messages to pass on to Michael later after he returned?"

"No, sir. In fact, the only...well, it was nothing, actually."

"Pardon?"

"It was nothing," she said with a sharp shake of her head. "I misspoke."

"Oh," said St. George as he paused a moment. "Please do not misunderstand my intent, Mrs. Sperling, but you have not struck me as the kind of person given to misspeaking. No matter how trivial the matter may appear to be, it still might have some bearing somewhere."

"Chief Inspector, your flattery is welcome but borders on the criminal. The order, if you will—reminder was more like it—that Mr. Pont gave me was not for Michael but for me. And that was to be sure the copier was fully loaded with paper and toner before I left. The reason I said it was nothing was because it is one of our standard chores before closing shop for the weekend."

"Ah, yes, to be all ready first thing Monday morning."

"That's right."

"But given the excitement of the day, I suppose, he went out of his way to remind you to do something you always did anyway."

"Yes, but I don't really do that. Mary Gates has that responsibility."

"The *junior* secretary."

"Yes," replied Edith Sperling with a fleeting smile.

"Mr. Pont aware of that, was he?"

"I don't know, it didn't really matter as long as it got done."

"If you were absent, even for a moment, would Mr. Pont ever go ahead and convey orders or requests directly to the others?"

"He could have, I suppose, but I don't believe he did. That just wasn't our protocol, if you will."

"Ah! You received such requests and then you passed them on to the relevant people. The gatekeeper, in other words."

"Yes. In this case, I reminded Mary and I'm sure she took care of it. Why? Was there a problem with the copier?"

"Not that we're aware of; I just wanted to be clear on the proper procedure."

At that point, Dr. Austen interrupted with his admonition that Mrs. Sperling should retire early that evening and asked that the detectives bring their interview to a close. Poole could see his boss was sorely tempted to protest but his hesitation showed he thought better of it. Thus, after an exchange of courteous adieus, the coppers found themselves riding back toward West Calder.

On the way, Dougall fielded a radio message that Dr. Woolsley wanted to meet with St. George and the team that evening if at all possible. The Chief Inspector suggested they all rendezvous at the Squire's Inn at 9 P.M. for snacks and dessert, his treat, and asked the good doctor to reserve the table. St. George correctly interpreted the moments of "dead air" which followed as reflecting Woolsley's shock and surprise. He smiled. Touché.

21

BACK AT THE police station, each man took his turn visiting the loo, and then they gathered in the murder room to unlock the secrets of Geoffrey Pont's personal computer.

With his colleagues looking over his shoulder, Poole powered up the machine, typed 'macbeth' in the password window space, and tapped the 'enter' key. Without protest, the password window instantly disappeared, leaving him in full command of the machine. Too fast for St. George to follow, Poole called up the C-drive window showing all the folders, applications, individual files, and programs contained therein. Nothing was labeled 'VES' or 'Viscount.' A folder labeled 'Review' was empty.

"That 'review' folder is suspicious to me," the sergeant said. "It's the kind of thing I'd use if I was doing some off-the-job work."

Dougall then pointed to an icon in a top corner. "The empty wastebasket says we've got someone who tidies up each time before he shuts down. Got a bloke like that here at the station."

"Tidies up?" said St. George.

"Doesn't leave discarded or deleted files around," Poole said. "They accumulate and take up valuable space on the hard drive and in the random access memory. So what he really needs, he keeps. The rest he discards into the wastebasket file which he then empties before he shuts down. It's an extra step but a safety measure so you don't accidentally and irretrievably remove something you really want to keep."

"Sounds like my kind of precaution," replied the Chief Inspector. "That's always been my fear—losing forever the Yard's entire database."

"The question is," Poole continued, "did he just read what he wanted off the disc—which would be in the A-drive—or did he copy anything onto the hard drive to save it to compare with later?"

Dougall had a suggestion. "What say we run 'Find' to search for anything labeled 'VES' or 'Viscount'? Maybe it's buried somewhere."

"Wait a minute!" Poole said. He smoothly slid the pointer down to the 'Start' button in the screen's lower left-hand corner. The short Start menu popped up as before but now he moved the pointer past 'Find' straight to the word 'Documents.' Immediately to the right appeared a vertical submenu listing 10 files bearing the letters 'VES' in their otherwise tightly abbreviated names. "Yes!" he exclaimed.

"Bravo, Laurence!" rejoined his mentor. "How in the world—?"

"Late-model computers like this one keep track of the last few files you have opened, even if by mistake. You can change the setting for how many it remembers. The idea is that you can access them here right away using these shortcuts without going through the entire tree. Most everybody forgets this list is here, but it shows our man worked on at least this number of VES financial files. Perhaps more."

"Well, maestro, let's bring one up for examination, shall we?" said St. George, who noticed with pleasure that Dougall was nodding in appreciation of the junior detective's efforts.

Poole clicked on the first file listed, and immediately, there was a mild sound from the CPU. Despite being a relative virgin regarding computers, St. George knew he was listening to the spinning hard drive searching for the digital record. But then came a broad window with lettering saying the computer could not find the requested file.

"Means he erased it or changed the name," Poole said. "Let's try another..."

Same result, but the third one also triggered a humming sound from the floppy disc drive which, however, was empty.

"That file was read off the A-drive directly," explained Poole. The same thing occurred for the remaining files. "So, in summary then, I'd say he copied down the first two files to compare with the ones he read later off the disc."

"All right, let's jot down those file names for future reference. Any chance anything might show up with the search tool the Inspector mentioned?"

"Let's see..." and with that Poole returned to the Start menu, chose 'Find,' then 'Folder' in the submenu, typed in one title, and clicked on the appropriate button and waited. Seconds later the computer reported the file was in a folder labeled 'Recent'. "Ah," he said. "If I'm right..." He then initiated a search for that folder and discovered it was inside the platform's main directory. Seconds later they had opened the folder and were perusing the same 10 file names. "As I thought, just another name for the 'Documents' folder. But we can try one anyway..."

Immediately the 'cannot find' window appeared.

"So it means," Dougall said, "that the records themselves are not in this machine unless he changed their names."

"Let's try the rest anyway," said the Chief Inspector. "No point wasting the opportunity."

The next few minutes passed quietly as the search continued for the other eight VES files. None were found.

"I've heard," said Dougall, "that even deleted files can be read off the hard drive using special software."

"Yes," Poole said, "if you're a computer geek and you're ready to take the bloody machine apart. But then, we must remember our guy *was* a computer geek."

"So he may have already thought to cover himself on that?"

"Wouldn't surprise me. And there might be a problem with integrity of evidence if we have the hard drive searched."

"Oh well, we tried," said St. George with a sigh. "For now, I'd say discretion was the better part of valor. Yes, Inspector?"

"Another problem, perhaps," said Dougall. "Do we know for sure *when* Pont reviewed these files here? It could have been anytime in the past month. Remember, Mrs. Pont admitted she's not conversant on the subject of computers so Defense could challenge her on what she claims she saw."

St. George winced. "Point well taken. Laurence, any hope?"

"Yes, actually," replied Poole as he right-clicked on the third file name. Instantly a submenu of options appeared. The choices ranged from 'send to' and 'print' to 'cut,' 'copy,' and 'delete.' He dropped the pointer down to 'Properties,' which he clicked. This produced a square gray window bearing several lines of lettering. Before St. George or Dougall had time to read them, Poole clicked on the 'General' tab at the top of the window and reached a second page, so to speak, with even more information. In the same instant, all three pairs of eyes fell on the same entries:

>Location: A: \ VES-xxxxx
>MSDOS Name: VES-xxxxx
>Created: November 23, 1992 10:42 A.M.
>Modified: February 14, 1996 3:13 P.M.
>Accessed: July 24, 1996 8:15 P.M.

Beaming with pride, it was everything St. George could do not to pat his man on the back with a hearty "well done!" He could tell Dougall was very impressed, and he thought: *Well, he should be: us Yard blokes aren't dummies after all. Provided, of course, you choose the right associate ...*

"Don't know what got modified in February," said Poole who was trying mightily not to show off. "The key thing for us is that some-body—who else but Geoffrey Pont—opened this file on this com-puter last Wednesday evening."

"Wife places him in his study," said Dougall. "Bloody hell, we got it!"

With a loud sigh of satisfaction, St. George asked Poole to check the same 'Properties' page for the other nine files. As Poole had pre-dicted, seven files had come off the A-drive (disc) and two from the 'Review' folder on the C-drive. All had been opened in the evenings between Tuesday, the 23rd and Friday, the 26th. Geoffrey Pont had died on the 27th.

Their last task before shutting down was to check the e-mail pro-gram. Again Geoffrey Pont had been fastidiously tidy, leaving no record of any sent or deleted messages. The one in-box message was an unopened weekly newsletter from a computer services company in Edinburgh. They checked his 'address book' but found only other executives listed along with brother Michael and cousin Edward and banker Muir. Attorney Leslie Brohm was not included.

"Hmmmpf!" St. George uttered as he shoved his hands in his pockets.

"I can't help thinking," said Dougall as Poole shut down the com-puter, "that if the company itself were the problem, then would not YAMATSU have tumbled to it and called off the deal?"

"Excellent point, Inspector, and it parallels my own concern. It certainly is conceivable that something arose last week without warning or preamble. But then why not alert Michael and Barrows and the others? Straighten it out before YAMATSU catches on. But the utter secrecy of the thing makes me think Pont was concerned about someone within the company, someone whose actions showed up in the financial records. That someone must be an employee...and a prominent employee to be mentioned in such records. Be sure all of this is documented, Inspector. Better set up a log so that we can prove who had access and when—starting with us right now. We'll wait and as soon as you're finished, we'll go join Marcus. And eat!"

"Thought you weren't fond of eating late," said Poole as Dougall left the room.

"Generally I'm not, gives me indigestion in the early morning. But damn it, strange as it sounds, all this traveling makes me hungry, makes me feel like I'm on a cruise ship. And I was once, years ago, and it was three full meals and then devour a huge buffet between 10 and 11. Gained a full 12 pounds. But oh, was it wonderful!"

"Well, maybe next time you could take me along as your official taster."

The Chief Inspector regarded his aide with a puzzled look.

"Laurence, I wasn't at risk for being poisoned."

"I know, but I thought I might have to eat half of each portion before deciding it was safe for you to have the rest."

The Chief Inspector's guffaw could be heard all the way out in the reception area, much to the consternation of the staff on duty.

22

THEIR PLACES CLEARED, only drinks and coffee remaining, St. George called the meeting to order just as Chief Superintendent Stallings arrived, apologizing for being delayed by traffic. Though it grated, St. George had felt obligated to invite the region's top cop to the meeting, especially after receiving a radioed apology for the 'misunderstanding' of earlier in the day. So he had thought the invitation preferable to simply having the man show up at his own initiative because unquestionably the local roster—Dougall included—would be under orders to summon Stallings should anything develop. After all, this was his home turf. Indeed, the London men had no delusions about the fealty of the local coppers to their head man—one's ultimate allegiance must lie with his superior. Therefore, withholding the invitation might prove the surest way to antagonize and alienate the very staff St. George and Poole would need to bring this case to a successful conclusion.

"Right...Well now, we are here to receive Dr. Woolsley's preliminary report," said St. George as Stallings took an end seat. "Marcus, the floor is yours."

The lanky Medical Examiner stretched before shifting his chair and reseating himself.

"Byram, I do hope you have even the faintest glimmer of the travail you have put me and mine through. As if it's not bad enough that you go gallivanting about the countryside while us mere mortals grunt and sweat under a weary life..."

"Oh, Marcus, spare us the Shakespeare, will you? It is getting late...."

"Well, just know that with this little exercise you will owe me. I can't calculate what it will be until I get back to London, but believe me, it will be considerable. And for the record, let me enter the usual and customary disclaimer, i.e., the obvious: we cannot possibly have everything inventoried and analyzed and verified for at least three weeks."

"Your disclaimer is duly noted."

"Thank you," Woolsley said, glancing at Stallings who was sitting rigidly at attention, thoroughly puzzled by the banter. "Right. Well, I can give you some initial results. To begin, we concur with Chief McSwain's negative findings as far as they go. About what was *not* there. No globs of wax, no spring-driven timers, no cigar butts, no cigarette stubs, no matchbooks, no sawdust, no broken light bulbs..."

"No sawdust?" Dougall said. "What...?"

"You pack a bunch of it around a bare 40-watt bulb and turn on the current. Wood is a marvelous insulator and traps the heat around the bulb. When the temperature reaches 1,500 degrees Fahrenheit, the sawdust catches fire."

"Right."

"So anyway, like McSwain, we went down your basic checklist and even repeated the ultraviolet exam. Nothing. We even used hydrocarbon sensors in case the roof's collapse had extinguished the fire soon enough to leave puddles of liquid behind. Granted, four days after the fact is a problem, as was the rain, but we tried. Again nothing. Same for the dog."

"Dog? You mean like for drugs?" Stallings asked.

"The very same. Brought the pooch in from Glasgow. In fact, a dog's nose is many times more sensitive than the bloody machine. But again there was nothing to find. Next, the fire brigade mentioned seeing yellow-brown smoke as they arrived. That color is typical of burning wood products, paper, and photographic filmstuffs. So the *absence* of thick, black smoke at the outset is another mark against conventional petroleum products being used as accelerants. You know, of course, that there are some 250 separate compounds in gasoline. We'll run the gamut of tests, of course, even energy dispersion X-ray spectroscopy to check for bromine and lead. However, I believe what is most important in this case was what was *not* smelled or detected. Meaning that the accelerant must have been completely consumed by the fire."

"And that would be...?"

"Acetone, obviously."

Woolsley paused to be sure everyone understood before proceeding.

"Byram, your point about the discrepancies in combustion temperatures was well taken. The hottest temperature in a fire is always up along the ceiling. Runs around 1,700 degrees Fahrenheit. Halfway down to the floor in a standard eight-foot room, the temp drops to about 850 degrees. Now, we should note the condition of the windows which were set at about the halfway mark, or about four feet off the floor. First, glass melts at 1,400 degrees ... but the glass was not melted. Second, the metal window frames and sills—mostly aluminum—would melt around 1,700 degrees or so, but none of them were affected. And third, a professional crematorium uses *2,000* degrees to incinerate a body. Therefore...such temperatures as would be required to incinerate this body, as it has been described, *never existed* in this building. *Except* ... for the body *itself!* Clearly, then, the *body* was a *second* act of arson. The killer thoroughly saturated it with acetone and set it alight."

Poole noticed Stallings jaw drop open.

"Could the man have torched himself?"

"Absolutely not."

"And why?"

"Because he was already dead."

St. George pointedly did not look in Stallings' direction but Poole watched the man's unabashed shock and surprise.

"That's music to my ears, Marcus," St. George said, "but you know we will need tangible proof for the prosecution."

"Have I ever failed you?" asked the Medical Examiner petulantly.

"No, but I just wanted to remind you of our high expectations."

"Bah! You and your bloody expectations!"

"So, pray continue. Cause of death?"

"The man was stabbed to death. We knew it first because of the blood-soaked toilet paper we extracted from the sewer line draining that dry toilet. Meant someone had bled and bled quite a bit. Yet Luminol showed nothing in the office area except for the blade of the sword-like letter opener on the Sperling woman's desk. That's where the body was found, against her desk. The opener rested in a iron base—supposed to represent Excalibur in the rock, I guess. I've got something like it at home. Anyway, hers has two sharp edges; had been deliberately sharpened. Sensible since she apparently opened everything that came in."

"Bravo!"

With a flourish and a deep bow, Woolsley answered, "As always, your obedient servant."

"Question," Poole said. "Why bother to clean up if the killer was going to torch the place anyway?"

"I wondered that as well," Woolsley replied. "Then it came to me. The victim is stabbed, probably repeatedly, and the natural result is that the killer has very bloody hands. He knows he cannot wash them because he's already shut off the water. And he cannot turn the water back on without leaving a bloody trail at that valve. So he does the best he can. He washes them in the toilet bowl, follows up with a spit bath, and then flushes the goods down the loo."

"What about blood type? DNA?" said St. George.

"We'll try, but don't hold your breath. I doubt any will belong to the killer. It will merely confirm my hypothesis."

"Excuse me." It was Chief Superintendent Stallings. "You say Mr. Pont was stabbed repeatedly with the letter opener. The state of that place, there is no way you can tell whether any such violence occurred."

"Actually, my premise is that there was very little violence. I surmise Mr. Pont was taken by surprise, probably coshed and rendered unconscious if only for a minute. Long enough for the assailant to open the man's clothes and deliver several well-aimed blows. Then he buttoned him back up."

Stallings's jaws clenched firmly

"All right," said St. George, "so the killer then set the fire and made a clean getaway."

"Right. The secret was using an accelerant with a very low boiling point. One that evaporates quickly and leaves no residue behind. Acetone fits the bill perfectly and was readily available in large amounts. In fact, the three carboys received here the week prior should have lasted for at least three months. Yet a one-month supply was gone in a week. And we're to believe that was normal usage? Balderdash! Rather than be splashed about, the 15 liters were sprayed throughout the place using an atomizer. A simple garden insect sprayer, I suspect. Easy to acquire, easy to carry, easy to dispose of. The volume was quite sufficient to saturate the air inside the plant. Remember, the place was not that large. Start in the west end and work back to the offices. However, the key to figuring the whole thing out were these…"

Woolsley slipped some photographs from his pocket and passed them around.

"Excuse me," Stallings said. "You speculate the killer went about the building spraying this acetone everywhere…"

Woolsley started to object to the 'speculate' but held his tongue and merely said, "Yes?"

"That would be impossible because the atmosphere would be quite toxic."

"Correct. I believe, therefore, that our culprit used one of those small scuba tanks—pony bottles they call them—which would be sufficient for the task. Something like 6 to 15 cubic feet of compressed air. Relatively lightweight, and again easy to carry, easy to conceal, easy to dispose of. Anyway, as for these photographs, they're numbered in sequence….to show these two tightly wadded-up little objects we found lying under a desk a few feet from where the body was found. They were compressed rather than merely crumpled up as one would ordinarily do with gum wrappers. So we unfolded them… to find that once upon a time…they were foil packets…which contained…"

"Yes?" prodded the Chief Inspector.

"Condoms."

* * *

Had the Archbishop of Canterbury announced his conversion to Judaism, the collective shock around the table could not have been more complete. In contrast, Woolsley was visibly delighted with the consternation he had created.

"My God!" gasped Dougall. "That means Geoffrey Pont was having a tryst there—with that woman who called it in, no doubt—and it went wrong or her husband came in and …"

"Wait, Inspector," St. George said, hand up like a crossing guard. "I believe Dr. Woolsley has more to add. Clearly, Marcus, you're thinking of something else?"

"Indeed. I must confess my first reaction was the same as Inspector Dougall's. Nothing like a juicy scandal to make a difficult situation infinitely worse. However, although we cannot say exactly *when* these packets were opened and emptied of their contents, we should note that the place was cleaned and left tidy at the end of business Friday. Therefore, it is highly implausible *and* highly improbable that they were merely overlooked from an earlier time. And then, come on! Someone doing the nasty in such a place, so accessible to anyone in the building, with people so close by? I mean, *really*. I've heard of risk-takers, but that would be too much. Even for Scotsmen. And leave such tangible evidence of your encounter just lying around for anyone to find? I rather think that these packets instead point to something sinister."

Poole snickered. "Unless they were all into some group thing over the noon hour. You know, the lord and master and his six love slaves?"

"Laurence!" chortled St. George as he glanced at an unsmiling Stallings. "We're trying to be serious here. All right, Marcus, grant us mercy. How was it done?"

"Well, it's an old tried-and-true method, and the condoms are the key. Very reliable timers, actually. What you do is sit the body against the desk and make a nest of toilet paper in the dead man's lap. The only things you've brought with you are a bug sprayer for dispersing the acetone and a large sandwich bag filled with a mixture of common granulated sugar and potassium chlorate. You empty the mixture into the bowl-like nest of paper. Next you open the condoms and insert one inside the other to give you a two-layer sac. You then siphon off some sulfuric acid from the company's supply into this latex sac and ligate it with a thin thread. You carefully place the sac amongst the sugar-potassium mixture and then get the hell out. The sulfuric acid eats steadily through the latex and contact with the mixture produces an immediate, very intense flame. In a split-second you first turn the body into a roaring bonfire, which then ignites the vaporized acetone to create a giant fireball and an explosion. The double latex layer would give you about a 16-minute delay to ignition."

St. George smiled at his friend before exclaiming, "Marvelous!"

"Thank you, thank you, thank you," said a beaming Woolsley. "But now, in good conscience, I must also give you the bad news. That's how the fire happened, but unfortunately all the chemicals, the latex, the paper, were all converted to water, carbon dioxide, fine ash, and trace amounts of salt. None of it evidence of anything. Except for the condom packets, there is no tangible proof that any such event occurred. Other than the killer knowing where to find the acid and the acetone, you have nothing that could lead to a conviction."

"What about knowing *how* to make the igniter?" Dougall asked.

"Anyone who can read can get that from a library, a bookstore, or the Internet."

The following moment of absolute silence ended with the Chief Inspector's mumbled, "Bloody hell."

* * *

After glumly congratulating Woolsley on his work, Stallings abruptly took his leave while St. George and the others prepared to bring their long day to a close. What mattered most to the Medical Examiner was the private expression of profound appreciation he received from St. George moments later in the restaurant's vestibule. He would sleep better and his next day's labor would be all the more tolerable as a result. To have his work valued so highly by a fellow senior professional thrilled him immensely, though he was loath to ever let anyone suspect that truth. However, he was all too aware that St. George knew it was his Achilles' heel.

Before the team adjourned for the night, St. George handed out the assignments for Friday. Cobb was driving him to Edinburgh to catch another early flight to London. He anticipated not returning until Saturday morning. In the meantime, Dougall and Poole were to interview Mary Gates at Viscount's temporary Livingston office to see if the emphasis on the copier was mere happenstance or actually reflected Geoffrey Pont's intent on returning to the plant Saturday morning. Thereafter, Dougall was to confirm Edward Cargill's Edinburgh alibi, preferably by retracing his journey using the receipts the man had provided as a guide. Poole was to do the same for Michael Pont's trip to St. Andrews, though obviously by phone. Then, through Superintendent Wallace, Dougall was to set up meetings for Saturday at their homes with Edward Cargill, Michael Pont, and James Barrows. Finally, as much as he wanted to put each suspect under surveillance, as yet they lacked sufficient evidence to establish probable cause.

With a fervor he had not felt in years, he prayed that the situation would soon change.

Friday

23

MARY GATES WAS surprised to see detectives Dougall and Poole
enter her office. She recognized the local man but viewed Poole with
a suspicion unexpected for her 32 years. Using what passed for his
most consoling bedside manner, Dougall reassured the young
woman about the benevolent nature of their visit and then, between
interrupting phone calls, guided her through an inventory of her
responsibilities at VES. On St. George's instruction, Poole made no
effort to take notes.

Dougall quickly established that the young woman was a combination receptionist, word processor typist, backup secretary, file
clerk, and "go-fer." As a direct result of these assorted functions, she
possessed a broader picture of VES office activity than either Edith
Sperling or her more compartmentalized coworkers. On the flip
side, she usually had little direct contact with Geoffrey Pont other
than exchanging passing greetings. Edward Cargill had spoken to her
once in four years. She was more likely to have conversations with
Michael Pont, James Barrows, Ted Manning, and others of lesser rank.

When Dougall brought their discussion around to the preceding
Friday, Mary Gates reinforced Edith Sperling's impression that
Geoffrey Pont had shown no particular change in behaviour despite
the pressure of meeting the important Japanese visitors.

"Mrs. Sperling said that part of preparing the office for work the following Monday was to add paper and toner to the copying machine. Was that correct?"

"Yes. In fact, I've done that ever since I started working here. It's no big deal. Takes a couple of minutes is all. Did she say something was wrong? I've never missed, not once. Neither have any of the other girls if I was gone."

"No, she did not, just that Friday afternoon Mr. Pont specifically reminded her to prime the copier. And that she had passed his request on to you. Is that right?"

"Yes, she did."

"Any idea why he would make such mention? Had it given trouble?"

"The copier? No, sir. Not that I know of. I just took it to mean he was going to use it over the weekend to finish work he couldn't get done, you know, what with the Japs coming and all."

"Oh, I see. Yes, that does make sense. He'd done that before, I suppose....working on the weekend?"

"Not that I know of. The place is always locked up tight as a drum."

"Did anyone happen to comment to you that Mr. Pont might be coming out to the plant Saturday?"

"No, sir, I don't know if anyone else knew."

"And he did not happen to elaborate on his plan with you, am I right?"

"No, sir, he did not."

"About the copier paper, do you know if he specified a particular kind—you know, weight, finish, and so on?"

"No, but we only use one kind for everything. Besides the newsletter, I mean. That's heavier stock, canary yellow. Just one page usually, sometimes both sides, birthdays and anniversaries, of course, but then children's accomplishments and promotions and then company reminders and stuff like being sure to review the safety manuals and so on, just a chatty little piece that helps keep everyone in touch with everyone else no matter how busy they are, makes everyone feel closer, like a family kind'a..."

"Sounds very commendable. Promotes loyalty, I would imagine."

"And then some! It's the only place I've worked where you could trust everyone else there. I mean, at first, us ladies always took our purses with us but occasionally we'd forget. But we'd laugh and go on and when we got back there they'd be, nothing touched..."

"So despite the high-tech environment, you get to move about quite freely."

"Oh, yes. Everybody knows everybody else."

"Right...well, I think that will be all, Mrs. Gates, unless the good sergeant has something...?"

Though he knew tact and protocol required him to demure and pass the shoe, so to speak, Poole could not turn down the opportunity.

"Uh, yes, thank you, Inspector, just a quick one, to clarify if I might...Mrs. Gates, do any of the other executives come to you directly with requests?"

"Oh, yes, all the time. About the post, is it in yet, or something for the newsletter, or a memo, and so on."

"I see. But in contrast, Geoffrey Pont was not in the habit of dealing with you directly on such matters."

"That's right. He always went to Mrs. Sperling."

"Good. Now, just for the record then, later on Friday, did Geoffrey Pont call you to confirm that you had prepared the copier?"

"No, sir. Just Michael."

The sergeant paused

"Michael Pont called you?"

"Yes. But not about the copier. Well, I mean I mentioned it, but he was calling about the usual. Schedule changes, if there were any."

"What schedule changes, may I ask?"

"Oh, meetings with his brother and Mr. Cargill or with Mr. Barrows or with clients, any number of things. I'm sort of his pocket organizer," chuckled Mary Gates. "He's gone so much of the time and he hates voice mail so if he's been away for any length of time, it's just easier for him to call me and find out what's happening."

"And he calls you at the office?" said Dougall who felt compelled to reestablish his primacy over this British interloper.

"No, home."

"Home?" said both coppers in unison.

"Why yes, he does it all the time. Well, not *all* the time, but maybe once a week or so."

"Why does he not just call his brother?" Dougall asked, visibly uncomfortable at the prospect of Poole having perhaps opened a Pandora's box.

"He said he didn't like to bother his brother at home, and I can see why because he usually got home later than anyone expected."

"I'm surprised," said Dougall. "I thought if anyone would carry one of those digital calendars and what not, it would be one of these computer guys."

"Oh they do, especially Mr. Barrows. But Michael doesn't like them and Geoffrey had Mrs. Sperling to watch out for him."

"Clarification again, if I may," said Poole with a deferential nod toward Dougall, "but you said Michael gets home later than expected. Such as?"

"Oh, nothing sinister, just that he's a wealthy bachelor, and he's got a bird in Edinburgh and I think another one in Glasgow. Makes quite a few side trips, he does."

"While otherwise on company business?"

Mary Gates smiled bashfully and nodded as though by remaining silent she was not gossiping.

"Your husband is not upset by all these calls?" said Dougall.

"Oh, he was at first – he's quite the jealous sort. But after listening in the first dozen times, he realized I've acquired quite a position here. I mean, I'm sort of the centerpost, if you will."

"Had Michael ever suggested stopping by your home?"

"Oh no, never. It's all quite platonic. I'm just his message service."

"In keeping with that," said Poole, "has Michael ever asked you to answer calls for him? Or make calls for him?"

"Well, I do at the office all the time. But never at home. Strictly that he wants to know what's going on. Just like Friday night. Like asking about the files."

"Files?" said Dougall, unable to conceal his surprise. "On what?"

"Business office files. Mr. Geoffrey had been taking some home for about a week. I don't think he wanted anyone to know, but I saw him take them from the main file room."

"Without asking either you or Mrs. Sperling to get them?"

"Uh-huh. That's what made me notice."

"Well, could not have been too sinister," said Dougall with a forced chuckle, "if Michael already knew about them."

"Oh, right, of course."

"Did Mr. Pont ever ask you to return those files to the file room?"

"No, though I'm sure he did himself. He was very conscientious."

The interview ended very pleasantly moments later, the coppers expressing their thanks and appreciation for her time and cooperation, and a relieved Mary Gates beaming in importance as they left. What they did not see as they climbed into their car was her picking up the phone to call Edward Cargill at his home.

24

As his plane touched down at Heathrow, St. George expressed a silent prayer of thanks for the turbulence-free flight. One could never have too many of those.

In London, a young constable was waiting for him at curbside, a cell-phone-equipped staff car at the ready. While his driver negotiated the heavy traffic, the Chief Inspector phoned the financial section at the Yard only to learn that they had fallen behind in analyzing the VES records. Acting on a flash of inspiration, he ordered them to hold everything and he would pick them up momentarily. Twenty minutes later, they pulled up to Harald Burklund's prize bastion: a tall, steel-and-concrete edifice that dominated its neighborhood as a medieval castle had intimidated the surrounding countryside.

In the surprisingly spartan lobby, he presented his credentials to the uniformed security guard manning the reception desk. In return, he received a clip-on plastic pass bearing a bar code which gained him access to the manned elevator serving only the top two floors. Despite the appearance of casual openness, St. George had no doubt he was under intense surveillance, starting with his approach to the front door. The lone guest passenger on the elevator, he noted how the operator's trim uniform failed to conceal his muscular physique. He also guessed that behind the control panel's metal door labeled PHONE was a loaded .357 or something equally powerful. He sensed an aura of "OK, buddy, just try something—I dare you."

As they reached the top floor, the door pulled back to reveal an immaculately attired male aide waiting for him in a small vacant vestibule. Consistent with proper corporate protocol, the man— about 30, slim, well-groomed—smiled constantly as though St. George were the most welcome sight of his life. He quickly ushered the visitor through three sets of opaque doors that 'whooshed' open at their approach. They reached a small waiting room which contained three, Danish-modern, thinly cushioned armchairs facing a tiny table barely wide enough to hold the short stack of business magazines. At no time had St. George seen any doors or side corridors, something that fit his preconception about many corporate types—that they had a penchant for insulating themselves behind an impenetrable labyrinth of hallways, passages, and offices. Sort of, he thought, like turning video games into real life.

He declined an offer of a beverage and then sat down as the aide disappeared through the last set of doors. Having arrived five minutes early, he expected to be admitted into The Presence in very short order because Scandinavians, like Germans, valued punctuality. However, a quarter-hour led to a second and a third one by which time he had resolved he'd show this bloody Swede who could outlast whom. Until now he had discounted the idea that top business moguls were either excruciatingly prompt or maddeningly laggard in keeping appointments. The tacitly understood maxim was that you did the first to curry favor and the second to show dominance and to unsettle your opponent. The corollary was that storming out in a huff showed weakness, not strength, and rarely gained a second appointment. Recalling Silas Muir's comment about slacks, the Chief Inspector realized his own were rather snug, but he thought being a government official here on official business more than compensated for the inadequacy of his attire. After all, the industrialist could not afford to offend Her Majesty's government. And so, while seething inwardly, St. George adopted the posture of someone very comfortable with mindless waiting, all the while certain he was under more fiberoptic surveillance. *Play it for the cameras, old boy.*

Suddenly, a brief swish across the room produced an aperture through which the aide popped out and, apology delivered, beckoned the man from Scotland Yard to follow. They had gone no more than a dozen paces when they entered a spacious yet modestly-furnished office with two large abstract paintings on the walls. Facing him was a stocky, square-shouldered, balding gentleman with a bullet-shaped head, piercing gray eyes, pug nose, and tight thin lips. *Not your classic Viking*, thought St. George as he approached this dynamo who was feared and respected in any industry in which he wished to operate. The firm handshake and greeting were brief and efficient.

"Let me add my own apologies to those Hans expressed," said the man in Americanized English. "Like you, I'm sure, every day is a busy one, but we seem to have lost control of this one."

"I fully understand," replied the Chief Inspector with a quick half-smile while taking his seat. Was his own insincerity apparent, he wondered?

"Well, to tell you the truth, Chief Inspector, I'm as glad to see you as you are to see me."

Bloody hell you are.

Many years earlier, St. George had learned that, among executives, the first 30 seconds determined who would control the conversation. And thus, who would win the negotiation and the deal. He had found that it wasn't all that much different when detectives grilled a suspect—though minus all the gloss. He had also learned that catchwords like "to tell the truth" usually signaled that what immediately followed was a lie.

"Indeed. How might that be?"

"Well, you're here, of course, to find out what I know of Viscount Electric. Probably, I imagine, because of my conversations with Edward Cargill. I was hoping your visit might afford me a comparable opportunity to learn something as well."

"Really now! How interesting. Not being intimately familiar with the ways of the high-level business world, I suppose your anticipation of a two-way flow of information would be a reasonable expectation. However, I'm afraid as I'm here on official police business, that flow must be unidirectional—toward me. I'm sure you understand."

"Of course. Nonetheless, you've told me a great deal already."

"Oh?"

"Yes. I expected I would hear from the police somewhere along the line, but the fact that the Commissioner of Scotland Yard himself scheduled you in was, I thought, remarkable. Then having someone of your seniority actually make the visit was doubly meaningful."

"Really."

"Oh, I mean no disrespect to your colleagues, Chief Inspector, but to simply question me about my limited contacts with VES could have been accomplished by any one of your junior men. Or women. So your being here adds a whole new dimension."

"Mr. Burklund, flattery is nice but places demands upon the recipient. After all, one does not want to seem ungrateful or impolite. Therefore, may I suggest we get down to cases."

"And I'm doing just that. In fact, as a token of my good faith, I'll tell you that some years ago—I think it was about six or so—I had a brief liaison with Myra Pont."

Burklund paused as though studying his visitor's reaction to the news. A thin smile barely creased his lips before he continued.

"I wasn't trying to shock you, but I thought you would get word from her or someone else and so I might as well say something. We met through one of the charitable foundations we support, and before long one thing led to another. I also mention this at the outset because that was the very first time I had heard of VES. Since we broke it off—amicably, I might add—we have had absolutely no further contact or communication. I'm aware it's your prerogative to confirm this with her although I would hope you could forgo it. It's very old news."

"Well, as you say, if this was all years ago, then it might not have a bearing on current events." *Except*, he thought, *for your 10 percent interest in the new project.*

"Thank you," replied the industrialist with a slight bow of his head.

"Speaking of past years, have you ever been to Italy, by chance?"

"Oh, numerous times. For business."

"Rome, Venice, Naples?"

"Yes."

"Turin?"

"No."

"Milan?"

"Oh, about 30 years ago when I first set out to make my fortune. Not since."

"Getting back to the present, your contacts with VES were only through Edward Cargill?"

"Yes. What I learned was meager but enough for me to judge that VES was an interesting but not exciting prospect. I have never had real need for such a company in my empire; its acquisition would have been either a diversion to mislead competitors in other fields or a bargaining chip for future mergers. *However...*your being here tells me that VES is extremely important to the government and other people who have probably never set foot in Scotland. All of which tells me I need to rethink my position."

"Your contacts with Edward...how many?"

"We've met a total of four times, and there have been an equal number of phone calls, including the one last Saturday informing me of the tragedy."

"If your contacts have been so casual, so informal, why should he have felt any obligation to call you?"

"Well...we're not what you'd call friends. We're acquaintances. I think for him it was simply good business etiquette—which I appreciated. He strikes me as someone who is eager to please. I suppose it might have come from the time when I expressed some interest in possibly buying a few shares in Viscount."

"Indeed. And did you ever purchase—"

"No. However, as I said, I'm going to have to rethink my position."

"What was your reaction to the news?"

Burklund smiled. "Shocked, of course."

"Why are you smiling?"

"No offense intended, Chief Inspector, but this interrogation reminds me of ones I've seen on television. As tactful as you are, it's clear you consider me a suspect in the man's death. And the fire. You're looking for a motive."

"Should we consider you a suspect?"

"For the sake of the process, I suppose. But the fact is Viscount was not a target."

"What about Myra Pont?"

"What?"

"You claim your affair ended, but surely you can understand how someone could wonder if you were still in pursuit of the lady and looked upon her husband as an obstacle to be removed."

"Ah, more melodrama. No, sir, the affair was over long before I met the illustrious Edward Cargill."

"I see. So when you heard the news of the fire and so on, did you feel any sense of relief?"

For just an instant, Burklund's forehead contracted into a frown.

"Relief? Why should I...what a strange thing to ask. Why should relief come into it?"

"The elimination of a competitor?"

"A-hah! Is this where I'm to jump to my feet in joy and celebration?"

"If it is, please don't deny yourself on my account."

"Then I'm sorry to disappoint you, Chief Inspector, but no, I was not relieved. Or sad, for that matter, beyond feeling sympathy for Edward's loss. And as to VES being a competitor, they were not and are not."

"Do you think VES is finished?"

"Yes."

"Why?"

"I can give you two good reasons: their names are Michael and Edward."

"Have you met Michael?"

"No. Never talked with him, either. Never had reason to."

"So why do you have such a low opinion of the two men?"

Burklund began swiveling slowly in his chair.

"Chief Inspector, have you ever heard of remoras?"

"Yes. Fish that swim with sharks."

"More than that. They actually attach themselves to the shark so that the beast carries them along on a free ride. They have to expend virtually no energy to find food. Lazy bastards. Now mind you, I'm not saying Geoffrey Pont was a shark. From everything I've heard, the man was a decent sort whose handshake was his bond. Just as good as his signature on a contract. Something that's almost unheard of anymore. But take his two relations. Well, Edward's your basic parasite. Been at it all his adult life. And Michael—he was instrumental in their start-up, but I hear he's had no marketable ideas since. And neither one of them has a clue for managing day-to-day operations."

"For having such limited, even superficial, contact with the company, you seem to have deep insight into the company's performance."

"Thank you, but it's not as deep as you might think. Strictly a matter of keeping one's ears open."

"Be that as it may, it's your judgment they are incapable of keeping the thing afloat."

"I would say so. But that's between us. I'd rather not be quoted."

"What if they bring in outside help?"

"Such as?"

"Bankers?"

"Oh, God no!"

"Yourself, perhaps?"

"What could I bring to the table?"

"Your 10 percent interest in Silas Muir's limited partnership."

Harald Burklund's cherubic face suddenly morphed into a stone mask as though, like a snail, he had withdrawn inside himself to assess a new threat. But in a matter of moments, it relaxed, and like the snail reemerging, the congenial businessman reappeared.

"You've done your homework. Except Muir was to keep that information extremely secret."

"I made him an offer he could not refuse."

Burklund smiled grimly. "Well, the effort you obviously expended to acquire that information only reinforces what I said earlier about Viscount's previous value. As VES alone, no interest. As for the new project, great interest. So yes, I have a stake in the partnership, but I have no lock on any particular parcel. What troubles me is that I may lose my entire investment if the company fails to resume operations in a timely fashion. Leave us with just vacant pastureland."

"But aren't computers part of your...empire?"

"Only to use, not produce. They're already assembled. My companies don't deal in components. True, in some manufacturing, it's beneficial to get in on the ground floor and secure the raw materials for yourself, but not with computers. And as for my future plans, they always depend on where I see probable expansion. However, as of this morning, I have no indication that VES in and of itself has any such appeal."

"All right, let me ask you this: In your estimation, what is the likelihood that a direct competitor to VES hired someone to blow up the place?"

Burklund visibly relaxed and again smiled, only this time broader and longer.

"The classic loaded question. First of all, Chief Inspector, I did *not* have the place blown up. Second, it is very unlikely that anyone would for the same reason as my own; namely, that it made no economic sense. They are small potatoes in the entire scheme of things."

"I see. But how do you square that with the government contracts they've serviced?"

"Again it's a matter of scale. How much were those contracts worth? How much money did Her Majesty pay out? Very little, actually. Oh yes, I suppose there might be an equally small company somewhere feeling the pinch of competition, but I would have no idea who they would be. On the other hand, YAMATSU is a whole other matter entirely."

The industrialist paused and leaned back to enjoy the look of surprise on his visitor's face.

25

"YOU KNEW ABOUT YAMATSU from the partnership?" St. George asked.

"Oh, long before that. Got the word from Geoffrey himself. Industry trade show about seven months ago."

St. George could barely sit still.

"Interesting...do tell."

"I was there scouting another company—textiles—when at one point I found myself sharing cocktails with Geoffrey and some other man. Well now, after a few sherries, the old boy just wouldn't shut up! Practically spilled out the whole life history of the company. And his plans for this big deal with the Japanese. Fortunately for him, the other chap was in even worse shape and probably remembered nothing of that entire day. For myself, I took pity on the man, I mean he was a friendly sort, and so I got him out of there and back to his room."

"The height of sportsmanship, one might say, until one considers that you might have then availed yourself of an unparalleled opportunity."

Burklund smiled again.

"True. The fact is, however, that he had nothing left to tell me; he had spilled it all out at the bar. But then imagine how embarrassing it would be to have had all the advance information and yet fail to buy them out *before* the YAMATSU deal was consummated. Be terrible for my reputation. However, at the time, that project had no place in my empire, as you call it. It was appropriate, though, for me to keep it in mind should some future investment opportunity arise—as it did. And let me add one more thing in my favor. Had I thought he was a scumbag, I probably would have invited the entire room over to listen in and to profit from the knowledge. But I did not."

"When was this trade show?"

"Last November."

"And the other gentleman at the bar—know him?"

"No."

"Ever see him again? Talk with him again?"

"No."

"Think he might have made use of Geoffrey's revelations?"

"No, and here's why. If he were a reporter, you would have seen something in the papers forthwith. If he were a competitor, he would have taken some kind of action long before this past week to scuttle the project or to substitute his own company into the deal. And if he were a speculator, he would have probably tried to blackmail Geoffrey into buying his silence. Apparently none of those things happened."

"All right, let's turn to Edward. Did he approach you or did you approach him?"

"The latter."

"When?"

"That was in late March. Purely social gathering. I was on the hosting committee and so I knew ahead of time he would attend. As you intimated, our meeting was no accident. I wanted to follow up and see if anything new had transpired. If there might be something useful. There wasn't."

"Were you disappointed?"

"No. Funny thing is, however, to this day Edward believes he's such good company. We're first names all the way," chuckled Burklund as he held up one hand with two fingers crossed.

"In your...interviews...of Edward, did you pick up anything that might suggest problems at the plant?"

"Problems? No. Such as?"

"What about hard feelings between the top three?"

"Nothing I would take seriously. Remember that I heard everything from *his* viewpoint which was that he was the resident genius and had to wait for the others to catch up."

"Did you ever try to establish similar contacts with Geoffrey or

Michael or James Barrows, the Chief Engineer?"

"No need to. I had my pipeline through Edward. He was really most accommodating. As for their employees, no one could give me the unfettered access that Edward accorded me. Besides, Michael was too sharp, too analytical, too calculating to ever be open with someone like me. And Geoffrey? He had too much business sense—when he was sober—to ever be caught off-guard. But then, what else could he add that he hadn't already told me?"

"Next question: Did you hire someone to burgle the place?"

"No. First, there was nothing for a burglar to steal. Whatever value lay with VES, it was not in tangible hardware. They had no tool or device or piece of exotic metal to steal. The components they made and used are a dime a dozen. The value lay in their software, and *that* you get at electronically. Through a modem and phone lines."

"Were you aware their computers were not linked to phone lines?"

Burklund hesitated and then smiled again.

"No, I did not, but that's very clever. Fits with a small operation. A large enterprise cannot survive without easy, rapid access to the outside world. That's where all those high-priced security companies come into play. I should know...I own one."

"So, one might wonder if you or someone working for you might have employed such expertise to bypass the security system and enter the building?'

"Great idea for a mystery story but doesn't fly here for the same reason as before—what are you going to do once you're inside?"

"Burn the place?"

"Why? What's to gain?" Burklund asked as he shrugged and held his palms up. "And consider something else: hiring a spy can be very tricky because, more often than not, his own agenda probably does not match yours. On the other hand, I could count on Edward's loyalty because of his assumption that I would bring him along with me as my personal assistant or some such after the takeover. So rather than trying to destroy the company, he'd work like hell to protect it. I think you'll agree there's quite a difference."

"I do."

"And then you should consider this: even a rumor that I'm sniffing around the henhouse would immediately compromise several other *very* important and *very* lucrative projects I have underway. No one in his right mind would undertake the risks you suggested."

"Have you had any contact with the remaining Viscount stockholders?"

"You mean Edward's suffering siblings? No. To my knowledge, Edward kept our meetings to himself."

"I mentioned James Barrows a while ago. Your impression?"

"He's the real head of R&D."

"If he were available, would you consider finding a place for him in your organization?"

Burklund threw his head back and laughed. "Chief Inspector, you never give up, do you? You're about as subtle as an American three-dollar bill. *Of course*, I'd hire him! He's extremely talented. Fortunately for VES, neither he nor they have any idea just how talented. However, the worst thing for me to do is try to raid another company. Sure, there can be short-term gains, but in the long run, the raider loses out to yet another raider and on it goes. As for VES, it's best to wait until all the demons have been exposed. And so no, I did not torch VES so that Barrows would be unemployed and available."

St. George nodded.

"You indicated Edward believes he would play a prominent role should you acquire the company. Could you elaborate?

"First, we never talked about it. Second, I was giving you my read on his mind-set, his personality. It would be terribly risky for me to ever voice such a thought to someone like him. So whatever he has conjured up is from his own imagination. If you would excuse my speaking bluntly..."

St. George gestured that his host should continue.

"Edward is a Milquetoast. He was acutely afraid that somehow the YAMATSU deal would fall through. Part of his concern was genuine—VES had not put out a new product for three years. And then a minor one at that. The industry was about to tag them with the label 'stagnant.' The resulting loss of confidence would lead inevitably to a sale, after which Edward would probably get the sack by the new owner. Typical chain of events. Happens all the time."

St. George now chose to use the tidbit of information the Commissioner had picked up when scheduling the appointment.

"On to something else for the moment. Can you tell me the purpose of your trip to Aberdeen Saturday?"

"Business. I can put you in touch with the principals if you like. Involves a woolen mill I own through a subsidiary. I got there about 10 A.M. and was back here by 4 P.M. So I was airborne when the fire occurred."

"Good," said St. George, smiling broadly for the first time. "Well, that concludes the official inquiry portion of my visit..."

"You're most welcome," Burklund said, standing up but looking puzzled that his guest remained seated.

"So now it's time to get to the business portion," said the man from Scotland Yard affably.

"I'm sorry?"

"Please sit down. We're into Part Two."

The industrialist's cagey eyes darted here and there and bespoke the man's surprise and uncertainty about what was coming. He sat down but on the edge of his seat.

"I want to hire you as an official consultant for the Yard."

"What?"

"For a fee. I don't have the voucher with me, but I'm seeking a top-notch opinion and we expect to pay for it," said the Chief Inspector who had not yet figured out how he was going to slip this one past his superiors.

Burklund sat back in his chair as though seeking its support. The gregarious *facies* of a minute before was now replaced by the impassive, inscrutable mask of the absolute corporate ruler. His eyes were drawn to the stack of 3.5-inch floppy discs St. George set on the desk.

"We want your professional assessment of these financial records. We want to know if there is anything irregular or out of the ordinary."

"I don't understand. You can get that information from any accountant."

"Yes, but we're not interested in matching debits and credits and receipts, and ledger mavens are only interested in whether the records conform to the tax code. No, I want you to put yourself in Geoffrey Pont's place and see if everything makes sense. Clearly you did not rise to the level you have without having that ability."

Burklund did not react to the compliment.

"Those are Viscount's confidential statements?"

"Yes, and I have every confidence they shall remain private. And uncopied."

The smiling Burklund now reappeared as he recognized the honor that Her Majesty's government was bestowing upon him. Refuse him citizenship year after year, but when the chips were down, to whom did they come, hat in hand?

"Very well, I will do as you ask. What's your time frame?"

"Could I have your report and the discs by tomorrow noon?"

"I'll do you better than that," Burklund said as he slipped one of the discs into the 'A' drive of a small, secondary computer resting on a wheeled cart next to his desk. From his seat, St. George could see a series of icons and bar-graphs-in-motion and finally a small white window with some lettering. Burklund explained, "Just a routine check for viruses and Trojan horses. It's clean. I'll check the others as well."

"Trojan horses?"

"Viruses that leave your computer open for access and remote control by someone else far away."

"How lovely. However, these were prepared by Silas Muir's bank."

"All the more reason to check..."

Burklund retrieved the disc and slipped it into his main desktop computer and began scrolling. "You've got me intrigued. I've also got highly trusted associates who can help. May take a few hours. Where can I reach you?"

"You have my office number. I'll be there or close by. But take all the time you need. Haste may defeat my purpose."

"Understood. We'll meet someplace later," replied the industrialist who could not take his eyes from the screen.

From nowhere Hans suddenly materialized and escorted St. George back to the elevator for the hushed trip to the lobby. Feeling exhilarated, the Chief Inspector turned in his pass and signed out. And the as-yet-nonexistent voucher? Alea jacta est, the die is cast, he reflected with only moderate concern as he left the building.

26

FOLLOWING THEIR MEETING with Mary Gates, Dougall, and Poole
went their separate ways, the inspector and Cobb heading for
Edinburgh and the detective sergeant for the murder room in the
West Calder station where he would track Michael Pont's movements before, during, and after the crime. The surviving brother had
provided the names and phone numbers for the people and places he
had visited around his Bathgate home and VES and in London and
his used airline tickets and boarding pass stubs. In the folder labeled
'Michael Pont' was Dougall's report of their earlier corroborating
interview with the man's Edinburgh girlfriend. It would have been
nice to have the pre- and post-travel mileage recorded, but Pont's car
had not been in for servicing and he denied fueling up until reaching
Edinburgh late Saturday afternoon.

As expected, the moment he identified himself as a policeman,
the other party became cautious and hesitant and so it took patience
and time to check out Michael's alibi, especially with the London
banker. Or rather, the bank officer's assistant who kept putting
Poole on hold while he went and conferred with his principal before
issuing an answer. However, in each case, he was able to confirm the
person, time, and place of the meetings Pont claimed he had. He also
had the good sense to inquire how long the meetings took, and it
struck Poole that the London matter had been concluded rather

quickly; within minutes, in fact. Having traveled a bit himself, he was familiar with the constraints of airline travel, so his policeman's mind now raised the question of how Michael Pont had spent the four hours before returning to Edinburgh.

His calls to St. Andrews were equally straightforward, yet left him feeling strangely unfulfilled. At the Rusacks, yes, Michael Pont had met the YAMATSU executives there—how did they know?—Michael had called the manager Friday evening to say he would do so and to please render the YAMATSU people whatever assistance they could. But no, he had not signed for anything. At the Links Clubhouse, he learned that all purchases had been prepaid in full by a line of credit from Geoffrey Pont. And that was all. The next person who had seen Michael was his Edinburgh girlfriend. Altogether, quite unremarkable, he thought as he checked his watch: it was high noon.

* * *

Exactly at the stroke of 1:00 P.M., Harald Burklund's limousine pulled up to the curb outside 10 Broadway just off Victoria Street where St. George was waiting. The Chief Inspector had spent the intervening two hours preparing the voucher request to cover Burklund's fee, clearing some cases from his desk, and then strolling through the building, staying on the move lest he encounter the AC/CID who would undoubtedly demand a full accounting. On one of his passes by the department came word from the industrialist that he was finished and wanted an immediate meeting. No sooner was St. George ensconced in the car's luxuriant rear seat than Burklund handed him a slim attaché case.

"Inside is my report. Also a statement for services rendered and your discs. Uncopied."

"I must say, such service is impressive. As is the transportation."

"Well, aside from my office and certain very noisy restaurants, this car is the most secure place I know."

"So you found something."

"Yes. A couple of things. The documentation is in the report. Let's start off by thinking of the business world as a food chain. VES makes components, but they, in turn, have to obtain raw materials and subcomponents before they can manufacture a thing. One interesting item is their source for the basic matrix upon which they do their work. It's sort of a wafer. Now this wafer is a very standard item throughout the industry, though marketed under three different brand names. Price and quality are comparable. Now...like any other industry, if you find a good reliable supplier for something, you stick with him if at all possible. Just like a butcher or car mechanic."

"Right."

"So here's the queer thing: Two years ago, VES changed the vendor supplying them with these wafers. I checked the board minutes, the Executive Committee minutes, office memos, but nothing gave any clue as to *why*. They just up and changed...which is odd because such topics are commonplace at management meetings. So I then checked invoices and found that the new vendor—called Greenock Manufacturing—has been charging VES substantially more for the same wafer. Yet Greenock is getting the stuff from the original vendor at the original price."

"That makes no sense."

"Oh, yes it does. Greenock is a dummy company. Address is Glasgow. It's an investment thing, all perfectly legal, but still a sham in my opinion. Designed to produce either income or a tax loss. What you do is form an unnecessary shadow company and then insert it into the food chain. The shadow does absolutely nothing but shuffle invoices but takes a cut for its effort. So Greenock buys the wafer from the original supplier and then turns right around and sells it to VES for a profit. Aside from an office, all they need is a delivery van with their name on the side."

"It's a phantom middleman."

"Right. Just between us, I've done it myself a few times, and it's a neat trick when it's done right. But the point here is *why* do it? And why would VES ever allow itself to be overcharged like that?"

"Makes you think someone on the inside had their finger in the pie. Who signed for Viscount?"

"Michael Pont. Anyway, I wanted to find out who was behind Greenock because I recognized the name and the signature on the wafer contract."

"You *know* the person?"

"Just by correspondence. A guy named Richard Fogger. He's a principal in an investment company called Loch Capital Ventures. A couple of months ago, they contacted me about the idea of joining a takeover of VES."

"*What?*"

"Naturally I was intrigued about who else was involved, and so I called some people I know and discovered that Loch Capital is a wholly-owned subsidiary of another dummy called Stuart Investments. Today I learned who the real owners are."

"And ...?"

"Chief Inspector, this morning you really didn't have a prepared voucher back at the office, did you."

"Uh, no, but I do now. I have it in my pocket."

"Well, I didn't tell you everything this morning because you didn't ask about everything. But I admire the calculated risk you took asking me to review these records. So I'm providing this at no charge. The owners of Stuart Investments are Richard Fogger and Michael Pont."

St. George gasped, thunderstruck. Unbelievably—finally—he had a possible motive, albeit from a totally unexpected quarter. "Wait a minute. You just said Fogger and Michael signed the Greenock agreement."

"Greenock is another Stuart subsidiary. They kept it all in the family. Undoubtedly, the profits are funding their takeover effort. As I said, it's all legal, but in my opinion, what Michael Pont is doing amounts to embezzlement."

"Amazing! By the way, may I ask where we're going?"

"Heathrow. My personal jet is waiting to take you back to Edinburgh."

St. George was completely flabbergasted. Like others among the lay public, he had read about such people who could just up and fly off on a minute's notice, but they had all seemed so fictional. Dear God, it felt terrific!

"Your generosity is...well..."

"It's not a bribe, Chief Inspector. Oh, yes, I suppose someday I might need a favor from Her Majesty's government, but let's just say I consider it my civic duty to get you back there as quickly as possible."

* * *

Poole checked with the staff and learned that Superintendent Wallace had indeed arranged the Saturday morning meetings with the three top VES executives. Woolsley would have nothing further on physical evidence until the following week and the documentation on the computer was complete. With nothing to do and hungry, he climbed into the rental compact and headed to a local diner for lunch. When he returned an hour later, he found Dougall and his driver back from Edinburgh. They quickly compared notes and brought the official file up-to-date. Just then a message came through to the main desk from St. George that he was airborne and in two hours would be landing at the Executive Terminal in Edinburgh. He asked that Dougall please reschedule the Pont, Cargill, and Barrows meetings for that same afternoon and evening—mandatory, no excuses accepted—and then initiate covert surveillance on all three VES men. Also to begin discreet inquiries into the backgrounds of Michael Pont and one Richard Fogger. Explanations to follow.

Dougall at once set things into motion between calls to report developments to Superintendent Wallace and Chief Superintendent Stallings. As for Poole, he settled into the empty murder room to wait out the half-hour before they left for the airport. For the lack of anything better to do, he rummaged through the week's accumulation of the local newspaper. Compared to the brassy London tabloids, this was a chatty neighborhood publication which reported births, deaths, new residents, and hospitalizations. His eye fell on a short paragraph entitled "Pilot Released." He always read aviation articles because of his compulsive concern for his older brother who was a commercial pilot. Though brother Stephen had never had a close call, Poole was certain it was his daily prayers and his dogged perusal of aviation articles that crossed his path that had created sort of a protective mantra. Kept the demons at bay, in other words.

He read the piece and then, stunned, he reread it and then read it twice more, reluctant to accept what his eyes were showing him. "Hallo!" he shouted to no one as he switched to a chair at the table and reached for a phone. While making a series of urgent calls, he double-checked the article yet again. Within minutes, he had confirmed the story's facts. One Dennis McGann had been discharged the day before from the hospital in Linlithgow after being treated for injuries sustained during the crash landing of his glider the preceding Saturday morning. The cause of his difficulty had been the lack of wiper fluid to wash away the soot from his windscreen after he had accidentally flown through the column of smoke coming from the fire at Viscount Electric Systems near West Calder. The man was resting at home and was expected to make a full recovery.

Before dashing to his car, Poole asked the desk sergeant to please inform Inspector Dougall not to wait up and ask him to convey his apologies to the Chief Inspector, that he would meet everyone later.

27

ST. GEORGE LUXURIATED in being the sole passenger aboard Harald Burklund's corporate jet, mixing such enjoyable thoughts as "If Silas Muir could see me now..." and "What would the office say?" with his disgust at Michael Pont's unbridled duplicity combined with worry that possibly Burklund was adroitly manipulating him. Yet the industrialist's report was as complete as it was concise. Everything was assiduously documented. The man's power, influence, and connections had produced results that the Yard might never have duplicated on its own. In any case, given such a road map, verification now would be easy.

His initial euphoria upon learning of Michael's secret plot was quickly tempered by the fact that the younger brother had an airtight alibi for the time of the murder. No matter how objectionable his actions, Michael Pont could not have been in two places at the same time. Especially two places a couple of hundred miles apart. Unless, of course, he hired the job done. The saboteur Burke, perhaps?

And then, what about this man Fogger...?

As he devoured the hot roast beef dinner that had been served by an equally "hot" young stewardess, he contemplated the world of private security. Many of his former brethren had been seduced into leaving the ranks of public service to sign on with private companies specializing in the protection of companies and wealthy individuals.

As he cleaned his plate, he marveled at all the wealth and glamour surrounding him. Just as quickly, though, he realized that the "grunt," the hourly-wage bottom feeder on the corporate ladder, earned about as much as a young constable. True, the top security man made considerably more, and could revel in his complete authority and his unrestricted access to his employer's luxury lifestyle, but the price he paid was eternal 24/7 availability. Something only a genuine workaholic would enjoy...or accept. Which is why, as he departed the limousine, the Chief Inspector had respectfully declined Burklund's offer to become the head of his London security team.

Inspired by his new information, he decided to tackle another bothersome problem: the computer printout. Nibbling at his dessert, he began studying the bloody thing once again. Moments later, he finished eating and leaned back in his seat, staring intently at the document for some 10 minutes when suddenly the answer came to him. He smiled broadly, laughing so loudly that 'Ms. Hot' came by to see if something was wrong, and then folded the printout and replaced it in his pocket. The clouds of uncertainty had evaporated.

Dougall met him at the executive terminal, suitably impressed by this London copper's ability to secure such stylish transportation. He explained Poole's mysterious absence—"said he's found a witness"—as they headed for their car, adding that the office would call as soon as the sergeant reported in. He was surprised at St. George's bland reaction ("Fine"), contrasting with the twinkle in the man's eye. Cobb had the engine running and they were off without delay.

"Time to put on the pressure," said St. George who then laid his discoveries before the local detective.

"Michael Pont two-timing his own! And that pig of a cousin!"

"Now, now, Inspector, calm yourself. We cannot appear outraged or even angry at someone we now consider a prime suspect. And with Edward the weakest of the three, I want to tackle him first. But before we get there, tell me what you found out."

"Well," said Dougall as he fished out his notebook, "he took his family for lunch and shopping all right. Ate at the King James Thistle Hotel..."

"My, my, expensive!"

"...located at 107 St. James Centre, 1 Leith Street. He signed a credit card voucher—we have both the copy he gave us and that from the hotel. Signatures are identical, the one being a carbon. They then patronized five department stores and a petrol station, making a credit purchase at each one."

"The amounts?"

"Sizable except for one—merely three pounds. Would make you wonder why not pay cash."

"Except to leave a paper trail, perhaps? Do we know if he phoned his office at any time?"

"No. He says not, and his office confirms, but if he called in to his answering machine there or at home from a pay phone, we would have no way of knowing. So if he was timing his trip to last until after the fire was reported, we cannot prove it."

"Interesting."

Set on 50 acres of rolling wooded countryside, the Cargill estate was as well manicured as St. George anticipated, in truth a reflection of its fastidious owner. Edward, the fourth generation of Cargills to live there, governed the residence that his brother and two sisters had fled as soon as they reached majority. Yet for all intents and purposes, his own authority had been only titular until his mother died four years ago. Since coming into "his own," he had managed the place with adequate if not sterling efficiency and had provided his wife and three children with a comfortable lifestyle.

The master of the estate greeted his guests at the front door and escorted them onto a tastefully but formally furnished sunporch. He explained that he had sent his family out shopping: "It's been hard enough on them as it is, but to have to sit and listen to talk about Uncle Geoffrey being an arsonist or murdered is simply too much. But lest I forget my manners, does anyone wish something to drink?"

The detectives declined, with thanks, whereupon Edward excused himself to fetch a chilled Perrier. He returned in less than a minute and settled into an elegantly upholstered armchair.

"Very well, gentlemen," he said, "what is it you wish to go over?"

"Well, to come to the point, Mr. Cargill," said St. George, "we would like more information about your encounters with Harald Burklund."

"Burklund? Why in Heaven's name for? Nothing came of it."

"I beg to differ—quite a lot came of it. I've talked to Burklund. And he said that he pumped you for information which you apparently willingly provided."

"I did no such thing! I can't imagine him making such a claim."

"He said your initial meeting was anything but coincidental."

Edward Cargill looked from one detective to another, his embarrassment growing by the second.

"Are you trying to make me out the fool?"

"No, just trying to dissect the morass that was Viscount Electric Systems. You see, he was very serious when he told you he wanted to buy Viscount. He also revealed that he knew all about YAMATSU from the very beginning."

"Impossible!"

St. George related the story of Geoffrey Pont's drunken disclosure. Edward's surprise and distress appeared genuine.

"You think he had something to do with the fire? With Geoffrey's death?"

"Not directly. VES is not a competitor. And I believe him when he says the plant is worth nothing to him burned."

"Oh, dear God! This is unbelievable! You must believe me, Chief Inspector, I swear to you I *never* thought I was betraying any company secrets."

"Not trade secrets, no R&D material, but perhaps comments about staffing, layoffs, taxes, insurance—you handle that, don't you?—and benefits, overtime, innocuous things like that which, when juxtaposed, may help construct a picture of the operating performance of your company."

Edward Cargill shook his head with new grief. "And all the time I thought it was just banal chitchat. You know, the market and Whitehall's policies and imports and so on. It seemed we talked more about his companies than we did about mine. Or maybe that was just my impression."

"Well, the fact is Geoffrey laid the groundwork and your commentary added the polish. You yourself commented to us about the extent to which industrial espionage occurs."

"My God...you read about such things, you hear it on the news, you think how stupid could someone be, and then...to hear you've possibly done the very same. You've not made my week any better, gentlemen."

"Be that as it may, we are left with but three possibilities. Someone wanted to bring down VES. Or someone wanted to remove Geoffrey Pont from the picture. Or both."

"Oh...Oh no, this can't be happening."

"What do you know about Greenock Manufacturing?"

"Who?"

St. George explained about the wafer supplier while Dougall took notes.

"I'm sorry, the name really doesn't ring a bell. But, yes, there was a switch in some supplier a ways back, but I never really caught the name. If Michael signed for it, then he obviously had the authority to do so."

"How about a venture capital group named Loch Capital?"

"Loch as in a Scottish lake or Locke as in the philosopher?"

"The former."

Edward Cargill tried mightily to concentrate.

"No, not that I can recall. No...Why?"

"Stuart Investments?"

Edward Cargill shook his head, concern and fear etched in his face.

"Never heard of them. Was I supposed to?"

"Even though you follow the stock market?"

"Especially because I follow the market."

"Well, it appears Burklund was negotiating with Loch Capital toward buying Viscount."

"No! Impossible! We would've known! No one ever made any such offer."

"Well, perhaps Geoffrey received an offer he kept to himself. Or knew one was coming."

"Oh, no, he would never do that. We all agreed at the very beginning that anything of the kind would be reported to the others. No, I'm sure he would have told us."

"Well, you see, perhaps that was the problem. Perhaps one or two of you wanted to sell out. More likely just one because I imagine it could become extremely frustrating always to be outvoted two-to-one."

"What are you saying?"

"That Geoffrey, for example, had grown tired of coming in second to you and Michael. There is also the possible motive of someone such as yourself wanting full voting control. The easiest way to gain that is to eliminate one of the Ponts."

"You can't be serious!"

As if adding punctuation, Edward dropped his glass, which splintered on the floor. The meeting was in recess for several minutes while the homeowner clumsily cleaned up the mess. When he was again seated, St. George continued.

"We've learned that your cousin phoned his London solicitor very late Friday evening. The lawyer who set up the company. Demanded a meeting first thing Monday morning. He did not state the reason for the call, but we surmise he was upset about something involving the company. We also know that you and Geoffrey have disagreed with increasing frequency over the past year or so. Myra could always tell when you and Michael had voted against her husband. We know about your history of insider trading which seriously limited your opportunities for a substantial independent income. Your family aside, you have a sizable estate and lifestyle to maintain, and that takes a lot of money. Now we factor in Burklund's interest in the company, that he deliberately seeks you out for conversation, and it is but a short easy step to conclude that, in fact, you wanted Burklund to come in and take over. With the understanding that you would assume the top chair of the new subsidiary."

"That's absurd! Even obscene!"

St. George ignored the protests and looked implacably at his witness. "Or suppose Burklund in fact wanted to buy the company, actually conveyed the offer through you, but Geoffrey balked. You've stated you have many contacts outside this area. It is not implausible that you could have hired someone to come in, eliminate your cousin, and set the fire as a cover. In fact, such a saboteur has indeed gone missing."

Edward Cargill sat aghast and trembling.

"After all," St. George said, "you more than anyone knew the insurance would pay for all the rebuilding and replacing the equipment. And just to be sure you were in the clear, you left these receipts throughout Edinburgh like a trail of bread crumbs for the police to follow afterward. You see, that's what troubles us—your paper trail is really too perfect. Too obvious."

"You're accusing *me* of setting the fire? Of *murder?* You think..."

"We believe we have good reason to include you on our short list of suspects for the reasons I just mentioned. So may I suggest that you retain a solicitor and also please do not leave Edinburgh without giving advance notice to Superintendent Wallace in Livingston."

"I can't believe this!"

Edward remained seated, fixed in place, as St. George and Dougall got to their feet.

"There is one other possibility we're looking into—that either you and Michael together hired it done or that the three of you did it."

"The three—?"

"And James Barrows. Thank you for your time. We'll see ourselves out."

28

EN ROUTE TO Bathgate, they received a radio call that Poole had returned to the West Calder station. A constable would drop him off at the Livingston police headquarters for pickup. St. George smiled.

"Pardon me for saying so," said Dougall, "but are we really that close to naming Edward a suspect?"

"Yes and no. On the one hand, I want to shake up that secure cage he and the others have been in since the fire. With Muir and Stallings and McSwain all working overtime to cover up any hint of murder, let's see if anyone panics and betrays himself. On the other hand, Edward Cargill would not be my first choice for a leader of anything. Harald Burklund had a particularly unflattering adjective for him. And remember, it was not Edward who pressured the authorities to declare the death accidental. That was Muir. And it was not Edward's idea to acquire power of attorney and send the remains to the oven posthaste. That again was Muir."

"So that leaves us with dear Edward as a follower."

"Yes, a remora , if you will."

"Huh?"

"A remora. The fish that swims with the sharks. Yet it is safe because the sharks consider it harmless."

"Well, he does have that paper trail for an alibi."

"Oh, there is no doubt he was there signing his name like some rock star. But as long as that saboteur remains unaccounted for, Edward cannot be discounted. Nor Michael for that matter. Or Barrows."

"But if all three were behind it, why would Barrows not have gotten himself an alibi for sure?"

"*That's* the right question, Inspector. That's why I think all three together are *not* behind it. Michael and Barrows are far too intelligent to gamble their lives on some psychological gimmick that could easily backfire. Like predicting that we would automatically discount Barrows because he was too obvious a candidate. No, Barrows is the odd man out. If he hired anyone, he would have left a trail someplace with someone to cover that time...Ah! There's Laurence!"

St. George could tell his aide was bursting with excitement as he jumped in the front seat and squirmed around to face them.

"I've got us a witness!"

"So we heard," said St. George. "Out with it!"

"A glider pilot. Flew right over the bloody fire just as it started. In fact, the smoke soiled his windscreen so that he crash-landed when he got back to his home field. He just got out of the hospital yesterday. I saw the notice in the local paper. Last night's edition."

"Capital, Laurence! So when do we see him?"

"Oh...I don't know. I just interviewed him. He lives near Falkirk."

St. George could not help but smile again. He had always preached "sensible" initiative to his men but here was one who had actually gone and done it. He could not have been prouder.

"Well, I guess that means I best be careful the next time I choose to leave the area. Might find my self replaced! No, no, don't apologize. You did exactly the right thing. So what did the man tell you?"

"Well, for starters, he can only describe the smoke as gray at first, then brown, and then black."

"Explosion?"

"Didn't see one but at that time he was still miles away. He remembers the flames spreading real fast and he caught a glimpse of the fire trucks coming on-scene. He also remembers the Mercedes sitting in front right up by what he guessed was the front entrance."

"Doors open or closed?"

"Closed."

"Anyone around the building? Another car?"

"No one on the grounds. He saw another car on the road, driving erratically toward Woolfords Cottages. Then his attention went back to the fire."

"Almost certainly our woman caller. Go on."

"He wasn't sure where the second car came from. I mean, he couldn't say if it came out from VES or not."

"Good point."

"But...he did see someone else leaving the area. Heading in the opposite direction. North toward the A71 ... on a bike."

"And the woman saw a biker! Must be the same one! They passed!"

"That was my thought," said Poole. "The pilot's name is Dennis McGann. His brother is big on cycling so he's familiar with all the gear and such. He says the rider wore a white helmet, a vivid yellow shirt, and black pants. Same as James Barrows."

"Capital!"

"But here's the kicker. He said the cyclist was not going fast. That's really why he noticed him. He says his brother is like all the other bikers, they ride along at a fast clip on the open highway. But this guy was just sort of coasting along."

"He's sure it was a man?"

"No. Not from that height."

"Did the cyclist pass the fire trucks?"

"No, they were coming in from the east-northeast. The car was headed south-southwest and the cyclist north."

"Why was the man not pedaling faster? Surely he wanted to call in the alarm..."

"Just like the woman," said Dougall.

"But then..." St. George said, "...what if he saw nothing when he passed the plant? What if he heard nothing? What if he was already past the plant when the fire started? Heading south, the woman would have seen the fire up ahead. But heading north, the cyclist would not; it would be behind him. So perhaps he truly was unaware. Then again, what if the biker were the culprit—but then would he not dash away from there at top speed?"

"Unless he believed that was the surest way to draw attention," said Poole. "You know, running from the scene. And especially with the fire sirens approaching. I mean, wouldn't he stand out, going away from the fire when everyone else was going toward it?"

"Point."

"My other thought was this," Poole continued. "What if the biker could not go faster? What if he wanted to clear the area right away, but the bike simply could not go any faster? Maybe stuck in second gear."

St. George frowned and then nodded. "Another good point. It would help, of course, if you came up with ideas that *simplified* the case, Laurence, not made it more complicated. You checked out Michael?"

"Yes, sir. Mr. Pont spent the day Friday in London, flew down in the morning, did business with one banker there who confirmed his presence, and returned by train later in the day to Haymarket station and then drove home."

"Using his own car?"

"Yes."

"But if he flew in the morning..."

"Oh, right. He parked at Haymarket and then cabbed to the airport."

"Right. Continue."

"Saturday morning he drove to St. Andrews, left early because they had a 10:10 tee time. Met his party, the Japanese chaps, at their hotel, The Rusacks, 16 Pilmour Links..."

"Yes, yes, Laurence," said the Chief Inspector, "we already know that."

"Right. The luxury package Michael described. Two-night stay. They got off on time and finished about 2:00 P.M. They stopped in both the Links golf shop and the 18th green shop for more souvenirs and then about 3:00 P.M. they all departed for Edinburgh, the Japanese for the airport and Mr. Pont for his lady friend. As previously determined, she confirms his presence with her from late afternoon until about 11 P.M."

"You said the Japanese were booked for two nights..."

"Yes, sir, that was the package but apparently they had no such intention. Time only for one round of golf and then back to London. I have fax copies of the hotel and golf club statements."

"Statements? You mean receipts."

"No, statements. The bills themselves. Mr. Pont signed no receipts. That from The Rusacks has a notation that Geoffrey Pont placed a 50 percent deposit for the reservation and that he personally was to be billed afterward for the balance. I checked—that bill has come through to his business address. Being held at the post office."

"Who registered the threesome when they signed in?"

"Their leader. Chap named Tamura."

"Hmmmpf. Michael could have done that as host had he been there. However, I suppose nothing like according the honor to your guest. Rather an adroit move, actually. And the golf?"

"A chap named Montcrief secured the reservations. He's an old friend of Geoffrey's."

Dougall interrupted by announcing, "Here's his street."

They turned onto a tree-lined boulevard filled with fancy homes and two-story duplex condominiums. A minute later they found Michael's two-story, chalet-style home sitting proudly on a small rise overlooking the city. The owner answered the door and invited his guests inside.

"It's not often that anyone in this neighborhood receives a delegation from the police," Michael said as he gestured for the three detectives to take their seats. "Especially on such short notice. What can I do for you?"

St. George was about to reply when he stopped, looked to his left, and then ducked into the adjoining den.

"A trophy room!" he gushed as he turned from wall to wall, each one covered with all sorts of sports mementos. Two side tables held numerous trophies of various sizes. "Laurence, come! You must see this!"

Poole obliged, followed by Dougall and their sheepish host.

"I always wanted a room like this," continued the Chief Inspector as his eyes swept the room like a child in a toy store, gorging himself on the photographs and certificates for soccer, fencing, and cricket. One wall was devoted exclusively to golf. On it were two vertical rows of framed scorecards from some of the most famous courses in the nation. Dougall was thoroughly puzzled at the digression, while Poole noticed how their host seemed actually embarrassed. Something else bothered him but he could not pin it down.

"Really, gentlemen, they're strictly for my own enjoyment," Michael said. "Wasn't meant to be any sort of display. I guess I just got carried away."

"Oh, no, I wasn't criticizing at all, I'm envious is what I am. And I just wanted the sergeant to see that I am not the only one who gets excited about golf. I always wanted to excel at sports, but except for golf, I was just too damned clumsy. Get my two feet in motion and I was done for. However, keep them set in one place and I could do all right. Ah, you've played Turnberry! And Lytham & St. Anne's. Too bad you did not have the presence of mind to keep your score Saturday. Now *that* would have been a card to frame!"

Michael agreed, yes, it would have, but then he suggested everyone would be more comfortable back in the living room. At a nod from St. George, Poole coughed harshly and asked for a drink of water. Michael promptly led him away to the kitchen. No sooner were they out of sight than St. George took several quick steps back into the den and peered closely at one portion of the golf wall. When Michael and Poole returned, the other two detectives were already seated.

"A lot of accomplishments there to be proud of," said St. George. "Probably on a par with the creation of VES, I'd imagine."

"Well, obviously the plant has...had...*has* more permanence and more impact. Any news?"

"Well, yes, we've come up with a few things on which we'd like your feedback."

"Surely," said the surviving brother as he settled back in his cushioned chair, his posture casual, yet his eyes wary.

"Right. We were just speaking with Edward. Tell me, how well did he get along with your brother?"

"Get along? Famously, I would say. Why?"

"Did they share the same view of the company's future? Direction? Objectives?"

"I would say so. Oh, we might disagree here and there, but once a vote was taken, it was all for one. What are you driving at?"

"Well, we're a bit bothered by Edward's paper trail through Edinburgh. It's too perfect. It's like he was saying: Look everyone, here I am!"

"You've lost me."

St. George recited the scenario he had painted for Edward Cargill. "So his family aside, he has a sizable estate and lifestyle to maintain, and that takes money. If he could move Geoffrey out of the way, then he would be ascendant."

"That's absurd! Edward's totally dedicated to the company."

"Or suppose Burklund in fact wanted to buy the company but Geoffrey balked. It is not implausible to surmise that, to ingratiate himself with Burklund, Edward hired someone to come in, eliminate your brother, and set the fire as a cover. Again, he knew the insurance would pay for everything so the financial risk was a wash. And just to be sure, he leaves his markers throughout Edinburgh for the police to follow afterward."

"No! I can't believe you're serious!"

"You would forever be a minority shareholder."

"That's nonsense! Sheer nonsense!" Michael said, jumping to his feet to stand beside his chair. "Edward couldn't conspire his way out of paper bag! Sure, he has ideas of grandeur, but who doesn't? For Edward to do such a thing would be positively suicidal. He needs

VES for his income, to maintain that lifestyle. He has nothing else. What you're proposing is sheer lunacy."

"Well, a saboteur could not possibly circumvent the security system on his own and find his way around without help from someone on the inside."

"Chief Inspector...you're crazy!"

"We also have a scenario for Mr. Barrows."

"You *what?*"

"Did you know that he had sent out resumes and had scheduled employment interviews for this week?"

Sitting to the side, sipping his water, Poole noticed how the anger on Pont's face changed to shock.

"He did *what?*"

"He denies it, but I think he deeply resents the fact that you three never invited him to share the frosting on the cake. Never offered him any shares in the company."

"I had no idea!"

"He claims he was worried about the world market and whether the YAMATSU project would succeed, but I think he was worried about something else at VES. It's also possible he was selling secrets to your competitors. Geoffrey found out, confronted him, and well, we know the rest. You see, we have two witnesses who place a lone cyclist within a mile of the plant that morning. A cyclist wearing the colors James Barrows always wears. And unlike you and Edward, he has no alibi whatsoever for that morning."

"Why are you telling me all this?"

"As I said, we need feedback."

"Feedback? What you're suggesting is absurd. James is as loyal as they come."

"Perhaps he was at one time. But he had the motive, the means, and the opportunity."

Pont shook his head. "I can't believe it."

"Well, then how about you?"

Michael Pont's jaw dropped.

"After all, you were trying to buy the company from under your brother's nose."

Michael just stared, speechless.

"You and Mr. Fogger, I believe his name is. Stuart Investments? Loch Capital Ventures? Not to mention Greenock Manufacturing and the wafers? Oh, yes, we know all about them. I understand the wafer deal is perfectly legal...but also unethical and immoral. I've heard the scheme described as nothing less than embezzlement."

Michael stood perfectly still, lips tight, his eyes blazing.

"It could have gone something like this. Let's say Geoffrey discovered your little plot—or maybe it was just the embezzlement. He needs to find out what legal redress is available to him. So he calls his lawyer in London. The one who drew up your original charter. You suspect he's going to reorganize the company—and kick you out of it. You have to silence him. You contact this Burke, and he comes up Saturday to do the deed while you're playing golf at St. Andrews. In a way, your presence there is just as overly conspicuous as was Edward's. Or how about this—Geoffrey has the incriminating information at the plant. Burke is to burn the plant to destroy the information. Again, as with Edward, you know the insurance will pay for everything so there will be no financial loss. Burke comes up to do the job but Geoffrey is there and pays the price. I think you will agree you fit the culprit's seat far more dramatically and effectively than does dear Edward."

Michael Pont hesitated a moment while he took a controlled deep breath. "But as you said, I was up at St. Andrews. I couldn't be in two places at once."

"Of course not, but that's not the point, you see, not if you *hired* the job done. You could have been at Windsor Castle dining with the queen. In either event, your alibi is worthless. In fact, we are looking for a certain saboteur who's gone missing. We're anxious to have a talk with him. Because an outsider like him would have to have information about the plant and that means one of you had to give it to him."

Michael seemed to stand straighter and yet more relaxed at the same time.

"If there is such a man, he wasn't hired by me. You've got nothing on me. Nothing at all. In fact, it's a good thing you're here and seated because I'm going to shoot down your whole case right here and now. You see, Geoffrey knew all about Greenock. Everything."

"Oh, come now," snorted St. George.

"Really. It was his idea. The buyout, I mean. We were fed up with Edward, period. We decided we wanted him out and Geoffrey came up with the idea of forming a dummy corporation to buy VES. Edward could then take his money and be gone. I came up with the idea of the purchasing intermediary to help siphon off money to fund the purchase with Edward none the wiser. We'd be rid of him and have ownership completely to ourselves."

Poole could tell his mentor was as shocked as he by these revelations. He also wished that Dougall would close his mouth, which was open and ready to catch flies.

"But surely YAMATSU would hamper such a plan," said the Chief Inspector.

"Not in the least. In terms of capitalization, we're about 18 months from being fully funded for the takeover. As for YAMATSU, we would discreetly inform them that we were simply streamlining ownership. Something they would undoubtedly appreciate."

St. George turned to Poole who could see that his mentor was still forcing his nonchalance. "Laurence, you have those VES file names with you? From Geoffrey's computer?"

"Right here," replied the sergeant as he flipped through his notebook. "Read them off?"

"No, show them to Mr. Pont, if you will."

Poole obliged. Michael took only a quick glance at the list.

"And you think these mean what?"

"Your brother apparently spent each evening last week studying them at home. We believe what he found there caused him to call Mr. Brohm in London..."

"Really," said Michael a bit sarcastically.

"...yes, and then to go out to the plant the next morning. Perhaps you could tell us what those files contained."

"Certainly. Purchasing matters mostly. Minutes and contracts and receipts. In fact, you will find most of the material about Greenock in there. Geoffrey was worried that we had not covered our tracks well enough and so I suggested he simply take the time and review the files on his own with no one the wiser. And that's what he did. So sorry, gentlemen, but I have no motive. Geoffrey was in on the whole thing."

"You wouldn't, by chance, have a corroborating memo or letter, transcript, video, or audio tape somewhere?"

"No, everything we discussed was verbal. The first time my signature appears anywhere is on the application for the charters for Greenock and Stuart. Because yes, we had something to hide, but nothing illegal...or dishonest, I may add. But the fewer pages flying around, the less likely Edward would accidentally tumble to our little scheme."

"Pardon me for making an outsider's observation," said Dougall, "but that seems a poor way of rewarding someone who helped give you your start."

Michael Pont leaned forward on his chair.

"Oh, absolutely, Inspector! You're perfectly right! But the man has grown insufferable. Our committee meetings are pure hell because he has to be sure we remember he's as important as we are, that's he's got the bloody extra five percent. He's so bloody cute about it! Who gets the treat this week? So yes, we owed him originally, but not any more. He's made a fortune off the insurance coverage and that should be enough. Time to move on."

Michael Pont now began pacing behind his chair.

"Of course, if you're coming to talk to me about him, then no doubt you spent some time talking to him about me. Well fine, if this all comes out now, so be it."

"What would that do to VES? And the new project?"

"You have to ask? Isn't it obvious? Down the crapper, I'd say. Of course..."

"Yes?"

"Well, everything's been signed, the project goes ahead. *Provided* we can get on the property to clear it. Beyond that, it all depends on what Geoffrey's will stipulates. The meeting with the lawyer was postponed until Monday, by the way, thanks to your investigation. So I guess you'll still be listing me as a suspect until then. Well, tell you what, I'll save you some time as long as you've made the trip. Go ahead and search the place."

"How's that?"

"Search my home. Right now. Top to bottom. I'll save you the trouble of a search warrant. You have my full permission."

"Why should we think a search is necessary?"

Thanks to St. George's teaching, Poole recognized how Michael had taken the offensive and thus had seemingly turned the meeting in his favor. The question in his mind, however, was why his boss was letting the man get away with it?

"You know that I cycled quite a bit in my younger days. You saw my pictures in there from the university. And I still do some now and then. Better on the legs than jogging. Well, my bike's been in the shop for repairs—new cables and brakes. It's in Corgan's shop down-town here. Call him. Well, in the morning, obviously, but he'll tell you it's been there since Wednesday last week. And I have not signed out a rental in the meantime. Oh, and another thing. I don't own any racing togs, period. Certainly not the kind James wears. So you're welcome to search my closets and storeroom and everything right now. In fact, I insist on it."

"That won't be necessary at this time."

"No, I insist! I've had no chance to prepare anything! So go ahead!"

St. George looked at a perplexed Dougall.

"Inspector, on second thought, I think Mr. Pont's generous offer is not at all unreasonable. So would you please accompany him and do the honors? The sergeant and I'll wait here."

While Pont led the local detective around the house, Poole looked quizzically at his boss who sat deep in thought. In less than 10 minutes, the search was over.

"Clean as a whistle," said Dougall.

"We shall make a note of that, Mr. Pont," said the Chief Inspector, "...as well as your exemplary cooperation."

"Oh wait! There's something else. I *do* have another bike. For emergencies. In the boot of my car. Only used it a couple of times."

"The boot?" said Dougall. "But there's no room..."

"Yes, there is. Come—I'll show you. Then you'll have no more surprises."

Michael led the group out to his garage where he unlocked the trunk and with a flourish lifted the lid. Lying peacefully on one side was a mass of shiny chrome and wire and clean black rubber. He explained that it was a folding mini-bike for just such temporary use as he described. St. George commented on the frame's stubby metal struts.

"Well, it's not for *racing*," replied Michael. "It's just to get you to the nearest farmhouse or garage."

"So one just moves along."

"Right. Why would you need anything else? Everyone seen enough?"

Upon the Chief Inspector's "Yes, thank you," Michael slammed the trunk shut and, with another flourish, waved everyone back inside.

"So there you have it, gentlemen. Geoffrey and I were trying to gain control of the company. But burning it down and killing my brother would ruin everything, not bring our plans to fruition. And as for opportunity, as you grandly describe it, I do own a touring bike, but I have not had it in my possession for more than a week, and the emergency bike in the boot would hardly speed me anywhere. And finally, again, and most importantly, I was more than a hundred miles from there at the time of the fire. If that still does not convince you, send my picture to the Japs—they'll identify it."

"Oh, we have," said St. George. "Well, thank you again for your cooperation, but please keep in touch with the Inspector here should you desire to travel. And you might think of retaining counsel—just in case."

"I hardly think I shall need one."

"As you wish. Well then, good day."

29

IT WAS ALREADY dark when they pulled up to James Barrow's split-level duplex. Standing under the porch light, they strained their ears for sounds from inside like radio telescopes seeking the noise of intelligent life coming from outer space. After knocking a third time, they heard hurried footsteps inside. Then the door opened and the resident genius of VES stood before them.

"I knew it," he said as he ushered the detectives inside. "You're late and so I thought I would have time to visit the loo but, sure enough, I'm no sooner in place than here you come."

He showed them into his sparsely furnished living room which obviously doubled as a study area with stacks of books and journals everywhere. On cue, Poole coughed, asked for water, and followed Barrows to the kitchen. St. George took the opportunity to stroll into the dining room which he discovered had no food function whatsoever. Instead it was the nerve center of the man's cyberworld. Arrayed there was a three-sided, two-level workstation built around a large computer and its 17-inch color monitor.

"Pentium 200," said Barrows as he returned. "Not supposed to be available until next year. But I got one. Got OS/2 plus Warp plus anything else you could want. 28K bpm Boca modem. It's a beauty. I can go anywhere."

"Really," said the Chief Inspector. "We have more modest affairs at the office. As Laurence can tell you, I'm always afraid I'm going to push the 'delete' or 'escape' button and erase everything."

"Well, no chance of that happening here. I'm strictly a nonviolent sort, Chief Inspector, unless you try to touch my friend here. Then I consider it self-defense."

"Indeed. Well, if you've got the sergeant taken care of, then let's go back and sit down. We won't keep you long. Just need to clarify some things if we can."

"About what?"

"Well, for starters, do you have your riding gear back from the cleaners?"

"Why...uh, yes...I, uh, picked it up Wednesday."

"May we see it, please?"

"What? Now?"

"Yes, if you wouldn't mind."

Poole thought Barrows looked positively alarmed.

"Well, yes, as a matter of fact, I do mind. What have my togs got to do with anything? Are you saying somebody is accusing me of being out there? Is that it?"

"Someone wearing a yellow top, black bottoms, and a white helmet was seen leaving the area, yes."

"Well, it wasn't me."

"Nonetheless, may we see your outfit? We could, I suppose, obtain a search warrant despite the hour."

"Oh, dammit, all right. Want me to fashion a noose while I'm at it as well? Save you the cost and the bother?"

"Only if you feel it's appropriate."

James Barrows left the room in a huff. While he was gone, Dougall commented on the somewhat ascetic appearance of the place to which Poole added, "Looks like he's put everything into that computer station. Not the sort of thing you'd expect from someone pursuing great wealth."

"Indeed," replied St. George. "No fancy car or clothes or furniture. Just like the chap who spends it all on customizing an old jalopy. Leaves nothing for a rainy day...Here he comes."

The Chief Inspector motioned for Barrows to show the plastic-wrapped garments to Dougall and Poole first. The jersey was indeed a vivid yellow, and the padded tights a shiny coal black. Barrows stated that the bright yellow and the three strips of white reflective tape front and back were so that he could be easily seen by drivers, day or night.

St. George took the parcel and turned it around and over, stopping to peer at a chit stapled to one corner. Poole was not sure but he thought he heard Barrows emit a slight groan.

"Interesting," said the Chief Inspector evenly, "this ticket is for last month. Hmmmm, so then, Mr Barrows, you were not out riding at all Saturday morning?"

"No, no, no, I was, really. Oh, all right..." said the software engineer with a sigh of defeat. In seconds he was back with the smelly garments.

"Not done the wash yet, I see," St. George said as he pulled back from the stinky wad Barrows held out to him. "And where is the grease, by the way?"

"The grease? Oh. There isn't any."

After a short pause, St. George said, "All right, thank you."

The contrite engineer now stood ill at ease, shifting his soiled garments from hand to hand. "So does that get me off the hook?"

"Not in the least. Had you been unable to produce them, then you would have been on two hooks."

"Two? But why?" said Barrows, amazed.

"Because then we would have had absolutely no reason to believe your story. As it is, we know you were out riding and working up a sweat any time from Sunday on. In fact, you could have waited until after we talked Wednesday to do it."

"Oh...damn!" Barrows said as he tossed the dirty clothing into the rear hallway.

"But at least there's a chance you're telling the truth. So let's move on. Have you ever heard of Greenock Manufacturing?"

"Greenock? No."

"How about Loch Capital Ventures?"

"No. Why?"

"Stuart Investments?"

"Look, if this is 20 Questions, I was never any good at it. If it's some type of *Trivial Pursuit*, I was no good at that, either. What's the point?"

"Does the name Burke mean anything to you?"

"No."

"How about Kurtz?"

"No, again. OK?"

"The reason we're asking is that someone may have hired a known saboteur named Burke to burn the plant. Real name is Horst Kurtz from Hamburg but he uses the Anglo name over here. Prefers fire to bombing. He's gone missing for the past week and we think he may be responsible."

"But why would I know such a person?"

"Oh, you could have hired him to torch the plant while you were busy pedaling to Glasgow."

"That's absurd! God, you really think I'm that stupid? I'd hire a guy to burn the place and kill my boss and then la-de-da-de-da go riding into the countryside where no one could remember seeing me? What type of a dumb-ass do you take me for?"

"One who gets upset when he is wrongfully accused."

"Huh?"

"I don't mean you're free of suspicion, but your present anger has thus far been your best and only defense."

"What are you talking about? What defense?"

"Against the witnesses who saw a solitary cyclist riding north away from the plant just as the fire started. Wearing your yellow-and-black combination. Makes one wonder just how many times you can allow your lack of an alibi to rise up and bite you."

Barrows slumped into an empty armless wood chair and cursed.

"Tell me," said St. George, "when you ride, how fast do you go? Your average speed?"

"All depends."

"On...?"

Barrows regarded the Chief Inspector as though he were a dunce. "The bloody hills, man! They can be killers."

"Of course, but I'm interested in level ground."

The computer genius looked askance and then at the other two detectives.

"You mean like out near the plant."

"Yes, actually."

"I'd go like a bat out of hell. No, not really, that would be reckless. But we like to cruise along at a good speed. Maybe 20, 25 miles per hour."

"Which would only make sense since there would be no point otherwise in using such lightweight bikes."

"Exactly."

St. George pursed his lips. "Interesting. All right, for the moment, let's switch tack, let's suppose you're not a suspect. We're coming to you for feedback."

"Feedback? What kind?"

"We're concerned that Edward might be involved."

"You're kidding."

"Why?"

"Dear prissy Edward? How do you figure?"

"Hired it done. He's been playing it rather close with an entrepreneur who wanted to buy the company. It's possible Geoffrey was standing in the way. Then, again, perhaps he just wanted voting control which he would achieve with Geoffrey gone."

"And you want my reaction?"

"If you would, please."

"Oh, of course he's your man! Bloody damn obvious! That way I'm in the clear!"

"I'm trying to be serious, Mr. Barrows."

"Well, so am I. OK, as for Edward, I'd say not on your life. He hasn't got the moxie, for one thing. And he hasn't got the smarts, for another. You may as well know that he got into trouble in his younger days with a bit of illegal trading. Damned near got acquainted with the inside of a gaol. Pretty dumb stunt he pulled. So I don't see him suddenly becoming some great criminal mastermind."

"How did you learn of his indiscretion?"

"Is that what they call it? Indiscretion? Heck, I got it from one of my buddies on the Web. The Internet. Chap in one of the ministries in London."

"Ah, yes. All right, how about Michael?"

"Why would he want to do anything? He's got a sweet ride as it is. I stare at the screen and he plays golf."

"It happens that he was trying to buy the company outright."

"Michael? Naw! Go on!"

"On the sly no less."

"Really? Why?"

"We were hoping you could shed some light."

"Not me. Sounds crazy. Got nothing to gain and everything to lose."

St. George nodded and looked at his shoes for a moment. "All right. What about this Manning chap. Head Technician."

"Don't know why he'd do anything. He's got the best job in the whole area. He's paid way above scale and he knows it."

"Does the name Harald Burklund mean anything?"

"He's a big industrial wheeler-dealer down in London."

"Ever talk to him?"

"No."

"Write to him?"

"No."

"Why not?"

"No reason to."

"Has he ever written to you?"

"No."

"Didn't send him your resume?"

"No. He doesn't do anything with computers. And he's already got loads of engineers working for him. No place for me to fit in."

The interview concluded shortly thereafter, and the detectives left the bewildered Chief Engineer standing in his doorway, trying to decide whether he should get a lawyer as they had advised or try and wing it on his own. Watching the police sedan disappear into the night, he decided he had a better idea – he'd get on the 'Net' and get ideas from some of his friends.

30

BACK AT THE station, all parties agreed on take-out for supper, but not on the source. After negotiations stalled, each went his own way and so the following half-hour saw a procession of deliverymen bearing country-fried chicken, Chinese beef and vegetables, pepperoni pizza, fish filets with fries, and double-beef cheeseburger with tomato, lettuce, onions, special sauce, and fries. Even Marcus Woolsley showed up, courtesy of St. George's invitation, and surprised everyone by devouring a medium supreme pizza all by himself. Finally, amid belches, burps, and "Excuse me's", the table was cleared, and St. George— soda can in hand—called the team's second general conference to order.

"Right...I should like to mention that Five have located our man Burke. Chap's been in the hospital for the past week. Gallbladder trouble. Went in jaundiced. Stone in his common duct, they say. Has a 12-inch incision. Just now getting up and around. Going home this weekend."

"So much for him being the outside saboteur," said Dougall.

"Yes, and it also makes it far less likely another local professional was involved. Theoretically, had well-financed entities such as Herr Burklund or YAMATSU had it done, the firebug would have been out of the country by that evening. Certainly hope that's not the case. However, that notwithstanding, I believe we can place the saboteur idea on the inactive list. Any objections? No? Very well, let's move on to the other employees. Inspector, what else do we know about them?"

Dougall cleared his throat and began. "They've all got their alibis for that morning. Almost all were in the presence of someone else. We really never got into who might have a motive. Seeing as how they've all been there so long, guess we'll need to get on that."

St. George frowned, slouched down in his seat, crossed his arms, and stared at the floor.

"No one fired, no one quit, or reprimanded?"

"Not that we know of. Of course, what information we have comes from the office staff. No independent confirmation...yet."

"No one denied promotion—like Barrows?"

"No, sir."

"All right. What of your interview with Mary Gates this morning?"

"Didn't really have much to contribute," Dougall began. "She's quite the busy person, I guess, fills in with several tasks. And—if you'll grant me permission to extrapolate a bit—I think serves as the office gossip. As for the copier, she voiced the opinion that Geoffrey was coming out to the plant Saturday to work. Even told Michael that when he called her at home."

"Michael? Not Geoffrey?"

"Right. Geoffrey never said a word. But it seems Michael calls her pretty regularly to find out what's going on in the office in his absence. She says it's only about schedule changes and meetings, but I think she enjoys bending the ear of the Number Two man. Gossip again. She's also of the opinion he has a girlfriend in Glasgow as well as Edinburgh."

St. George snorted. "Glasgow seems to be a popular destination. First Barrows, then Michael the thief, and now Michael the lover."

Dougall hesitated and then continued. "Mrs. Gates did say that she had seen Geoffrey take files out of the main file room. Not send anyone to do it for him. She thought he was taking them home. She was concerned that maybe something was wrong but Michael assured her there was no problem."

"*Michael* knew Geoffrey was taking files home?"

"Yes, sir."

"This man becomes more remarkable with every minute! How interesting! On Friday evening, he's in full knowledge of his brother secretly checking company files. Which presents us a fine kettle of fish, does it not? If we attach a 'sinister' tag to that knowledge, then we have Michael alerted that he's about to be found out about either the Greenock deception or the buyout plot or both. He thus has incentive to move quickly and burn the plant and dispatch his brother."

"Buyout plot? What buyout plot?" asked Chief Superintendent Stallings, who had suddenly appeared. He, too, had been invited by St. George to attend the supper but had declined. In fact, all three London men just could not picture the man gnawing away at fried chicken or pizza. He was just not the type.

St. George recounted, for the Chief Superintendent's benefit, the revelations about Michael Pont's conspiracy with Richard Fogger.

"That's positively awful!" Stallings said.

"Quite. And I'm very unsure whether I believe him about Geoffrey being in the know. Sounds awfully clean, awfully tidy. If true, it wraps up the entire disclosure in a harmless neat package."

"How so?" said Stallings.

"Well, if Michael and Geoffrey were truly in the thing together to free themselves of Edward's participation in the company, then Michael could not have been surprised by Mrs. Gates's Friday evening disclosure. That knowledge would then qualify as 'innocent.' So how do we wish to read it? Oh, what a lovely war!"

"Sir? A question?" said Poole. "Do we have any indication that Barrows had the same knowledge? About Geoffrey and the files, I mean?"

"I don't believe so unless someone is deliberately withholding. Why would Barrows even be interested—Of course! If he were stealing company secrets, he would be on the watch for any sign of someone checking company files!"

"Well, then," said Poole, "consider this: Suppose Geoffrey was on to Barrows for stealing secrets. Only Barrows has no idea that Geoffrey is on his trail. And he has no idea that the copier is primed for use Saturday morning. And he has no idea when Geoffrey intends to be out there. So Geoffrey would stumble onto Barrow's arson plot only by the sheerest coincidence rather than be deliberately invited, if you will, by Michael."

"Excellent summation, Laurence! Inspector, our surveillance teams in place?"

"Yes, sir. Four shifts of six hours."

"All right. As for the remaining employees, let's put some men to questioning them starting tonight."

"You're thinking an employee could be the weak link?" Dougall asked.

"For questioning, hopefully so. Yet he or she would have to be the mastermind. And would have hired an outsider, the same as we postulated for Edward and Michael. However, my reason for expanding the inquiry is to try and make somebody nervous. Make them afraid we've uncovered something they overlooked. In the meantime, let's continue pressuring our four chief suspects."

"Four?" said Stallings.

"Yes, we're still up against the idea that Geoffrey was the culprit. His entry card was used at the plant Saturday and his Mercedes was the only vehicle on-site."

"Oh, right, of course."

"Very well, then," said the Chief Inspector as he straightened in his chair, "let's start with Geoffrey. He had opportunity, obviously; the means, possibly—though how did he dispose of the sprayer since it was not in his car; motive unknown, especially if Michael's story is true and he and Geoffrey were trying to unload Edward. Agreed?"

A gentle murmur circled the room.

"Then Michael: no opportunity except through a hired agent, no means, but one hell of a motive. Or, according to him, no motive at all. Objections?"

There were none.

"Then Edward: no opportunity but, like Michael, the possible hire of an accomplice; as for motive, we turn to Harald Burklund. Altogether, however, a much weaker candidate than Michael.

"And finally James Barrows: opportunity certainly—he could bike his way to hell and back, the means certainly in terms of knowledge and taking the paraphernalia with him, and twin motives."

"Two?" said Dougall. "Pardon me, I must be dense."

"No, no, that's why we're talking this through. His first motive is resentment at being excluded from an ownership position. Being unappreciated. We must not forget that lack of recognition for one's efforts is the most common cause for employee dissatisfaction and disaffection. And even violence. The second motive—as yet unproven—involves selling company secrets. Now then, all in all, the one strong factor linking all four men to the crime is their intimate knowledge of the place. The crime simply could not have been committed without one or more of them contributing that knowledge to the arsonist-slash-killer. That's our one absolute."

"Mind an extra problem?" said Poole.

The Chief Inspector's reply was a pair of raised eyebrows.

"Edward has never had a card for the grounds or the building. And how could he supply a hired bug with the means to get by the security system so cleanly unless he had such a card?"

"Good point. I think it would be necessary for the infiltrator to have either one of the five magic cards or a duplicate."

"Yet all five cards were quickly and easily accounted for," said Dougall.

"Which rules out simple loss or theft unless one of those five is the duplicate."

"All five were the originals," said Dougall. "Actually, that should be four since Geoffrey's was burnt and melted. Although I suppose that could have been the duplicate. Effective way of disposing of it."

"Yes...except ... then what would the killer do with the real card key? He could not risk being caught anywhere near it. And to have Geoffrey's card show up would only point to an accomplice. No, I think Geoffrey's card was on his person when he died. If there were a duplicate, the killer took it with him and I'm sure destroyed it."

Poole raised his hand. "But you can't really copy one of those cards, can you? You'd have to make a twin of the original, a clone if you will, and that would mean using the in-house computer system. I mean they must have the necessary software stored somewhere just as a precaution. Anyway, that would point to both Michael and Barrows."

"Indeed. Oh, by the way....speaking of computers..."

St. George produced the now-wrinkled security system printout and asked Dougall to make copies for everyone.

"It's ironic," the Chief Inspector said, "but when people are preconditioned to expect something complicated and intricate, they will not see what is plain and straightforward. As I believe this record is here. Inspector Dougall made a valuable comment the other morning—that the Ponts installed a simple security system because it was far less likely to develop anomalies and glitches over time. Their concern was with unauthorized visitors and industrial spies lingering after hours. Yet everyone who has reviewed this record says the system malfunctioned and that, aside from Geoffrey's entry at 9:17, the record is gibberish. But if we're to do our job right, we must give a look at the other side. What if their simple, binary, on-and-off system actually worked the way they intended? What if this record is accurate? What then?" He paused as Dougall handed out the copies.

"To begin, look at the right-hand columns for the temperature and humidity for the work area, R&D, and the business offices. We know the fire started around 10 A.M. because of the fire alarms and because the electricity cut off shortly thereafter. The entire plant was climate controlled. Laminar flow ventilation was used in R&D and the work area. So we would expect very little environmental change over an hour's time, and indeed, until 9 A.M. that was the case. But then the temperature in the office rises a bit right after 9 o'clock. And then again at 9:20 and stays there until 10 A.M. I submit this represents the presence of two warm bodies within that space. Geoffrey Pont and his killer. Then notice another rise at 10 A.M.— which I believe represents the fire's ignition. Marcus, you agree?"

"Hmmmm. Plausible."

"Next, examine the readings for the work area. Everything's boringly status quo until 9:30 when the humidity rises a notch. As sensitive as such instruments must be, there has to be a substantial change in the atmosphere of that entire section to register any change at all. I submit this was the result of the acetone being sprayed about the building."

"Ahem!" coughed Woolsley politely. "Cautionary word, if I may. I'm not a physical chemist, but I'm not sure that the pressure exerted by the acetone vapor would be measured by the hygrometer. If it was, then you're on solid ground. But if not, then I'd suggest not making the humidity thing central to your argument. As I see it, your main point is that the systems for measuring the temperature and humidity and the systems for compiling and printing that data all remained operative until the bitter end. Thus, your thesis about the security system data being valid as well has merit. That's all. You may continue."

"Oh, *thank* you, O Exalted One!"

"As always, your obedient servant, sir," said Woolsley with another flourish and a bow.

"All right, getting back to my brilliant deduction....Consider the security system as two distinct parts. You have the grounds and you have the building itself. Take the building first and start with the end of the record and work backward. Ignore the letters for the time being. Look at the 'access' column. Look at the four entries right there at 9:20. The system is turned on, then off, then on, then off. Just like flipping a light switch. On-off-on-off. Simple. But how can you turn the system ON unless it was already OFF? The only answer possible is that the entry at 8:51 is *correct*—the security system was turned *off* at that time. Nearly a half-hour *before* Geoffrey Pont passed the guard shack.

"Now...look at the time column and the entries at 9:01 and 9:05. The inner door is opened five times in rapid succession...and then *left* open. Something placed as a doorstop, I would imagine. Again *before* Geoffry ever shows up."

Dougall spoke next.

"What if Geoffrey got onto the grounds, did all this, then left and drove back with his car, parked out front..."

"All for the purpose of framing himself?" said St. George.

"Uh, right, not much point."

"For the moment, gentlemen," the Chief Inspector said, "let's just say that someone got onto the grounds and at 8:51 A.M. shut off the security system with the proper card. They then waited outside the building for nine minutes before opening the inner door twice and later three times and bracing it open. Keep in mind that stepping on the doorsills does not trigger anything. One must step on the flooring. Anyone halfway athletic could easily accomplish this. So, Geoffrey passes the guard shack at 9:17 and finds the place wide open. He's surprised and shocked—or was he? Did he expect to find someone already there? In any case, I submit he died promptly upon going inside. His killer then flipped the system on-and-off, leaving the impression that Geoffrey had done so. As we have discussed before, only someone intimately acquainted with VES and its security system could know it could be so easily manipulated."

"Well done, Byram, I concur," said Woolsley. "There's also the three-minute interval between the man's arrival at the gate and his supposed entry into the building. Three minutes to do what? Daydream? The fact that he parked his car right at the front door suggests to me he was quite upset and agitated. Certainly wouldn't take him three minutes to find his way inside. Might have taken someone three minutes to kill him, however."

"Yes!" said St. George. "Marcus, you're a genius!"

"Come on, you know flattery will not reduce your debt to me one whit."

"So that puts Edward and the other employees on the back burner, does it not?" said Poole. "And if it were Barrows, biking there and back, how did he get onto the grounds without being detected by the system?"

"Aye, there's the rub," replied the Chief Inspector, "and I believe I have the solution. All right, as for the little matter of gaining access to the grounds ... Inspector Dougall, will you please recount for us the distribution of the infrared beams and the outdoor pressure sensors?"

"Yes, sir. The beams are inside the building when the security system is activated. The pressure sensors are set under the pavement alongside the guard shack. Where you come up to the crossbar. Once past, you're clear. But then they've got sensors under the sod alongside the driveway and then all around the perimeter of the paved ground. So anyone trying to walk around the crossbar or across the grassy boundary will be detected before they ever get to the concrete surface. Again it's a simple system, but effective."

"And I believe you told us that the sensors do not directly abut the driveway or the pavement but leave a gap of about two inches."

"Correct. Far too narrow for anyone to walk along. Even heel-toe. Absolutely impossible."

"Indeed. So again we're looking for someone who *knows* where the sensors were placed. Someone who *knows* about that two-inch gap."

"Back to Geoffrey, Edward, Michael, and Barrows," grumbled Dougall.

"A bicycle?" said Poole.

"Exactly. I believe someone rode a bicycle along that narrow ribbon of turf. He came riding past the guard shack, past the lowered crossbar, and up to the unwired pavement. He left the same way."

"Which would eliminate Geoffrey because no bike was found at the scene," said Poole.

"That's the way I read it," said St. George as he leaned back and stretched.

"And both Barrows and Michael ride bikes," said Dougall. "I don't think Edward does. Probably ought to check that out anyway."

"We can do that tomorrow. All right, then, let's go over alibis again. Barrows has none and must go to the top of the list. Inspector, will you review what you found for Edward and Michael?"

With an eye on his superior at the far end of the table, Dougall put on his most professional performance, trying to emulate what he had observed in St. George and even Det. Sgt. Poole. The result was a surprised and then pleased look on the part of Chief Superintendent Stallings. When the inspector finished, St. George had a question.

"But it leaves us with sort of a curious oddity, wouldn't you say,

Marcus?"

Woolsley had busied himself during the recitation with looking bored beyond human endurance but now rousted himself into a more upright position.

"It seems one man signed his name all over southern Scotland while the other didn't bother to make his mark anywhere."

"Yes. Interesting, don't you think?" St. George said. "Here we are, smack dab in the middle of a murder case, and we have an almost burdensome amount of tangible proof supporting the alibi of one of our prime suspects. For another we have literally none, and for the third, only a distant mirage. But as long as people will vouch for Michael during Saturday morning, his position seems unassailable."

"Even if we discount his alibi," added Poole, "Michael's bike was not available on Saturday; but Barrows' was."

St. George frowned. "Ah, yes, but remember your idea from before? That perhaps the mystery bike could not go fast? And Michael's reply tonight when I commented about the heavy, short struts on his fold-up bike? When he said it was not built for speed? What if his accomplice parked somewhere within range and then pedaled over?"

"Either bike could have passed by the sensors," said Dougall.

"Gentlemen!" snapped Chief Superintendent Stallings. "You're overlooking something very fundamental. As Dr. Woolsley pointed out, the people at St. Andrews vouch for Michael. And that includes the Japanese who would have recognized an impostor. We sent over an old newsphoto by fax and they confirmed it was he. So Michael could not have been down here."

"Not so, actually," said St. George. "The Japanese never laid eyes on Michael Pont before Saturday. He was conveniently out of town all day Friday. And newsphotos tend to be grainy and indistinct. So in the end, like Barrows, all we really have for proof is his word. And as for Barrows, unless somebody unexpectedly comes forward, there is no possible way of pinning down his movements. However...we can make or break Michael's alibi."

"How so?" asked Stallings.

"By going to St. Andrews. Inspector, would you be so kind as to make train and bus arrangements for us? For first thing in the morning? And return, of course." Dougall rose and left the room to pass on the assignment. "And Laurence, see if you can find that chap who made the golf reservations. Have him meet us at the R&A."

"Right, sir," said Poole, who reached for a file on a side table.

With visibly increased confidence, Stallings posed the question: "Well, then, think of this: if Michael Pont did not play golf at St. Andrews, then who did?"

Saturday again

31

ST. GEORGE HAD been up since dawn, pacing first the hotel and later the police station as he put the finishing touches on the day's agenda. Woolsley had left at first light, packing his van the evening before. Excluding their own adventure to the Kingdom of Fife, most important was Dougall's assignment to complete the dossier on Richard Fogger. Initial inquiries from the day before had as yet gone unanswered and so aggressive follow-up was needed. Operating under Chief Superintendent Stallings' oversight and with clearance from the Yard's financial division, Dougall settled into his office to begin his daunting task. The remaining West Calder officers that could be spared commenced their questioning of the remaining VES employees either by phone and or in person, their objective being to leave the impression that a dragnet was underway. All the while, everyone operated under strict instructions to communicate *nothing* about the case to *anyone*—especially to Michael Pont, James Barrows, and Edward Cargill. Any calls from Silas Muir, his associates, or Myra Pont were to be passed on to Chief Superintendent Stallings.

Poole had privately questioned trusting the local commander, but St. George explained that he had informed the policeman by phone late the previous evening that his land partnership investment was now official evidence. Stallings needed no prompting to understand that any semblance of laggardly effort on his part would be seen as compromising the investigation for his own financial gain. Therefore, St. George felt he and Poole were leaving the West Calder end in reliable hands, Silas Muir or no Silas Muir.

As for the Scotland Yard men themselves, Cobb got them under way promptly at 8:30. Awaiting them on the rear seat were two messages and an envelope. The first was a fax from Woolsley's office that the lot numbers from the condom packets came from a shipment to Glasgow earlier that summer. "Glasgow, again" Poole said. Next, a lone partial fingerprint was too smudged to be useful. Third, the envelope contained the old *Times* newsphoto of Michael Pont that had been faxed to Kobi, Japan. An attached notation stated that the three YAMATSU executives identified the photo as the man with whom they had played golf. The Japanese could not understand why such a question was being asked by a police agency. That they expected an answer was clearly implied.

"'Bout does it, huh, Gov?" said Poole, affecting his best Cockney manner.

"Perhaps," said the Chief Inspector as he slid the photo back inside the envelope. "Nevertheless, it won't hurt to confirm Michael's alibi on-site. Were the situation reversed and he had played in Tokyo, then I think one could complain about our traveling there in light of other seemingly positive evidence. But I have to say, with this particular photo, I think the best one could do is speak to resemblance rather than outright identification. In any case, I think it's still to our advantage to be away today for I imagine about now Herr Muir is receiving his own query from Japan about that picture. As if questions from the Chief Constable were not enough. We can do without his outrage until this evening."

"But if Michael was playing golf, then he had to have hired somebody to kill his brother."

"Well, ironically, as Stallings indicated, if he was not on the Old Course, then he becomes our prime suspect. And we're still left with discovering who did the actual murder and burning. But if he *was* on the Old Course, then it falls to James Barrows as prime suspect. That's what I don't like—having too many options about whom to arrest. To me that spells missing links and a weak case. It's bad enough that the evidence against Barrows is only circumstantial. And worse yet, mind you, neither man ever threatened the victim. So we have a great deal at stake on this trip. Nevertheless, we can still enjoy it."

They rode in silence thereafter until they reached Waverly Station, where they bid Cobb farewell and then sought out their train. A bit Sherlockian, thought Poole as they picked up their tickets, boarded, and took their seats. Maybe St. George had an old Bradshaw's in his hip pocket? All in all, he had to concede his mentor's idea of a day trip by rail and bus made for a nicer hiatus than traveling by car. And he relished the chance to get away from the intense silent scrutiny in West Calder.

During the one-hour train ride, the two men commented on the sunny Scottish countryside and St. George provided some factoids about St. Andrews golf—such as play on the Old Course was banned on Sundays, except when big tournaments were held there. Not to force the people into church, he cautioned, but for a far more important reason—to give the course a day's rest. At Leuchars, they debarked, confirmed their return reservations, and then hiked past an old railway signal hut and the corner of the RAF base with its high-wire fence to the bus stop where they soon boarded the blue-and-white Stagecoach bus #94 for the short haul to their destination. Poole was surprised by his mentor's peevishness at demanding the port-side window seat, but all became clear as they rode along the A91 into town: spread across acres of open ground were more golf holes than he had ever seen in one place— 99 of them, actually, according to his companion. The detective sergeant glimpsed dozens of people out playing and realized that this journey was, indeed, a homecoming of sorts for his fellow copper. As they passed the turnoff to the large Petheran Bridge Car Park, St. George reached up and pushed the stop button and indicated they should move up front. Shortly, they stepped off at the Pilmour Links bus stop where St. George inhaled two lungsful of clean sea air before beating his breast and proclaiming himself ready for action.

"Let's start at The Rusacks right here and then head for the clubhouse," declared the senior man as he set off at a surprisingly brisk pace, leaving Poole to wonder what happened to his gimpy leg. *Reminds me of a child entering bloody Disneyland*, he thought just as St. George called over his shoulder, "Did you know this is a university town? Founded in 1411, it was."

"Yes, sir, I did."

"And that the flag of Scotland derives from an event that occurred right here in the sixth Century?"

"Yes, I believe a Greek monk named St. Regulus, alias St. Rule, tried to bring the bones of St. Andrew here."

"Except that his original destination was elsewhere," St. George said, "specifically Albion, coming from the Latin word alba meaning 'white' which, of course, refers to the white cliffs at Dover. But Rule and his chaps fell victim to the proverbial tempest which blew them off course and beached them here on this stalwart peninsula between the Firth of Forth and the Firth of Tay. Now way back then, the resident savages were the lovely Picts with their delightful bright blue faces and their unpleasant habit of charging forth and braining newcomers. However, on this fateful occasion, a meteorite or some such flashed overhead just as they attacked the stranded party. Left behind a giant white cross slashed across the blue sky. Stopped them dead in their tracks, it did. And damned if they weren't converted to Christianity right on the spot. So Rule and his party were spared and decided to stay and put down roots—and thus the town of St. Andrews was born."

"And later the national flag bearing the white cross on the blue field."

"Exactly."

With more assertiveness than he intended, the sergeant added, "There is another theory—about Scandinavian hunters coming across the North Sea around 8,000 B.C. or so."

"Oh, undoubtedly someone crossed over, but did they settle the place? Besides, does it not stir your blood to have the Almighty Himself step forward and save you and yours from being smashed by a stone ax?"

"I suppose. Guess I need more romance in my soul."

"Ah, here we are," said St. George as they entered one of the city's premier hotels.

The manager had all the relevant documents ready for their inspection. The YAMATSU reservation had indeed been made by phone by Geoffrey Pont himself using the VES company credit card. Follow-up correspondence under the company letterhead and bearing his signature had accompanied full payment of the package which replaced the credit card guarantee. The cheque had been drawn on the Viscount Electric Systems corporate account at Silas Muir's bank. No extraordinary charges appeared on the statement, a copy of which had gone out by the Monday post.

St. George inquired, "I know everything today is electronic, but by chance, did anyone actually sign a register of sorts?"

"Why yes, as a matter of fact, they all did. A distinction accorded only to those availing themselves of our luxury-level accommodations. If you'd like," the manager said as he opened a ledger lying atop the main counter, "you can see for yourself." Finding the appropriate page, he turned the book around so that the coppers could read the entries, among which both Poole and the Chief Inspector recognized names from the worlds of motion pictures, sports, and government. But most prominent were three vertical sets of Japanese characters beneath which were printed the Anglicized names Tamura, Sameki, and Suchawa.

TAMURA   SAMEKI   SUCHAWA

The Chief Inspector commented, "The printing, it's by the same person?"

"Yes, sir, our clerk."

"So if I understand, Mr. Michael Pont signed or printed nothing here on Saturday morning."

"That's correct, sir."

"How about when the Japanese folks checked out?"

"Their assistant or whatever did that."

After passing around Michael's photograph which generated little reaction, the two Londoners thanked the manager and his staff and were again outside and stepping lively, yet a bit slower back up the rising Pilmour Links toward the intersection with Golf Place, the street that would take them to the Royal & Ancient clubhouse.

"Ever stay there?" asked Poole.

"The Rusacks? No, though I've had dinner there a couple of times. Full service establishment, very famous."

"And expensive I should imagine."

"Well, anything bordering the linksland is premium property. Now if you want expensive, may I refer you to the Old Course Hotel that sits alongside the 17th hole? Five-star resort, it is, with prices to match. I mean, when you see a sample menu that includes entrees like ravioli of crab and coliander or medallions of monkfish, you know you'll be forking out top dollar—though you must remember that many people get a thrill from such extravagance. But I say, just how long can such a meal last? Once it's over, it's over. So you fork over your money and minutes later, there's nothing left to show for it."

"Full amenities, then."

"Oh, yes. Even have a golf pro on staff. But you know my preferences, that I am a modest man, and so the availability of an aroma therapist, a reflexologist, and a beauty therapist simply are not among them."

"Hah! You're saying you rough it?"

"I suppose some might think so. Depending on circumstances, I generally choose a remote hotel with good bus service. Failing that, I look for a bed-and-breakfast closer in."

Further discourse was interrupted by their passing Auchterlonie's golf emporium on the corner at Number 2, Golf Place, then quickly crossing the street, and heading north past another shop at Number 6 that specialized in handmade wooden putters. While glancing at other stores like the Niblick Bar and the Quarto Bookshop, St. George commented on the plethora of golf emporiums.

"I always feel like Ulysses tied to the mast when I pass by. You know, fighting the sirens' song. It's a curse I must bear, however..."

"Really..." Poole said, grinning.

They continued along the now gradual downslope past the Dunvegan Hotel and toward Hamilton Hall and beyond that to the solitary, stolid, weatherbeaten grey sandstone edifice that had served as the clubhouse for the Royal & Ancient since 1854.

"Ah, Laurence, you see before you *grand* history! More than 500 years of it. Mind you, these St. Andrews chaps were not the very first to bring formal structure to the game. That honor went to the Honorable Company of Edinburgh Golfers who organized themselves in 1744 and agreed upon a set of governing rules for the game.

Actually, they were playing in Leith at the time, but that's just a detail. Mind you, though, there is a claim that, in 1735, a group of Leith freemasons formed the Royal Burgess Golfing Society. However, that order's passion for secrecy precluded any written documentation and so the claim remains heresay. But not so on May 14, 1754, when "twenty-two noblemen and gentlemen" gathered to form the Society of St. Andrews Golfers—later to become the 'Royal and Ancient'—and to set down the rules of golf in writing."

"Really," said Poole, this time trying to sound genuinely interested.

"They didn't have an actual clubhouse in those days; no one did. So, in 1836, they expropriated Hamilton Hall here, which, at the time, was called The Union Club. They renamed it the Union Parlour Club and remained there for 18 years until completion of the original clubhouse in 1854. The Union Parlour Club then became the Grand Hotel until the university bought it and converted it into a dormitory under its present name. You see that large gray-white cupola on the outside corner? It used to be lead but it melted during a fire some 25 years ago so they replaced it with a fiberglass replica painted to look like lead. Anyway, I think you'll agree it's quite distinctive. It's also highly visible from anywhere on the course, so you can use it to guide you on certain blind shots. Just a bit of what they call 'local knowledge'."

"I see," said Poole who added silently, *Said the blind man to his deaf son.*

"Comes under the heading 'course management.' In other words, rather than just flailing away and leaving the rest to chance like roulette, you deliberately place your shots in specific landing areas. Oh, and did you know that Mary, Queen of Scots, was an avid golfer?"

"You don't say. That must have been dicey."

"Oh, how so?"

"Well, the rules were not fixed until the mid-1700s."

"Right. First consensus, you might say. Before then, every group kind of made their own variations."

"So someone in her foursome was going to say, 'Sorry, Your Majesty, but you cannot tee up your ball in the rough? You must play the ball where it lies?' Quick trip to the dungeon, I should think."

"An extreme example, Laurence, I'm sure, but then again, not unlike many corporate outings today where the underlings somehow find a way to be sure their president wins the trophy. Bad for morale if the chap loses badly. But we digress," said the Chief Inspector, clearly relishing his docent's role. "Last I heard, the Royal and

Ancient had some 1,800 members. Not quite half come from overseas. Men only, of course, and possessing either wealth or social position. Businessmen per se are assigned to the New Club while trades-
men join the St. Andrews Club. Don't think they've set a place yet
for us coppers."

Feeling a bit like Sancho Panza, Poole dutifully followed his mentor up to the front doors and cast a critical eye over the bold white
letters etched in a large brass plaque:

MEMBERS OF
ROYAL & ANCIENT
GOLF CLUB
ONLY

Inside, St. George presented his credentials to the Club Porter
and explained that Mr. Robert Montcrief was expecting them. After
a momentary wait, the man they sought came bustling into the foyer
with hearty greetings and then escorted the pair to The Big Room, a
broad salon 60 feet by 27 feet with a 25-foot ceiling. Six-foot-tall
wooden lockers lined the three inside walls. The outer fourth wall
held a giant bay window formed by eight very tall glass panes that
commanded an unparalleled view of the 1st tee and the 18th green.
What wall space remained was covered by innumerable portraits of
notables from the Duke of Windsor to the immortal golfing tri-
umvirate of Vardon, Braid, and Taylor.

Speaking in the subdued tones so typical of Scotsmen when out in
public, Montcrief asked if either detective had been at the Club before.

"Sgt. Poole has not had the pleasure," replied the Chief Inspector.
"So this is his baptismal visit. I myself have been fortunate enough
to have caught both the Amateur and the Open here. In fact, I was
present in '78 when Nicklaus won the Open and in '84 when
Ballesteros prevailed. Got a quick peek inside then. "

"Wonderful!" exclaimed Montcrief with genuine good humor.
"You sound like quite an advocate of the game."

"That would be an understatement," St. George said as Poole
looked away to conceal his smirk.

"Well, for me, it's in my blood, I'm afraid. One of my ancestors
was Sir Robert Henderson, 4th Baronet of Fordell."

"One of the 22!!" gasped St. George with what Poole thought was
the unabashed delight of a groupie encountering a rock star.

"Quite. Tell me, have you ever played the Old Course?"

"Alas, no, never had the opportunity. I have walked it numerous times during tournaments, however."

"Oh, yes, of course. Well, should you ever find sufficient time to do so, and have the desire, please call me and I will make the arrangements for you. And Sergeant Poole as well. I would only ask that you give me at least eight weeks' notice."

Poole thought he saw his boss stagger a bit upon receiving what he himself perceived as merely a courtesy bid.

"*Thank* you," replied the Chief Inspector. "You have no idea of the certainty with which I shall take you up on your offer."

Poole felt obliged to express his thanks as well but wisely held back from revealing that he had never played the game. Somehow he thought such disclosure would be counterproductive under the circumstances.

"You'll need caddies, of course, rather than bag carriers if you're to have a good round. They go for around £25 plus a £3 administration fee. Payable in cash."

"Must be requested, I believe," said the Chief Inspector. "With some modicum of humility, I've heard."

"Quite true. That's because the caddies are what's now termed 'independent contractors.' Each man for himself and not obligated to anyone else except to be registered with the Links Trust."

"Which trust?" asked Poole innocently.

"The Links Trust. Set up by Parliament in 1974 to manage the six courses here. They're all public, you know."

"Six?" said St. George. "Oh, yes, I forgot Balgove, the nine-hole."

"Right. Anyway, the Trust supervises all course operations, the whole lot. I should mention, Chief Inspector, we do have motorized trolleys if that's your desire, but only on summer afternoons, I'm afraid. And motorized buggies are limited to the New, Strathtyrum, and Balgove. But all that aside, I know you're not here about golf. I understand that Geoffrey is really dead. That it's no longer just a terrible rumor."

"I'm afraid so."

"What happened?"

St. George finished a brief recounting with the comment that officially they were just routinely checking Michael Pont's alibi while—in strictest confidence—they were availing themselves of the opportunity to visit the city. Nodding with full comrades-in-arms understanding, Montcrief asked about the widow, explaining that he and Geoffrey had been school chums all the way through university. However, once VES got rolling, the two old friends had seen less and less of each other.

"Do you know Michael well?"

"Not really. Met him once at one of Geoffrey's gatherings. Quite some years ago."

St. George produced the newsphoto. "Does this look like him?"

"Yes, I'd say so," replied the member after a quick glance. "Fairly good likeness.

"When was the last time you saw Geoffrey?"

"Last Christmas, in fact. He and Myra came up for a visit. My God, what do you suppose his death will do to that Japanese deal they were working on?"

"*You* knew about it?"

"Oh, yes, well, of course, because he had to explain why all the intrigue."

"I see. Well, as to the project...," St. George went on, "it's hard to predict. Perhaps nothing beyond some slight delay. Did Geoffrey mention any details?"

"No, just that his people had come up with something that would put them way ahead of the world competition. 'Leapfrog' was the word he used."

"And the last time you spoke with him?"

"Friday afternoon. I called him to tell him the ballot results. That we had got his people on the Old Course for 10:10. Quite a coup. I'm sure it made him quite the big man with his new partners. Certainly made them the envy of their colleagues back home."

"You made those reservations yourself?"

Montcrief hesitated and smiled bashfully. "Yes and no. In general, tee times are reserved at least four weeks in advance by phone, fax, or mail. And for Jubilee, Eden, and Strathtyrum, one may phone in the day before to take whatever openings remain. On the New Course, you cannot; you simply show up and wait standby. However, the Old Course is of necessity quite different because it accommodates some 42,000 rounds per year."

"Bloody hell!" Poole gasped.

Montcrief smiled again, this time in amusement while St. George merely looked on in rapt attention. "Quite so. Obviously that makes the lead time greater and we anticipate that for the coming millennium they may have reservations out a year ahead."

"Amazing!" said the Chief Inspector.

"Well, keep in mind that for the entire year, almost half the times are consigned to a lottery, or ballot as we call it. You submit your group by 2 P.M. the day before and then they make the draw. Availability varies, of course, with the demands of the seasons. I submitted the top man's name—Tamura, it was—for the maximum two slots and we got one. Pure luck with that, however."

"How do you mean?"

"Well, the New Course reservation was pretty much a sure thing. You see, the Royal and Ancient built the New Course and paid for it...so understandably our members get preference."

"Such plotting!"

Montcrief laughed. "Occasional, tactful *orchestrations*, if you will, are tolerated, Chief Inspector. As it was, I was only too happy to help Geoffrey get his way."

"When you talked to him Friday afternoon, was he worried about anything?"

"No, just paying attention to details like being sure the hotel was set and so on. I must say again, providing his new business partners with a round of golf here was quite a feather in his cap."

"So he did not sound distraught? Depressed? Anxious?"

"Oh, no, none of those things. No, he seemed perfectly natural. Well, considering we had just come through with the ultimate golf surprise."

"So I take it you did not play."

"No. Family reunion later that day in Dundee. Been in the works for almost a year. I didn't dare back out. I would have enjoyed it, however."

"Did you happen to meet any of the party?"

"No, though I was around here in the morning."

"Reason, may I ask?"

"Oh, uh, for a committee meeting. And later to meet some friends."

"Have you received any feedback about the visit? How it went? Word from the Japanese, for example?"

"Not from them, of course, but according to the Links Clubhouse staff, apparently everyone left happy. The shop manager on duty last Saturday is there today as well. He said he'd be glad to talk with you if you wished. Perhaps he might have some information."

"Yes, good idea, we shall do just that. Thank you for lining him up. His name?"

"Kirkland. Brad Kirkland."

"Good...Well, I think we need detain you no further, Mr. Montcrief. But, oh yes, there is one other little thing: did you know that Michael did not get up here until Saturday morning? That he was called to London Friday?"

"No, I didn't. But that explains it."

"Explains what?"

"Why he did not show."

"Pardon?"

"He was to leave a prospectus for me here at the Club."

"What kind of prospectus?"

"Shares in the new project. Geoffrey wanted my assessment and even offered me some shares before they went public next year. He was that confident in the outcome."

32

MONTCRIEF ESCORTED HIS visitors back to the front lobby where vigorous handshakes and more awkwardly effusive thanks and appreciation ended the meeting. The R&A member then disappeared within the clubhouse while the two coppers nodded to the Club Porter and stepped outside.

"You heard him, didn't you?" said St. George urgently as they skirted the wide 1st tee and started along the bordered footpath that would take them to their next destination. The white railings on either side reminded the sergeant of a horse paddock.

"Sorry?" said Poole as he again found himself hurrying to keep pace.

"Oh, Laurence, do tell me your heard him. Please don't disappoint me."

"I believe I heard everything that was said by either of you. What specifically...?"

"The invitation, man! To call him for a tee time! I can't tell you how many men would kill for a chance to play the Old Course during their lifetime, let alone have an R&A member book it for them, and here I have the opportunity handed to me on a silver platter! It was everything I could do not to sign up right then and there! What was wrong with me?"

"Wrong?"

"That I didn't do it!"

"Well, you're not one to take advantage."

"Bull-roar! Wherever did you get that crazy notion?"

"Uh, from you, sir. You said so, once."

"Oh...well, there was no reason I could not have signed up for next summer."

"Except you haven't played for how many years, sir?"

"That's beside the point. I've had a brace constructed at my own expense and I could get back into shape over the winter. Really, it could be done."

"Yes, sir."

"Oh, come on, it's not that unreasonable, is it? Oh, this is the Starter's Box right here..."

The 'Box' was a small, one-man, white cabana with a peaked-roof set upon a wooden deck a respectable distance from the 1st tee. About 20 yards further back was a larger squat structure.

"And that's the caddie manager's lair, called the Caddies Pavillion."

"Right."

They crossed an immense undulating putting green called the Himalayas before reaching the Links Clubhouse, a new two-story, gabled concrete building with a shingled roof, a central observation turret, and a full-length outside balcony. A long ramp covered in AstroTurf conveyed them to the second-floor entrance where St. George commented to Poole that the building's design reminded him of an Anglo-Saxon fortress.

"But don't ever breath a word of that around here," he cautioned as they stepped inside. "The Angles and Saxons were not very popular."

The staff person manning the long, curved reception counter informed them that Mr. Kirkland had been called home due to sickness in the family.

"Nothing serious, I hope?" said the Chief Inspector.

"Afraid so. Their youngest boy has cystic fibrosis and needs daily therapy. They've done quite well with him at home, very aggressive they are, jump on every little cough, they just have to be, and Brad springs home at the slightest sign of trouble. He said he'd be back about 2:30. Will that be all right?"

"Cutting it a bit thin," said St. George as he checked his watch, "...but yes, we'll manage. Thank you."

Outside, Poole asked, "Are we really cutting it close? I thought you meant this to be an all-day affair."

"I do...and it shall be. But never let others believe that you have all the time in the world, lest they hold you to that. But come, we can accomplish no more until the man returns and so we have three hours to occupy ourselves."

As they started to leave, St. George paused to point across the small piazza to a dark gray granite water fountain and, beyond that, the Jubilee Course's Starter's Box. "The fountain and the course commemorate Queen Victoria's 50 years on the throne. I wonder if the Yard will do something like that for me..." When Poole refused to take the bait, the Chief Inspector went on, "Anyway, I propose we see what the shops over on The Links have to offer and then grab some lunch. We can cut across over there—" He pointed to Grannie Clark's Wynd, the public walkway that crosses the 1st and 18th fairways to and from the West Sands.

Poole responded, "I say, but would you mind terribly if we went for a bit of a walk instead? I mean, you already know the golf shops like the back of your hand."

St. George pretended not to be startled by his aide's audacity as he removed his hat and let the mild sea breeze ruffle his hair.

"Well...I suppose we could...after all I *was* up here just last summer...as long as we can stop in now and then..."

"I thought we might start at West Port. All right?"

"West-what?"

"Come on, I'll show you. I know a shortcut," whereupon the sergeant set off along the footpath. Caught off-guard, St. George hesitated a moment before falling in behind his compatriot, wondering where the bloody hell his faithful deputy was headed.

33

POOLE STRODE PAST the R&A Clubhouse and into the large car park fronting the seashore, stopping finally at the tall standard bearing the stylish Park-and-Ride logo. Nodding at the sign, he remarked, "Every 10 minutes. Free during summer. Next stop is a stone's throw from West Port. Mostly backtracking the way we came, but saves us an uphill climb."

"Really," replied the Chief Inspector, embarrassed that he had overlooked the detail his deputy had remembered—namely that, except for the linksland itself, the city sat on a bluff some 50 feet above sea level. Going up the slope on Golf Place would be a very noticeable and perhaps uncomfortable strain for St. George's gimpy left leg, its residual weakness the result of an on-duty encounter with two bullets long since relegated to an evidence box. As he had explained to Poole, when attending the Open or the Amateur, he commuted by commercial bus, special event shuttle, or once even by bicycle. That last had been a genuine brainstorm until he grew tired of traffic wardens constantly telling him to park elsewhere. And then, too, pedaling in the dark along some rural road had not proven the safest thing to do—especially when fatigued and burdened with a fully-fed stomach. So as his finances permitted, he gradually moved closer and closer to the golf course. Along the way, he had seen buses around and about, but had never thought he had the need of taking

one. On this occasion, however, he expressed his appreciation to
Poole for his thoughtfulness. The latter smiled and then went on to
mention that the bus route had eight other stops: the Petheram
Bridge Car Park at city's edge, St. Mary's Place, Church Street, the
Cathedral, North and Union streets, and the car parks at Argyle
street and the bus station.

The Chief Inspector was about to pose a question when along
came a standard model Stagecoach Fife bus, all pure white with a
full-length, broad midstripe of orange, red, and blue plus the Park &
Ride logo. The marquee spelled out 'Park & Ride' and the white
bumper carried the bold black characters K490FFS.

They rolled south back along the embankment, past the club-
house and Bow Butts, and then on Golf Road past Hamilton Hall. At
North Street, they zigzagged to the right and forged ahead on City
Road past the central bus station to the four-way intersection with
Market Street to the east and Double Dykes Road to the west.

"We're next," said Poole, glancing back at his companion as though
checking on a wandering nephew. The bus surged forward again, and
moments later, they debarked near the intersection of City Road,
Bridge Street to the south, Argyle Street to the west, and South
Street to the east.

Walking up to a massive stone arch, Poole declared, "Here's the
main entrance to the old city." St. George noticed that the ancient
structure was wide enough to accommodate only one lane of traffic.
"What you see is one of the few remaining city gates in all Scotland.
I'm not sure when it was first erected, but I do know it was restored
in 1589." He added that the twin side arches and a statue of King
David I had been added centuries later.

"This King David chap...Scot, I presume...how come...why...?"

Poole chuckled, "He was the reigning monarch who granted the
citizens here permission to organize themselves formally into the
Royal Burgh of St. Andrews. Somewhere between 1144 and 1153."

While St. George reached out to touch one of the blackened
stones, Poole explained that the city centre had been laid out along
three main streets running parallel to the seashore: Northgait,
Marketgait, and Southgait. As was appropriate for medieval times,
all three venues terminated at the cathedral to the east overlooking
the harbour—symbolically important because the first rays of the
rising sun would strike the cathedral's bell tower. A fourth street
along the sea cliffs, now called The Scores, had originally been

named The Swallowgait. Secondary streets divided the intervening land into 10-metre-wide parcels with buildings set hard upon the pavement. In some cases, an arched opening called a 'pend' permitted access to rear courtyards while a narrow alley called a 'close' would service still more buildings. Over the centuries there had been the expected mergers and subdivisions of lots so that today, a map might have a somewhat helter-skelter appearance. However, the city's centre faithfully maintained the cheek-by-jowl terraced housing of yesteryear. And not surprisingly, Market Street and South Street continued to serve as the city's primary shopping venues.

"Laurence! You quite amaze me! I had no idea you were into things historical."

"Well, not everything by a long shot," said his companion as they walked beneath the ancient arch and started up the broad tree-lined street. "But my ancestors came from here. Some were Catholic and some were Protestant."

The Chief Inspector confessed sotto voce to being a thoroughly fallen Anglican.

"You're kirk, then."

"Pardon?"

"You're Protestant. The Holy Trinity Church up ahead is also known as the Town Kirk. On the other hand, 'chapel' is generally reserved for Catholic churches. So if people ask you whether you're either kirk or chapel, they mean are you Protestant or Catholic."

The Chief Inspector shook his head. "But that's all so needlessly divisive!"

"It used to be, but St. Andrews has become so cosmopolitan that any residual animosity is highly diluted. Unlike Northern Ireland."

"So only your parents moved to England?"

"Yes. But we've always made a point to keep in close touch up here. By the way," Poole said as he gestured toward the pancake emporium dead ahead at Number 177-179, "in case you're interested sometime..."

"Hah! I'd love to! But I'm afraid you'd have to carry me back!"

Knowing the last thing St. George appreciated at mealtime was a roomful of hungry people accompanied by a chorus of crying infants, Poole dared tease him by adding, "Well, in fairness I suppose you should know that they can seat 100 *and* have baby-changing facilities."

"Oh, no!" St. George sighed, his anguish apparent even beneath his beard. "Tell me you jest."

"Well, it is a family restaurant."

"That wasn't fair, Laurence; it really wasn't."

"Yes, sir," said Poole as St. George pointed to their right toward a dark domed relic across the street.

"That's what's known as the Blackfriars Chapel," Poole explained. "It's what's left of a Dominican friary established in 1274 and destroyed in 1559. Casualty of the Reformation. You know, back then, there was a lot of bloody hell raised here. Major reason was that St. Andrews was the headquarters for the Roman Catholic Church for all Scotland. Accordingly, the cathedral here was the largest in the entire country."

"I say! That would tend to make feelings run rather high, wouldn't it."

"But then there are the positives..." and as they continued on at a leisurely pace, Poole explained that the University of St. Andrews—junior in age only to the fabled institutions at Oxford and Cambridge—was now composed of several colleges. However, in times past, revolutions and plague had slashed the census, once as low as only three students in 1558. Not to mention another time when King Henry marked the entire town for extinction but never got around to following through.

"Bloody Hell!" exclaimed St. George. "Then we'd have Manchester or Liverpool or something worse as the home of golf! Perish the thought!" The Chief Inspector suddenly stopped and stared quizzically at a group of young people wearing bright scarlet cloaks.

"University students," explained Poole. "An old tradition holds that wearing the red cloak makes it easier to see the student entering a brothel. In other words, shirking one's studies. Of course, no such establishments around here nowadays. Rather predated our modern ankle alarms, though, wouldn't you say?"

They moved on until they came to the important buildings bracketing the Church Street intersection. Holy Trinity Church and its tastefully understated, deeply black, wrought-iron fence occupied the northwest corner. On the northeast corner stood the three-story home of the St. Andrews *Citizen* and its ground-level J&G Innes, Ltd bookstore; across the street was the three-story, steeply gabled town hall and a barbershop.

Further on they passed a cyclery at Number 77, Renton Oriental Rug at Number 72 (where St. George commented on the incongruity of selling such merchandise in the land of the tartan), a high fashion emporium at Number 73, and a heraldry office at Number 61. Slowing the pace, Poole took time to point out St. Mary's College and St. Leonard's School situated just beyond Abbey Street.

"Ever hear the expression 'to have drunk at St. Leonard's well'?"

"Cannot say that I have," replied the Chief Inspector who again chastised himself for being so ignorant of this golfing mecca's complicated background.

"Well, because so many of its students supported the Reformation, the expression denotes those who spent their time listening to Protestant propaganda."

"Drinking in the Protestant version of the Good Word."

"Exactly. It's a girl's school now. The library's located in a house that Mary, Queen of Scots, once occupied...as did Charles II later."

The Chief Inspector now caught sight of a three-story, cylindrical, stone tower attached to the corner house at the end of the street. At ground level was a mitre-shaped blue door.

"Called the Roundel," explained Poole. "Part of a 1590 townhouse. Not sure of its purpose, but architects seem to get excited about it."

"And over here?" said St. George as he gestured to another ancient gothic stone archway immediately to their right, this one dark, sullen, and foreboding. Poole answered that it had been the guardhouse entrance to the abbey that had once shared the grounds with the cathedral.

"Officially called The Pends. Altogether gives some idea who had primacy back then."

"Indeed. I don't think I would have done very well in those days. Would have been branded with two I's for 'insolent insubordination'."

A quick laugh escaped Poole's lips.

Now at the far east end, they found themselves facing the ruins of the once majestic cathedral. Founded in 1160 and built over two centuries, the centerpiece of Scottish Catholicism had succumbed to the Reformation and had long since been stripped of its Papist trappings and ornaments.

"Remarkably," said Poole as they gazed at the surviving 60-foot-tall, twin-peaked bell tower, "its structural demise came not from pillaging but from disuse and disrepair. Also some question about the quality of the original design and construction. However, once no longer consecrated ground, the townsfolk scavenged the stones for their homes, the town defenses, and the main pier, which is down below on the other side. Still, the twin towers are impressive."

"I should say so," said St. George respectfully. "I've seen them, of course, from a distance, from the other end of town, and in photos, but up close, they're positively striking!"

"Not to mention that they receive more appreciation now with the rest of the structure gone."

"Right—OK, where to next?"

"Well, are you game for a bit of exercise before lunch?"

"Exercise? Besides the walking? I'm not sure...what are you suggesting?"

Poole pointed to the imposing, 108-foot-tall, square, stone tower standing apart from the cathedral.

"Called St. Rule's Tower. What remains of yet another twelfth century church. I hear the view from atop is fantastic. I've never been up there, so I thought ..."

Common sense told him he was daft, but the Chief Inspector surrendered to his aide's infectious enthusiasm. "Oh, all right. Bloody hell, I thought I was in charge of this excursion..."

He waited by the tower's narrow entrance, contemplating the tall multispoke turnstile set to the inside while Poole diverted to the visitor centre to purchase their admissions. The centerpost's four vertical arrays of seven U-shaped tubular prongs each reminded him of the farm combine's rotating reel that gathers in the unsuspecting grain for harvest. Try as he might, he could not easily envisage himself, or rather his ample abdomen, slipping gracefully through the portal. Just as he mentally questioned the small copper bell anchored to the wall, Poole returned with two gold-colored tokens about the size of a quarter or a 10-pence bearing an eagle and the word 'Freedom' on the one side and 'No Cash Value' on the other. Rather uninspiring, he thought, but then the pieces were never intended as keepsakes, were they? Following his companion, he plunked his token into the gray box and squeezed through and then lumbered up the tight spiral of 155 unforgiving stone steps until he eventually joined Poole at the top.

Despite his discomfort with heights, St. George felt a bit denied when he found that a modern, chest-high, wooden deck fence kept him and Poole (and the six people who had followed him) a full three feet back from the tower's original waist-high stone parapet. This sensible protective measure reduced their observation platform to no more than about 10-foot square, leaving everyone to jostle politely but determinedly for their preferred vantage points.

The two coppers looked out in awe at the panorama beneath them: miles of rolling countryside followed by the expanse of the North Sea and then the medieval portion of St. Andrews spread out before them like tribute to a reigning monarch.

Still wheezing and panting, St. George managed one distinct "Magnificent!" as he turned around slowly to absorb the view. He appreciated the city centre's sensible symmetry that was not apparent at ground level. To the northwest he espied the Old Course and, closer in, two landmarks that he greeted like old friends.

"There's the cupola of Hamilton Hall...and there, to its left, that's the steeple of St. Salvator's Tower. Very helpful for your tee shot off Number 15."

"Oh, yes? Well, it didn't always have the steeple. Originally was flat like this. The French used it in 1546 for a gun battery to besiege the castle."

"The devil you say!"

"No, the French weren't concerned with tee shots in those days. Anyway, whenever you see airborne photos of the city, this is where they were taken. It's absolutely perfect, isn't it?"

"I must confess I've never seen anything like it. Despite the labor, I should have done this long ago..."

"If I may ask, why didn't you?"

"Well..." said the Chief Inspector as he drank in the vista, "my focus has always been on the golf: the tournament, the players, autographs when I can get them, the conversation, the shops, the exhibits. And when you've saved your money all year to attend, you must of necessity concentrate on the essentials, on what brought you, and strive to get as much out of the experience as you can. And I have. So that doesn't leave much room for sightseeing. Which has been fine by me because I'm not the passive person as I think one has to be to ride around and just watch things. Oh, I've gone to cinemas and bookshops and last year I even stopped by the castle over there, but that's about all. However, you've already shown me how much I've missed. And for that, Laurence, I must thank you."

"Oh, well..." replied his aide bashfully.

"Of course, having demonstrated your proficiency, I believe you may now carry on with your presentation. For example, down near the cliff there, is that an old foundation?"

"Indeed it is. The Church of St. Mary-on-the-Rock. Believed to have been the first house of worship here. Built on another site some time before 600 A.D. by an order of monks known as the Culdees. In the 1100s, they moved the church to this site, some think to avoid high tides. Over time the order faded away, and next came the Church of St. Rule and this tower. Ironically, no one's exactly sure when it was built. But then that church disappeared to be replaced by the cathedral."

"Not unlike the evolution of man from Homo habilis onward," St. George observed.

"Pardon?"

"One species of man holds forth until a more advanced version shows up and supplants it. Then that species holds sway until Homo sapiens arrives on the scene and takes over. Similarly, one sect holds sway for a while only to be replaced by another who then are replaced by still another, newer sect, and so on."

"Uh...I suppose so."

St. George pointed next to a crooked stone finger jutting out into the water toward the bay.

"The pier," answered Poole. "Of great importance in olden days of yore to maintaining the harbour's integrity but now primarily a fixture of tradition."

"And all those people parading back and forth down there? Some occasion?"

"Another tradition from the dim mists of time. Both students and citizens march out to the pier's end, inspect the water, and then march back. Shall we?"

"No, thank you. Climbing your Scottish Matterhorn was quite sufficient. You go ahead and do the honors for both of us. You know, Laurence, if I didn't know better, I'd suspect you were plotting to do me in from overexertion and then take my place back at the office."

"Zounds! Alas! I've been found out! I must flee!"

While Poole hurried down to join the pilgrims marching to the pier, St. George finally descended at an unhurried pace after two false starts. The first time he encountered someone on the ascent with a girth greater than his own, and being but 20 steps from the top, he chivalrously retreated back up to the top rather than exercise his right-of-way under mountain law. Then on his second attempt, he twice became momentarily wedged against first another portly individual and then, near the bottom, a stocky woman carrying a canvas knapsack and two shopping bags. Wiggling and squirming amidst appropriate mutual apologies finally achieved safe passage to the ground.

He then wandered among the headstones that occupied fully half of the ground covered by the original cathedral. Turning back toward the tower, he suddenly spotted a unique white monument set along the abbey's southern perimeter wall. From a distance, he fancied it featured the full figure of a man at address with a golf club. Intrigued, he walked over to discover it was just that—the grave of Tommy Morris, four-time British Open champion of the nineteenth century. Tragically, the young man died at age 24, consumed by alcoholism and the grief brought on by the deaths of his wife and unborn child. His father, "Old Tom," was the venerated patriarch of the Old Course, considered the nation's best player until his son succeeded him as Open champion. Fittingly, in death, father and son lay side-by-side.

St. George was still daydreaming when Poole rejoined him, slightly breathless and eager for lunch. They agreed to seek out simple fare and had just entered Market Street when St. George exclaimed "There!" and made straight for a parked white van with the name 'Murray's Chippy' written in bright purple letters. Moments later, clutching their fish-and-chips and sodas, the two touring coppers retreated curbside to devour their meal.

"Reasonable facsimile," offered Poole between bites.

"It serves," agreed his companion after a swallow. "Whenever I feel put upon by derivatives of the original, I just stop and remember that at least we invented it."

"How do you mean?"

"Fish-and-chips. It is an original of Great Britain. Not like chop suey or pizza."

Poole stopped in mid-chew and stared at his mentor. "We didn't invent them?"

"Neither did the Chinese or the Italians. Both came out of New York City, I believe."

"No! I had no idea!"

"Oh, yes," said St. George as he zeroed in on his last morsel. "Ready?"

Sated, they walked down Market Street past Luvians Bottleshop at Number 66 and then more greengrocers, gift shops, bakeries, bookstores, wine bars, and art galleries. Along the way, St. George repeated that previously he had confined himself almost exclusively to the vicinity of whatever links he was visiting and yes, especially the golf shops lurking nearby like a school of hungry red piranhas for his hard-earned-but-eagerly-spent money.

"Make no mistake, Laurence, I've spent many happy hours immersing myself therein. And if those various proprietors included my patronage in their annual budgets, then I must confess they did so with good reason."

"Ah! In other words, you're hooked."

"Yes, I suppose you could say so. But that makes it sound rather pathologic. After all, it's not like I'm a gambler."

Always sensitive to his mentor's sensibilities and moods, Poole hastened to add, "Of course not. Just sounds better than 'compulsive' or 'addicted'."

"Let's just say 'focused' and leave it at that."

"All right. Pathologically focused."

St. George guffawed and sent a playful punch in his associate's direction.

They passed the Bank of Scotland's white facade and detoured by the tiered Whyte-Melville Memorial Fountain and the crowded weekly farmers' market assembled around it. A block later they came to the intersection with Greyfriars Gardens where Poole indicated they could cut over to North Street. Minutes later, St. George seemed relieved and acted like he had found an old friend.

"Ah, yes, here we are! The cinema's right over there and the University library just up a ways. And there..." said the Chief Inspector pointing to a stately, three-story, graystone Georgian townhouse filling the northeast corner of North Street and Murray Park "...is *the* place to stay. Called Burness House. Serves as a bed and breakfast year-round. I had the good fortune to bivouac there last summer when the Open played here."

"Ah, yes, right."

"Quite a tournament, by the way. That American chap John Daly won it. Huge drives but a marvelous touch around the greens. Very unorthodox swing but he got the job done."

Poole shook his head: "Sorry, but somehow I still cannot imagine you in a B&B."

"Why not?"

"I would picture you in a more formal setting."

"Simply because of my seniority?"

"Yes, I suppose so."

"Well, be assured Burness House is not 'just' a B&B. Strangely enough, prior to finding this place, I would have told you that there was no sense paying for a room when one knows he is not going to be in it except at night when he is asleep. The rest of the time, the room lies vacant because I'm chasing around the tournament. For example, there's a popular establishment on the edge of town in which Jack Nicklaus books the same room every time he plays here."

"Jack who? Oh, right, the American player."

The Chief Inspector's shoulders sagged in momentary discouragement, but then he continued. "The place is a bloody estate with 10 acres of formal gardens. Beautiful place, yes, but at those prices, I would feel obliged to stay there and admire the gardens for at least five hours a day just to get my money's worth. So I'm just not comfortable anywhere. And besides, in too many places, I'm just a room number."

"And at this Burness House, it's different?"

"Oh, my yes. The fact is, I was spoiled rotten. I mean, imagine this: breakfast cooked to order, everything fresh that day, linen table cloth and napkins fresh that day, your place setting of sterling silver, very attentive service, not to mention getting a solid night's sleep. Bloody hell, I didn't want to leave! I even found myself—and God help your career if your repeat this to a soul—I even found myself quitting the golf shops early to return and simply read in the parlour."

"Well, certainly not your usual, I grant you," Poole said, "but lodging no more than two blocks from the golf course ... it's got to cost a fortune!"

"Well, ahem, yes, there is a bit of a premium on location, that's true...brisk sea air in the morning and then all the tantalizing aromas from the neighborhood eateries in the afternoon. Not to mention what it saves on transportation..."

"Just how much of a premium?"

"Ahem, well, I had the lone single room, third floor, which goes for around seven times the rate during low-season. Nice view of the ocean."

"Bloody hell! I'd look for a relative!"

"Yes, Laurence, but that's only because you *have* them."

"Oh...sorry about that," said Poole, remembering too late that his boss had been an orphan.

"Never mind. In any event, my experience was so enjoyable I resolved to make a yearly stop up here just for the relaxation of it. Starting next year; this one's already taken."

Poole chuckled, "Yes, I can see how *that* would appeal. All right, so at your present grade, how did you get in there in the first place?"

"By accident and good fortune. One of my neighbors works for a brokerage that was renting the whole house for the week. He was to be in the single, but two days before leaving, he's in the hospital and he can't go. I happened to stop by to wish him well and, seizing the moment, offered to take his place and reimburse his people. Done and done. My last payment is next month."

"And then...?" Poole asked, one eyebrow raised.

"Hah! Yes, yes, I'm saving my sheckels. Have to put down half with your booking a year in advance. Come to think...let's go over."

St. George fairly jumped out into traffic and hurried across to the establishment's Murray Park entrance. Poole was right at his heels, wondering what in blazes was afoot.

"Separate party owns the ground floor and uses the North Street entrance," explained the Chief Inspector as he fumbled around in his pockets before opening the outer storm door and entering the vestibule. Beyond a second door, Poole could see a short hallway leading to a set of stairs. "We have individual color-coded keys for these doors and our rooms upstairs..."

"A bit of 221B, have we?"

"Come again?"

"221B Baker Street?" said Poole. "Vestibule, stairway to second floor rooms, comfortable sitting room with fireplace, reading materials available, and a long-suffering resident manager who cooks for a demanding detective?"

"Hah! Nice try, but I assure you the thought...well, I mean, certainly not consciously, anyway. As it is, our Mrs. Hudson closes breakfast promptly and irrevocably at 9 A.M."

Poole craned his neck to see what his boss was printing on his business card. He could make out only two of the words.

"Porkie pies?" he inquired, knowing the slang phrase meant 'to tell lies.'

"An inside joke. I just want to leave a gentle reminder about next year. Oh, right, we have to use the letterbox on the storm door..."

With his note duly deposited, St. George suggested they move up North Street a short ways to the police station at Number 100. The reason given was simply to pay a courtesy call on the local gendarmes of the Fife Constabulary. Moreover, it might actually convince their superiors back in London that they really were in St. Andrews on official business. Poole's tactful response was 'Of course' as the two men exchanged smirks.

No. 100 was an unprepossessing, gray, three-story structure that one would never mistake for a police station were it not for the small, plain, white-with-blue marquee sticking out over the two-door entrance and the emergency phone box set next to the arched entryway to the car park within the enclosed courtyard. Once inside, the Chief Inspector employed a humble, gosh-darn demeanor as he emphasized that he and Poole were assisting the West Calder police, who had requested they come to St. Andrews. The gesture was well-received by the inspector-in-charge, a husky middle-aged chap named Grogan, who offered to help when and if needed.

Mission accomplished, the London men proceeded next along Butts Wynd toward The Scores. On the way, Poole commented that they were following the traditional path that led to the city's original archery range at the Bow Butts behind the R&A Clubhouse.

"Shades of Robin Hood," joshed St. George.

"Seriously though, in the early days, well-trained archers were the main defense against the hated British."

"I know," St. George answered, "and because everyone was busy playing golf, James II feared that archery practice would be abandoned and he would have no one to defend his realm. So in 1457 he insisted the Scottish Parliament issue a decree banning golf altogether. Fortunately, everyone outside the King's retinue ignored it."

"And the rest is history."

"Not right away. James III issued a similar ban in 1471, as did his successor James IV 20 years later. However, I guess The Fourth got the message because he converted in 1502 and acquired his own set of clubs. And then the rest is history."

Upon reaching The Scores, they paused to admire St. Andrews Bay, during which time St. George glanced to his right and said, "You say the French shelled the old castle up there?"

"Yes, during the siege of 1546."

"I missed that information somehow. Of course, I really stopped there to see the dungeon. Hideous place. I remember bumping into a chap who was taking photographs for a computer panorama. He said as a youngster he had once watched a performance of *Macbeth* staged within the castle ruins. Certainly would lend the proper atmosphere, I'd say."

"Yes, it was a rather nasty place," Poole said sadly. "Construction began in 1200. Served as the palace for the presiding Catholic cleric. Ironically, also served as the site for many executions."

"Mmmmm, yes, I read something to that effect," replied the Chief Inspector. "Anything to do with the siege?"

"Oh, quite definitely. It all began when a Roman Catholic cardinal sat atop the castle wall and at his leisure watched an unfortunate Reformer named Wishart burn at the stake right below him. Then two months later, Wishart's friends stormed the palace, captured and butchered the cardinal, and hung his body from the battlements. You might say they had a different view of due process in those days."

"God, I knew such atrocities happened in London, but *here?*"

"Absolutely."

"And in the name of religious purity, of course."

"Of course. Mind you, this was no sleepy little shepherd's village. That dormitory, Hamilton Hall? Named for another bloke who burned for six hours before dying. You might say the Catholics back then had trouble keeping their fires going. And that obelisk behind your clubhouse?"

"A monument, I believe. I've never really looked."

"Commemorates all the martyrs who died at the stake for heresy. Hail to the Pope Almighty!"

Taken aback at his aide's outburst, St. George suspected that such a fate had befallen one of Poole's ancestors, but before he could say anything, the young detective completed his story of the French fleet besieging the castle and eventually forcing the surrender of the Protestant insurgents. As they approached the Martyr's Monument, both men were uncomfortably silent, and St. George felt obliged to remain so, head bowed for a moment, out of respect for his colleague...and friend. Then, wordless, they continued down the slope to the railing in front of the clubhouse to watch a foursome play their approach shots to the 18th green. As though having crossed some invisible boundary, St. George picked up the narration.

"You know, they've played golf here for more than 500 years. And what may appear to be wasteland is in reality an extremely unique piece of real estate. It is the only golf course in the world that has *evolved* over time rather than being designed and constructed. All the ridges, swales, mounds, the wave-like undulations, the gorse, heather, and rough you see out there were created by nature. Man had nothing to do with it."

"Oh, come now!...Sir."

"No, really. Take the sand bunkers. They came from sheep digging hollows out of the natural sand dunes to create shelter from the wind. Man has simply kept them trimmed and filled."

"So no one laid it out on paper and then hired a contractor."

"Absolutely not. Oh, there have been some relatively minor modifications here and there, but what you see has been here for centuries."

"And they've always had 18 holes?"

"Surprisingly, no. Originally, each course had its own number. Here they began with nine holes, got up to 22, and then for aesthetic reasons took out four and settled for 18. Of course, then there is the theory of gematria."

"Gem-what?"

"Gematria. It's an ancient form of numerology that assigned numerical values to words. 'Eighteen' happens to be the numerical equivalent of the Hebrew word chai which means 'life.' So I suppose you could call golf the game of life. But the Old Course goes that one better. You're aware that usually each hole has its own green?"

"Right."

"But not here. Only on four holes: 1, 9, 17, and 18. The rest share double greens and the *numbers* for those holes always total 18. So you have 4 and 14, 5 and 13, 6 and 12, and so on. In fact, the double green serving the 5th and 13th holes is the largest green in the world. Some 50,000 square feet, I believe. White flags mark the outward-bound holes, red flags coming in. Players seldom cross paths because the two flags are usually 65 or more yards apart. However, some players have had putts over 100 yards."

"It's so wide open...how can it be so difficult?"

"That's the genius of the place. It's so very deceptive. But generally, playing down the left side of the hole is the safest although, for scoring purposes, the best approach angle to the pin is usually from the right. Another feature is that, almost always, a shot that lands off the fairway will bounce directly toward a bunker. I once heard an apt description that playing the Old Course was akin to navigating on the sea: tacking back and forth with the wind. So one must decide how much risk one will stand because a careless shot receives no mercy. Some time ago I came across a passage written by an American author named Dawson Taylor to the effect that, let's see, the Old Course will 'encourage initiative, reward a well-played, daring stroke more than a cautious one, and yet...insist that there must be planning and honest self-appraisal behind the daring'."

"So no simple flailing and hoping for the best."

"Correct."

"Just like a murder investigation at Scotland Yard, right?"

"Hah! Smart-aleck!" St. George paused to glance at his watch. "The time is upon us. Let's go find Mr. Kirkland."

As they started down the footpath for the second time, Poole brushed his hair back. "Usually this breezy?"

"Oftentimes. In fact, the wind is the major determinant of what shot you'll play. The yardage listed on the scorecard is merely a base-line value upon which you factor in the current weather conditions."

In the distance, a group of joggers were doggedly making their way along the beach known as the West Sands.

"Look familiar?" said Poole.

"The view or the people?"

"Both. Remember the film *Chariots of Fire*? The opening and clos-ing scenes in which the Olympic track team is running on the beach during training?"

"Oh, yes, quite. Wait a minute, you're not suggesting..."

"Yes, sir. Filmed it right here. In fact, you can glimpse the club-house and Hamilton Hall in the background."

"How embarrassing! I should have caught that!"

"Well, pity us, if only someone had caught Michael Pont on film."

34

AT THE LINKS Clubhouse, Brian Kirkland, a tall blond man in his 40s, met them at the door and ushered them into his small office. He apologized for his absence that morning.

"Think nothing of it," said St. George. "Family should always come first. Your boy is better?"

"Yes, thank you. We just had to loosen up a bit of phlegm. He's fine now. Mr. Montcrief said you might be by. How can I help?"

In a replay of his performance at the police station, St. George adopted the *persona* of the humble civil servant, emphasizing that he and Poole were in St. Andrews only at the behest of the West Calder authorities. He explained that details could be divulged only with the permission of Chief Superintendent Stallings. "I'm sure you understand."

"Oh, yeah, guess that makes sense. Go ahead, ask away."

"Thank you. We understand you were on duty here at the shop last Saturday."

"Yes, I was. All day, in fact."

"The fellow we're asking about is Michael Pont. Name sound familiar?"

"Well, only because Mr. Montcrief mentioned it. He was with three Japanese gentlemen, right?"

St. George smiled. "That's what we're supposed to ask you."

"Ah yes, well, I remember the Japanese gentlemen, all right. I mean we do get quite a number of foreign players and tourists passing through but these blokes were unusually formal as a group."

"Formal? How do you mean?"

"Oh, all the reciprocal courtesy, you know, the bowing back and forth, and what not. No problem telling who was Number One."

"You waited on them?"

"No, I was with other customers. Actually, I'm not sure who did." St. George produced the newsphoto. "Did you see this gentleman?" Kirkland took a quick glance and grimaced.

"I really can't say. Like I said, I was over at another counter. Is this supposed to be your Mr. Pont?"

"Do you think one of your staff might remember?"

"From Saturday? No, they're not in today. However, after Mr. Montcrief called, I did check the register receipts. The group bought a bunch of merchandise before and after they played."

"How did they pay?"

"Line of credit secured by another member. Oh right, his name was Pont, too."

"A brother."

"Oh."

"In your review, did you see if Michael Pont happened to sign any chits?"

"You mean receipts? No, not here in the shop. Everything was covered by the line of credit. All they had to do was say they wanted something and they got it."

St. George paused a moment. "They used caddies, I imagine?"

"Yes. Our Japanese guests frequently like to use trolleys, you know, their love of all things mechanical. But trolleys are permitted only in the afternoons....Let me check with the caddie manager. Just a moment..."

"In this day of riding carts?" whispered Poole as Kirkland reached over and tapped in an extension number on his phone.

"Oh, yes," St. George answered quietly. "Walking is the tradition here. Carry your own or pull your own. Then they have what Montcrief referred to as caddies and bag carriers. The latter do nothing more than that—carry the bag and keep your clubs clean. No-frills service. The true caddie, though, is sort of a guardian angel who guides you through, around, and over the hazards of the course. Even for the pros, he or she can literally be priceless. Ironically, the very first golf professionals were the best players among the caddies. It was only much later that they diverged into separate groups."

"Sort of a golfing Homo habilis."

"Well, yes, it was, actually. Earliest record of a caddie was in 1833. Rather a shaky start as they were not regarded very highly by either the paying public or the nobility. In fact, some were downright disreputable. Even hostile toward their customers. But that got straightened out and then about 100 years ago they evolved again. Some fishermen wanted to supplement their incomes and so joined the ranks. The thing was they continued wearing their traditional jackets and caps and gradually that combination became the standard apparel...."

"Sorry again to keep you waiting," said Kirkland. "Yes, they hired four caddies."

"By any chance would any of those men be out here today?"

"I really can't say. But Tom Laird, the caddie manager could tell you."

"Then I believe he shall be our next stop. Oh, I almost forgot, they played the Old Course. May we see the register where they signed in?"

"Oh, no, sir, they would not sign in here. The daily lists are kept with the respective starter."

"But they paid their green fees here."

Kirkland shook his head good-naturedly. "No, sir, those playing unreserved times or by ballot would pay at the starter's box. The rest of the week, advanced reservations are placed and paid for through the Reservations Centre at the Trust office in Pilmour House. Just off the A91."

St. George stopped and gawked at Poole. "What a dunce!" he muttered. "How bloody stupid of me! A lesson to you, Laurence. The times I have been here and I never bothered to ask. I always assumed the obvious...Mr. Kirkland, so I don't compound the error, may I inquire whether Pilmour House is open today?"

"No, sir, just Monday through Friday."

"Ah! So there is no way we can check on how the greens fees were paid."

"Not today. First thing Monday, though."

"How about the starter. Might he know?"

Again Brian Kirkland shook his head kindly. "I doubt it. Whoever it was probably won't recall exactly because of the number of players he has to get through. Especially since he has to confirm each player's official handicap certificate and identification. Tourists often use just a letter of introduction from their home club. However, they are beginning to give serious consideration to changing the requirement to a photo ID of some sort. You know, driver's license, passport, visa, what not. Too many people try to sneak in under somebody else's name."

St. George responded with a sympathetic "tsk, tsk" as though he encountered the very same problem every day. "About to do that, are they?"

"Not for quite a while, in my opinion. Lot of resistance. Folks kind of consider it inhospitable in a way. Even unfriendly."

"So as it is, the player has to present some kind of convincing evidence he is who he claims to be."

"Correct. And if you're still thinking of receipts, whatever the starter had he'd turn back to the office at Pilmour House."

"Yes, well, then I suppose there's nothing for it but wait until Monday..."

The men from Scotland Yard expressed their heartfelt appreciation to Kirkland and departed. "Well, so much for my record of infallibility..." said St. George as they set off at a quick step for the Caddies Pavillion. Poole noticed how his superior's embarrassment accentuated his limp.

"How will we handle Monday?" Poole asked.

"I'm not sure at the moment. I'm more annoyed than anything else. A credit card chit would end the matter because, with no advance reservation, there would be no advance payment. It would all be done at the Starter's Box. Either credit or sterling. That's it. The thing is I have the feeling there's something we haven't uncovered, although I haven't a clue what it might be."

"Well, if the starter let him on, then that proves it was he."

"Yes, I suppose so..."

As they approached the building, they could see an older yet burly man watching them through the windows. An assortment of other men, young and old, stocky and tall, wiry and thickset, were standing or sitting on benches alongside the building. None said anything but every eye watched the two strangers enter their domain.

After the introductions, St. George got right to the point and Tom Laird responded.

"Yeah, Brian mentioned you were asking about a group last Saturday so I checked and, yeah, they hired four men. As a matter of fact, Roger and Mac were here this morning. Mac was with your Mr.

Pont. But he's called it a day. Roger's gone out for his second run."

"Have you any idea where we might find Mac?"

The caddie manager scrunched up his face in that universal, time-honored fashion of foremen, bartenders, shop stewards, and others who regularly find themselves interposed between their employees and the public—should they admit knowing anything or should they play dumb? Sensing the latter, the Chief Inspector explained that Mac was not under investigation but that he could possibly prove an important witness.

"Well, that's just it, Chief Inspector. Mac's as solid as they come, and I wouldn't like to see any bother comin' to him."

"Of course not."

"Especially any lawyerin' harm. Those bastards are worse than hemorrhoids."

It was the coppers' hearty chuckles at the blatantly impolite declaration that broke the ice and right off they learned that Mac, full name William MacKenzie, often stopped in at the Jigger Inn, a popular drinking establishment alongside the Old Course Hotel. St. George knew the place and jokingly commented how one American gourmet magazine described it as "dark, smoky, and mysterious." The caddie manager averred that Mac would probably descend upon the place within the next half-hour, whereupon the Chief Inspector gazed longingly out the windows toward the 1st green.

"I realize it's highly irregular, and I wouldn't ever think of asking if it were not for the investigation, but might we borrow one of your buggies? Two reasons. First, to save us time getting to the Jigger Inn and back and secondly, it would be most helpful if we could check in on Number 11."

Laird looked at the man from Scotland Yard as though he were thoroughly daft.

"Eleven? High Hole? What in heaven for?"

"Something just occurred to me that may have great bearing on the case."

"I'm sorry, but use of the buggies is strictly limited and never on the Old Course. Not safe enough."

"Yes, I'm quite aware, thank you, but this is midsummer and it *is* now afternoon..." referring, Poole recognized, to the official policy cited by Montcrief, "and we are here on official business, so it would greatly assist us..."

"Uh, I dunno," countered the caddie manager. "You're gonna need a medical reason."

"He's got one!" exclaimed Poole.

"Huh?"

"Laurence..."

"He's got one. Go ahead, sir, show him your leg."

"Laurence!" snapped the Chief Inspector. "This is not a frivolous request, sir, it is central to our completing our assignment here..."

The caddie manager started shaking his head when Poole interrupted again.

"You want bloody medical, just check his left leg! Bloke took two bullets in it on the job protecting yours and mine—"

"LAURENCE!! I'll thank you to—"

"That a fact?" said Laird, one eyebrow raised. "All right, then, let's see it."

"See WHAT?" exclaimed an incredulous St. George.

"Your precious leg. That is, unless you'd not be wantin' that buggy anymore..."

Five minutes later the two coppers were rolling smoothly and quietly over the links in their borrowed electric golfcart. Once past his second embarrassment, St. George had complimented Poole for his initiative, though he cautioned him never to do anything like that again. They frequently halted as puzzled players executed their shots and more than once drew scowls from players and caddies alike. Despite his steadfast belief in the correctness of his maneuver, the Chief Inspector could not help feeling he and Poole were trespassing.

* * *

The 11th tee is an unassuming flat mound of grassy turf with a crouching thicket of thorny green whins in front. A posted 172 yards away, due west toward the River Eden, is the double green serving both Number 11 and its mate, Number 7. Besides the River Eden lurking in the background, other major hazards confronting a player are the rapacious sand bunkers in front: Hill Bunker, Strath Bunker, and Cockleshell Bunker. Hill Bunker is large and deep—would you believe perhaps eight feet?—and the great Gene Sarazen once needed three attempts to get his ball out and back into play. Guarding the right side of Number 11's landing area is the circular but equally deep and dangerous Strath Bunker. Cockleshell is usually only a threat to approach shots on the 4-par 7th hole. Finally, all too obvious is the green's rather steep pitch from front to back.

* * *

St. George explained it all to Poole, who replied that the only way he could ever extricate himself from one of those bomb-like craters was using the proverbial 'hand-wedge.'

St. George laughed and said, "A sentiment shared by many. Indeed, one can be ambushed even in the best weather."

"Ambushed?"

"Absolutely. Not a tree in sight, wide-open grassland as far as the eye can see, and it's just a simple toss with a mid-iron over to the green, right? But watch that chap on the rear edge who's putting..."

Poole dutifully stared as the man, standing motionless, barely tapped his ball. Even from that distance, the sergeant could see the ball quickly pick up speed, make a broad curving arc to the left, and roll devilishly off the front of the green.

"No way!"

"That's why you *always* want to have your shot finish in the front half of the green. Leaves you an uphill putt, which is much easier to control. Now today, even though the breeze is against us, coming out of the west toward the sea, it's quite mild and so something like a four-iron or five-iron would be sufficient. But imagine if you had a gale blowing against you—which has happened more than once in tournaments. Last year, in fact, during the Open. The most famous example of all occurred in 1930, the year of the Grand Slam. That summer, the famous American amateur Bobby Jones won both American and British Open Championships and both American and British Amateur Championships. Put the pros to shame and no one has ever equaled it. Anyway, our Amateur was played here, and one match set Jones against our defending champion Cyril Tolley. Wind was blowing like hell, blowing the sand from the bunkers, and giving the ball incredible distance when coming from behind. But here the wind was dead against. Tolley was a power hitter and used an iron which, being lofted, necessarily got the ball up in the air. However, the wind took the ball straight up as it soared over the green and then blew it 30 yards *backward* to land out there in the fairway."

"You're kidding!"

St. George held up a cautionary finger. "I never kid about golf, Laurence. The point is that one must respect the conditions. Of course, at other times, the fog and mist roll in until you can't see the end of the club. That's when man surrenders...and..."—St. George checked his watch—"...so should we. Questions?"

"No, sir."

"Then let's be off. When we get back to 18, we'll swing over to The Links and then up to the inn. Hopefully we won't get noticed. Might be banned for life."

Once underway, Poole put forth a question. "You've lost me about this caddie. What's he going to tell us that we haven't learned already?"

"Well, to begin, he's more than just a witness. His participation is essential to a solid game. There are so many nuances to course strategy beyond proper shot and club selection that the lone player simply cannot fathom. Even some pros have been humble enough to acknowledge that partial credit for their victories belonged to their caddies. Two famous caddies I recall specifically are Guy Gillespie who caddied for Gary Player and "Tip" Anderson who worked with the great Arnold Palmer and Tony Lema."

"We're going to show him the photo?"

"Oh, yes, but there's more to be gained than that, I hope. I've grown increasingly curious how Michael shot his remarkable round. So let me put it this way. Someone wants to write a chat-up piece about you and your work for the Sunday paper. You would expect that they would want to obtain as much accurate information as possible in the shortest amount of time. So now they can talk to your rental agent who sees you once a month, your grocer who sees you once a week, your neighbor who sees you once a day, or me—your beloved superior—who sees you hours on end."

"They'd choose you, naturally, since I spend the greatest amount of time with you."

"Exactly! And this Mac fellow spent several hours in very close proximity to our man. If there is anyone who can tell us about Michael Pont, it is his St. Andrews caddie."

"You sound like you're really not satisfied that Michael was up here."

"Let's just say I'm not comfortable with what we have thus far. Consider how the usual corporate host behaves. He shepherds his guests around, paying and signing for everything, leaving his financial scent-marks all over the place like Edward Cargill did in Edinburgh. Yet here it's as though Michael went out of his way *not* to leave any such trail behind. Not even fingerprints. We have no tangible evidence that he *touched* anything. All we have is less than wholehearted recognition of a grainy photograph. It makes no sense. Unless, of course, he was *not* up here, that he was elsewhere, that someone as yet unidentified came here to impersonate him for the day, in which case it was imperative that no telltale fingerprints or handwriting be left behind."

"Or souvenir photographs."

"True. But then there is this problem. You're going to play the Old Course, so you know one of the requirements is identifying yourself if even in the most rudimentary fashion. So what would you pull out and display?"

"On duty or off?"

"Off, naturally."

"My driver's license."

"Exactly! Now if our premise that Michael hired someone to kill his brother is true, then he was here and so surely he did the same thing to establish his presence."

"Although he had not availed himself of other, earlier opportunities to do so," Poole countered.

"Correct. You see how odd it is? Now then, if he was not here, if he used a stand-in, then how the bloody hell did the stand-in get by the starter? He surely could not take the chance of loaning out his driver's license for the obvious reasons. So what could the stand-in have used?"

"I would think a letter of introduction would be hard to come by on short notice," Poole ventured.

"Indeed. So what's left?"

The next 20 seconds passed in silence before St. George exclaimed, "Yes!"

"Sir?"

"It fits. I only hope it doesn't fit too well, that I'm wishing it to fit where it should not, but here goes. Remember Pont saying that his brother set up a temporary R&A membership for him? I'll bet you that is what he gave his stand-in. Royal & Ancient recognition is about as much carte blanche as you could ever need."

The Chief Inspector paused a moment while Poole navigated around a foursome. "And then, I've been bothered by his disinterest in his fabulous score. Had it been me, I would have been talking it up for weeks. But his reaction is 'Oh well, ho-hum.' Yet there are his pictures and mementos on his trophy wall, and then the paneling, some places dark, some lighter...but we're getting ahead of ourselves. Onward, my good man!"

$$35$$

THEY TURNED WEST off Granny Clark's Wynd onto The Links which ran snugly alongside 18 and part of 17. As they cruised past pedestrians and parked cars and the windowed dining room of The Rusacks, St. George increased his sergeant's fund of golf knowledge by relating tales and legends he had heard about famous St. Andrews caddies of the past.

"One of the most colorful was a chap named Donal' Blue, a fisherman who took up the game and became a very good player as well as a good caddie. He also worked part-time as Keeper of the Castle and even had picture postcards of himself printed for sale to tourists. Quite an enterprising fellow for those days. Others succumbed to The Dark Side and did more than was allowed. One chap named 'Trap-door' Willie Johnson wore a large shoe on the pretext that his legs were of different lengths. The truth was he had a golfball-sized hole in the bottom of the larger shoe. He'd go along through the rough and step on an opponent's ball, pick it up in his shoe, and the opponent would be penalized for a lost ball."

"That's cheating! I thought you said this was such an honest game!"

"Of course it is. But it evolved into one. Let me give you another example. Early in the last century, you teed your ball on a small pile of sand scooped from the ground or a sandbox or a bunker. Actually, they do the same thing in Saudi Arabia today. Anyway, wood tees would not come into being until much later. The caddie had the responsibility to tee the ball the proper height for his player—called a *man*, by the way. Using his tongue, a good caddie would wet his thumb thoroughly and thence the ball, so that grains of sand would adhere to the ball and produce backspin."

"Ugh!" was Poole's only reply while he concentrated on avoiding oncoming traffic.

As advertised, the Old Course Hotel dwarfed the Jigger Inn's white cottage which St. George pointed out had originally been the residence of the railroad's stationmaster. "Accounts for its cozy ambiance, I'd say. A caddie haunt for years, but I understand there's pressure to make way for the hotel's higher-priced clientele."

They parked right by the front door, the Chief Inspector predicting aloud that no one would be anxious to confront anyone so audacious as to commit such an indiscretion. Once inside, they straightaway made the acquaintance of the barkeep and asked for Mac, aka William MacKenzie, while taking pains to drop the names of Brad Kirkland and Tom Laird along the way. The barkeep replied that their quarry had not yet shown but was expected shortly. Taking their beers, the detectives sauntered over to a corner table and took their seats. Several sips and 15 minutes later, an older, grizzled gentleman dressed in durable yet neat khaki jeans, shirt, cap, and official windbreaker appeared and signaled the barkeep. In return, the barkeep pointed out the men from Scotland Yard and delivered the man's drink. William MacKenzie eyed the two detectives from a distance and then cautiously made his way to their table.

"Robert there said you was lookin' *foor* someone."

"For a caddie named 'Mac'," answered St. George. "Mr. Laird said we could most likely find him here. Might you be the man?"

"I suppose I could be," said the newcomer whom they had learned from the caddie manager had worked the Old Course for 30 years. "And you two are coppers?"

"Yes, from London," said the Chief Inspector who produced his ID. "The local police at West Calder asked us to help with a little matter near there. Chief Superintendent Stallings, in fact, asked that we come up to check the alibi of a person who claims he played the Old Course last Saturday morning. Played host to a Japanese threesome."

Hands shoved in his pockets, 'Mac' stared down at the scarred wood table.

"London, huh? That means Scotland Yard. Must be awfully important to drag Scotland Yard into it."

"It involves a murder, actually."

Mac's eyebrows rose for just a split-second. "You don't say. So what can I do for ya?"

"Well, we understand you caddied for the Caucasian in that group. The Scotsman. We were hoping you might be able to tell us something about him. Won't you please join us?"

Mac nodded once and pulled out a chair and sat down. "Well, I'll do what I can...not that I know very much. Last Saturday, you say?"

"10:10 tee-off. Four of you grasshopping."

Mac screwed up his face as though the extra muscle action would increase his concentration.

"Aye, I remember the group," replied the veteran caddie as he sipped his drink. "Roger and Dave and Alex and I."

"Was this your *man?*" said St. George as he held out the newsphoto. Mac gave it a quick look.

"Probably so. I pay more attention to a player's game than to his looks. Looks can be mighty disappointing."

"Indeed," said the Chief Inspector as he replaced the photo in its envelope. "I imagine you and your colleagues must have had a busy time of it 'working the tools'?"

Mac squinted at St. George and grinned.

"We had our hands full, all right. Leastwise, my three lads did."

"How did the Japanese fellows play?"

"Nae gowf," said Mac sadly. "More like pasture pool for them. They was all over the place. But they seemed to enjoy themselves. Talked all the time, they did."

"And how about Mr. Pont? Was he polite and courteous?"

Mac shrugged.

"He was all richt. Dinna say much."

"How did he play?"

"He did all richt."

"What? You call a 76 'all right'? Bloody damned good, I should think."

"That it would be."

"Well then...wait...what do you mean 'it *would* be'?"

"If a fella shot a 76."

To Poole, the Chief Inspector seemed stunned, even lost, his mind momentarily elsewhere.

"Are you saying Mr. Pont did not shoot 76?"

"Well, he *dinna* keep a card..." said Mac who now was eyeing his drinking companions sideways.

"Oh, come now, Mac, you and yours carry a running total for everyone you carry for. Are you telling me he didn't break 80?"

Mac took a long sip and then for a moment looked out the nearest window as though studying the far horizon. When he was ready, he looked back.

"Shot a bit more than that."

"How much more?"

Mac shrugged. "More like 95, I guess."

"Ninety—!"

St. George shot forward in his seat, his surprise unmistakable. "We're talking, aren't we, about last Saturday? One week ago?"

"Aye, but remember, Chief Inspector, it was blowin' gey strang."

The eyes of caddie and copper locked. Neither blinked. Poole had seldom seen his boss so alert and intense.

"Blowing hard like during the Open last year?"

"Pretty much."

"Perhaps like the Tolley match?"

Mac's eyes narrowed and his thin lips spread into a grin: "Damn near."

"High Hole," St. George snapped.

"You're meanin' 11."

"I am. Wind against?"

"Aye, it was."

"Might you tee off with a putter?"

Mac smiled and said, "Been done."

"And was it?"

"Wisnae."

Eyes shimmering with excitement, St. George turned sharply to Poole, a triumphant smile stretched from ear to ear.

"WE'VE GOT HIM!"

36

THE HECTIC NEXT two hours began with the London men cajoling the skeptical caddie into accompanying them to the police station to sign a sworn statement covering everything he had just discussed. Inspector Grogan was as good as his word and made his staff and facilities readily available.

"But I need to have a word with you, Chief Inspector, for a moment, if I may."

"Why certainly, of course," said St. George. "What is it?"

"Well, sir, from our official position, we don't really see it as a problem, we're sure you had good cause, but well, sir, we've received quite a few complaints about your...well, not really your conduct but your cruisin' about here and there."

"I'm sorry?"

"Well, Tom Laird, the caddie manager, was watchin' you through his binoculars ridin' around the course, and he got all fussed when he saw you take off down the street, and then he got a bunch of complaints about your being out on the course with that buggy in the first place, and so he told 'em to call here and then we started hearing about you heading up to the hotel, people swearing you were drunk, and well, all in all, you got quite a lot of people upset."

St. George stood stock-still, completely dumbfounded. "I what? I don't believe it."

"So I'd like to be able to tell them something official was going on," Grogan added, almost apologetically.

"Inspector, you may do exactly that. Please inform Mr. Laird that his kind permission to use the buggy enabled us to complete our inquiries sooner than expected and to identify our murderer. For that we are indebted to him and to his fellow citizens for their indulgence."

Grogan smiled and replied, "Thank you, sir, I think that will help immensely." He then left to squelch any further protests, leaving the Chief Inspector and Poole to work the phones to West Calder, Livingston, and London lining up Stallings, Dougall, and their men for the impending showdown that evening. Finally, with profuse thanks to all, the London men headed for the bus stop, passing Auchterlonie's golf shop on the way.

"Yes, Laurence, it's taking great willpower for me not to pop in for even a minute. In fact, my goal is someday to have enough saved to have them create a set of clubs for me. However, we've reached a crisis point, and the sooner we get back to West Calder, the better. According to the schedule, the next bus should be here in a matter of minutes."

"One quick question?" said Poole as other shops receded into the background.

"Certainly."

"I caught only part of your call to Stallings. You said something about a union? What union?"

St. George smiled. "The Scottish Golf Union. I implored Stallings to pull rank and get them to check Michael's handicap records this afternoon. It's a long shot, but it's the best we've got."

After a three-count, Poole said, "I'm lost. I thought we caught Michael in a barefaced lie that broke his alibi completely."

"Yes, we did, but I fear that what we have will not be enough to convict. Imagine what an unscrupulous defense lawyer might do to poor Mac. And I seriously doubt the Reservations Office here keep any records of receipts or tee times after a week or two."

"Well then, what about Fogger?"

"Yes, but does he truly know enough to say the right things? We can't know that until we catch him and when will that be? So time is critical and it's time we're about out of, pardon my preposition. No, our problem is that we need something tangible to pin down Michael's round of 76, and we need it now. Perhaps even a witness. I mean, I have no doubt he actually shot such a score, just that it was not last Saturday. So when? That's the rub. I suspect it was in the fairly recent past, maybe two or three years."

"Well, we can rule out the girlfriend; they've been together only seven months. What about Mary Gates?"

"I don't trust her," St. George replied. "The company's central gossip. The confidant of the Number Two man who is now under suspicion—she may very well lie for him. Of course, on the other hand, she may truly know nothing. Either way, we can't take the chance."

"Well then, how about Edward?"

"If he knew anything—which I doubt—he'd have said 'Oh, Michael, you mean you shot another 76?' No, his only value will be gaining us access to company records to see what Michael charged off to business expense. But that must come later lest Edward alert Michael that we're poking around."

"You mean regarding this evening."

"Yes."

"Okay, so how does Michael's handicap help us pin down his 76?"

"It's in the method, Laurence. A fixed number of the most recent *recorded* scores are used for the calculation, generally between 20 and 30, the most recent being listed first. What I am hoping is that his 76 is there. But if it's not, then it's not."

The first five minutes at the station were spent trying not to act impatient, the second five pacing back and forth in a gentlemanly manner, and the third five petitioning the stationmaster for information and relief. To their mutual dismay, they learned that, practically speaking, the printed timetable was merely a first approximation. The usual vagaries of the route to and from Leuchars was this day complicated by engine trouble in the bus which had brought them to town. Another vehicle had been diverted to assume the route and was expected "momentarily." Connecting with the return train was now problematical as well, their worst fears confirmed with a phone call to the station. Finally, St. George had no choice but to call Dougall to say they would be delayed at least two hours.

"Anything yet about Fogger?....Brussels? Well, that makes sense. What about the phone intercepts?" One of the Chief Inspector's first commands for Dougall was to tap the phone lines to Michael's home, temporary office, and the Glasgow headquarters for Stuart Investments, etc. It was imperative that, if at all possible, Fogger and Michael not communicate to preclude Fogger going underground if

Michael suspected the police were closing in. "Thank God! Good work, Inspector! Keep on it and we'll see Cobb at the station."

St. George rang off and turned to Poole. "*That* was a near thing. Two minutes after they get the Stuart Investments intercept operational, a call came through from Brussels. Hotel Demarche, whatever that is. The operator pulled it off, though, and convinced the caller there was line trouble in the building and that it would not be fixed until noon tomorrow at the earliest."

"Fogger?"

"Very likely. Anyway, Stallings jumped on that like hot coals and got the word to Interpol. If it was Fogger, they should be knocking on his door right about now, I'd say."

"Put on the pressure and see if he'll crack."

"Exactly. Like what Michael did with his preemptive maneuver at his home, insisting we search his place and inspect his car. He wanted to fluster, put us on the defensive. It's all move and countermove, Laurence. And timing. And right now, I don't want Michael Pont feeling *any* pressure. I want him to believe we are fools. I want him to feel that he has succeeded. I want him to enjoy a strong sense of accomplishment. Of security. Again, not unlike what many golfers do to their opponents in match play."

"Back to golf again?"

"Of course! You see, match play is mano-a-mano, shot for shot, strategy for strategy. With every stroke, you're trying to outwit, outhit, outthink, outplay your opponent. And while nothing exerts pressure on an opponent like a brilliant shot that leaves you at the pin while he's many yards away, psychology is also at work between shots. Each player is watching the other for signs of stress. Pacing, fiddling with clubs, repeatedly picking up grass to check the wind, shifting tee position, facial tics, fussing with the glove or clothes, furrowing of the brow, tightening of the lips, you name it."

"Like we've been doing for the past quarter-hour."

St. George blinked, "We have?"

Poole smiled and nodded.

"Well anyway, one of the classic traps is early on to concede your opponent his remaining three-foot putt rather than make him putt out. Unwitting players accept the offer as though it were a gracious, courteous gesture. A bit of jolly good sportsmanship. But the reason behind the ploy is that in the closing holes, when the match is on the line and the pressure mounts with every stroke, very frequently those same three-foot putts can either tie, lose, or win the hole and the match. That's when the gullible player suddenly discovers he has not made a three-foot putting stroke all day and is now woefully unprepared to do so. Thus, his chances of missing and losing are extraordinarily high."

"So you want to leave Michael a three-foot putt."

"Exactly!"

Poole smiled as he fully grasped the strategy. "Interesting. Speaking of Michael, mind if I bring up something that's bothered me for a while? It's probably nothing."

"No, no, go on," said St. George as their bus arrived and they jumped on board and took the last seats available.

"Well, sir, in the interest of trying to observe everything, that wall in his den that you were looking at, the one with all the golf stuff..."

"Yes?"

"Well, I thought it seemed a bit odd compared to the others."

"Odd? In what way?"

Poole was so preoccupied formulating his question that he missed the slight smile on his mentor's face.

"The way everything was arranged. Especially on the side near the window. Seemed somehow disorganized. Unbalanced. Yeah, that's the word I've been looking for—unbalanced. Seemed kind of odd for someone whose work requires precision, perhaps even symmetry."

St. George's smile lengthened.

"Laurence, you've hit upon the core of this case. And it points us to the only thing that will bring Michael Pont to justice. I certainly don't want to hand the Crown a case based solely on the testimony of one Richie Fogger. That's why we're going to pay Michael a visit this evening—to look at that wall."

The Chief Inspector refused to elaborate further or expand on his fuss with the caddie about the wind. Instead, once aboard their train, he slouched down for a catnap that ended with their arrival in Waverly Station. Cobb and Dougall greeted them and soon the team was making its way through the early evening outbound traffic from Edinburgh. Dougall reported that, as instructed, he had called Michael and told him St. George had good news for him and would call him later in the evening.

"Naturally, he wanted to know what it was, but I said I was not at liberty to say. So he thanked me and that was it. So he should be home."

"Good. Surveillance?"

"In place."

"Excellent. And Fogger?"

"Interesting bit there. He's been gone about a week according to his landlady. No one knew where. But he's in Brussels, all right, and Interpol's got him. Expect him back here in a couple of days."

"Great! He's *incommunicado?*"

"For the moment. The embassy is having trouble finding the appropriate attaché to handle his requests to make calls back here—if you get my meaning. Probably can't keep someone from reaching Pont after tomorrow morning."

"Anything more?"

"Yes. I happened to ask Edward Cargill if he had heard of this guy, and to my surprise he said 'yes'. Said Fogger and Michael were school chums years back. Even attended university together. Fogger went for an economics degree while Michael went into computer science. At any rate, Edward mentioned that he met Fogger one summer when the two paid a visit to the Cargill family's summer home. Couldn't really describe him except that, with moustaches, they both sort of looked alike."

"Aha!" said St. George with a wink toward Poole.

"I caught up on that," Dougall continued, "and asked if there might be any pictures around, you know, family album stuff, and he said the one person who might was his Aunt Sarah who lives across town. Apparently she's got entire scrapbooks filled with family pictures. Anyway, he calls her, she's home, and I go there and meet the old bird. Nice old lady but talks your leg off. Got her to show me some albums which she's more than happy to do—old gal is lonesome, I think—and sure enough here's a couple of Michael and his buddy Fogger. Damned if they couldn't be twins."

"And you have...?"

"The originals and a copy of each," said Dougall as he proudly produced his evidence. Even in the dim twilight inside the car, the detectives had no trouble recognizing the resemblance between the two friends, now plotters. With a word of hearty congratulations, St. George handed the pictures back.

"All right, gentlemen, I think we've solved the case—Michael killed Geoffrey while Fogger played golf in his stead. *But* ... every piece of evidence we have is fully deniable by the killer and his accomplice. That's why we must pull off our little charade tonight without a hitch. Barrows will be home?"

"Yes, and I told him to speak to no one."

"And Edward?"

"Told him to expect a call from you sometime this evening," Dougall said. "I should imagine he'll stay put as well. Think we should record these calls?"

St. George paused. "No, I wouldn't take the chance of anything mechanical being heard. Same for the echo of a speakerphone. The calls are just supposed to be me calling them personally and privately. But your point is well taken."

The team stopped at a fast-food diner for supper before continuing on to the police station where they found Chief Superintendent Stallings waiting for them. Within minutes, all was ready and St. George called James Barrows to explain the plot they had created for him.

"Good evening, Mr. Barrows, Chief Inspector St. George calling.... Yes, well, we appreciate your making yourself available. Tell you why I've rung you up, we have a favor to ask of you, for this evening in fact, within the hour actually.... Yes, we'd like to drop by and we'd appreciate it ever so much if you would allow us to arrest you..."

Next he called Edward Cargill. The VES comptroller's shock at learning that James Barrows was the killer was profound and genuine. The would-be aristocrat numbly agreed not to do anything until he heard back from the police later that evening.

"Which means he will be promptly on the horn to Michael," Stallings commented as he stood around the desk with Dougall and Poole.

"I hope so. Nothing like a bit of independent corroboration for our man, wouldn't you say? Let's give them a few moments, shall we?" said St. George as he stood and asked where he could find the soda machine. In a minute, he was back, retook his seat, set his soda on the desk, and dialed Michael's Pont's number.

"Mr. Pont?...Hello, St. George here. We've had some developments. I thought you'd like to hear straightaway...Well, first off, we've confirmed your alibi for Saturday. No problem there.... Yes, that's right, you've been cleared of any suspicion—which brings me, however, to something unpleasant. We have solid evidence that Mr. Barrows killed your brother....That's right...no question at all....Vengeance through and through....Well, for not inviting him to join the Executive Committee. For not giving him a larger share of the profits. So burning down the plant was his revenge....As for

Geoffrey, it was simply his very bad luck to go out to the plant and surprise Barrows in the act....Well, Geoffrey's off the hook completely and since Barrows is not an owner or an officer or a shareholder, his arson cannot be laid at the company's doorstep. Looks like Walcott's people will have to pay off....Quite simple, actually, he rode his bicycle on the grass strip alongside the driveway...Tell you what, if you'll come to Inspector Dougall's office after 10 tomorrow morning, we can fill you in on the particulars....Because we're preparing to arrest Mr. Barrows this evening...within the hour, in fact...Thank you, yes, good luck does come in handy sometimes. Oh, one more thing, however—for your own safety, please stay home. *Do not* come by to watch. I'm fully aware how that would be natural, under the circumstances, this being so tragic and painful for you, but Barrows has already killed once and with the fire committed violence twice, and we cannot predict how he will behave. If he sees you...well, we don't need another victim. So please stay away. If you feel you must confront him, you can do so tomorrow after his solicitor's seen him....Right. Until tomorrow then..."

St. George rang off and sighed heavily. He saw that several constables had now joined the others, all of them watching him intently. Chief Superintendent Stallings could not resist posing the obvious question.

"I'm still not clear on why you believe he should want to watch the arrest."

"Were he innocent, he wouldn't," answered St. George as he slouched back in his seat. "He would be so relieved he would want to rest, let down and recover from all the tension of the case. A bit of fanciful psychology, I grant you, but I wanted to plant the idea that he should witness the culmination of his plot. See for himself that, yes, we truly did not suspect him of anything. That he was genuinely free and clear. Call it the forbidden fruit or seeing greener grass on the other side of the fence or what have you, it's all toward doing whatever we can to keep him away from that scorecard...wherever he's put it. So I'm hoping he'll find the temptation irresistible and do a 'Stapleton'."

"A 'Stapleton? I don't..."

Over a quick chuckle, Poole explained. "I believe he's referring to *The Hound of the Baskervilles,* sir. Where the villain Stapleton leaves his house to watch his murderous hound attack Sir Henry on the moor."

The Chief Superintendent's look of disgust was immediate as was his next question: "About that scorecard...you explained it over the phone, but there needs to be more. The Crown Prosecutor was not pleased with what little I had to tell to him. In fact, we were granted the warrant only because you were so specific in what you were after."

"Certainly, but may I suggest we get underway first? We don't want to keep Mr. Pont waiting."

"Right, but before we go," said Stallings as he held out a piece of paper, "here are your results on Michael's handicap scores."

"Oh, yes!" barked St. George as he jumped from his seat and snatched the paper in midair. His eyes eagerly scanned the row of 20 numbers ranging from 71 to 78. There were four 76s, two of them marked with an asterisk.

"They only keep the 20 most recent scores," Stallings said. "Chap indicated those at the end were actually from 1994. That 76 with the asterisk at the end was from St.Andrews. The Old Course."

St. George favored the Chief Superintendent with a smile and a hearty "Well done!" which caught the senior copper pleasantly by surprise. Before there was time for explanations, he hurried every-one outside and to their cars.

37

THE CONVOY OF four cars set out, radios tuned to a rarely used frequency. The three detectives plus Stallings rode in the second car with Poole driving, Dougall alongside. Two surveillance teams, one of them from Bathgate, were already in position around the homes of James Barrows and Michael Pont. They reported that both subjects were still home.

"Right," said St. George. "The lynchpin of our entire case is the scorecard from Michael Pont's remarkable play on the Old Course two years ago. The one in which he parred the 11th hole on his way to shooting a 76. He is already aware that it can convict him; that is why he removed it from the wall in his den and tried to rearrange the other framed mementos to cover up its absence. As long as he believes his deception is secure, he will leave well enough alone. That's why we must not alarm him."

"Yes, but how is this scorecard so damned important?" Stallings asked.

"Because it catches him in a barefaced lie of monumental proportions and destroys his entire defense. It provides him with the missing ingredient for arrest and prosecution—opportunity to commit the crimes. You see, I'm an avid golfer and I've been to St. Andrews several times. So my curiosity was piqued when I heard that Michael had not only been there a few days before but had recorded such a magnificent score. As a devotee of the game, I was eager to learn how he played one hole in particular, the 3-par 11th, a favorite of mine. It has been the scene of many disasters and triumphs over the years, yet this man reached the green in regulation and two-putted for par. A worthy achievement, indeed, by anybody's standard.

"Despite all his cunning and planning, however, Michael never anticipated the possibility that someone would actually ask for details about his supposed round of last Saturday. It is pointless to speculate 'why,' but he believed all he would ever have to do is say he had been at St. Andrews and that would be it. All conversation would focus on Geoffrey's death and the YAMATSU project. Then I came along and asked for specifics. That left him with only three options—admit he was never there and instantly become Suspect Number One, make up a fictitious round which might trip him up later, or describe an actual round from another day. An ironic case of telling the truth being the safest choice."

"So the key," Stallings said, "was not to let anyone see the real scorecard, which would show that the round was actually played two years earlier."

"Exactly. That and the caddie's testimony about the weather last Saturday which made it impossible to duplicate the score. Laurence, in fact, confirmed that with the local weather service. But give the devil his due, Michael finessed the situation very smoothly. He drew upon that memorable round and discussed it as though it had occurred only yesterday. And that's what has hung him. Fogger as Michael shot a 95 in near gale-force winds which is light-years from a 76 shot in nearly perfect weather. So in sum, on Saturday last, Michael could not have played the 11th hole the way he claims. Which, in turn, means he was unaware of the strong winds up there because he was never there."

"Question?" said Poole over his shoulder.

"Certainly."

"Any idea what he did with all his time in London before he returned here? Could he have bought his scuba gear then? The mask, tank, and so on?"

"I believe that's exactly what he did."

"The bastard!" muttered Stallings. "So we have to find the score-card before he destroys it."

"Yes. It is a prized memento to be treasured for the rest of his life, *unless* it becomes the only thing standing between him and freedom. That's why I want to keep him confident in his genius and savvy and his triumph over us lowly civil servants."

"But how the pictures hang," said Stallings, "could have any number of explanations. Surely there must have been something else?"

"Certainly: the portions of paneling not bleached by the sun. The interface between the original dark stain and the faded areas clearly show the corners and edges of the frames in their original positions. So certain items had only very recently been moved. Why? And then there was the absence of dust. He was astute enough to realize that handling the repositioned frames would disturb their coating of fine dust which would be a dead giveaway. So he went to the effort to clean off everything on that wall...but then forgot to do the same to the rest of the room. So you have to ask, 'Why dust only one wall?' It all adds up."

"Still circumstantial, though," Stallings pouted as he crossed his arms.

Nothing more was said until they arrived at James Barrows' residence. Just then, Dougall's handset crackled and they heard the partially garbled report that Michael Pont had left his home wearing jogging attire and riding his bike. He appeared to be headed in the direction of the home of James Barrows.

"YES!" said St. George as he smacked his hand. "All right, everyone, let's get to work!"

* * *

Twenty minutes later, with CS Stallings in the lead, two burly constables hustled a struggling, protesting James Barrows from his home and into a patrol car. Dougall's handset chirped once again. The conversation was short.

"He's up there all right. Top of the hill to our left. Watching through binocs."

"Glasses? That makes it bit dicey. OK, everyone keep on being busy. The binocs means he's checking details so we must make this as real as possible. Tape, the whole works. Your boys still concealed?"

"Right."

"All right. Tell them to move in and secure the house. Your forensics man ready?"

"Yes."

"Then let's get on with it..."

As the others stood by, Stallings climbed into the front seat and gave the order to drive on, destination the Bathgate station. Minutes later, a second call came over Dougall's radio: Michael was still on the hilltop, still watching.

St. George winked to the surprised detective as he said, "Good thing we decided to follow the thing through, eh? Perhaps he's merely savoring his victory or maybe he wants to make certain we mean business. Either way we would have come up a cropper had we just up and gone away. Two things on our side, however—the more time passes, the more legitimate we should appear, and he cannot afford to stay up there all night. Someone would report him."

For the next 20 minutes, St. George played the stereotypical role of the authoritarian superior while alternately Poole and Dougall came up to him ostensibly to report something before moving on with new orders. The uniformed constables lugged empty suitcases and boxes out to the cars as though they were laden with heavy contents, the pièce de résistance a discarded 456 Mhz computer tower exhumed from its resting place inside a bedroom closet. It was then that St. George worried they might run out of removable 'evidence.'

* * *

Michael Pont stood expressionless in the darkening shadow of a shade tree and watched the police prepare to leave James Barrows' home. Subconsciously he had counted the items carried to the waiting police cars and a grim smile appeared as, one by one, the coppers climbed in and drove away. Except the last car, which backed up and paused while the fat one got out and walked up and said something to the lone guardian constable at the front door. Then he, too, was gone, leaving the constable to deal with the small crowd of neighbors that had gathered.

Yes, thought Michael, he had played the thing well. Particularly having the foresight to prepare a fallback position. No one else would have done so. Yet Michael would not give his ego free rein, mindful as he was of the role luck had played. Obviously the coppers had tumbled onto something illegal concerning Barrows, as evidenced by all the stuff they had seized. Certainly much more effective than if he had tried to plant something in the man's home or office. In truth, he had grown weary of the computer engineer's whining and complaining about never being included in anything. Well, my friend, you're included now...

Darkness had settled over the neighborhood. Warm, friendly light spilled out of windows and from porch lights and driveway lamps. Time to go home for a little celebration—and to rehearse his shock and anger and outrage for tomorrow's meeting with the coppers. Yet Michael found it difficult to tear himself away; he did not want to leave, not just yet....

* * *

Constable Reynolds, most junior member of the Bathgate force, checked his watch as the last of the curious bystanders moved off into the fading twilight. As usual, darkness discouraged onlookers because, porch lights and streetlights notwithstanding, there was very little to see compared to midday. He was grateful because this was his first big assignment and, according to the Chief Superintendent, would end at midnight with the change of shift. Well, at least *somebody* knew what he was about, Constable Reynolds judged, unlike that bearded bloke from London who had come back expressly to tell him to be alert for a man on a bike, wearing jogging clothes, who might try to pump him for information. Final order was to tell such a man absolutely *nothing*. Yes, sir! Well, there hadn't been such a man, now had there—?

Constable Reynolds gawked as he spotted a cyclist, a male cyclist, wearing jogging clothes, cruising down the dimly lit street. To his disbelief, the man slowed to a stop in the driveway, got off, and flipped out the kickstand. Reynolds suddenly felt very alone.

Sorry, sir, you'll have to move on....Not at liberty to say, sir....Yes, that's police tape and this is an official police crime scene which means civilians are not permitted to loiter...Not at liberty to divulge such information, sir. Now would you please move on?...I'm sorry, sir, you'll have to leave....I must insist....Have a good evening....

Reynolds later reported how edgy the man seemed, excited even, as he looked again and again at the house like a prospective buyer. Despite the poor lighting, the constable would identify the man as Michael Pont.

38

WITH BARROWS ENJOYING a catered dinner at the Bathgate station, the Chief Inspector's posse converged on Michael's residence just as a report came through that the surviving brother was on his way home. Minutes later, Inspector Dougall and a half-dozen constables were waiting outside when Michael turned the corner to discover his house cordoned off by police cars, flashing barricades, and police tape. He slowed to a stop in the middle of the street, still 30 yards away, and just sat there, hands on the grips, feet on the pavement. For several long seconds, nobody moved. Then at Dougall's quiet command, two constables moved forward, one to each side. As they approached, Michael remained motionless and then, without protest, dismounted and handed off the bike to the curbside officer, whereupon both constables escorted him down the street to Dougall.

"What's going on?" said the clearly puzzled owner.

"Evening, sir. The Chief Superintendent and the Chief Inspector would like a word with you. Inside, if you please."

The remarkably docile brother entered his home to find all the lights on and policemen everywhere. Dougall led the way into the den where Stallings and the men from Scotland Yard were waiting. Upon seeing St. George, Pont exploded.

"What is the MEANING of this?" he shouted at Stallings. "Why are all these POLICE here? How did you get into my HOUSE? What RIGHT ...?"

Stallings held out a folded paper.

"We have proper cause and this is a proper warrant. And the rear door was open."

Michael took the paper and threw it down.

"But what are you DOING here? You just arrested Barrows...."

"Quite, but there is another matter. The Chief Inspector will—"

"Damn him! He's a bloody foreigner! He has no business here! You're the one in charge!"

"Enough!" snapped Stallings as he held up a cautionary hand. "You may have some influence in these parts but that does not extend to police matters, so I'll thank you to keep a civil tongue. And as the Chief Inspector is in charge of this investigation, you will give him your full cooperation, do you understand?"

Fear, confusion, contempt, and rage all swept across his countenance before Michael reluctantly turned toward his stony-faced antagonist and sneered, "So what's this big deal that gives you cause to take over my home?"

"The murder of your brother," answered St. George in a level tone. "And secondly, the burning of the plant."

"But you've already arrested Barrows for both."

"And you've prepared a bit of celebration, have you?"

"Huh? What?"

"The tin of caviar and the champagne in your kitchen. Not the usual way to assuage one's grief." Pont said nothing as the man from Scotland Yard continued. "Afraid they've both warmed to room temperature by now."

"So what?" said Michael as he looked to Stallings as though seeking relief from this moron. "I just went for a ride."

"Yes, we know you did. We've had you under surveillance the entire time."

"You *what?* Oh, so now it's against the law to leave one's house and ride around?"

"Of course not. The point is, we were expecting you to do so and you did not disappoint."

"Expecting? I don't believe this!"

"Oh, believe it, sir, believe it fully. That warrant on the floor covers our searching your entire premises. For as long as it takes and as much work as it takes. Even if it means taking down every wall. We have a full complement of sledge hammers and pry-bars out there in the van. But as we've all had a long, arduous day, there is an alternative, and so I'll simply ask you to deliver up the scorecard."

Michael Pont's mouth dropped open as shock and fear competed for primacy. Eyes wide, he watched St. George walk slowly across the carpeting like a panther stalking wounded prey.

"I repeat, will you produce the scorecard or do we tear your home apart to find it?"

"What scorecard? I...I don't know what you mean!"

St. George pointed to the golf trophy wall from which more than half the photos and mementos had been removed and laid on nearby tables.

"This is OUTRAGEOUS!" screamed Michael. "You had no right to touch ANYHING!"

"We've documented everything with photographs, by the way," St. George said. "This wall has a southern exposure so it receives both direct and indirect sunlight for most of the day. With the pictures removed, you can see how that sunlight has faded the stain on the paneling not covered by the frames. By the way, we checked, and you added this den when you bought the place, which explains the cheap construction in this room compared to the rest of the house. Such as this low-grade veneer which bleaches out rather easily. Anyway, you will see this rather rectangular patch along the border has less discoloration which tells us that whatever hung there had not done so for very long. Certainly not as long as the other mementos. Perhaps no more than two years."

"You're full of crap!"

"I submit what hung there is the scorecard from your magnificent round on the Old Course in late 1994. The day you shot the 76."

"You're crazy! I shot that last Saturday!"

St. George shook his head emphatically.

"The caddie identified me! You said so!"

"I lied. What he actually said was your picture only *resembled* the man who played as you in the YAMATSU foursome. He really paid more attention to *how* your substitute played. The man was terrible. Your man Fogger. Incidentally, Inspector Dougall has found school photos showing the remarkable resemblance between you two. No, what got us on the wrong track was presuming you had gone to St. Andrews and your accomplice went in and did the dirty work. But in fact, it was the other way around. Quite clever, actually."

"Go to hell. You can't prove a thing."

"Oh, but we can. See those toothpicks in the wall? They're in the
nail holes we found centered for each dark area. Now if you'll give us
a minute," St. George said as he motioned to Poole and Dougall.
Together, the three detectives hung the displaced photos and
mementos back on the wall like a jigsaw puzzle, each frame now
matching its outline perfectly. Along the border was a vertical row of
four individually framed scorecards. Only the rectangular area
directly beneath them remained.

"We cannot know in what order you hung these scorecards, but
that is irrelevant. What counts is that the single space remaining
here is for something exactly the same size and shape as the other
four. And here is the last toothpick waiting for it. Specifically, the
card from 1994, which hung here until last week. So again, do you
hand it over or do we tear the place apart? Mind you, out of fairness,
I should warn you that many of these trophies and such might be
inadvertently damaged or even destroyed should we have to rum-
mage around. Be a shame..."

Michael's features drooped, his eyes conveying defeat. For nearly
a half-minute, he remained mute before speaking in a quiet voice.

"H-How did you know?"

"A round of 76 on the Old Course is worth treasuring forever. And
you did by having the card framed like these others. But when I
asked you about your game last Saturday, I caught you unprepared.
You realized that making up something was pure folly, and so you
had to grasp at the only factual material you had at hand – the round
you played two years ago. But having done that, you then could not
risk anyone seeing the actual card on the wall and see the real date.
Left you with an unplayable lie, if you'll forgive the metaphor."

Michael shoulders sagged. "Go on."

"So you came home, took it down, hid it, and then set about rear-
ranging the rest of your...exhibits, shall we say...to cover you in the
event we stopped by. The proof that you thought you were safe, that
you had escaped exposure and detection, was when you challenged
us with that bit of bravado about searching your place and your car.
No doubt you planned on returning the card to its rightful place
sometime in the future."

"You're wrong. I tell you, I don't have any such card."

"Oh, but you do. You could never part with it. Just as you could
never bring yourself to alter it. Such as trying to change the date. You

may not believe it, but I fully comprehend the emotional value of such a relic. So it's here. Now will you produce it, or do we ransack the place?"

Michael looked all around, his eyes darting about like a cornered animal, seeing nothing but coppers everywhere.

"Oh, I should mention we have Fogger in Brussels. They say they can't shut him up."

Michael paused and looked St. George straight in the eye, his face contorted with the pain of exposed guilt, not remorse. Then he suddenly became calm and relaxed.

"All right...all right...it's in the hall closet. In the overcoat bag."

"Constable?" said Dougall as he motioned to the officer nearest the closet. The officer opened the door and carefully moved aside the coats and other garments on the rack until he said "It's here." Then the forensics team leader put on his latex gloves, reached in, and brought out a long black zippered garment bag. At a nod from Stallings, he opened it to reveal a buttoned wool topcoat that seemed a bit full in the chest. Pausing to allow the photographer to snap his pictures, the forensics man next unbuttoned the coat and displayed a framed scorecard suspended from the hanger by a length of twine.

At St. George's direction, the coat was removed and, without touching it, the frame was lowered into a large fresh specimen bag along with the twine and sealed inside.

"That," said St. George to Michael, "guarantees that the only fingerprints on that frame are yours and the framer's." Turning to Dougall, he added, "No planted evidence, in other words."

Through the clear plastic, everyone could see a pristine scorecard from the Old Course set within a beautiful walnut frame. Michael Pont looked sullen as the Chief Inspector stepped over to Stallings and pointed out the date, the score, and the '3' on Number 11.

"You'll notice how this is professionally framed. Sealed in back so that air cannot reach the contents. To be preserved for all time—"

"WAIT! HALT!"

39

IT WAS DOUGALL'S cry as Michael Pont suddenly lunged forward, knocked down the constable closest to him, and dashed into his kitchen with Poole in hot pursuit. The others followed to the sounds of scuffling and then a grunt and found Poole in the killer's grasp, bent backward, a long serrated steak knife denting the skin of his throat.

"No, Chief Inspector," Pont snarled, "We're through doing things your way. We're going to do them mine."

The wicked-looking knife held the policemen transfixed. Glancing only now and again at Michael's eyes, St. George ordered everyone out of the kitchen and permitted Pont and his prisoner to edge forward into the dining room. Gratefully, St. George noticed that the knife tip was now merely resting against Poole's skin.

"Very good," said Pont, his face perspiring, his left arm binding Poole in a tight hammerlock. "Now get all the coppers behind you so I know where you all are....DO IT!"

St. George issued the order without giving any thought to protocol. Chief Superintendent Stallings be damned—if he had done his job, this wouldn't be happening. As if reading those thoughts, Stallings spoke up, his delivery like someone reading from a B-movie script: "You can't get away."

"SHUT UP! I'll get away if I damn well please or you can just try and get the blood back into this bloke if my hand slips just the wee little bit. Serrated knives do so much more damage than the plain ones. Understand? Better tell him, Chief Inspector."

"I don't doubt you for a minute," said St. George who involuntarily recalled slicing through steak only the week before. He reached out and politely laid a restraining hand on Stallings' arm. "However, if you will permit me, I'd like to point out that we are also concerned about an accidental slippage, should you intend to keep that knife in that position. I mean, it will be rather awkward leaving here."

Pont smiled. "Got that covered. Open that center drawer in the credenza."

St. George complied.

"OK, now reach in back and you'll find a small pistol. Take it out by the barrel and put it on the table and then back away."

St. George quickly found the weapon, a small snub-nosed revolver. As he brought it to light, he saw the knife point again denting Poole's skin.

"All right, you can release the pressure."

"Once you've put it on the table and backed away."

To St. George, this was not the time for resistance. Yes, they could charge Pont and subdue him, but not before he fatally plunged the blade deep into Poole's neck. Likewise if they stalled handing over a weapon that would put all of them at risk—a quick glance at the cylinder showed it held at least five slugs—but again, his faithful aide would suffer first. So if they were to save Poole, they had to take the risk of handing over the loaded weapon. Accordingly, St. George gently laid the gun—.32-calibre he thought—on the dining table and stepped back.

"A bit more toward the edge, if you please? I prefer to keep my balance."

St. George complied.

"Very good, very good, Chief Inspector, you see the whole picture. That's why I think we'll make progress. All right now..." Michael paused as he moved the knife point no more than a millimeter from Poole's skin, leaving St. George feeling sick at the sight of an immediate drop of bright red blood at the site. "...what we're going to do now is this. You coppers back up to that wall there so I can keep an eye on you...Come on, I haven't got all day!...Good, now Sergeant, you just ease forward a bit at a time so you don't run into this blade and we'll just stop by and pick up that gun..."

Pont did not see the quick visual exchange between Poole and St.

George, the one questioning whether he should make a play despite being the hostage, the other responding with an abrupt twitch of the head to say 'No'. After 15 tense seconds, Pont was standing even with the waiting pistol.

"Now then, just to remind you gentlemen, by the time you reach me, I will have regrabbed this knife and shoved it into the sergeant's neck here. He'll be dead before you lay your first hand upon me. And if you're slow, then I'll have time to grab the gun and blow someone's brains out as well. All right, do we understand each other?...And Sergeant, I can feel your balance shifting so if you so much as try anything, I shall kill you without hesitation. Understood?"

"Yes," gasped Poole.

"Fine...let's see, oh, Chief Inspector...you naughty, naughty boy...if I were not so anxious to be away from here I'd kill the sergeant right now for that little move. Will you be so good as to release the safety? Pointing the thing toward that wall?...You see, I always leave it off."

A sheepish St. George again came forward, pointed the gun away from Pont and released the safety. *Damn*, he groused silently: another two seconds, another criminal without such an analytical mind, and they would have had the bloke cold.

"All right, now I think we're ready..." and with a quicker move than any thought he was capable, Michael Pont tossed the knife toward the coppers, who ducked while he picked up the gun and pressed the barrel against Poole's temple.

"There! Now that wasn't so bad, was it? You all did very well. Now the Sergeant and I are going for a little ride so we shall require whichever of your cars has the most petrol. Chief Inspector, I want you to stay here. Send one of your constables out to check the gauges..."

St. George did not take his eyes off Pont as he walked to the front door and turned the lock.

"You're going nowhere."

Michael Pont stared in utter disbelief as did everyone else. Poole first looked puzzled and then frightened.

"It's over, Michael. The crime at the plant was cleverly done. Well conceived and well executed. Quite commensurate with your level of intelligence and—if I must say it—your genius, but *this...this* is not your style at all. It's crude, vulgar, pedantic—the act of a plain mugger."

"OPEN THAT DOOR AND GET ME A CAR! OR ELSE!"

"Yes, yes, I know we'll all be dead, but you see the real point is that *you* won't be. Yes, you've committed one murder and you're going to prison for it. But which prison? Aye, there's the rub. After all, there are detention facilities for the white-collar types like yourself and there are prisons and then there are dungeons. Oh, yes, we still have them, believe me. In solitary lockdown 23 hours a day. No one to talk with except in your imagination. Nothing to read except perhaps the cover of an old magazine. No mail in or out because the office just is not quite sure where you are. Meals once a day if the warder happens to remember how many people live in your cellblock. Perhaps becoming the object of another, larger prisoner's affection? Think you could make it through 40 years of such a life?"

Michael Pont started to speak but stopped, his forehead glistening with sweat.

"Your one victim will get you a decent sentence, no question about that, but even *one* police scalp will bring you eternal damnation in the worst purgatory we have. And speaking personally, should you draw so much as one more drop of blood from Sgt. Poole, I will see to your eternal damnation myself. There's not a barrister in the country who can save you from it."

Pont said nothing as he looked questioningly at this Scotland Yard bastard. He cursed as he began waving his gun around in an increasingly wide arc to cover everyone.

"Remember," St. George continued, "that the white-collar units are little more than country clubs with electrified fences. Decent bedding and food, quite a bit to read, satellite television, other chaps with half-a-brain with whom to converse. A damn sight better than the dungeon."

The killer's gun lowered halfway. Still no one moved.

"All for a bloody scorecard," Michael growled.

"Oh, yes. It was your play on Number 11 that pinned you down. The par which you recorded. Hit a five-iron, you said. Back in 1994, yes; last week, no. Impossible. Totally impossible. What you did not know is that Saturday had a nearly gale-force wind directly against the tee shot. Your five-iron could never have reached the green. Not even close...Ever hear how the great Bobby Jones played it?"

"Who? The American?"

"The same. In a match under similar conditions, he used a putter off the tee and ran the ball along the ground and onto the green."

Michael Pont's jaw dropped slightly. Then he smirked and spat out an expletive.

"You see it now. Your mistake was you never asked your man Fogger about the playing conditions and he never thought to tell you. And why should he? He's a hacker; he doesn't know any better."

The killer shut his eyes and the gun muzzle dropped further. Remaining motionless, St. George lowered his voice.

"So you were never there Saturday. Fogger was. Instead, you were out at Viscount. Killing your brother."

Slowly, Michael Pont took a deep breath and lowered his gun all the way. "It was designed to be all so simple," he said in a monotone. "Then Geoffrey had to go muck it all up."

At the Chief Inspector's command, Michael released Poole, who stumbled out of reach. He then laid the gun on the floor and stepped away. Dougall immediately swooped in and scooped up the gun with his handkerchief while three constables hustled forward to take Pont into custody.

St. George motioned for Poole to follow him outside as Chief Superintendent Stallings somberly pronounced, "Michael Pont, I arrest you for the murder of your brother Geoffrey Pont. Anything you say..."

Epilogue

AT SCOTLAND YARD three weeks later, Poole approached his mentor's office and rapped twice on the metal doorframe. In his hand were three pages of curled paper filled with single-spaced print.

"Fax, sir, from West Calder. Inspector Dougall. The Pont case."

St. George looked up from the final draft for a case report and glanced warily at the flimsies. "Wordy fellow, isn't he. Could you somehow find it in your heart to summarize for me?"

The Chief Inspector's disinterest in reading the communique for himself did not surprise Poole, who thought his boss had seemed distracted all day.

"Right. Michael's made a clean breast of it. Seems things came to a head that last week when he called Geoffrey at home and Myra told him his brother was locked in his study going over financial reports. Checking with the office girl, he learned which files his brother was reviewing."

"Purchasing and the like."

Poole nodded. "He decided he dared not wait and so he laid plans to torch the place. Bought the biking apparel and scuba gear that Friday in London and then afterward cut it up, bagged it, and dispersed the parcels in several dumpsters."

"And the mask and tank?"

"Thrown into different lakes. They've found the tank. And as we

thought, the London trip was completely unnecessary for the project but essential so that the Japanese would never lay eyes on the real
Michael before Saturday."

"Damn, we're good!" said St. George impishly but without smiling.

"Let's see, what else...he used his folding bike like we thought.
Parked behind a vacant house a couple of miles away. Bike went so
slow he was afraid he wouldn't clear the area in time."

"Which was the very point you raised," St. George said. "Oh, there's
one thing I forgot to mention—how terribly clean those bike tires
were. Too clean for just lying unused in the boot like he claimed. Dust
inevitably gets in and settles. As though they were brand new or
newly washed. But go on—what about his encounter with Geoffrey?"

"When he got home Friday evening, there was a message for him
from Geoffrey. Very cold sounding. Told him they were now playing
the Old Course and to enjoy his golf. Told him they must meet very
first thing Tuesday morning and rang off. He thought that was very
odd—why not Monday? That's when he tried to call Geoffrey and
got Myra. He already had Fogger on standby and so he called him and
sent him to St. Andrews straightaway. Stayed in Leuchars overnight."

The Chief Inspector nodded with somber understanding.

"Remarkably," Poole continued, "Fogger claims he believed he was
making it possible for the two brothers to meet and work things out.
That Michael was going to offer Geoffrey a piece of the action."

"Your impression?"

"Officially, I'm reserving judgment for now."

"Unofficially?"

"Cattle excrement."

"Laurence!" yelped the Chief Inspector in mock horror. "Such lan-
guage! And on a weekday, no less! I think I shall faint..."

"More excrement, that, sir. Begging your pardon..."

"Hah! All right, all right. Anything else?"

"Well, with owner Michael responsible for the fire, Walcott's
company doesn't have to pay a dime. Worse yet, to save money with
lower premiums, Geoffrey had waived his double-indemnity clause
in his personal policy. End-result is that VES was on the rocks."

"Was?"

"Enter the Viking knight in shining PVC armor."

"Burklund."

"Indeed. Bought them out for rock-bottom price, but the good
news is that he's going to rebuild the same plant on the same site and

retain all the old employees. Guess he decided to venture into new territory after all."

"What about Barrows?"

"Stays on as the YAMATSU project director."

"And dear cousin Edward?"

"Not too shabby. Burklund retained him as his personal representative to the YAMATSU crowd. After all, I guess he's the only executive they know personally. Oh, and his brokerage is being allowed to bid for the insurance business on the new project. He seems quite relieved."

"I should think so. And the widow Pont?"

"Put away her widow's weeds now that there will be no trial. Investing her sale proceeds."

"Ah, wherever he is, Geoffrey must be positively overwhelmed by all the sentimentality," said St. George as he leaned back in his chair. "Anything about Stallings or McSwain?"

"Yes, they both put in for early retirement. Stallings came under fire for his mishandling of Pont's body but his active role thereafter bought him some grace. In any case, both have left the spotlight hoping, I guess, to cash in on their investment. They apparently had some unpleasant nights before Burklund rescued their investments. Dougall thinks Stallings may try and go for Head of Security at the new plant."

"And how about Dougall himself?"

"Received a commendation for his work. And he thanks you for some letter to the Chief Constable. I didn't know you wrote one."

St. George smiled and looked down at his work. "We do what we can."

Poole hesitated a moment: he knew the Chief Inspector's reputation for firing off scathing memos about incompetent subordinates, colleagues, and bureaucrats. What was unknown to all but himself and a few others was the man's penchant for dispensing kudos as well, but with no fanfare. His introspective pause ended when his boss looked up.

"Yes, Laurence, there's something else?"

"Yes, sir, if you forgive my mentioning it, but I've noticed you've seemed not quite yourself all day. Like you had something else on your mind. Anything wrong?"

St. George sat back in his chair, his face puzzled, his eyes twinkling.

"That obvious, is it?...Well, yes...there is some news...double dose, in fact. First off, our beloved National Health has bailed on me regarding my leg brace. Sent a lovely note, together with all their sincere regards, that they've changed their mind and will not cover any of the cost. They say it's medically unnecessary. So I'll have to cash in more savings, which takes away from my travel fund—but that's not your problem. Besides that, the bloody thing needs some adjustment."

"For what?"

"For bearing the strain of all my weight shifting forward during the downswing! Believe me, I have no intention of getting out there and swatting at the ball with only my arms like an old woman. But that's not the worst part. I had written Robert Montcrief about signing up for the Old Course...thought I would do it early next summer...got his reply today...seems he forgot to mention that one must have an official handicap to set foot on the Old Course...and the New Course as well...nothing over 24 permitted...I should have anticipated there would be some such requirement....presents rather a formidable problem."

"How so?"

The Chief Inspector produced a wan smile. "Well, with this gimpy leg, I certainly have never entertained any thoughts of playing as well as I used to...and yes, my weight will probably get in the way, and despite my stretching exercises, I'm not limber enough for golf, not yet, so the reality is it will be a long time before I can play consistently below that 24 limit."

"How long?"

"The truth? I haven't the faintest idea. As for the handicap, I shall sign up as an associate member with the English Golf Union. They accept informal rounds, whereas a golf club would take only rounds played in formal competition. Clearly I could never do the latter. The catch is I have to find three other EGU chaps to play with and have them sign my scorecard. However, there is certainly no point lining anyone up until I break the 24 barrier."

For a moment each man paused, alone with his thoughts.

Then Poole said, "How about playing one of the other courses there. The Balgove, for example. Nine holes, isn't it?"

"Yes, yes, that's an option, but that would be a consolation prize. It really would not be the same...not the same at all."

"Well then," Poole sighed, "in the meantime, I guess there's nothing for it but to keep on chasing murderers."

St. George's features brightened, he chuckled, and then he scrawled his name on the finished report.

Notes

The Gaelic and Scottish phrases used in the story have the following meanings:

Grasshopping = carrying golf clubs.

Working the tools = providing the player the proper club on every shot.

Nae gowf = not golf.

All richt = all right.

Gey strang = very strong.

Wisnae = was not.

Acknowledgments

I would like to thank the following for their invaluable assistance:

saint-andrews.co.uk website and webmaster Kenneth Cochran.

Heather McQueen, owner/proprietor, Burness House, Murray
      Park, St. Andrews, Fife, Scotland FY16 9AW.

Lachlan McIntosh, Membership Secretary, Royal and Ancient
      Golf Club, St. Andrews, Scotland.

Kyle J. Peterson, Phoenix, Arizona, for Japanese signatures.

Dawson Taylor, St. Andrews — Cradle of Golf, A.S. Barnes & Co.,
      New York, 1976.